P9-CBE-686

Winamac, Indiana 46096

"To the future Duchess of Alzacar!"

There were gasps across the crowd, the largest of which was probably mine. But Alejandro continued to hold up his flute, so everyone else did, too. He drank deeply, and a thousand guests drank, too. Toasting to our engagement.

My body trembled. All I wanted to do was turn and flee through the crowd, to disappear, to never come back. To be free of him—the man who'd once destroyed me. Who could, if he tried, so easily do it again—and more, since now our child could be used against me.

But that child also meant, in a very real way, that I was bound to Alejandro for the rest of my life. We both loved Miguel. We both wished to raise him.

Which meant, no matter how fiercely I wished otherwise, that no matter how I'd tried to deny it, I would never be truly free of Alejandro—ever.

Putnam County Public Library
737 South Riverside Drive

Dear Reader,

For my twenty-first book for Harlequin®, I wanted to try something new. I wanted my heroine, Lena Carlisle, to be able to tell her own story—in her own words.

Writing the book, I wanted to feel the joy and anguish and passion of her story as directly as if it were happening to me. I wanted to be gripped with emotion as I went, with Lena, from being neglected and ignored—"invisible," as she says, "like a ghost in my own home"—to becoming, through the love of a wealthy, handsome Spanish duke, the strong, beloved woman she was always born to be.

Alejandro's thoughts are never directly revealed in the story, but I hope you can still feel his anger and grief and passion, as Lena does. And come to love him, as I did.

Lena has nothing but her baby, her courage and a pure heart; Alejandro has money, wealth and power, but is in danger of losing his soul. She is the only one who can save him. She can give him hope, and give him a future, with her love. If he'll just let her in...

I hope you enjoy their story.

With love,

Jennie Lucas

Jennie Lucas

—

Uncovering Her Nine Month Secret

If you purchased this book without a cover you should be aware
that this book is stolen property. It was reported as "unsold and
destroyed" to the publisher, and neither the author nor the
publisher has received any payment for this "stripped book."

Recycling programs
for this product may
not exist in your area.

ISBN-13: 978-0-373-13742-8

UNCOVERING HER NINE MONTH SECRET

First North American Publication 2014

Copyright © 2014 by Jennie Lucas

All rights reserved. Except for use in any review, the reproduction or
utilization of this work in whole or in part in any form by any electronic,
mechanical or other means, now known or hereinafter invented, including
xerography, photocopying and recording, or in any information storage
or retrieval system, is forbidden without the written permission of the
publisher, Harlequin Enterprises Limited, 225 Duncan Mill Road,
Don Mills, Ontario M3B 3K9, Canada.

This is a work of fiction. Names, characters, places and incidents are
either the product of the author's imagination or are used fictitiously,
and any resemblance to actual persons, living or dead, business
establishments, events or locales is entirely coincidental.

This edition published by arrangement with Harlequin Books S.A.

For questions and comments about the quality of this book,
please contact us at CustomerService@Harlequin.com.

® and TM are trademarks of Harlequin Enterprises Limited or its
corporate affiliates. Trademarks indicated with ® are registered in the
United States Patent and Trademark Office, the Canadian Intellectual
Property Office and in other countries.

Printed in U.S.A.

All about the author...
Jennie Lucas

JENNIE LUCAS had a tragic beginning for any would-be writer: a very happy childhood. Her parents owned a bookstore, and she grew up surrounded by books, dreaming about faraway lands. When she was ten, her father secretly paid her a dollar for every classic novel (*Jane Eyre, War and Peace*) that she read.

At fifteen, she went to a Connecticut boarding school on scholarship. She took her first solo trip to Europe at sixteen, then put off college and traveled around the United States, supporting herself with jobs as diverse as gas station cashier and newspaper advertising assistant.

At twenty-two, she met the man who would become her husband. For the first time in her life, she wanted to stay in one place, as long as she could be with him. After their marriage, she graduated from Kent State University with a degree in English, and started writing books a year later.

Jennie was a finalist in the Romance Writers of America's Golden Heart contest in 2003 and won the award in 2005. A fellow 2003 finalist, Australian author Trish Morey, read Jennie's writing and told her that she should write for the Harlequin Presents® line. It seemed like too big a dream, but Jennie took a deep breath and went for it. A year later Jennie got the magical call from London that turned her into a published author.

Since then, life has been hectic, juggling a writing career, a sexy husband and two young children, but Jennie loves her crazy, chaotic life. Now if she can only figure out how to pack up her family and live in all the places she's writing about!

For more about Jennie and her books, please visit her website at www.jennielucas.com.

Other titles by Jennie Lucas available in ebook:

THE SHEIKH'S LAST SEDUCTION
THE CONSEQUENCES OF THAT NIGHT *(At His Service)*
A REPUTATION FOR REVENGE *(Princes Untamed)*
DEALING HER FINAL CARD *(Princes Untamed)*

To Pete

PROLOGUE

HE SEDUCED ME EASILY. He broke down my defenses as if they were paper. You wouldn't have been able to resist, either, believe me.

After so many years of feeling like a ghost in my own home, invisible, unloved, I think I would have fallen into his arms for one dark glance—one husky word. But Alejandro gave me so much more than that. He looked at me as if I were the most beautiful woman on earth. Listened to me as if every word on my lips was poetry. He pulled me into his arms, made me burst into flame, kissed my grief and cares away. After so many years of living in a cold gray world, my life exploded into color—because of him.

There was no reason why the Duque de Alzacar, one of the richest men in Spain, would want someone like me—plain, poor—rather than my beautiful, wealthy cousin. I thought it was a miracle.

It was only later that I realized why Alejandro had chosen me. He hadn't seduced me out of love—or even lust. It was many months before I realized the selfish reason that had caused him to overwhelm me with his charm, to dazzle me, to make me love him.

But by then, it was too late.

CHAPTER ONE

THE GRAY, LOWERING sky was falling like a shroud across the old colonial city of San Miguel de Allende when I heard the words I'd feared in nightmares for the past year.

"A man was here looking for you, Señora Lena."

Looking up at my neighbor, I staggered back, clutching my five-month-old son in my arms. "What?"

The woman smiled, reaching out to chuck the cooing baby's pudgy chin. "*Gracias* for letting me watch Miguelito for an hour. Such a pleasure..."

"But the man?" I croaked, my mouth dry. "What did he look like?"

"*Muy guapo,*" she sighed. "So handsome. Dark-haired and tall."

It could be anyone, I told myself desperately. The old silver mining town in central Mexico was filled with American expatriates who'd moved here to enjoy the lovely architecture and take classes at the famous Instituto. Many single women had come here to start new lives, pursuing new businesses as artists and sculptors and jewelry makers.

Like me. A year ago, I'd arrived pregnant and full of grief, but I'd still managed to start a wonderful new life. Perhaps this dark stranger was looking for a portrait of his sweetheart, nothing more.

But I didn't believe it. Fear was cold inside me. "Did he give his name?"

Dolores shook her head. "The baby was fussing in my arms when I answered the door. But the man was well dressed, with a Rolls-Royce. A chauffeur. Bodyguards, even." Her smile spread to a grin. "Do you have a rich new boyfriend, Lena?"

My knees went weak.

"No," I whispered.

It could be only one man. Alejandro Guillermo Valentín Navaro y Albra, the powerful Duke of Alzacar. The man I'd once loved with all my innocent heart. The man who'd seduced and betrayed me.

No. It was worse than that.

"He's not your boyfriend, eh?" My neighbor's voice was regretful. "Pity. Such a handsome man. Why did he come looking for you, then? Do you know him?"

Beads of sweat broke out on my forehead. "When was he here?"

She shrugged, looking bemused. "A half hour ago. Maybe more."

"Did you say anything about—about Miguel being my son?"

Dolores shook her head. "He didn't give me the chance. He just asked if you lived in the house two doors down. I said yes. He pulled out his wallet and asked me not to mention his visit, because he wanted to surprise you. Can you imagine?" She flourished some bills from her apron pocket in delight. "He paid me a thousand pesos for my silence!"

Yes. I could imagine. I briefly closed my eyes. "But you told me anyway," I whispered. "Bless you."

She snorted. "Men always want to arrive with a flourish of trumpets. I thought it better for you to be prepared." She looked at my shapeless white sundress and plain sandals with a moue of disapproval, then at my long, casual ponytail and makeup-free face. She sighed. "You have a good figure, but in that dress you look like a marshmallow. You don't make the most of yourself. It's almost like you don't *want* to be noticed!" She shook her head. "But tonight you must be at your most irresistible, your most sexy, *sí?* You want him to want you!"

No. I really didn't. Not that he would want me anyway, now his evil plan had succeeded. "He's not my boyfriend."

"So picky!" She made a *tsk* sound. "You don't want *this* billionaire, you don't want *that* one—I tell you, wealthy, handsome men are not so thick upon the ground as you seem to think!" Dolores glared at me. "Your son needs a father. *You* need

a husband. Both of you deserve every happiness."
Her expression turned suddenly sly. "And the man
at my door looked like he would bring a *lot* of happiness to a wife. Every night."

"No doubt," I said over the razor blade in my
throat. It was true. Alejandro had brought me intense joy for one summer. And a lifetime's worth
of anguish since. "I should go."

"*Sí.* It's almost Miguel's nap time, isn't it,
pequeño?" she crooned.

My baby yawned, his fat cheeks vying with his
sleepy dark eyes for cuteness. Those eyes just like
his father's.

I exhaled, running a hand over my forehead. I'd
allowed myself to think we were safe. That Alejandro had given up looking for me. *I should have
known.* I should have known better than to start
sleeping at night, to start making friends, to start
making a real home for myself and my son. *I should
have known they would someday find me....*

"Lena?" My neighbor frowned. "Is something
wrong? You do not seem happy."

"Did you tell him when I'd be back?"

"I wasn't sure when you'd be done, so to be safe
I said four o'clock."

I glanced at the clock in her brightly painted front
room. It was only three. I had one hour. "Thank
you." In a burst of emotion, I hugged her, knowing that she'd been kind to me—to both of us—but

I would never see her again after today. "*Gracias,* Dolores."

She patted my back. "I know you've had a hard year, but that's in the past. Your life is about to change for the better. I can always feel these things."

Better? I choked back a laugh, then turned away before she could see my face. "*Adios....*"

"He'll be your boyfriend, just wait and see," she called after me gleefully. "He'll be your husband someday!"

My *husband.* A bitter thought. I wasn't the one Alejandro had wished to marry. He wanted my wealthy, beautiful cousin, Claudie. It was the whole reason he'd seduced me, the poor relation living in the shadows of Claudie's London mansion. If he and Claudie wed, together they'd have everything: a dukedom, half of Andalucía, political connections across the world, billions in the bank. They'd have almost limitless power.

There was just one thing they could never have.

My eyes fell on my baby's dark, downy head. I clutched Miguel tightly against me, and he gave an indignant cry. Loosening my grip, I smoothed back his soft hair.

"Sorry, I'm so sorry," I choked out, and I didn't know whether I was begging my son's forgiveness for holding him too tightly, for tearing him away from his home or for choosing his father so poorly.

How could I have been so stupid? How?

Hurrying down the small street, I glanced up at

the heavy gray sky. August was the rainy season, and a downpour was threatening. Cuddling Miguel against my hip, I punched in the security-alarm code and pushed open the heavy oak door of my brightly painted home.

The rooms inside were dark. I'd fallen in love with this old colonial house, with its tall ceilings, its privacy, its scarcity of windows on the street. I could not have afforded the rent in a million years, but I'd been helped by a friend who'd allowed me to live here rent-free. Well—I thought of Edward St. Cyr as a friend. Until a week ago, when he'd—

But no. I wouldn't think of that now, or how betrayed I'd felt when the friendship I'd come to rely upon had been revealed for what it was.

I'm tired of waiting for you to forget that Spanish bastard. It's time for you to belong to me.

I shuddered at the memory. My answer had sent Edward scowling from this house, back on his private jet to London. There was no way I could remain in this house, living rent-free, after that, so for the past week, I'd looked for a cheaper place to live. But it was hard to find any place cheap enough for the income of a new, self-employed artist. Even here.

San Miguel de Allende had become my home. I would miss the city's cobblestoned streets, growing flowers in my garden and selling portraits in the open-air *mercados*. I'd miss the friends I'd made, Mexicans and expats who'd welcomed an unmarried, heartbroken woman and her baby, who'd taped me up and put me back together.

Now I took a deep breath, trying to steady my shaking nerves. "I can do this," I whispered aloud, trying to make myself believe it. I knew how to grab passports, money and clothes and be out of here in five minutes. I'd done it before, in Tokyo, Berlin, Istanbul, São Paulo and Mumbai.

But then, I'd had Edward to help me. Now I had no one.

Don't think about it, I ordered myself, wiping my eyes. I'd go on foot and hail a taxi on the street. Once at the station, my baby and I would take the next bus to Mexico City. I'd use the emergency credit card Edward had left and fly to the United States, where I was born. I'd head west. Disappear. Once I found a job, I'd pay back Edward every penny.

I'd raise my child in peace, in some small town in Arizona or Alaska, and this time, I'd make sure Alejandro would never, ever find me....

A lamp flicked on in the foyer.

Alejandro was sitting in a chair across the room, staring at me with eyes that burned like fire.

I halted, choking out a gasp.

"Lena Carlisle," he said in a low voice. "At last."

"Alejandro," I breathed as terror racked through me. My hands instinctively tightened on my baby in my arms. "What are you— How did you…"

"How did I find you?" He rose to his feet, tall

and broad-shouldered. "Or how did I get in to your house?" His voice was low and husky, with only the slightest accent, blurred from growing up in Spain, followed by years of running a billion-dollar business conglomerate from New York and London. "Do you really think any *security system,* no matter how expensive, could keep me from being where I wanted to be?"

He was even more handsome than I remembered. Seeing him in the flesh, after a year of being tormented by sensual dreams, made my knees tremble. I clutched Miguel closer, willing myself not to faint.

Alejandro's cold eyes never left mine as he walked toward me. He was dressed in black from his well-cut coat to his glossy Italian shoes, draped in *power.*

"What do you want?" I choked out.

He looked from me to my yawning, drowsy-eyed baby.

"Is it true?" His voice was deadly quiet, but the words burned through my heart. His face was grim. "Is this my baby?"

His baby. Oh, God. Please, no. I stumbled back in blind panic.

"My men are outside. You won't even make it to the street...."

I ignored him. Grabbing the wrought-iron handle, I pulled open the heavy, weathered oak door and started to run. I stopped.

Six hulking bodyguards stood outside my house,

in a semicircle, in front of the expensive sedan and black SUV now jamming the slender residential lane.

"Did you think," Alejandro said softly behind me, "that when I finally found you, I would leave anything to chance?"

He stood close behind me, so close I caught the scent of his cologne. So close I could feel the heat emanating from his powerful body. Briefly closing my eyes, I shivered at being so close to the man who had once possessed me, body and soul.

Unwillingly, I turned back to face the ghost who still haunted my heart. His hot black gaze held mine, and in the dark embers of that fire, I was lashed by memories I'd tried so hard to forget. I'd loved him hopelessly from the moment he'd first come to call on my beautiful, wealthy cousin. I'd watched from hallways, made them tea, organized their dinner parties. I'd done it all with a smile, any and all work my cousin required, ignoring the ache of my heart when she bragged after he left that she was going to catch the uncatchable Spanish duke. "He's nearly in my grasp!" Claudie had crowed. "I'll be a duchess before the year is out!"

Then, to everyone's shock, he'd suddenly jilted her.

For me.

He was the first man who'd ever noticed me—really noticed me—and I'd fallen like a stone beneath the sensual onslaught of his power and glamour and dangerous, sexy charm. For six reckless, miraculous weeks in London last summer, Alejandro had held me in his arms, and I felt as if I owned the world.

Memories of the hopes I'd had, the naive girl I'd been, ripped through me now like a torrent of blows. Alejandro's expression was stark, but I could remember his playful smile. The intensity of his dark gaze. The sound of his husky voice whispering sweet words in the night. I could remember hot kisses, and the feel of our naked bodies intertwined in his London hotel suite. In the back of his limo. And once, against the wall in the back stairs of the Carlisle mansion.

Our affair had seemed as infinite as the stars in the sky. But on that bright summer day when I finally gathered the courage to tell him I was in love with him, his smiling face had changed in front of my eyes.

"*Love me?*" Alejandro had repeated scornfully. "You do not even *know* me."

Two minutes later, he was gone, leaving me bereft and bewildered. But the broken, truly broken, came later…

Now, Alejandro took my hand, glancing up and down the quiet Mexican street.

"Come back inside, Lena. We have much to talk about."

Feeling the electricity of his hand wrapped around mine, I looked up with an intake of breath.

He was so close now. Touching me. My lips parted. He was somehow even more devastatingly handsome than I'd remembered. He had the kind of face that could break a woman's heart into a million pieces, to little shimmering fragments of gray dust, leaving you too dazed with his power and beauty to feel anything but gratitude as he lazily destroyed you.

Without my notice, he led me back into the foyer. Reaching over my head, he towered over me, his arm brushing against my hair, his body pressing against mine. I shivered, clutching my baby close. But he merely closed the heavy door with a sonorous bang behind me.

The hard-edged billionaire duke, in his sharply tailored clothes, stood out starkly against my comfortable, bohemian home, with its warm tile floors and walls I'd decorated with homemade paper flowers and my own paintings, one of the Parroquia de San Miguel, but the rest of my baby, the first from when he was just six days old.

Looking down at me, Alejandro said softly, "Is what Claudie told me true? This baby in your arms—it is mine?"

Trembling, I pulled away. Gathering my wits, I glared at him. "Do you really expect me to answer that?"

"It's an easy enough question. There are only two possible answers." Reaching out, he stroked my cheek, but there was no tenderness in his gaze. "Yes. Or no."

"You'd be a horrible father! I won't let my sweet boy be turned into a heartless bastard like—"

"Like me?" His voice was dangerously low. His dark eyes gleamed in the shadowy foyer. "Is that what you really think of me—after all we once shared?"

Caught in his gaze, I trembled. Once, I might have believed so differently. I'd managed to convince myself that beneath his wealth and power and aristocratic title, Alejandro was decent and good. Like generations of women before me, I had seen what I wanted to see. I'd been blind to the truth, until, against my will, the blindfold had been torn from my eyes.

"Yes. That's what I think of you."

A strange expression flickered across the chiseled planes of his face, an emotion I couldn't identify before it swiftly disappeared. He gave me a sardonic smile.

"You are right, of course. I care for nothing and no one. Least of all you, especially after you and your cousin have gone to such lengths to blackmail me over this child."

"Blackmail you?" I gasped. "You're the one who deliberately seduced me, and got me pregnant, intending to steal my baby away so you could raise him with Claudie!"

He grew very still.

"What are you talking about?" he ground out.

My body was shaking with emotion. "You think I didn't know? When I found out I was pregnant, you'd already left me and gone back to Spain. You wouldn't return my calls. But fool that I was, I was still desperate to share the news, because I hoped you might care! So I begged Claudie for enough money to fly to Madrid. I was scared to tell her why I needed the money. She'd planned so long to marry you. But when I told her I was pregnant, she did something I never imagined."

"What?"

I took a deep breath.

"She laughed," I whispered. "She laughed and laughed. Then she told me to wait. She went into the hallway, but she left the door open and I heard her call you. I heard her congratulate you on your brilliant plan! *Thanking* you, even! How brilliant you were, how clever, to seduce her lowly cousin, the poor relation, to provide the heir you knew she could never give you! Now the two of you could get married immediately." My voice turned acid. "Just as soon as her lawyer forced me to sign papers terminating all my parental rights."

"Yes. She called me." His eyes narrowed. "But I never…"

"'Don't worry, I'll get Lena to sign her baby away,' she said!" My voice trembled as I remembered the terror I'd felt that day. "She asked you to send over a few security guards from your London office, just in case I tried to fight!" My voice choked and I looked away. "So I ran. Before either of you could lock me away somewhere for the duration of my pregnancy and try to steal my child!"

Silence fell. His eyes narrowed.

"From the day, from the *hour* Claudie told me you were pregnant, I've had investigators trying to track you down, chasing you around the world. Yes, she had some crazy idea that it was her inability to have children that kept me from marrying her. She was wrong." He came closer. "I raced to London, but you were already gone. And ever since, you've always managed to disappear in a puff of smoke whenever I got close. That, *querida,* is expensive. And so is this." He motioned at the high ceilings of the two-hundred-year-old colonial house. "This house is owned by a shell company run out of the Caymans. My investigators checked. So why don't you just admit who's helping you? Admit the truth!"

Something told me not to mention Edward St. Cyr. "And what's that?"

"Once you found out you were pregnant, you knew I would never marry you." His voice softened, his dark eyes almost caressing me. "So you came up with a different plan to cash in, didn't you? You struck a deal...with your cousin."

Whatever I'd expected, it wasn't that. I stared at him. "Are you crazy? Why would Claudie help me? She wants to marry you!"

"I know. After you disappeared, Claudie told me

she knew exactly where you were, but that you refused to let me see the child until we could guarantee a stable home. Until I married her."

My lips parted in shock. "But I haven't spoken to Claudie for a year. She has no idea where I am!" I shook my head. "Did she really try to blackmail you into marriage?"

"Women always want to marry me," he said grimly. "They think nothing of stealing or cheating or lying for it."

I snorted. "Your ego is incredible!"

"It's not ego. Every woman wants to be the wife of a billionaire duke. It's not personal."

Of course it is, I thought unwillingly, my heart twisting in my chest. How could any woman not fall in love with Alejandro, and not want him for her own?

"But what I want to know is…" His voice became dangerously low. "Is this baby in your arms truly mine? Or is it just part of some elaborate plot you've set up with Claudie?"

My head snapped back. "Are you asking me if my son is some kind of *stunt baby?*"

"You would be surprised," he said tightly, "how often in life someone pretends to be something they are not."

"You think I'd lie about this—for money?"

"Perhaps not. Perhaps for some other reason." He paused. "If you were not working for Claudie, perhaps you were working for yourself."

"Meaning what?"

"You hoped that playing hard to get, disappearing with my child, would make me want to pin you down. To marry you." He lifted a dark eyebrow. "Not a bad calculation."

My mouth had fallen open. Then I glared at him. "I would never want to be your wife!"

"Right."

His single small word was like a grenade of sarcasm exploding all over me. For an instant my pride made me blind with anger. Then I remembered the dreams I'd once had and my throat went tight. I took a deep, miserable breath.

"Maybe that was what I wanted once," I whispered. "But that was long ago. Before I found out you'd coldheartedly seduced me so you could marry Claudie and steal my baby."

"You must know now that was never true."

"How can I be sure?"

He shook his head. "I never intended to marry Claudie or anyone."

"Yes, you said that. You also told me once that you never intended to have children. And yet here you are, fighting for a DNA test for Miguel!"

"I do not have a choice." His expression changed as he said sharply, "You named the baby Miguel?"

"So?"

"Why?" he demanded, staring at me with a sudden suspicious glitter in his eyes that I did not understand.

"After the beautiful city that took me in—San Miguel became our home!"

He relaxed imperceptibly. "Ah."

Now I was the one to frown. His reaction to our baby's name had been so fierce, almost violent. Had he wondered if I'd named him after another man? "Why do you care so much?"

"I don't," he said coldly.

My baby whimpered in my arms. Fiercely, I shook my head as I hugged him close, breathing in Miguel's sweet baby scent, feeling his tiny warm body against me. I nuzzled his head and saw tears fall onto his soft dark hair. "If you didn't get me pregnant on purpose, if it happened by accident and you don't want a child…just let us go!"

His jaw tightened. "I have an obligation…."

"Obligation!" I cried. "To you, he's just someone to carry on your title and name. To me, he's everything. I carried him for nine months, felt him kick inside me, heard his first cry when he was born. He's my baby, my precious child, my only reason for living." I was crying openly now, and so was my baby, either in sympathy or in alarm or just because it was past his nap time and all the adults arguing wouldn't let him sleep. Miguel's chubby cheeks were red, his eyes swimming with piteous tears. I tried to comfort him as I wept.

Alejandro's expression was stone. "If he's my son, I will bring both of you to live with me in

Spain. Neither of you will ever want for anything, ever again. You will live in my castle."

"I'd never marry you, not for any price!"

"Marriage? Who said anything about that?" His lips twisted. "Though we both know you'd marry me in a second if I asked."

Stung, I shook my head furiously. "What could you offer me, Alejandro? Money? A castle? A title? I don't need those things!"

He moved closer to me, his eyes dark.

"Don't forget sex," he said softly. "Hot, deep, incredible sex."

In the shadowy hacienda, Alejandro looked at me over the downy head of the baby that we had created. My breasts suddenly felt heavy, my nipples tightening. My body felt taut and liquid at once.

"I know you remember what it was like between us," he said in a low voice. "Just as I do."

I lifted my gaze to his.

"Yes," I whispered. "But what use are any of those things really, Alejandro? Without love, it's empty." I shook my head. "You must know this. Because the money, the palaces, the title—and yes, even the sex… Have those things ever made *you* happy?"

He stared at me. For a long moment, there was only the soft patter of the rain against the roof, our baby's low whimper, and the loud beat of my aching heart.

Then abruptly, for the first time, Alejandro looked,

really looked, at our son. Reaching out, he stroked Miguel's soft dark hair gently with a large, powerful hand.

As if by magic, our baby's crying abruptly subsided. Big-eyed, Miguel hiccupped his last tears away as father and son took measure of each other, each with the same frown, the same eyes, the same expression. It would have been enough to make me grin, if my heart hadn't been hurting so much.

Suddenly our baby flopped out a tiny, unsteady hand against Alejandro's nose. Looking down at him in surprise, Alejandro snorted a laugh. He seemed to catch his breath, looking at Miguel with amazement, even wonder.

Then he straightened, giving me a cold glare. "There will be a DNA test. Immediately."

"You expect me to allow a doctor to prick my baby's skin for a blood test, to prove something I don't want to be proved? Forget it! Either believe he's your son, or—better yet—don't! And leave us in peace!"

Alejandro's face looked cold and ruthless. "Enough."

He must have pressed a button or something—or else he had some freaky bodyguard alert, like a dog whistle I couldn't hear—because suddenly two bodyguards came in through the front door. Without even looking at me, they kept walking through the foyer, headed across the courtyard toward the bedroom I shared with Miguel.

I whirled on Alejandro. "Where are they going?"

"To pack," he replied coolly.

"Pack for whom?"

A third bodyguard who'd come up silently behind me suddenly lifted Miguel out of my arms.

"No!" I cried. I started for him, arms outstretched, but Alejandro held me back.

"If the DNA test proves he is not my son," he said calmly, "I will bring your son back to you, safe and sound, and I'll never bother either of you again."

"Let me go!" I shrieked, fighting him—uselessly, for with his greater power and strength, his grip was implacable. "You bastard! You bastard! I will *kill* you! You can't take him from me—Miguel! *Miguel!*"

"You are so sure he is mine?"

"Of course he is yours! You know you were my only lover!"

"I know I was your first...."

"My only! *Ever!* Damn you! *Miguel!*"

Something flickered in Alejandro's eyes. But I was no longer looking at him. I was watching as the bodyguard disappeared through the door, my baby wailing in the man's beefy arms. I struggled in Alejandro's grip. "Let me go!"

"Promise to behave, Lena," he said quietly, "and I will."

How I wished I could fight him. If only I had the same power he did—then we'd see who gave orders! If I had his physical strength, I would punch him in the face! If only I had a fortune, a private jet, my own bodyguard army…

My lips parted on an intake of breath.

Edward.

Would he help me? Even now?

That wasn't the question.

Would I be willing to pay the price?

"I don't want to separate you from the baby," Alejandro said, "but I must have the DNA test. And if you're going to fight and scream…"

I abruptly stopped struggling. Nodding, I wiped my eyes. "I'll come quietly. But please," I said softly, looking up at his face, "before you take him to Spain, could we stop in London?"

He frowned. "London?"

I nodded, trying to hide my eagerness—my desperation. "I left something at Claudie's house. Something precious. I need it back."

"What is it?"

"My baby's legacy."

He lifted a dark eyebrow. "Money?"

"And also," I said on a wave of inspiration, "if we could talk to Claudie, together, we could force her to admit how she played us both. Then maybe we could actually trust each other, going forward…."

Alejandro rubbed the back of his head, then nodded. "That would be better. And to be honest, there are a few things I'd like to discuss with your cousin myself."

His voice was grim. I believed him now when he said he didn't want to marry Claudie. Maybe Alejandro hadn't deliberately planned to get me pregnant after all.

But I'd been right about one thing. He still planned to steal my baby. He intended to keep Miguel at his side, to raise him as his heir in some cold Spanish castle, until he turned him into some heartless, unfeeling bastard like himself.

And Alejandro didn't intend to marry me. So I'd be powerless. Expendable.

"So we have a deal?" Alejandro said. "You'll allow the DNA test, and if he is my son, you'll come with us to Spain?"

"With a stop in London first."

"Yes. London. But after that, Spain. I have your word?"

"I honestly hate you," I whispered with feeling.

"I honestly do not care. Do I have your word?"

I glared at him. "Yes."

He looked down at me in the shadows. For a moment, there was a current of electricity between us, sparking in the shadows of the room. His fingers tightened. Then he abruptly released me.

"Thank you," he said coldly, "for being so reasonable."

Hiding the cold determination in my heart, I left him without a word, and nearly sprinted toward my baby.

Alejandro thought he owned me now. But I

wasn't as helpless as he thought. I had one card left to play, if I was willing to pay for it.

Was I?

For my son?

Yes. I was.

CHAPTER TWO

THE FIRST TIME I saw London, I was a grief-stricken fourteen-year-old, newly orphaned, just arrived from New York. My grandmother, whom I'd never met, sent her driver to collect me from Heathrow. The sky was weeping and gray. I remembered trembling as I walked up the steps of the tall white mansion in Kensington, a house roughly the same size as my entire apartment building in Brooklyn.

Brought in by the butler, I'd found my grandmother sitting at her antique desk in the morning room. I stood in front of the fireplace for some moments, my eyes stinging and my heart aching, before she finally looked up.

"So you're Lena," she'd said, looking me up and down, from the lumpy coat my mother had made before her hands grew frail in illness, wasting away like her heart since my father's death six months previously, down to my feet crammed into cheap, too-small shoes that had been all my loving but sadly unskilled father had been able to side me in the back of the limo, now sleeping in blessed silence. "You go. I'll stay here with Miguel." Which would also be the perfect way for me to sneak to Edward's house, at the end of the street.

"Dowell can watch him."

I glanced at the driver doubtfully. "No."

"Then bring Miguel with us."

"Wake him up?" I whispered, scandalized. I narrowed my eyes. "Of course *you* wouldn't worry about that. You're not the one who spent the whole flight walking in circles trying to make him sleep."

Alejandro set his jaw. "I offered to take him…."

"You could have offered again." I was dimly aware that I sounded irrational. There was no way he could have taken Miguel from me on the jet except by force, which wouldn't exactly have gone over well, either. My cheeks got hot. "It doesn't matter."

He lifted a dark eyebrow. "You do know how to take care of Miguel better than I do."

His tone told me whom he blamed for that. "I had no choice. I thought you were going to steal him from me."

"So you stole him first?"

I blinked. I hadn't thought of it that way before.

"You could at least have called me directly," he ground out.

Now, that was unfair! "I tried! You wouldn't take my phone calls!"

"If I'd known you were pregnant, I would have."

His jaw tightened. "You could have left a message with Mrs. Allen...."

"Leave a *message* with some faceless secretary at your London office to let you know, oh, hey, I'm pregnant with your baby? Seriously?" I lifted my chin. "You should have just taken my damn call!"

Alejandro stared at me, his lips pressed in a thin line. "This argument is over." He turned away. "Unlatch the baby carrier and lift it out of the seat. That won't wake him up, as you know perfectly well."

My cheeks burned slightly. Yes, I'd known that. I'd just been hoping *he* wouldn't.

When I didn't move, Alejandro started to reach around me. With a huff I turned and unlatched the seat. Miguel continued softly snoring in sweet baby dreams, tucked snugly in the carrier with a soft blanket against his cheek.

As the driver closed the door behind us with a snap, I stood on the sidewalk, staring up at the cold white mansion.

I'd never wanted to return to this house. But there was one silver lining. I hadn't been lying when I'd told Alejandro I wanted to come back for Miguel's legacy. Something I'd been forced to leave behind that had nothing to do with the inheritance I'd lost.

As I looked up, the soft drizzle felt like cobwebs against my skin. Like memories. Like ghosts.

"What now?" Alejandro was glaring at me as if I wasn't his favorite person. I couldn't blame him. He wasn't my favorite person right now, either.

Although at this moment there was one person I liked even less. I swallowed.

"I'm scared," I whispered.

He stared at me. "Of Claudie?"

I nodded, not trusting my voice.

"You don't need to be scared," he said gruffly. "I'm here with you now." Reaching out, he took the baby carrier from my trembling hands. "Come on."

Alejandro carried our sleeping baby up the stone steps and knocked on the imposing front door.

Mr. Corgan, the longtime butler, opened the door. His jowly face was dignified as he greeted Alejandro.

"Good morning, Your Excellency." Then he glanced at me and his eyes went wide. "Miss Lena!" He saw the sleeping baby in the carrier, and the usually unflappable Mr. Corgan's jaw fell open. "It's true?" He breathed, then glanced at Alejandro, and the mask slipped back into place. Holding open the door, he said sonorously, "Won't you both please come in?"

He led us into the elegant front salon, with high ceilings and gilded furniture. Everything looked just as I remembered—vintage, French and expensive. I'd been allowed in this room only a handful of times, the last being when I'd begged Claudie for money to fly to Spain. The day my life had fallen apart.

Mr. Corgan said, "I regret that Miss Carlisle is… out…at the moment, but she has a standing order to welcome you at any time, Your Excellency, if you care to wait."

"*Sí,*" Alejandro said coldly. "We will wait."

"Of course. She will be so pleased to see you when she returns. May I offer refreshments? Tea?"

Alejandro shook his head. He sat down on the pink striped couch near the window. He seemed incongruous there, this dark, masculine Spaniard with severely tailored black clothes, in a salon that looked like a giant powder puff, with the powder made of diamond dust.

He set down the baby carrier on the white polished marble floor beside the sofa. I swiftly scooped it up, and exhaled in relief now that my sleeping baby was safely back in my possession. I followed Mr. Corgan out of the salon and into the hallway.

Once we were alone, the butler's mask dropped and he turned to face me with a happy exclamation.

"We missed you, girl." He hugged me warmly. I closed my eyes, smelling pipe smoke and brass polish. Then I heard a crash and pulled back to see Mrs. Morris, the housekeeper, had just broken a china plate in the hallway. But she left it there, coming forward with a cry.

A minute later, both of them, along with Hildy, the maid, were hugging me and crying and exclaiming over Miguel's beauty, his dark hair, his fat cheeks.

"And such a good sleeper, too," Mrs. Morris said

approvingly. Then they all looked at each other. I saw the delicate pause.

Then Hildy blurted out, "Who's his father, then?"

I glanced back at the salon, biting my lip. "Um…"

Hildy's eyes got huge when she saw who was in the salon. Then she turned to Mr. Corgan. "You were right. I owe you a fiver."

His cheeks went faintly pink as he cleared his throat with a *harrumph*. "I might have heard some of your conversation with Miss Carlisle the day you left, Miss Lena." He shook his jowly head with a glare. "It wasn't right what she did. Driving you from the house a year before you would have got your grandmother's inheritance."

I was surprised for only a second. Then I gave a wry smile. Of course they knew. Household staff knew everything, sometimes even before their employers did. "It doesn't matter."

"But it does," Mrs. Morris said indignantly. "Miss Carlisle wanted your inheritance and the moment she convinced you to move out of the house, she got it by default. Just a year before it would have finally been yours!"

I pressed my hand against my temple as emotions I had spent the past year trying to forget churned up in me.

When I turned eighteen, I could have left for college, or gotten a real job. Instead, I'd remained living in this house, working as a sort of house manager/personal assistant for my cousin beneath her unrelenting criticism as she tried her best to drive me away. I'd had a small salary at first, but even that had disappeared when she'd lazily announced one day that she was cutting the salaries of the staff by twenty percent. "They don't need it," she sniffed. "They are lucky, working all day in my beautiful house. They should be paying *me!*"

Mr. Corgan and Mrs. Morris and the rest had become my friends, and I knew they had families to support. So I'd given up my salary rather than see them suffer. Leaving me virtually destitute for years, in spite of working eighteen-hour days.

But I hadn't minded, not really, because I'd known all I had to do was remain in this house until I was twenty-five, just a few months from now, and I would have gotten the huge inheritance once destined for my father, before he'd been cut out of the will for the crime of marrying my mother.

Eight years ago, when my grandmother lay dying, she'd clutched his old teddy bear and dissolved in tears I'd never seen before as she remembered the youngest son she'd once loved best. She'd called for her lawyer.

If Robert's child proves herself worthy of the Carlisle name, my grandmother's will had read, *and she still lives in the house at the age of twenty-five, she may claim the bequest that would have been his.*

But now it had all reverted to Claudie. I hadn't cared a whit about the money last year, when I'd feared my baby would be stolen from me. But now...

"The house hasn't been the same without you, Miss Lena," Mr. Corgan said.

"Half the staff resigned after you left," Mrs. Morris said.

"She's been intolerable without you to run interference." Mr. Corgan shook his head grimly. "I've worked for this family for forty years, Miss Lena, but even I fear my time here is nearing an end." Leaning closer, he confided, "Miss Carlisle still insists she'll marry your duke."

"He's not my duke...."

"Well. He's the only man rich and handsome enough for *her,* though she says she'd marry any rich idiot who'd make her a duchess...." Glancing back over his shoulder, he coughed, turning red.

Turning, I saw Alejandro standing in the doorway of the salon. I wondered how much he'd heard. His face was half hidden in shadow, his expression inscrutable.

"Did you change your mind about the tea, Your Excellency?" Mr. Corgan gasped, his face beet red.

Alejandro shook his head. His eyes were dark, but his lips quirked at the edges. "We rich idiots prefer coffee."

The butler looked as if he wished the earth would swallow him up whole. "I'll get it right away, sir...."

"Don't bother." He looked at me. "Did you get what you came for?"

He'd heard everything, I realized. He thought I'd come for my inheritance. He thought that was the precious thing that had brought me here. It wasn't.

I turned to Mrs. Morris urgently. "Did she throw out my things?"

"She wanted to," she said darkly. "She told me to burn it all. But I boxed it all up and left it in your attic room. I knew she'd never bother to go all the way up there to check."

"Bless you," I whispered, and hugged her. "Stay and have coffee," I called to Alejandro. "I'll be back in a few minutes." I started up the stairs, carrying my sleeping baby with me.

Climbing three floors, I reached the attic. It looked even more desolate than I remembered, with only one grimy window, an ancient metal bed frame and stacks of boxes. Setting down the baby, I went straight for the boxes.

"What are you looking for?"

Hearing Alejandro's husky voice behind me, I turned. "These boxes hold everything from my childhood."

He stepped inside the attic room, knocking his head against the slanted roof. He rubbed it ruefully. "I can see why Claudie wouldn't come up here. This place is like a prison cell."

"This was my home for over ten years."

His dark eyes widened. "This room?" He slowly looked around the attic, at the rough wood floors, at the naked lightbulb hanging from the ceiling. "You lived here?"

I gave a wistful laugh. "From the time my parents died when I was fourteen, until I left last year when…well. It looked nicer then, though. I made decorations, paper flowers." A lump rose in my throat as I looked around the bare room where I'd spent so many years. The bare mattress on the metal bed frame where I'd slept so many nights. I gently touched the bare lightbulb and swung it on the cord. "I had a bright red lampshade I bought from the charity shop on Church Street."

"A charity shop?" he said sharply. "But you're Claudie's cousin. A poor relation, I know, but I'd assumed you were well paid for all your work…."

This time my laugh was not so wistful. "I was paid a salary after I turned eighteen, but that money had to go to—other things. So I started earning a little money doing portraits at street fairs. But Claudie allowed me so little time away from the house…"

"*Allowed* you?" he said incredulously.

I looked at him. "You heard about my inheritance."

"How much would it have been?"

"If I was still living in this house on my twenty-fifth birthday, a few months from now, I would have inherited thirty million pounds."

His jaw dropped.

"Thirty…"

"Yes."

"And you left it all?"

"To protect my baby. Yes."

"To protect our baby, you sacrificed more money than most people see in a lifetime."

He sounded so amazed. I shook my head. "Any mother would have done the same. Money is just money." I glanced down at Miguel, and a smile lifted my cheeks as I said softly, "He is my life."

When I finally looked up, his dark, soulful eyes were looking at me as if he'd never seen me before. My cheeks went hot. "I expect you think I'm an idiot."

"Far from it," he said in a low voice.

He was looking at me with such intensity. Awkwardly, I turned away and started digging through the top box. Pushing it aside, I opened the one beneath it.

"What are you looking for?" he said curiously.

Not answering, I pulled out old sweaters, old ragtag copies of books I'd read and reread as a teenager, *Rebecca*, *A Little Princess*, *Jane Eyre*. Finally, at the bottom of the box, I found the three oversize, flat photo albums. "Thank you," I whispered aloud when I saw they hadn't been burned, or warped from being left to rot in the rain or scribbled on with a venomous black marker, or any of the other images I'd tormented myself with. Pressing the albums against my chest, I closed my eyes in pure gratitude.

"Photo albums?" Alejandro said in disbelief. "You begged me to come to London for *photo albums?*"

"I told you," I said sharply. "I came for my baby's legacy."

"But I never thought..." Frowning, Alejandro held out his hand. "Let me see."

Reluctantly, I handed them over, then watched as he turned through the pages of the top album, at old photographs pressed against yellowing adhesive pages beneath the clear plastic cover.

"It nearly killed me to leave them behind," I said. "It's all I have left of my parents. My home." I pointed to a picture of a tenement building where the ground floor was a butcher's shop. "That was our apartment in Brooklyn."

He turned the page. "And this?"

My heart twisted when I saw my mother, young and laughing, holding a ragtag bouquet of flowers, sitting in my father's lap. "My parents' wedding day. My dad was a student in London. He fell in love with a waitress, an immigrant newly arrived from Puerto Rico. He married her against his family's wishes, when she was pregnant with me...."

Alejandro looked at me for a long moment, then silently turned more pages. My babyhood flashed before my eyes, pictures of me as a tiny baby, getting bathed in the sink, sitting on a towel on the kitchen floor, banging wooden spoons against a pot and beaming with the same chubby cheeks that Miguel had now.

Finishing the first album, Alejandro handed it to me without a word, and thumbed through the second book, then the third. My childhood passed swiftly—learning to ride a bike...my first day at school...

"Why are you interested?" I said haltingly. "Is it—to make fun of me?"

"To make fun?" He looked at me with a scowl. "You think I would taunt you about having a happy childhood?" He shook his head. "If anything, I envy you," he said softly, looking back at the pages that my tenderhearted mother had made for me when I was a child. Right up to the very last photo, of my father at Christmas, sitting beneath the tree wearing a Santa hat, smiling lovingly at the camera as he held my mother's homemade gift of a sweater. Two months later, he was dead. There were no more photos. The last few pages of the album were blank. Alejandro said softly, "I have no pictures of myself with my mother. None."

I blinked. "How is that possible? I mean, I'd think you'd have a million pictures taken...."

He abruptly looked at me. Without answering, he closed the photo album and handed it to me.

"Perhaps you're not who I thought you were."

"Who did you think I was?"

"Exactly like all the other women I've ever dated. In love with the idea of being a rich duchess." He looked down at me, his dark eyes infinite and deep as the night sky. "But I'm starting to think you're different. A woman who would willingly leave thirty million pounds… You were actually in love with me, weren't you?"

My breath got knocked out of me.

"That was a long time ago."

Our eyes met, and I suddenly had to get out of the attic. I picked up Miguel's baby carrier with one arm and carried the albums with the other. "I'll be downstairs."

Without looking back, I fled, rushing down the flights of stairs. My teeth were chattering, and I was shaking with strange emotion. *Edward,* I reminded myself. The other reason I'd come to London. I had to get his help before Alejandro could bully me into going to Spain. Although it actually wasn't going to Spain that frightened me. It was never being able to leave again. It was being separated from my baby. It was being completely under the control of a man who'd almost destroyed me once, just by making me love him.

As I reached the bottom of the staircase, I heard a car door slam outside. Through the windows, I saw a flash of purple.

Claudie had come home.

I turned to where Hildy was loitering at the bottom of the stairs. "Hildy!"

"Oh, hello," she said, blushing when she saw me. "I was just dusting the banister, Miss—"

"My cousin is here. Please." Grabbing Hildy's arm, I whispered, "I need you to take a message to Edward St. Cyr."

"Edward St. Cyr?" Hildy's eyes nearly popped out of her head. "Mr. St. Cyr himself? Are you serious?"

"Tell him I need to see him," I said with more assurance than I felt.

"Here, miss? You know he and Miss Carlisle hate each other...."

Hearing my cousin fumbling at the door, I shook my head. "Tell him...the Princess Diana Playground in thirty minutes."

With a quick, troubled nod, Hildy hurried toward the back door. Just in time, too. The front door slammed.

"Well. Look who's back."

My cousin's voice was a sneer. Warily, I turned to face her for the first time in a year.

"Hello, Claudie." She was wearing a tight, extremely short bandage dress, the kind you might wear to a club if you wanted a lot of attention, in a vivid shade of purple that almost matched the hollows beneath her eyes. "Late night?" I said mildly.

She glared at me.

"If you came to beg for your inheritance, forget it. My solicitors went through the will with a fine-tooth comb," she ground out. "You'll never..." Then she saw the baby and gasped in triumph. "You brought the brat here? I knew you'd see reason." She rubbed her hands together in glee. "Now I'll either make him marry me, or else I'll—"

"You'll what, Claudie?" Alejandro said coolly from the top of the stairs.

My cousin looked up, speechless for the first time in her life. But she recovered almost instantly. Smiling up at him, she put her hand on her hip, setting a pose that showed her figure to advantage, wearing her six-inch heels and skintight purple dress, trailing a cloud of expensive perfume. Her gorgeous, long blond hair tumbled over her shoulders, emphasizing the bone structure of her sharp cheekbones.

But as she licked her big lips, beneath her smile, her eyes were afraid. "Alejandro. I didn't know you were here."

He came down the stairs, looking down at her. He stopped in front of her. Even though she wore such high heels, he was still taller.

"You lied to me, Claudie," he said pleasantly. "Lena wasn't holding my baby hostage. You were."

She visibly trembled, then tried to laugh. Reaching into her crystal-encrusted bag, she got out a pack of cigarettes. "Darling, I don't know what kind of lies my precious cousin might have told you, but…"

He grabbed her wrist almost violently.

"Do not," he said coldly, "smoke near my son."

"*Your* son," she breathed, searching his gaze, then ripped her arm away. "Are you so sure of that?" Her beautiful blue eyes hardened. "How do you know he's yours? You should have seen all the men who used to come through here, Alejandro—trooping up to Lena's bedroom every single night—"

A little gasp escaped me, like an enraged squeak.

Alejandro lifted an eyebrow. "Then they must have been lost, on their way to *your* room, Claudie."

Her eyes narrowed. "I don't like what you're implying—"

"We did a DNA test," he said, cutting her off. "The baby is mine."

For a moment, she stared at him. But you could almost see her gather her forces. "He doesn't have to be." She looked from him to me. "If you don't treat him like your son, no one else will."

"You think I would abandon my own child?"

"Fine," she said impatiently. She flung a skeletal finger toward my sweetly sleeping son. "We can take her baby. She's nobody, Alejandro. She won't be able to stop us...."

With a gasp, I protected the baby carrier with my body.

"Just think." Claudie swayed her hips as she walked toward Alejandro with her hypnotic red smile. "Just think how perfect our future could be." She started to wrap her arms around him. "With your money and title, and my money and connections...the two of us could rule the world."

He looked down at her coldly. "Do you really

think I'd want to rule the world, if the price would be marriage to you?"

Shocked, she let her arms fall to her sides.

"You used Lena for years as an unpaid slave," he said, "then threatened to take her baby, for the sake of stealing what you wanted—her inheritance. And then you tried to blackmail me into marrying you!"

She licked her lips. "I…"

He held up his hand sharply, cutting her off. His voice was deep and harsh. "For the past year, you've lied to me, saying if I ever wanted to see my child, I had to marry you. Blaming Lena, making me think she was the one to blame. For that, you deserve to go to hell. Which I hope you will find—" he gave her a sudden, pleasant smile "—very soon. *Adios, Claudie.*" Scooping up the baby carrier, he turned to me gravely. "Shall we go?" Without another word, he walked out the front door.

"Alejandro, wait," Claudie gasped, but I was the only one left to hear. *"You."* Her face as she turned to look at me really did look like a snake's. Or maybe a dragon's—I could almost see the smoke coming out of her nostrils as her blue, reptilian eyes hardened. "You did this!"

For the past decade, I'd dreamed of what I would say to her if given the chance, after all my lonely years, crying alone in my attic. All the subtle and not so subtle ways she'd insulted me, used me, made me feel worthless and invisible for the past ten years. But in this moment, all those things fled from my mind. Instead, the real question came from my heart.

"Why did you hate me, Claudie?" I whispered, lifting my tearful gaze to hers. "I loved you. You were my only family. Why couldn't you love me? Why wouldn't you let me love you?"

My cousin drew herself up, all thin gorgeousness.

"Why?" She lit her cigarette with shaking hands. "Because you're not my real family." Taking a long draw on her cigarette, she said in a low, venomous hiss, "And you're not good enough for Alejandro. Blood always tells. Sooner or later, he will be embarrassed by you, just as I was. He'll take your child and toss you in the gutter, like you deserve."

My mouth fell open as her poisoned dart hit me, square in the heart.

"It didn't have to be this way," I choked out, and I turned and fled, still holding my photo albums against my chest, like a shield.

Outside, a sliver of sun had split through the dark clouds, through the rain. Stopping on the sidewalk, I turned back and looked up at the Carlisle mansion for one last time.

"Goodbye," I whispered.

Then I climbed into the limo, where the driver waited with my door open, and he closed it behind me.

"Enjoy a tender farewell?" Alejandro was already in the backseat, on the other side of Miguel, who had woken and was starting to whimper.

"Something like that," I muttered, trying to surreptitiously wipe my tears.

"I was surprised. It's not like you to let me walk off with—" His voice cut off as he saw my face. "What's wrong?"

"Nothing," I said. Turning to my baby, I pressed his favorite blanket against his cheek and tried to comfort him. Tried to comfort myself. My baby's tears quieted and so did his quivering little body, as he felt the hum and vibration of the car's engine beneath him. His eyelids started to grow heavy again.

"What did she say?" Alejandro said. Frowning, he looked closer at my face. "Did she…"

There was a sudden hard knock on his window. Miguel's little body jerked back awake, and his whimpers turned to full-on crying. Alejandro turned with a growl.

Claudie stood by the limo, her eyes like fire. "Open this window!" she yelled through the glass.

Alejandro's expression was like ice as he rolled it down a grudging two inches. She leaned forward, her face raw with emotion.

"We could have ruled the world together, Alejandro, and you're throwing it all away—for that little whore and her brat!"

Alejandro said softly, his face dangerous, "If you ever insult either my son or his mother again, you will regret it."

Claudie looked bewildered. To be fair, she'd insulted me for so long she'd probably forgotten it wasn't nice.

"But Alejandro…" Her voice had a strange begging sound I'd never heard from her. "You'll never find someone with my breeding, my beauty, my billions. I love you…."

"You love my title."

Her cheeks flushed red. "All right. But you can't choose her over me. She's…nothing. No one."

I swallowed, blinking fast.

"Blood always tells," she said. "She's not good enough for you."

Alejandro looked quickly at my miserable face. Then he turned back to Claudie with a deliberate smile.

"Thank you for your fascinating opinion. Now move, won't you? I need to take Lena shopping for an engagement ring."

"You're—what?" Claudie staggered back. I gasped. Miguel was crying.

The only one who looked absolutely calm was Alejandro. Turning away from her, he sat back in the plush leather seat, and said to Dowell, "Drive on."

Claudie stared after us, looking stupefied on the sidewalk, and almost forlorn in her tight club dress and bedraggled mascara. Looking back at her through the car window, I felt a strange wave of sympathy.

Because I, too, knew what it felt like to be left by Alejandro Navaro y Albra.

"You didn't have to be so cruel," I whispered.

"Cruel?" he said incredulously. "You defend her, after the way she treated you?"

"She's still my cousin. I feel sorry for her…."

"Then you're a fool," he said harshly.

I stroked my crying baby's cheek. My lips creased sadly. "Love makes us all fools."

"She doesn't love me. She doesn't even know me."

"That's what you said to me, too," I said softly. I met his gaze. "I wonder if any woman will ever truly know you."

For an instant, I thought I saw hunger, even yearning in his dark eyes as he stared down at me. Then the expression shuttered, leaving me to decide I'd imagined it. But even then, he continued to look at me, as if he couldn't look away.

"What are you staring at?" I put my hand to my messy ponytail, feeling suddenly self-conscious. "I must look a mess."

"You look…" His eyes slowly traced over my hand, up my arm, to my neck, to my lips. "You look like a woman who cares more about her baby than a fortune. Like a woman who works so hard and so well—for free—that she's beloved by the entire household staff. You look," he said softly, "like a woman who feels sympathy, even for the coldhearted creature who tried to destroy her."

"Are you—complimenting me?"

He gave a low laugh. "If you're not sure, I must be losing my touch."

I flushed. Turning away, I took a deep breath. And changed the subject. "Thank you for bringing me back to London. For these." I motioned toward the photo albums. "And for giving me the chance to finally ask Claudie something I've wanted to know all my life. I always wondered why nothing I did was good enough to make her love me." I looked out the window at the passing shops of Kensington High Street. "Now I know."

Silence fell.

"Are you all right?" he asked.

I nodded over the lump in my throat.

"I know how it feels," he said in a low voice, "to be alone."

"You?" I looked at him sharply, then gave a disbelieving snort. "No, you don't."

His dark eyes were veiled. "When I was young, I was good friends with...our housekeeper's son. We were only six months apart in age, and we studied under the same governess. Friend? He was more like a brother to me," he said softly. "People said we looked so much alike, acted so much alike, we could have been twins."

"Are you still friends?"

He blinked, focusing on me, and his jaw tightened. "He died in the same crash that took the duke, the duchess. The housekeeper. Twenty-three years ago."

"They all died in the same crash?" I said, horrified.

He looked down. "I was the only one to survive."

I thought of a young boy being the only survivor of a car accident that took his parents, his best friend. That made him a duke at the tender age of twelve. I couldn't even imagine the loneliness. The pain. Reaching out, I took his hand and whispered, "I'm sorry."

Alejandro drew away. "It was a long time ago." I saw tension in his jaw, heard it in his voice. "But I do know how it feels."

I swallowed, feeling guilty, and embarrassed, too, for all my complaining when he'd suffered worse, and in silence. "What was his name? Your friend?"

He stared at me, then his lips lifted slightly. "Miguel."

"Oh." I gave a shy smile. "So that's why you don't mind that I named our baby Miguel—"

"No." He seemed to hide his own private smile. "I don't mind at all."

I frowned, looking at him more closely.

His expression shuttered, and his dark eyebrows came down into a scowl. "His surname, however..."

I sighed. "I thought you might want to change that. But don't worry." I gave an awkward smile. "I won't hold you to your marriage proposal."

His eyes were dark and intense. "What if I want you to hold me to it?"

My lips parted in shock.

"What?" I said faintly.

His dark eyes challenged mine. "What if I want you to marry me?"

"You don't want to get married. You went on and on about all the women who tried to drag you to the altar. I'm not one of them!"

"I know that now." Leaning his arm across the baby seat, he cupped my cheek. "But for our son's sake, I'm starting to think you and I should be... together."

"Why?"

"Why not?" He gave a sensual smile. "As you said, I already broke one rule. Why not break the other?"

"But what has changed?"

"I'm starting to think...perhaps I can trust you." His eyes met mine. "And I can't forget how it felt to have you in my bed."

Something changed in the air between us. Something primal, dangerous. I felt the warmth of his palm against my skin and held my breath. As the limo drove through the streets of London, memories crackled through me like fire.

I remembered the night we'd conceived Miguel, and all the other hot days of summer, when I'd surrendered to him, body and soul. I trembled, feeling him so close in the backseat of the limo, on the other side of our baby. Every inch of my skin suddenly remembered the hot stroke of Alejandro's fingertips. My mouth was tingling, aching....

"That's not a good reason to marry someone. Especially for you. If I said yes, you'd regret it. You'd blame me. Claim that I'd only done it to be a rich duchess."

He slowly shook his head. "I think," he said quietly, "you might be the one woman who truly doesn't care about that. And it would be best for our son. So what is your answer?"

My answer?

I remembered the darkness I'd fallen into the last time Alejandro wanted me—then stopped wanting me. I'd never let myself be vulnerable to him ever again. I couldn't. He'd almost destroyed me once. I could never live through that again.

Sooner or later...he'll take your child and toss you in the gutter, like you deserve.

I couldn't give him control over me, ever again. I couldn't be tempted. My only hope was to get away. My only hope was...

Oh, heaven...what time was it?

"I need to..." As I saw the time on the dashboard of the limo, my heart nearly burst in panic. "Stop the car!" I leaned forward desperately toward the driver. "Let me out!"

Looking confused, Dowell pulled over on the side of the busy road.

"What are you doing?" Alejandro demanded, looking at me as if I was crazy. I felt crazy.

I unbuckled our baby, who'd just stopped crying and was looking drowsy. "Miguel needs a walk to help him sleep...."

"Is that a joke?"

I didn't answer. Cradling our baby, I stepped out on the sidewalk in front of Kensington Palace, and started running into the park, toward the playground. Toward Edward.

CHAPTER THREE

THE PRINCESS DIANA PLAYGROUND was in the corner of Kensington Gardens, just north of the palace. It was still early, and the playground had just opened, but in the midst of August holidays it was already starting to fill with children of every age, laughing and whooping as they raced toward the teepees and leaped on the ropes of the life-size pirate ship. It was a magical place, as you might expect of a children's playground, near a palace, based around a Peter Pan theme and named after a lost princess.

But I was here desperate for a different kind of magic.

Protection.

Edward St. Cyr had protected me more than once. We'd first properly met three years earlier, when I'd been walking up from the Tube late at night and I'd passed a group of rowdy teenagers on Kensington High Street. I'd been weighed down with groceries, and tried to keep my head down as they passed. But some of the boys had followed me up the dark street, taunting me crudely. As one started to knock the grocery bags out of my hand, there'd been a flash of headlights on the street and the slam of a car door, and suddenly a tall man in a dark coat was there, his face a threatening scowl, and the young men who'd scared me fled like rabbits into the snow. Then he'd turned to me.

"Are you all right, miss…?" Then his expression had changed. "But wait. I know you. You're Claudie Carlisle's cousin."

"Yes, I…"

"You're all right now." He'd gently taken my trembling hand. "I'm Edward St. Cyr. I live a few streets from here. May I give you a ride home?"

"No, I couldn't possibly. I…"

"I wouldn't mind a walk myself," he said briskly, and with a nod to the driver of his Rolls-Royce, he'd insisted on walking me home, though it took ten minutes.

"Thank you," I'd said at the door. "I never meant to impose…."

"You didn't." He'd paused. "I remember what it's like to feel alone and afraid. Will you let me check on you in the morning?"

I'd shaken my head. "It's truly not necessary."

"But you must." He'd lifted a dark eyebrow. "If for no other reason than it will annoy your cousin, whom I've despised for years. I insist."

Now, as I looked out at Kensington Gardens in the distance, I saw the paths where we'd once head. "This idea of marriage is just a momentary madness with you—it will pass...."

My voice trailed off as I saw Hildy on the edge of the playground, frantically signaling.

Alejandro frowned. "What is it?" He started to turn his head. "What are you..."

"On second thought, let me think it over," I said quickly. Touching his arm, I gave him a weak smile. "So much has happened since yesterday. Maybe I'm too exhausted to think straight." I pointed toward the outdoor café at the front of the playground. "Could you...please...get me some coffee?"

Alejandro's dark gaze flickered over my bedraggled dress, the dark circles under my eyes. "Of course, *querida*," he murmured courteously. Turning away, he started toward the outdoor café.

The instant he was gone, I rushed to meet Hildy.

"Where's Edward?" I said desperately.

She was already shaking her head. "Mr. St. Cyr wasn't home. They said he's in Tokyo."

Of all the bad luck! "Can I borrow your phone?"

"Yes...." She reached into her pocket, then looked up, her mouth a round *O*. "I didn't bring it! It's still at home!"

Alejandro was already handing over money at the café. I saw him pick up two coffees from the counter. No time.

My shoulders fell. "Thanks anyway. You'd better go."

"Good luck, miss…."

Defeated, I looked out across the green park, deep emerald beneath the lowering gray London sky. I suddenly wondered what the weather was like in Spain. Warm. Sunny. Blue skies. With the chance of a hot, seductive Spaniard demanding that I share his bed.

No! I couldn't let myself think about it! Just sharing custody of Miguel would be bad enough. I would never, ever be Alejandro's lover! And certainly not his wife!

"Here." Alejandro handed me a white paper cup that warmed my hands. The coffee smelled like heaven. I took a sip, then sighed with appreciation as I felt the heat melt me from the inside. It was sweet, and creamy.

"You remembered how I liked it," I said in surprise.

He took a sip of his own black coffee, and gave a wicked grin. "That's how all women like it."

"That's not true!"

He shrugged. "It's mostly true. Cream and sugar will calm a woman down every time."

I glared at him. "You are such a—"

"A heartless bastard?" He paused, then tilted his head. "Do you still think I'll be such a disaster as a father?"

He sounded wistful, even—hurt? No. Impossible. A man like Alejandro had no heart to injure. But still, guilt rose in me, making my cheeks burn. "Maybe you're not *completely* evil." I looked down at the cup. "You did get my coffee right. Even though you're completely wrong with your stereotype about women liking cream and sugar."

"Obviously," he agreed. He tilted his head. "Your arms must be getting tired from holding Miguel all this time."

"A bit," I admitted sheepishly. "He's starting to get too heavy to carry like this for long."

Finishing off his coffee, he threw the empty cup in the trash and reached out. "Give him to me."

I hesitated, then handed him over. I watched anxiously, but Alejandro was careful, holding him, even turning Miguel around so he could see the world around him. Alejandro caught my look. "How am I doing?"

"Not bad," I said grudgingly.

"Would you care to walk?" He lifted a dark eyebrow. "Since he needed a walk so badly that you almost jumped out of a moving car. This taking babies on walks must be a serious business. Or else you had some other reason for coming here that you don't want me to know about."

I looked at him sharply. Did he know something? Or was he just fishing?

He gave me a bland smile.

I shrugged. "It was what you said. Pure panic at your marriage proposal." I took a sip of coffee.

"Kind of like how you reacted last year when I told you I loved you. Instant disappearance." For a moment, we stared at each other. Then I turned away. "Yes. Let's walk."

The rain had eased up, and though gray skies were hovering, eager children of all ages, speaking many different languages, were now playing everywhere as we strolled past the pirate ship.

"So what is your answer?" he said casually, as if he'd been asking me out for a movie.

"About what?"

He looked at me.

"Oh." I licked my lips. "That."

"That."

"Be serious."

"I'm trying to be. But I've never asked any woman to marry me before. I'm starting to think I must be doing it wrong. Do I need to get down on one knee?"

"Don't you dare."

"Then what is it?"

I'm afraid you'd make me love you again. The cold knot near my heart, which had started to warm on the edges, returned to ice. "Come on," I mumbled, looking at the ground. "We both know that I'm not exactly duchess material."

"Are you trying to let me down gently?" he demanded. He stopped, leaning our baby against his hip as he looked at me. "Is there someone else?

Perhaps the person who helped you flee London last year, and travel around the world?"

"It's not like that."

"When a man protects a woman," he said grimly, "it is exactly like that."

"How do you know it's a man?"

"By looking at your face," he said softly. "Right now."

I looked away. My throat hurt as I took another sip of the rich, sweet coffee, watching all the mothers and fathers and smiling nannies hovering on the edge of their children's delighted play. Some of them looked back at me. They probably imagined we were a family, too.

But we weren't.

I would have given anything if Alejandro could have been a man I could trust with my heart. A regular guy, a hardworking, loving man, who could have been my real partner. Instead of a selfish playboy duke who didn't know the meaning of love, and if married would plainly expect me to remain a dutiful wife imprisoned in his castle, raising our child, while he enjoyed himself elsewhere. Why shouldn't he? If love didn't exist, I could only imagine what he thought of fidelity.

"Why did you seduce me, Alejandro?" I blurted out.

He blinked. "What?"

My voice trembled as I looked up at him. "If you

weren't trying to get me pregnant to provide an heir for you and Claudie, why did you seduce me? Why did you even notice me?"

"I don't understand."

"Are you really going to make me spell it out? Fine. You're—you—" I waved my half-full coffee toward him "—and I'm…" I indicated my white dress I'd worn for thirty-six hours now, wrinkled and possibly stained with baby sick I didn't know about, and I shivered in the cool morning air. "I believed Claudie's story last year because, for the first time, everything made sense. There was no other reason for you to… I mean, why else would a man like you, who could have any woman in the world, choose a woman like…"

Reaching out his hand, he cupped my cheek. "Because I wanted you, Lena. Pure and simple. I wanted you." Looking down at me, he said in a low voice, "I've never stopped wanting you."

My lips parted. I trembled, fighting the desire to lean into his touch. The paper cup fell from my hand, splashing coffee across the grass. But I barely noticed. Craning back my head, I blinked back tears as I whispered, "Then why did you break up with me like that, so coldly and completely? Just for telling you I loved you?"

Alejandro stared at me, then dropped his hand. "Because I didn't want to lead you on. I'd promised myself I'd never have either wife or child…."

"But why?" I said, bewildered. "Why wouldn't you want those things? You're the last of your line, aren't you? If you died without an heir…you would be the last Duke of Alzacar."

"That was my intention," he said grimly.

"But why?"

"It doesn't matter anymore." He looked down at Miguel in his arms. "Fate chose differently. I have a son." His dark eyes blazed at me, filled with heat and anger and something else…something I couldn't understand. "And I will protect his future. Right or wrong."

"You keep saying *right or wrong*. What is wrong about it?" I narrowed my eyes. "If you're trying to imply that he's not good enough—"

"Of course not," he bit out.

"Then it's me—"

He shook his head impatiently, his jaw tight. "I'm talking about me."

The great Duque de Alzacar, admitting some kind of fault? I blinked. I breathed, "I don't understand…."

"What is there to understand?" he said evasively. "Now that I am a parent, my priorities have changed. Wasn't it the same for you, when Miguel was born?"

I hesitated. It was true what he said, but I still had the sense he was hiding something from me. "Yes-s…."

"We have a child. So we will do what is best for him. We will marry."

"You didn't want to marry me in Mexico."

"That was when I thought you were a liar, a thief and probably a gold digger. Now my opinion of you has improved."

"Thanks," I said wryly.

"Why are you fighting me? Unless—" He gave me a sharp, searching gaze. "Are you in love with someone else?"

The image of Edward flashed in front of my eyes. I wondered if Alejandro would still keep his improved opinion of me if he knew I'd been living in another man's house. It would look sordid, even if the truth had been so innocent. At least—innocent on my side. Swallowing, I looked away.

"I'm not in love with anyone." My voice was barely audible over the noisy children at play.

His shoulders relaxed imperceptibly. "Then why not marry me?" His tone turned almost playful. "You really should consider it for the jewels alone…."

I gave a rueful laugh, then looked at him. "I'd never fit into your world, Alejandro. If I took you at your word and became your wife, we'd both be miserable."

"I wouldn't be."

I shook my head. "Your expectations of marriage are lower than mine. It would never work. I want—"

I looked down as my cheeks turned hot "—to be loved. I want what my parents had."

Alejandro abruptly stopped. We were in the far back of the playground now, in a quiet overgrown place of bushes and trees. "But what about our son? Doesn't he have some rights, as well? Doesn't he deserve a stable home?"

"You mean a cold, drafty castle?"

"It's neither drafty nor cold." He set his jaw. "I want my son, my heir, to live in Spain. To know his people. His family."

I frowned at him. "I thought you had no family."

"My grandmother who raised me. All the people on my estate. They are like family to me. Don't you think he deserves to know them, and they should know him? Shouldn't he know his country? Where else would you take him—back to Mexico?"

"I loved it there!" I said, stung.

"We will buy a vacation house there," he said impatiently. "But his home is with his land. With his people. With his parents. You of all people," he said softly, "know what it means to have a happy, settled childhood, surrounded by love."

I sucked in my breath. I felt myself wavering. Of course I wanted all those things for my son.

"You'll be a duchess, honored, wealthy beyond imagining."

"I'd be the poor stupid wife sitting at home in the castle," I whispered, hardly daring to meet his gaze, "while you were out having a good time with other, more glamorous women...."

His dark eyes narrowed. "I have many faults, but disloyalty is not one of them. Still, I can understand why you'd immediately think of cheating. Tell me—" he moved closer, his sardonic gaze sweeping over me "—did you enjoy having the use of Edward St. Cyr's house? His jet?"

My eyes went wide. My mouth suddenly went dry.

"How did you find out?" I said weakly.

"Before my jet left Mexico, I told my investigators to dig into the layer of the shell company that owned the house in San Miguel. If it wasn't Claudie who helped you," he said grimly, "I intended to find out who it really was."

Well. That explained why he'd stopped asking. "Why have you pretended all day you didn't know?"

His handsome face looked chiseled and hard as marble beneath the gray sky. "I wanted to give you the chance to tell me."

"A test?" I whispered.

"If you like." His eyes glittered. "Women always find the quality of danger so attractive. Until they find out what *danger* really means. Tell me. Did you enjoy using St. Cyr's possessions? His money? His jet? How about his bed? Did you enjoy sharing that?"

"I never shared his bed!" I tried not to remember the husky sound of Edward's voice. *It's time for you to belong to me.* Or the way he'd flinched at my reaction—an incredulous, unwilling laugh. He'd taken a deep breath. *You'll see,* he'd whispered, then turned and left. Pushing the memory away, I lifted my chin. "We've never even kissed!"

"I see." Lifting an eyebrow, Alejandro said scornfully, "He helped you out of the goodness of his heart."

That might be pushing it. I bit my lip. "Um… yes?"

"Is that a statement or a question?"

"He's a friend to me," I whispered. "Just a friend."

Alejandro looked at me more closely. "But he wants more, doesn't he?" The sweep of his dark lashes left a shadow against his olive skin, his taut cheekbones, as he looked down at our baby in his arms. After all this time, he still carried Miguel as if he were no weight at all. He said in a low voice, "I won't let my son keep such company. Because I, at least, have clear eyes about what *danger* means."

"And I understand at last," I choked out, "why you suddenly want to marry me."

He narrowed his eyes at me. "Lena—"

"You say he is dangerous? Maybe he is. But if it weren't for Edward St. Cyr, I don't think I could have survived the darkness and fear of the past year. He was there for me when you deserted me. When you left me pregnant and alone and afraid."

His face turned white, then red. "If you'd given me the chance—"

"I did give you a chance. You never called me back." I took a deep breath. "I know now you weren't the monster I thought you were. But I'll never be able to trust you like I did. It's lost. Along with the way I loved you."

Silence fell, the only sound the children playing on the other side of the trees. I heard their shrieks of joy.

When Alejandro spoke, his voice was low, even grim. "Love me or not, trust me or not, but you will marry me. Miguel will have a stable family. A real home."

I shook my head. He moved closer.

"You promised to come to Spain, Lena," he said. "You gave your word."

I threw him a panicked glance. "That was when—"

"Ah. You hoped you could break your promise, didn't you? Perhaps with St. Cyr's help?"

My silence spoke volumes. His dark eyes hardened. "You gave me your word that if I brought you to London, you would come with me to Spain."

He was right. I had. Now, I felt so alone and forlorn. Alejandro was starting to wear me down. To break my will. To remind me of a promise I'd never wanted to keep.

"It will only lead to misery," I whispered.

"Wherever it leads," he said softly, "whatever we'd once planned for our lives...you are part of my family now."

"Your family. You mean your grandmother?" I shivered, imagining a coldly imperious grande dame in pearls and head-to-toe vintage Chanel. A little like my own grandmother, in fact. "She will hate me. She'll never think I'm good enough."

He gave a low laugh. "You think you know what to expect? A cold, proud dowager in a cold, drafty castle?"

"Am I wrong?"

"My grandmother was born in the United States. In Idaho. The daughter of Basque sheep ranchers."

"Idaho?" My mouth fell open. "How did she...?"

"How did she end up married to my grandfather? It is an interesting story. Perhaps you can ask her when you meet her." His lips twisted grimly. "Unless you intend to break your promise, and refuse to go to Spain after all."

I swallowed, afraid of what it would mean to go to his castle. Surrounded by his family and friends. Surrounded by his *power*. How long could I resist his marriage demand then?

"Enough. You always spend too long in your mind, going back and forth on decisions that have already been made. End it now." Reaching into his pocket, Alejandro pulled out a phone and dialed a number. He pushed it into my hand. "It's ringing."

"What?" I stammered, staring down at the phone. "Whom did you call?"

"My grandmother. If you are breaking your promise to me, if you are truly not willing to bring Miguel to Spain to meet her, tell her now."

"Me? I can't talk to your grandmother!"

"No. *I* can't," he said coldly, "because I love her. *You* have no feelings for her whatsoever, so you should have no trouble being cruel."

"You think I'm cruel?" I whispered as the phone rang.

His eyes met mine. "Tell her she has a great-grandchild. Introduce yourself. Tell her I've asked you to marry me. Go on."

I stared at him numbly, then heard a tremulous voice at the other end of the line.

"*¿Hola?* Alejandro?"

It was a warm, sweet, kindly voice, the sort of voice that a grandmother would have in a movie, the grandmother who bakes cookies and is plump and white-haired and gives you hugs and tells you to eat more pie—or in this case, more paella?— because food is love, and she loves you so much that you're her whole existence, her light, her star. It was the type of voice I had not heard since my parents had died.

"Alejandro?" The woman sounded worried now. "Are you there?"

"It's not Alejandro," I replied, my voice unsteady. "But he asked me to call you. I'm a…friend."

"A friend?" The sweet tremulous voice gasped, her accent definitely American. "Has he fallen sick? Was he in an accident?"

"No, he's fine…."

"If he were fine, he'd be calling me himself, as he always does." A sob choked her voice. "You're trying to break it to me gently. But you can't. First I lost my children, then my…" Her voice broke. "Alejandro was all I had left. I always knew I would lose him someday. That sooner or later—" another sob "—fate would catch up with me and…"

"Oh, for heaven's sake!" I cried in exasperation. "Alejandro's fine! He's standing right by me!"

She sucked in her breath. Her tone changed, became curious. "Then why are you calling me on his phone?"

"He…wanted me to tell you the happy news." Glaring at Alejandro, I kept my voice gentle as I said, "You're a great-grandmother."

"A—" her voice ended in a gasp. A happy gasp. "Alejandro has a child?"

"We have a five-month-old son. I'm the baby's mother."

"You're American? Canadian?"

"Born in Brooklyn."

"Why didn't he tell me before? What's your name? Have we met?" She didn't seem like the snooty duchess I'd imagined. She continued eagerly, "Did you elope? Oh, I'll never forgive Alejandro for getting married without me—"

"He didn't tell you because—well, he wasn't sure about it. For your other question, we're not married." I gritted my teeth. "And we have no plans to be."

"You have no—" She cut herself off with an intake of breath. Then changing the subject with forced cheer, she said, "So when can I meet my great-grandson? I can hardly wait to tell my friends you're coming to live in the castle. The pitter-patter of little feet at Rohares Castle at last!"

"I'm sorry. We're not going to live in Spain."

"Oh." I heard the soft whoosh of her whimper. "That's…all right." She took a deep breath. "So when are you coming to visit so I can meet him?"

I bit my lip. "I don't know if we can…."

"I understand," she sniffled. "It's fine. Just send me a Christmas card with the baby's picture, and… it's fine. I've had a good life. I don't need to meet my only great-grandchild…."

My own fear of spending time with Alejandro, of allowing him more power over me, suddenly felt small and selfish compared with letting her meet Miguel—and even more important, allowing my son to have the family I myself had yearned for. What did I have, a heart of stone?

"All right." With a sigh, I accepted the inevitable. "We'll come to Spain in the next day or two. Just for a visit, mind!"

But even with that warning, her cries of joy exploded from the phone. I held it away from my ear, glaring all the while at Alejandro. "I'll let you talk to Alejandro," I told her, then covering the mouthpiece, I handed him the phone and grumbled, "I hate you."

"No, you don't." He took it from my hand, looking down at me seriously. "I'll win your trust, Lena. And then…"

"Then?"

He gave me a sensual smile. "You'll be my wife within the week."

There are many different kinds of seduction.

There's the traditional kind, with flowers, chocolates, dinner by candlelight. That's the way Alejandro had seduced me last summer. He called the Kensington mansion, asked for me, invited me to dinner. He showed up at the door dressed in a tux, his arms full of roses—to Claudie's rage—and greeted me with a chaste kiss on the cheek.

"You look beautiful," he'd murmured, and took me to the best restaurant in London. He asked me questions, listened aptly and physically grew closer and closer, with the innocent touch of his hand, the casual brush of his body against mine. He held my hand across the dinner table in the candlelight, in full view of the other patrons, looking at me with deep soulful eyes, as if no other woman had ever existed. Afterward, he took me to a club. We danced, and he pulled me into his arms, against his hard, powerful body. Closer. Closer still, until my heart was in my throat and I started to feel dizzy. In the middle of the dance floor, he lowered his head and kissed me for the first time.

It was my first kiss, and as I closed my eyes I felt the whole world whirling around me. Around us.

When he finally pulled away, he whispered against my skin, "I want you." I'd trembled, my heart beating violently, like a deer in a wolf's jaws. He'd looked down at me and smiled. Then took me back to his rooftop terrace suite at the Dorchester Hotel.

There had been no question of resistance. I was a virgin in the hands of a master. He'd had me from the moment he kissed me. From the moment he showed up at my door in a sleek tuxedo, with his arms full of roses, and told me he wanted me in his low, husky voice. He'd had me from the moment he'd seared me with the intensity of his full attention.

That was the traditional way of seduction. It had worked once, worked with utterly ruthless efficiency against my unprepared heart. But I knew the moves now—that is to say, I knew how they ended. With pleasure that was all too brief, and agony that was all too long.

But there are many different kinds of seduction.

Alejandro had decided we wouldn't leave immediately for Madrid, but would spend one night in London, resting at his usual suite of rooms at the Dorchester. He told me it was because the baby and I both looked tired. I was immediately suspicious, but as we left the park, he did not try to kiss me. Even after we'd arrived at the luxurious hotel, he did not look deeply into my eyes and tell me I was the most beautiful woman on earth, or pull me out onto the rooftop terrace, overlooking Hyde Park and all the wide gray sky, to take me in his arms.

Instead, he just ordered us lunch via room service, then afterward, he smiled at me. "We need to go shopping."

I frowned at him, suspecting a trick. "No, we don't."

"We do need a stroller," he said innocently. "A pushcart. For the baby."

I could hardly argue with that, since we'd left the umbrella stroller back in San Miguel. "Fine," I grumbled. "A stroller. That's it."

"You're very boring."

"I'm broke."

"I'm not."

"Lucky you."

"I can buy you things, you know."

"I don't want you to."

"Why?"

I set my jaw. "I'm afraid what they'd cost me."

He just answered with an innocent smile, and had his driver take us to the best shops in Knightsbridge, Mayfair and Sloane Street. He bought the most expensive pushcart he could find for Miguel, then pushed it himself, leaving the bodyguards trailing behind us to hold only shopping bags full of clothes and toys for the baby.

"You said just a stroller!"

"Surely you wouldn't begrudge me the chance to buy a few small items for my son?"

"No," I sighed. But Alejandro kept pushing the boundaries. All the bodyguards who trailed us were soon weighed down with shopping bags.

"Now we must get you some clothes, as well," Alejandro said, smiling as he caught me looking wistfully at the lovely, expensive dresses. I jumped, then blushed guiltily.

"No. Absolutely not."

"It's the least I can do," Alejandro replied firmly, "considering it was because of me that you lost your inheritance."

"That wasn't your fault…" I protested. He looked down at me with his big, dark, Spanish eyes.

"Please let me do this, *querida*. I must," he said

softly. "Such a small thing. You cannot deny me my desire."

I shivered. That was exactly what I was afraid of. That if I couldn't deny him this, I wouldn't be able to deny him anything. And soon I'd be putty in his hands again, like a spaniel waiting for her master with slippers in her mouth.

I'd end up married to a man who didn't love me. Who would ignore me. And I'd spend the rest of my life like a ghost, haunting his stupid castle.

Wordlessly, I shook my head. He sighed, looking sad.

I was proud of myself for sticking to my guns. But as we walked through the expensive shops, Alejandro saw me looking at a pretty dress a second too long. He gave one of his bodyguards a glance, and the man snatched it up in my size.

"What!" I exclaimed. "No. I don't want that!"

"Too bad," he said smugly. "I just bought it for you."

Irritated, I tried to foil Alejandro's plan by carefully *not* looking at any of the beautiful clothes, shoes or bags as we walked through the luxury department store and designer boutiques. But that didn't work, either. He simply started picking things out for me, items far more expensive and flashy than I would have picked out for myself. Instead of the black leather quilted handbag I might have chosen, I found myself suddenly the owner of a handbag in crocodile skin with fourteen-karat-gold fittings and diamonds woven into the chain.

"I can't wear that!" I protested. "I'd look a proper fool!"

He grinned. "If you don't like me choosing for you, you have to tell me what you want."

So I did. I had no choice.

"Dirty blackmailer," I grumbled as I picked out a simple cotton sweater from Prada, but his smile only widened.

The salespeople, sensing blood in the water, left their previous customers to follow eagerly in our wake. The size of our entourage quickly exploded, with salespeople, bodyguards, Alejandro, me and our baby in a stroller so expensive that it, too, might as well have been made of rare leathers and solid gold. Other people turned their heads to watch as we went by, their eyes big as they whispered to each other beneath their hands.

"I feel conspicuous," I complained to Alejandro.

"You deserve to be looked at," he said. "You deserve everyone's attention."

I was relieved to return to his suite of rooms at the Dorchester, even though it was so fancy, the same suite Elizabeth Taylor had once lived in. I was happy to be alone with him.

And yet not happy.

It took a long time for the bodyguards to bring

up all the packages. Even with help from the hotel staff.

"I didn't realize we bought so much," I said, blushing.

Alejandro gave a low laugh as he tipped the staff then turned back. "You hardly bought anything. I would have given you far more." He looked down at me. Running his hand beneath my jaw, he said softly, "I want to give you more."

We stood together, alone in the living room of the suite, and I held my breath. Praying he wouldn't kiss me. Wishing desperately that he would.

But with a low laugh, he released me. "Are you hungry?"

After I fed Miguel and tucked him to bed in the second bedroom, we had an early dinner in the dining room, beneath a crystal chandelier, on an elegant table that would seat eight, with a view not just of London, but of the exact place where, last summer, he'd pressed me against the silver wallpaper and made love to me, hot and fast and fierce against the wall.

All through dinner, I tried not to look at that wall. Or think about the bed next door.

I told myself he wasn't trying to seduce me. Maybe he wasn't. Maybe it was just my delusion, reading desire in his dark, hot glances. It had to be me. He wouldn't actually be intending to…

Alejandro suddenly smiled at me. "You are tired. It has been a long day for you."

"All that shopping," I grumbled. He grinned, taking an innocent sip of his after-dinner coffee.

"I meant before that. Mexico. Claudie. Your sleepless night on the plane…"

"Oh." I yawned, as if on cue. "I am a little tired."

"So go take some time for yourself. Take a nap. A shower. Go to bed. I will take over."

"Take over?"

"With Miguel." As I blinked at him in confusion, he lifted a dark eyebrow and added mildly, "Surely you can trust me that far—as far as the next room? If there is any problem, I will wake you. But there won't be. Go rest."

I took a long, hot shower, and it was heaven. Putting on a soft new nightgown straight from the designer bag, I fell into the large bed, knowing that someone else was watching our child as I slept, and I wasn't on call. That was the most deliciously luxurious thing of all.

When I woke, early-morning sunlight was streaking across the large bed, where I'd clearly slept alone. Looking at the clock, I saw to my shock I'd slept twelve hours straight—my best night's sleep in a year. I stretched in bed, yawning, feeling fantastic. Feeling grateful. Alejandro…

Alejandro!

He couldn't possibly have stayed up all night with

the baby! He must have left. Jumping out of bed in panic, I flung open the bedroom door, terrified that Alejandro had spirited away our baby and left me behind.

But Alejandro was in the living room, walking our baby back and forth, singing a Spanish song in his low, deep voice, as Miguel's eyes grew heavy. Then Alejandro saw me, and he gave me a brilliant smile, even though his eyes, too, looked tired.

"Buenos días, querida. Did you sleep?"

"Beautifully," I said, running my hands through my hair, suddenly self-conscious of my nightgown, which in this bright morning light looked like a slinky silk negligee. I tried to casually cover the outline of my breasts with my arms. "And you?"

"Ah," he said, smiling tenderly down at his son. "For us, it is still a work in progress. But by the time we are on the plane to Madrid, after breakfast, I think our little man will sleep. He's worn himself out, haven't you?"

I stared at the two of them together, the strong-shouldered Spaniard holding his tiny son so lovingly, with such infinite care and patience, though he'd clearly kept Alejandro up most of the night.

Miguel looked up with big eyes at his father. They had the same face, though one was smaller and chubby, the other larger and chiseled at the cheekbones and jaw. But I could not deny the look of love that glowed from Alejandro's eyes as he looked into the face of his son.

I'd been wrong, I realized. Alejandro did know how to love.

He just didn't know how to love *me*.

Turning back, Alejandro gave me a big grin, filled with joy and pride. Our eyes locked.

The smile slowly slid from his face. I felt his gaze from my head to my toes and everywhere in between. His soulful dark eyes seemed to last forever, like those starlit summer nights.

I looked at Alejandro in this moment, and I was suddenly afraid. Seeing him as a father, as a true partner in caring for the tiny person I loved so much, I trembled.

I could handle his gifts. I might even be able to handle the sensual awareness that electrified the air between us. I could keep my heart on ice. I could resist.

But this?

There are many different kinds of seduction. Some are of the body. Some are of the mind.

But others, the most powerful, are of the heart.

CHAPTER FOUR

I'M NOT GOING to lie. A private jet makes travel easier. Especially with a baby. We had a quick flight from London to Madrid. No standing in lines, no fighting for overhead space. And I felt much better than I had on the last flight. I was well slept, showered. My hair was brushed until it tumbled over my shoulders. I'd even put on a little mascara. Arriving in Madrid in my new soft pink blouse and form-fitting jeans, I felt almost pretty.

"Where's your diamond handbag?" Alejandro teased as we left the jet, going down the steps to the tarmac of the private airport, followed by his men carrying our luggage. "Don't you like it?"

I bit my lip. "Well…"

He put his hand on his heart, as if it had been stabbed with grief. "You don't!"

"Don't worry," I assured him. "I'll still use it. I was needing a new diaper bag."

He gave a low laugh, then sobered, his dark eyes resting on mine as he said softly, "I'll have to see if I can find some other gift to please you more."

I shivered at his glance, then looked out the window of the SUV. *He's not trying to seduce me,* I repeated silently to myself. *He's not. He's just trying to lure me into a loveless marriage of convenience—don't fall for it, don't...*

Madrid was beautiful, an elegant, formal city with its nineteenth-century architecture, spreading regally across the banks of the Manzanares River. All the gray clouds of San Miguel and London seemed a million miles away. Here, the August sky was bright blue, and the Spanish sun burning hot.

Alejandro's driver took us to his penthouse apartment near the Prado, the bodyguards and luggage following in the car behind. We arrived at the flat, which took the entire top floor, and were answered at the door by a middle-aged woman who seemed far too young to be his grandmother. He quickly introduced her as his longtime housekeeper, the only paid staff at the penthouse, Mrs. Gutierrez, who lived on a floor below.

Alejandro walked us around the enormous apartment, with its stark contemporary furnishings and enormous windows overlooking the city. "What do you think?"

"It's beautiful," I said slowly, "but so cold. You can hardly tell anyone lives here." Shivering, I cuddled my warm baby close. "You must not stay here much."

He blinked. "More blunt honesty."

"Was I rude?"

"I can take it." He shifted his weight, then clawed back his thick, dark hair. I wondered what it would feel like to… No! I stopped the thought cold. Oblivious of my inner struggle, he continued with a sigh, "My company is headquartered here. I am in Madrid all the time."

"Oh," I said, looking at all the sharp edges of the furniture, all the glass and chrome. "Um. Well. It's very—masculine."

He lifted a dark eyebrow. "Perhaps it needs a woman's touch."

In my current frame of mind, I wondered if he was talking about more than his apartment. My cheeks went hot and I cleared my throat. "I'm surprised your grandmother isn't here. She sounded so keen to meet her great-grandson."

"You'll meet her tomorrow. I have an event tonight in Madrid, and Abuela doesn't like to leave her roses, or all the people who count on her at the castle."

"The castle?"

"Rohares, near Seville. Where the Dukes of Alzacar have lived for four hundred years."

"Cold and drafty," I sighed.

"Exactamente." He gave me a sideways glance, seeming to hide a smile. "I can hardly wait for you to see it."

"Yeah," I grumbled. "How many rooms?"

"I lose count," he said, and I couldn't tell if he

was joking. But at least such a large building would create more space between us. Even this large penthouse felt too...close, when we were together. Every glance, every word, made me more attracted. It was dangerous.

As soon as his grandmother met the baby, I told myself firmly, I'd be out of this country and away from Alejandro. We'd come to some agreement over custody. Preferably one that involved Miguel living with me in Mexico.

Although it would be a shame to separate my son from a father who loved him, just because I was afraid of being hurt....

I pushed the thought away. "You said something about an event tonight?"

"A celebration—a ball, really. Hosted by my company. Starts in—" he glanced at his platinum watch and said calmly "—twenty minutes."

Thank heavens! I wouldn't have to spend the evening with him, trying desperately not to feel tempted! With real relief, I said, "Go and have a good time. We'll be fine. I'll tuck Miguel into bed and maybe read a book until..."

But he was already shaking his head. "Leave you alone with our son, giving you the opportunity to run away again? No."

"Why do you think I'd run away?"

"Why would I think you wouldn't?"

"You could post your bodyguards at the door," I suggested.

"You'd charm them and escape."

He thought I was charming? For an instant I felt flattered. Then I folded my arms. "You could just decide to trust me."

"I will trust you." He tilted his head, looking down at me with amusement. "As soon as you marry me."

"Never going to happen, and believe me, after this momentary madness—or whatever it is— passes, you'll thank me."

"Fine," he sighed, plunking down on the soft sofa in front of a wide-screen TV and a window with a view of the city. He reached for the remote control. "Shall we see if there are any good movies on tonight? Maybe order takeaway?"

I stared at him, my lips parted. "You can't miss your own party."

He shrugged. "Yes. It's a pity. Especially since it was to celebrate my company's upcoming IPO on the stock exchange. But I can miss it to watch a TV movie with you. No problem."

"Are you crazy? You can't miss something like that. You're the host! If you don't even bother showing up, what do you think it will do to your stock price?"

"It's fine. Really." He shrugged. "I don't have a date to the ball anyway."

"You honestly expect me to believe you don't have a date—*you?*"

"You have to admit it's kind of your fault."

Now we were getting down to it.

"How is it my fault?" I said suspiciously.

Tilting his head, he looked at me from the sofa. "I *did* have a date for tonight." He stroked his chin thoughtfully. "A beautiful Swedish swimsuit model, in fact. But when I called her yesterday and explained I wouldn't be picking her up in my jet because I'd just discovered a former mistress had my baby and I had to spend the day buying you presents instead of flying to Stockholm to collect her, well—for some reason, Elsa wasn't interested in flying coach to Madrid to be my date tonight."

I hid a laugh, tried to look mad. "Too bad for you. But it's really not my problem."

He nodded sagely. "You're scared."

"Scared? Of what?"

"Of spending time with me. You're scared you'll be overwhelmed with desire and say yes to everything, and wake up tomorrow morning, in my bed, with a ring on your finger."

In his *bed?* My mouth went dry.

"It's all right. I understand." He fluttered his dark eyelashes outrageously. "You don't trust yourself, because you want me so badly."

It was so true. "That's so not true!"

He lifted his eyebrows. "Then you'll be my date?"

I thought about the type of people I'd be likely to meet at his party. A bunch of wealthy, beautiful, *mean* people. Just like Claudie. "No, thanks."

"Why?" he demanded.

"The baby will wake up at midnight for a feeding…" I said weakly.

"I'll have you back by midnight. Via pumpkin coach if necessary."

"There's no one I can trust as his babysitter!"

"Mrs. Gutierrez raised four children, and has ten grandchildren. She's very trustworthy and experienced, and she's agreed to stay."

"You thought of everything," I grumbled.

"So say yes."

"I won't fit in with your friends, okay?"

"Always so afraid," he sighed. "Of me. Of them. Of your own shadow."

He was clearly taunting me, but I couldn't help but bristle. "Even if I wanted to go with you, it's too late. Your party starts in twenty minutes, and unless you bought a ball gown in London yesterday without me noticing, I have nothing to wear!"

Alejandro smiled. "Did I ever show you our bedroom?"

I shook my head with a scowl. "It's either yours or mine. Not *ours*."

"That's what I meant," he said innocently. Walking ahead in the hallway, he pushed open a door.

The bedroom was enormous, with an amazing view of Madrid, but sparsely furnished, with only an expensive, masculine bed. And, incongruously, a crib beside it.

But when I looked closer at the bed, I saw a flash

of pink. Coming closer, I gasped when I saw a pale pink gown, a delicious confection of flowers and silk, spread across his plain white bedspread. I picked it up with one hand, then dropped it when I saw the tag peeking at me. Oscar de la Renta.

A pumpkin coach, indeed! I whirled to face him. "You bought this yesterday. You always intended to bring me as your date tonight," I accused.

His lips were curved in a sensual smile, then his hands went up in mock surrender. "I admit it." Then he put down his hands, and his expression changed. His dark eyes became intent. Sensual. "I always get what I want," he said softly, searching my gaze. "And I don't give up. When something is difficult to possess, that only makes me want it more."

For a long heartbeat, we stared at each other in his bedroom.

Then I tossed my head, hoping he couldn't see how my body was trembling. "Fine. Have it your way. I'll come with you tonight, since it means so much to you. I'll do it for Miguel's sake, so your friends will know he wasn't just the result of some cheap one-night stand. But that's it."

His dark eyes burned into mine. "A cheap one-night stand? That is the last thing you were to me. You should know that by now."

A shiver went down my spine and through my soul. I straightened, locking my knees, and I handed him the baby. "I'll get dressed as quickly as I can."

Thirty minutes later, Alejandro helped me out of

the limo, holding my hand as we walked up a red carpet, past the flashbulbs of the paparazzi.

"I thought your company was a metals and real estate conglomerate," I murmured beneath all of the attention.

"It is," he said innocently, "among other things. We recently bought a movie studio. Look." I followed his gaze to see a beautiful movie star whom I'd admired for years just ahead of us in a tight sequined gown. "That's the reason for the paparazzi."

"She is beautiful," I said.

He looked down at me. "You're more beautiful than her on your worst day. Even when you are wearing a dress like a sack and barely brush your hair."

I snorted, expecting mockery. "You are so full of—"

Then I saw his expression, the frank hunger in his eyes as he looked at me, and my mouth went dry.

"Come on," he said roughly. "The sooner we get this done, the sooner we can go home."

I licked my lips, tasting lipstick, which was foreign to me. But in this pale pink ball gown, I didn't feel like myself at all. I might as well have been wearing glass slippers....

Alejandro led me into a large ballroom, filled with people dancing and drinking champagne beneath enormous crystal chandeliers high overhead. I watched as, ten minutes after we arrived, he went to the elevated dais and made a short speech into a microphone, congratulating the staff of his company, and thanking all their investors and friends, which was met by a roar of applause. When he left the microphone, he returned to my side.

"Now the work is done," he whispered, nuzzling my ear. "Let's have some fun."

He took me out on the dance floor, and I trembled, remembering the last time he'd held me in his arms on a dance floor, the way he'd slowly seduced me, until I surrendered in my first kiss. Now, I felt his arms around me, and I shuddered from deep within, feeling his warmth and strength beneath the tuxedo, breathing in his cologne and the scent that was uniquely him. When the music ended after the first dance, I pulled away.

"I—I need some champagne," I said unsteadily.

"Of course," he said huskily, his dark eyes intent, as if he saw through me, every inch and pore, down to my heart and soul.

For the rest of the night, Alejandro was the perfect gentleman, solicitous, getting me champagne, even cheerfully introducing me to the acquaintances who quickly surrounded us.

One of his friends, a German tycoon of some kind, looked me over appreciatively. "Where did you keep this beautiful creature hidden, Your Excellency?"

"Yes, you should have introduced us," a handsome Japanese millionaire said.

"You sure you want this guy, Miss Carlisle?" An actor I recognized from a big summer movie, where he'd gotten revenge against aliens who blew up Paris, gave me a big shiny grin. "You haven't given the rest of us a chance yet."

I blushed. The whole night seemed unreal, as if I were playing a part, with my hair pulled back into a high ballerina bun, wearing the petal-pink ball gown with tiny flowers embroidered over it. Remembering the part I was to play, I glanced at Alejandro. "Sorry. I only want Alejandro."

His relief was palpable. He smiled back at me.

"Awww, so sweet," the movie star said, somewhat ironically. "Well. Whenever the romance is over, feel free to…"

"It's not a romance," a man said behind us. "It's extortion."

Turning, I sucked in my breath. A man stood behind us, dressed exactly like the others, in a sharp black tuxedo. The man I'd been so desperate to see—and yet, oddly, he seemed out of place here. Handsome. But malevolent.

"Edward," I breathed. "I thought you were in Tokyo—"

His eyes softened. "My staff called me. I was glad to hear you'd gone to London to see me. But not so glad to hear who was with you." He glared at Alejandro, his jaw tight, even as he continued to speak to me. "Are you all right?"

"Of course I'm all right," I said, suddenly nervous.

The two men were glaring at each other, both of them straining the size of the ballroom between their shoulders and masculine pride. I had a sudden dismaying flash of two predators, growling over the same female—or the same prey.

Alejandro's eyes narrowed, but with a swift glance at me, he politely put out his hand. "Edward St. Cyr. I know you by reputation, of course."

The words were courteous and cool. Edward took them as the insult they were no doubt intended. Without taking the offered hand, he bared his teeth in a smile. "How gracious of you to say so. I know of you not just from reputation, but also from more…personal sources." He looked down dismissively at Alejandro's hand. "It does seem a little… tacky?…that after dragging Lena to Europe, you'd force her to pose as your date."

"I didn't force her."

"Of course you did," he said roughly. "What is it, some feeble attempt to project stability for the benefit of future shareholders? Or—no, don't tell me—some attempt to make her love you again?" Smiling his shark's smile, Edward held up his glass of champagne in salute. "You'd think destroying her once would be enough for you. But if anyone would be selfish enough to try for twice, it's you, Navaro."

No respectful *Your Excellency*. Just Alejandro's surname, tossed out with scorn. The entire group, including me, stared wide-eyed as Edward drank down the entire contents of his champagne glass. We looked at Alejandro.

He had dropped his hand, his eyelids now narrowed to slits. "Whatever you might have heard about me, it was a mistake." He glanced at me. "Lena now knows the truth."

Edward lifted an eyebrow. "Convinced her of that, have you?"

"What are you even doing here?" Alejandro's face hardened. "I don't recall sending you an invitation."

Setting his empty glass down on a nearby tray, Edward looked over the ballroom with a small smile. "I have plenty of friends. One was happy to bring me along."

"Who?"

"The Bulgarian ambassador." Edward turned back with lifted eyebrows and said mildly, "Surely you're not going to throw us out and risk an international incident?"

Alejandro looked at a gray-haired, distinguished-looking man across the ballroom, who appeared deep in conversation with someone I recognized from newspaper photos, who'd recently won the Nobel Peace Prize. He turned back with gritted teeth. "What do you want, St. Cyr?"

"I want Lena, since she's asked for me," he said softly. He turned to me, holding out his arm. "Shall we go, love?"

I heard a low, almost barbaric growl, and suddenly Alejandro was in front of me, blocking me from Edward's outstretched arm.

"So it's like that, is it?" Edward said. "She's your prisoner?"

"She's here with me of her own free will."

"*Free will.*" Edward's lips pulled back, revealing white, sharp teeth. "Meaning you probably black-mailed her over that baby. You have no real claim on her."

"I have every claim."

"Because she had your child?" He snorted, jerk-ing his chin. "Keep it," he said derisively. "If I'm the man she wants, I will give her more."

I gasped aloud at his cold reference to Miguel. *It?*

Edward couldn't have referred to my precious baby as "it." He couldn't have implied that he could get me pregnant and replace Miguel in my arms, in my life, as easily as someone might replace a new shoe.

Could he?

The black slash of Alejandro's eyebrows lowered. Every line of his hard-muscled body was taut, as if he were barely holding back from attack. He re-minded me of a lion, or a wolf, coiled to spring, with only a thin veneer of civilized reason holding him in check—but not for much longer.

The two of them were about to start a brawl. Right here, in this elegant gilded ballroom, sur-rounded by the glitterati of Spain and all the world. The crowd around us was already growing, and so were the whispers. I wished I'd never started this by trying to contact Edward. Desperately, I yanked on his sleeve. "Please. Don't…"

Edward looked down at me condescendingly. "It's all right, Lena. I'm here now. I won't let him bully you." His eyes were hard, and his broad shoulders were square, like a rugby player's. And the condescending smile he gave me, after the cold, contemptuous stare he'd just given Alejandro, made me wish he was a million miles away. "You're safe. I'll take over."

"*Take over?*" I repeated incredulously.

Just yesterday, I'd wished so ardently for Edward's help. I'd remembered only that a year ago, when I'd needed to escape London, when I'd felt desperate and terrified and alone, I'd been grateful for his strength. But now…

I'd forgotten what Edward was really like.

Forgotten the times he'd visited his house in Mexico after Miguel was born, when he'd seemed irritated by Miguel's cries when my son's tummy hurt or he was unable to sleep. Edward had made several dark hints about adoption, or sending the baby back to Claudie and Alejandro. I'd thought Edward's jokes were in poor taste, but I'd let it go, because I owed him so much.

But now—

Edward was no longer even looking at me. He was smiling at Alejandro, utterly confident—like a dog who couldn't wait to test out his slashing claws and snarling teeth, to prove who was the stronger, meaner dog, in the pretext for a brawl of fighting over a bone—me.

Alejandro's dark eyes met mine. For a moment, they held. Something changed in his expression. He seemed to relax slightly. He drew himself up, looking almost amused.

"Yes, Lena is the mother of my child," he drawled. "And because of that I have a claim on her that you never will. But that's not the only claim. I have one deeper even than that." He glanced at me. "We intended to keep it private for a few days more, as a family matter, but we might as well let everyone know, shall we not, *querida?*"

"Um, yes?" I said, as mystified as everyone else.

Still smiling that pleasant smile, Alejandro turned and grabbed a crystal flute and solid silver knife off a waiter's passing tray. For a moment I froze in fear. Even with a butter knife—heck, even with his bare hands—I knew Alejandro could be dangerous. Boxing and mixed martial arts were hobbies in his downtime, the way he kept in shape and worked out the tension from a hard day making billion-dollar deals.

I exhaled when he didn't turn back to attack Edward. In fact, he rather insultingly turned his back on him, striding through the ballroom, to the dais, as the crowds parted like magic. He climbed the steps to the same microphone where he'd given the speech before. Most of the guests, seeing him, immediately fell silent. A few continued to whisper amongst themselves, staring between him and Edward—and me.

Alejandro chimed his knife against the crystal flute, so hard and loud that I feared the delicate glass might break in his hand. The entire ballroom fell so quiet that I could hear my own breath.

"I know this is a business gathering," he said, "but I must beg your indulgence for a moment. I am, after all, amongst friends...." His eyes abruptly focused on me across the crowd. "I have some happy news to announce. My engagement."

No. My face turned red and my body itched in an attack of nervous fear beneath my pale pink ball gown as a thousand people turned to stare at me. The whispering increased, building like the roll of distant thunder.

"Many of you probably wondered if I'd *ever* get married." Alejandro rubbed the back of his dark hair then looked up with a smile that was equal parts charming and sheepish. "I confess I wondered that myself." His low, sexy voice reverberated across the gilded ballroom. "But sometimes fate chooses better for us than we could ever have chosen for ourselves."

No, no, no, I pleaded desperately with my eyes. He smiled.

He lifted his champagne flute toward me. "A toast. To Miss Lena Carlisle. The most beautiful woman on earth, and the mother of my baby son..."

The whispers exploded to a sharp roar.

"…to the future Duchess of Alzacar!"

There were gasps across the crowd, the largest of which was probably mine. But Alejandro continued to hold up his flute, so everyone else did, too. He drank deeply, and a thousand guests drank, too. Toasting to our engagement.

Only two people continued to stare at him blankly.

Edward.

And me.

My body trembled. All I wanted to do was turn and flee through the crowd, to disappear, to never come back. To be free of him—the man who'd once destroyed me. Who could, if he tried, so easily do it again—and more, since now our child could be used against me.

But that child also meant, in a very real way, that I was bound to Alejandro for the rest of my life. We both loved Miguel. We both wished to raise him.

Which meant, no matter how fiercely I wished otherwise, and no matter how I'd tried to deny it, I would never be truly free of Alejandro—ever.

Cheers, some supportive, some envious and some by bewildered drunken people who'd missed what all the fuss was about but were happy to cheer anyway, rang across the ballroom, along with a smattering of applause. Alejandro left the dais, where he was stopped by crowds of well-wishers, including the glamorous movie star I'd recognized and two heads of state.

Behind me, Edward seethed with disappointment and fury, "He doesn't own you."

"You're wrong," I whispered. I turned to Edward with tears in my eyes. "He owned me from the moment I became pregnant with his baby."

Edward's face went wild.

"No," he breathed. He started to reach toward my face, then he stiffened as he became aware of all the people watching us, the strangers starting to hover, no doubt awaiting their chance to congratulate me on snagging a billionaire duke into illustrious matrimony. Gorgeous, beautiful women in designer clothes, thin and glossy like Claudie, were already staring at me incredulously, clearly in shock that someone like me could possibly have captured the heart of a man like Alejandro.

The answer was simple. I hadn't.

This was my future. Everything I thought I'd left behind me in London, all the pity and dismissive insults. Except it would be even worse. Being described as a poor relation was practically a compliment, compared with the epithet that strangers would soon use to describe me: *gold digger*.

It would have been different if Alejandro and I had actually loved each other. Thinking of it, my heart ached. If he'd loved me, and I'd loved him, I wouldn't have given two hoots what anyone else thought. But as it was…

"You agreed to marry him?" Edward said incredulously.

"Not exactly." Swallowing over the ache in my throat, I breathed, "It doesn't matter. Now he has proof he's Miguel's father, he'll never let him go. And I will never leave my son. So we might as well be married...."

"Like hell."

Edward grabbed my arm, his eyes like fire. Without warning, he pulled me through the crowd. I had one single image of Alejandro's shocked face across the ballroom, watching us, before I was out the side door and down the hall, pushed into a dark, quiet corner of the empty coatroom.

Edward turned to me, his face contorted by shadows.

"Run away with me," he said urgently.

I drew back in shock. "What?"

"Navaro has no hold on you."

"He's Miguel's father!"

"Share custody of the kid if you must," he said through gritted teeth. His hand gripped my forearm. "But don't throw yourself away on a man who will never deserve you."

"What are you saying?" I tried to pull away my arm, but his grip was tight.

"He terrified you for a year—got you pregnant just to steal your baby—"

"I was wrong—he didn't! It was all Claudie! She's the one who said it, and I believed her."

"So he's innocent? No way," he said grimly. "But even if he is—even if he didn't do that one awful thing, what about the rest?"

"What do you mean?"

"He made you love him, then he *abandoned* you. Don't you remember how gray your face was for months afterward? How your eyes were hollow and you barely spoke? I do."

I swallowed. "I…"

"Where was he when you wanted to give him everything? When you tried to tell him you were pregnant? He *changed his phone number*. How can you marry him now? How can you forget?"

I flashed hot, then cold. Yes. I remembered.

"And after all that, he gets you back?" Edward pulled me closer, looking down at me in the shadowy cloakroom with a strange light in his eyes. "No. I was there for you. I took care of you. I'm the one who—"

"Get your hands off my woman."

The low voice was ice-cold behind us. With a gasp that must have sounded guilty, I whirled to face him. "Alejandro!"

His eyes were dark with fury as he looked at me. "So this is why you were so reluctant to marry me?"

"No, you—"

"Be silent!"

I winced.

"Don't talk to her that way," Edward said.

Alejandro didn't look away from me. He held

his body in a dangerous stillness as he ground out, "You have nothing to do with us, St. Cyr."

Either Edward didn't see the warning, or he didn't care. "Don't I? Who do you think was supporting her this past year? Who held her together after you blew her apart?" Coming closer to Alejandro, he said softly, with a malicious look in his eyes, "Who was at Lena's side at the hospital, when she gave birth to your child? Where were you then, Navaro?"

Alejandro slowly turned to look at him. I saw the hard set of his shoulders, the rapid rise and fall of his breath. I saw his hands tighten at his sides, and knew Edward was about to lose half of his face.

"Stop!" I cried, stepping between them in real fear. "Stop this at once!" I pressed on Edward's chest. "Just go."

He lifted his eyebrows in shock. "You can't honestly choose him over me?"

"Go. And don't come back." I glanced back at Alejandro and knew only the fact that I stood between them kept him from attack. I took a deep breath. "Thank you for everything you did for me, Edward. I'll never forget how you helped me." My jaw hardened. "But it's over."

Edward's face contorted. "You're throwing yourself away on *him?* Just because of some *stupid baby?*"

My sympathy disintegrated.

"That *stupid baby* is my son."

"Dammit, you know I didn't mean…"

But my heart had iced over. Releasing him, I stepped back, closer to Alejandro. "Yes, I choose him. Over you."

"You heard her," Alejandro said roughly. "You have thirty seconds to be out of my building, before security throws you out."

"Sending in your goons, eh?" he sneered. "Can't be bothered to do it yourself?"

"Happy to," Alejandro said grimly, pushing up the sleeves of his tuxedo jacket as he took a step forward, fists raised.

"No!" I grabbed his arm. My hand couldn't even fully wrap around the full extent of the hard, huge biceps beneath his tuxedo. "Please, Alejandro," I whispered. "Don't hurt him. He was good to me, when I had no one else. I never would have survived without him. Neither would Miguel. Please. For my sake."

Jaw taut, Alejandro slowly lowered his fist. "For your sake." His voice was low and cold as he turned to Edward. "Thank you. For protecting what I love."

Love? For a moment I stared at Alejandro, then I realized he was speaking of Miguel.

Edward glared at him. Obviously not realizing he'd just narrowly escaped death, he sneered, "Go to hell." At the door, he turned back and said, "I'll be back for you, Lena."

Then he was gone. And Alejandro and I were

suddenly alone in the cloakroom. But my relief was short-lived.

"No wonder he loaned you his house," he said. "No wonder he protected you. He sees you as his. Why does he believe that?"

I whirled to face him. The cold fury in his eyes was like a wave. But there was something else there, too. Hurt.

"He tried to kiss me last week," I admitted in a low voice, then shook my head. "But I just gave a shocked laugh and he left. Whatever he might have hoped, all he ever was to me was a friend—"

"*Friend*," he said scornfully. "You knew what he wanted."

I shook my head fiercely. "Not until last week, I never—"

"Then you were willfully blind. He's in love with you."

"You're wrong there." Shivering, I crossed my bare arms over my pink strapless ball gown. "If he'd really loved me, he would have loved Miguel, too. But he was always getting annoyed about him. Suggesting things…like I should send him away, farm him out for adoption…"

Alejandro's eyes darkened. "And you were willing to call him a friend? To let him near our son?"

I wanted to lash back at him. To tell him he was being unreasonable, or that I hadn't had a choice. Instead, I said the only thing that mattered. The only thing that was true.

"I'm sorry," I said in a low voice. "I was wrong."

He'd been opening his mouth to say more, no doubt cutting, angry accusations. But my humble, simple words cut him off at the knees. For a long moment, he stared at me in the shadowy cloakroom. Down the hall, we could distantly hear music playing, people laughing. Then he turned away, clawing back his dark hair.

"*Bien.* I wasn't exactly perfect, either," he muttered. Lifting his head, he glared at me. "But you're never to see him again. Or let him near Miguel."

"Fine," I said.

"Fine?"

"He stopped being my friend the moment he called my baby 'it.'"

"So," he said with a casual tone that belied the tension in his shoulders, "did you let him kiss you?"

I gaped at him. "Oh—for heaven's sake!" I stomped my foot against the plush carpet. "I'm not going to say it again!"

"I found the two of you here, talking..."

"And I just saw you talking to an actress in the ballroom. I didn't accuse you of making out! He made a pass at me last week. I refused. End of story."

"Once we are married..."

My cheeks went hot. "Married!" I stared at him, shocked. "Who said anything about marriage?"

Now Alejandro was the one to look shocked.

"I just asked you to marry me!"

"Asked?" My voice was acid. "When you asked, I said no. Tonight, you just *announced* it! In front of everyone! You may have asked—I never said yes!"

"We are going to be wed. Accept it."

"I will accept *an engagement,*" I retorted. "I will accept that we need to live in the same town, perhaps even the same house, for our son. A public front, a pretense for Miguel's sake, to make it appear we are actually a couple—that he wasn't just some *mistake!* But nothing more. There's no way I'm actually going to *marry* you. Do you think I would ever give you my body again? Or my heart?"

"I told you," he ground out. "I'm not asking for your heart."

"Then you can forget anything else—I won't give you my body, or take your name! I owe you respect as Miguel's father, but that's it," I said through gritted teeth. "Whatever you might believe, you don't own me, any more than Edward did!"

"I'm not Edward. I'm the father of your child." He grabbed my wrist, looking down at me. "I'm the man you will wed. I don't need your heart. But your body, at least, will be mine."

"No!" But even as I gasped with fury, heat flashed from his possessive grip on my wrist. Electricity crackled up my arm, to my throat, to my lips, to my breasts, down, down, down to my core. Pushing me back roughly against the coats, he looked down at me in the shadows.

"Did you really think," he said softly, "once I

found you, I would ever let you go? I gave you up once for the sake of a promise. I gave you up to *do the right thing*. But fate has thrown you back into my arms. Now you will be entirely mine—"

Lowering his head, Alejandro kissed me fiercely, his lips hot and hard against mine, plundering, demanding. I tried to resist. I couldn't let myself feel—I couldn't—

Then I melted as the banked embers inside me, beneath the cold ash of the past lonely year, roared to a blazing fire. My body shuddered beneath his ruthless, almost violent embrace, and I wrapped my arms tightly around him, holding him to me, lost in the sweet forbidden ecstasy of surrender.

CHAPTER FIVE

HIS LIPS SAVAGED MINE, his tongue hot and salty and sweet. I clutched his shoulders, desperate to sate my desire. I'd hungered for him every night, even when I hated him, against all reason, against my will.

Alejandro's hands ran along my bare arms then moved to the tangle in my hair, tilting my chin so he could plunder my mouth more deeply. Long tendrils of hair had pulled free from my chignon. I felt them brush against my naked shoulders as his hard, muscular body strained against me, towering over mine, overpowering me. But it wasn't enough. Not nearly enough…

His hot kisses moved slowly down my neck, as he murmured husky endearments in Spanish against my skin. My head fell back against the wall of coats, and I closed my eyes, feeling tight and dizzy. He nuzzled my bare skin over the neckline of my gown. His hands cupped my breasts straining against the pink silk of the bodice.

So sweet. So hot. My breath came at a gasp, and as my eyelids flickered, the world seemed to spin in whirling patterns of shadows and light, echoes of past love and longing. For over a year I'd longed for him. For all my life, I'd longed for this. And it was even better than I remembered, a powerful drug beyond imagining. Wrapped in his embrace, I forgot myself, forgot my own name, and knew only that I had to have him or die....

A low deliberate cough came behind us. Startled, I turned my head, and Alejandro straightened. The Bulgarian ambassador stood at the cloakroom door, with his wife draped in pearls behind him.

"Excuse us," he said gravely, and stepping forward, he took a black fur coat off the hanger behind us.

I heard his wife titter as they left, "See, Vasil? I told you it was a love match!"

"Poor devil deserves some pleasure, at least," the man's reply echoed back to us, "after the grasping creature tricked him into marriage with a pregnancy."

Shamefaced, I looked up at Alejandro. The air in the cloakroom suddenly felt thin and cold.

"Let me go," I said.

His hold on me only tightened. "Who cares what they say?"

"I care," I whispered.

"Bull," he cut me off ruthlessly. "You're too strong to be ruled by gossip." His hands moved slowly down the bare skin of my upper back, and I shivered, fighting my own desire. "It's this you're afraid of. This." He stroked my arms to my breast, then abruptly pulled me up to stand, hard against his body. "This is all that matters...."

"It's not," I choked out. "There's love. And trust...."

"Love for our son. And trust for your husband. Your partner."

For a second, I trembled. I did want those things. A real home. I'd already accepted that we would need to live in the same town, or better yet, the same house. Why not accept a partnership? We could share a life, a son, even a bed. Would it be enough, without romantic love? Could I live without that? Could I?

For Miguel's sake?

"Maybe I could accept a marriage without love," I said in a small voice. I took a deep breath and raised my gaze to his. "But there is no partnership without trust. Can you promise you've never lied to me? And that you never will?"

I watched as the brief triumph in his eyes went out. "No."

My lips parted in a silent gasp. I hadn't expected that. My heart twisted as I thought how, with just a few hot kisses and the dream of giving Miguel a real home and family, I'd been perilously close to giving up my dreams.

"Well, which is it, Alejandro?" I choked out. "Did you lie to me in the past? Or will you lie to me in the future?"

His jawline tightened. For a moment, his face seemed tortured. Then, as I'd seen happen before, his expression shuttered, becoming expressionless, leaving me to wonder if I'd imagined the whole thing. "Take your pick."

I stiffened. Hating him—no. Hating *myself* for letting him kiss me. Letting him? All he'd had to do was touch me and I'd flung myself into his kiss with the hunger of a starving woman at a piece of bread. "What have you lied to me about?"

"You expect me to tell you the truth about that?"

"Other women?"

He glared at me. "I told you. I believe in honor. Fidelity. No. My lie is about—something else."

"What?"

"Me," he ground out through gritted teeth. "Only me."

Which didn't tell me anything at all! "Fine. Whatever." I glared at him. "You shouldn't have kissed me."

He relaxed imperceptibly now that we were no longer talking about his secrets.

"This isn't the place," he agreed.

"I didn't just mean the cloakroom. I mean any-where."

"I can think of many places I'd like to kiss you."

"Too bad." My cheeks flamed, but I wouldn't let him distract me. "Take your kisses, and your lies, somewhere else."

"A marriage in name only?" He sounded almost amused. "Do you really think that will work?"

"Since I can't even trust you, let alone love you, there will be no marriage of any kind," I snapped. "And if you keep asking, even our engagement will be remarkably short."

"Why are you trying to fight me, when it's so obvious that you will give in?" he said. "You want to raise Miguel. So do I. What do you expect to do—live next door? In my stable?"

"Better that than your bed."

His dark eyes glittered. "That wasn't how you kissed me."

Heat pulsed through me. I could hardly deny it. I looked away. "Sex is different for women. It involves love!"

He snorted. "Right."

"Or at least caring and trust!" I cried, stung.

"Who is speaking in generalities now?" he said harshly. A cynical light rose in his eyes. "Many women have sex with strangers. Just—as you said—as many women prefer to drink their coffee black, without the niceties of sugar and cream!"

My cheeks flushed. "Fine for them, but—"

"Lust is just an appetite, a craving, such as one might have for *ensaladilla rusa*. No one says that you must be deeply committed to the mayonnaise in order to enjoy the taste of the potato salad!"

I lifted my chin. "Go seduce one of those salad women, then! I don't want you in my bed, I don't want you as my husband and I just regret I'm stuck with you as Miguel's father!"

"Enough." His voice was deadly cold. "You have made enough of a fool of me, making me beg— for the truth about Miguel, for the DNA test, for access to him. I even had to beg you to keep your promise to come to Spain. There will be no more begging, at least—" his eyes glittered "—no more begging from me."

Alejandro had begged me for stuff? I must have missed that. "I never—"

"You will marry me. Tonight."

"Don't be ridiculous!"

"Right now. Choose." His expression had hardened. "A priest. Or a lawyer."

"Are you threatening me?"

"Call it what you want."

I licked my lips, then tried, "Edward would help me. He has money and power to match even yours…."

"Ah." Alejandro came closer, softly tucking back a long tendril of hair that had escaped when he'd crushed me a few moments ago in his passionate embrace. "I wondered how long it would be before Mr. St. Cyr's name made an appearance. That was even quicker than I expected."

My cheeks went hot, but I lifted my chin. "He would still help me if I asked."

"Oh, I'm sure he would," he said softly. "But are you willing to accept the cost of his help?"

I swallowed.

"And the price to Miguel. Think of it." He tilted his head. "A custody war, when each side has infinite resources to pay lawyers for years, decades, to come." He gave a brief, humorless smile. "Miguel's first words after *mamá* and *papá* might be *restraining order.*"

I sucked in my breath.

"And the scandal… The press will have a field day." Pressing his advantage, he stroked my cheek almost tenderly. "Miguel will grow so accustomed to paparazzi he'll start to think of them as members of his family. With good reason, for he'll see them more frequently than he sees either of us." He dropped his hand. His voice became harsh. "Is that really what you want?"

"Why are you doing this, Alejandro?" I choked out.

"I won't risk having Edward St. Cyr as my son's future stepfather."

I shook my head. "It will never happen!"

"I'm supposed to believe that? A few minutes ago, you promised you'd never see him again. Now you're threatening to use his wealth and power in a custody battle against me."

He looked at me with scorn, and I didn't blame him. I wiped my eyes. "You're right. I shouldn't have done that—but you're forcing my back against the wall! I have no choice!"

"Neither do I." His sensual lips curved downward. "You think you can control him. You cannot. He's selfish. Ruthless. Dangerous."

I flashed him a glare full of hate. "Are you talking about him," I said bitterly, "or yourself?"

"Yes, I could be dangerous," he said softly. "If anyone tried to hurt someone I cared about. I would die—or kill—to protect someone I loved."

"But you don't love anyone!"

"You're wrong." His voice was low. His lips pressed together in a thin line. "So will it be marriage between us—or war?"

"I hate you!"

"Is that your final answer?"

Tears of hopeless rage filled my eyes, but I'd told Edward the truth. Alejandro had owned me from the moment I'd become pregnant with his child. I would give anything, sacrifice any part of myself, for my son. My heart. My dreams. My soul. What were those, compared with Miguel's heart, his dreams, his soul?

My baby would not spend his childhood in and out of divorce courts, surrounded by pushy paparazzi, bewildered by the internecine battles of his parents. Instead, he would be safe and warm and surrounded by love. He would be happy.

It was all I had to cling to. All I had to live for.

My shoulders fell.

"No," I whispered. "You win. I will marry you."

"Now."

"Fine! I hate you!"

He looked down at me, his expression sardonic. "Hate me, then. At least that I can believe. Far more than your so-called *love*. But you will be my wife. In every way."

Yanking me into his arms, he kissed me, hard. But this time, there was nothing of tenderness, or even passion. Just a ruthless act of possession, showing me he owned me, a savage kiss hard enough to bruise.

Pulling me out of the cloakroom and outside into the warm Spanish night, he called for his driver. The paparazzi were long gone, and the street was quiet, even lonely.

Alejandro took me to the house of a local official, where with a quiet word a certificate of permission to marry was produced in record time. Then to a priest, in a large, empty church, so old and full of shadows it seemed half-haunted with the lost dreams of the dead.

And so Alejandro and I were wed, in that wan, barren church, with only flickers of candlelight and ghostly moonlight from the upper windows lighting the cold, pale marble. My pink ball gown of silk and embroidered flowers, which once seemed so beautiful, now hung on me like a shroud.

There was no wedding dress. No cake. No flowers. And no one, except the priest and his assistant called as witness, to wish us happiness.

Which was just as well, because as I looked at the savage face of my new husband as we left the church into the dark of night, I knew happiness was the one thing we'd never have.

Alejandro looked across the front seat of the car. "You're going to have to talk to me at some point."

I looked out the window at the passing scenery as we drove south into Andalucía. "No, I don't, actually."

"So you intend to ignore me forever?" he said drily.

I shrugged, still not looking at him. "Lots of married couples stop talking eventually. We might as well start now."

We'd been alone in the car together for hours, but it felt like days. Alejandro was driving the expensive sports sedan, with Miguel in the baby seat behind us, cooing and batting at plush dangling toys. Three bodyguards and his usual driver were in the SUV following us. "I want some private time with my new bride," Alejandro had told them with a wink, and they'd grinned.

But the reason he'd desired privacy wasn't exactly the usual one for newlyweds. I'd given Alejandro the silent treatment since our ghastly wedding ceremony last night. Seething. It wasn't natural for me to bite my tongue. I think he was waiting for me to explode.

He'd gotten me home by midnight as promised. The instant we returned to his Madrid penthouse I'd stalked into the bedroom where my baby slept,

and though I couldn't slam the door—too noisy—
I'd locked it solidly behind me. Very childish, but
I'd been afraid that once Mrs. Gutierrez left, he
might demand his rights of the wedding night. Pulling on flannel pajamas, I'd stared at the door, just
daring him to try.

But he hadn't. About three in the morning, feeling foolish, I'd unlocked the door. But he never
came, not even to apologize for his brutish behavior. There was no way I would have let him seduce
me…but my nose was slightly out of joint that he
hadn't even bothered to try. Our marriage was only
a few hours old, and he was already ignoring me?

I didn't see him until this morning, when he was
coming out of the guest bathroom next door, looking well rested and obviously straight out of the
shower. His dark hair was wet, a low-slung towel
wrapped around his bare hips and another towel
hanging over his broad, naked shoulders.

I'd stopped flat in the hallway, unable to look
away from the muscular planes of his bare chest,
laced with dark hair, or the powerful lines of his
body, to the slim hips barely covered by the clinging white terry cloth.

Alejandro had greeted me with a sensual smile.
"Good morning, *querida*," he'd purred, then lifting
a wicked eyebrow as if he already knew the answer,
he'd inquired, "I trust you slept well?"

But I was starting to get my revenge. His lips
were now set in an annoyed line as he kept his eyes

on the road, pressing on the gas of his very expensive, very fast sedan. "We are husband and wife now, Lena. You must accept that."

"Oh, I do," I assured him. "But we're a husband and wife who happen to hate each other. So perhaps just not talking is best."

Alejandro exhaled in irritation, his hands tightening on the steering wheel. I turned away, staring out wistfully at the scenery of Spain flying past us. In any other circumstance I would have been in awe at the magnificent view. The farmland and soft hills of central Spain were turning to a drier landscape. Lovely thick bushes of pink and white oleander flowers separated the highway, a vivid, wild, unexpected beauty, much like Spain itself.

Oleander. I shivered a little. So beautiful to the eyes. But so poisonous to the heart.

Just like Alejandro, I thought. I wouldn't let him in. Husband or not, I'd never let him close to me. In any way.

We'd stopped only once since we left Madrid, to feed and change the baby, and to put gas in both cars. Alejandro offered to take a small detour and stop for lunch in Córdoba, to show me the famous cathedral that had once been a Great Mosque. But I'd refused. I didn't want him doing me any favors. Though later I regretted it, because I heard a lot about the famous Mezquita.

As the car flew south, turning on a new road, I blinked in the bright sun flooding the windows.

After weeks of rain in San Miguel, and London's drizzle and overcast skies, the Spanish sun had come as advertised, with a wide blue horizon that held not a single cloud. The arid landscape suddenly reminded me of Mexico. Which reminded me of the freedom and independence I'd had so briefly.

And Edward.

I'll be back for you, Lena.

"Stop it," Alejandro growled.

I nearly jumped in the smooth leather seat. "What?"

"I can hear you. Thinking about him."

"You can hear me thinking?"

"Stop," he said quietly, giving me a hard sideways glance. "Or I will make you stop."

"*Make* me—" I snorted derisively, then I looked at him, remembering his last ruthless kiss in the cloakroom. And the one before it, which had been even more dangerous. I remembered how it had felt, surrendering to his embrace, how it had made my whole body tremble with need.

"You're such a jerk," I muttered, folding my arms mutinously. "My thoughts are my own."

"Not if they are of a man like St. Cyr. Thoughts lead to actions."

"I told you, I don't even like him anymore!"

He snorted. "And that is supposed to inspire trust? You've made it plain you did not wish to marry me. Perhaps you're wishing now you took the other choice."

I looked at him. "What other choice?"

"A war between us," he said grimly. He was staring forward at the road, his jaw tight. "St. Cyr would be eager to help you with that."

My arms unfolded. "No." I frowned. "I don't want war. I'd never deliberately hurt you, Alejandro. Not now."

"Really," he said in clear disbelief.

"Hurting you would hurt Miguel." I looked out the window and said softly, "We both love him. I realized the truth last night, even before your marriage ultimatum—neither of us wants to be apart from him." Blinking fast, I faced him. "You're right. We're married now. So let's make the best of it."

"Do you mean it?" he said evenly. I nodded.

"Let's make sure Miguel has a wonderful childhood and a real home, where he'll always feel safe and warm and loved."

His hands seemed to relax a little around the steering wheel. He looked at me. There was something strange in his eyes, something almost like— yearning—that made my heart twist.

"If it's really true you'd never deliberately hurt me…" He seemed to be speaking to himself. "I wish I could…"

"What?"

He shook his head, and his jaw went hard. "Nothing."

What had he been about to say? I looked down,

blinking as my eyes burned. Telling myself I shouldn't care. Willing myself *not* to care.

My lie is about something else.

What?

I remembered the stark look in his eyes. *Me. Only me.*

Stop it, I told my heart fiercely. *Don't get sucked in! Keep your distance!*

Silently, Alejandro stared forward at the road. For long minutes, the only sound was Miguel cooing to himself in the backseat, chortling triumphantly as he grasped a soft toy hanging from the top of his baby seat, and making it squeak. I smiled back at my son. He was the reason. The only reason.

"I'm glad you feel that way. The truth is I don't want to hurt you, either." Alejandro tightened his hands on the steering wheel. He glanced at me out of the corner of his eye. "Our son is what matters. We'll focus on him. I'll never leave you or Miguel. Together we'll make sure our son is always well cared for."

Our eyes locked, and an ache lifted to my throat. Turning away, I tried to block the emotion out with a laugh. "Miguel will be a duke someday. That's crazy, isn't it?"

Alejandro turned his eyes back to the road.

"Sí," he said grimly. "Crazy."

I'd been trying to lighten the mood. But his voice sounded darker than ever. "Did I say something wrong?"

"No. You are correct. Miguel will be Duque de Alzacar." I frowned. But before I could figure out what lay behind the odd tension in his voice, he turned to me. "So you forgive me for forcing you to marry me against your will?"

I exhaled.

"It's a very complicated question."

"No. It is not."

Something broke inside me. And words came pouring out.

"You think I was silly and selfish to want to marry for love. But for the past ten years, that dream was all I've held on to." I looked at my hands in my lap. "Ever since I was fourteen years old, I've felt so alone. So unwanted. But then, last year, when I met you…" I lifted agonized eyes to his. "All my dreams seemed to be coming true. It was as if…I'd gone back in time. To the world I once knew. The one filled with love. The world where I was good enough. Wanted. Even cherished."

Alejandro's expression darkened. "Lena…"

"Then you abandoned me," I whispered. "You told me you didn't love me, that you never would." I looked at him. "But I still married you yesterday, Alejandro, knowing that. Knowing you've lied to me in the past and will lie in the future. I married you knowing that the loneliness I tried to leave behind me in London will now follow me for the rest of my life. Only now, instead of being a poor relation, I'm the gold digger who got pregnant to ensnare a rich duke. And everyone will say, weren't you so good and noble to marry me? Wasn't it an amazing sacrifice for you to make me your wife? How generous of you! How kind!"

He glowered. "No one will say that."

I cut him off with a low laugh. "*Everyone* will. And I know there will be days when I'll feel that marrying you was the biggest mistake of my life." I drew a deep, shuddering breath, then met his gaze. "And yet I can't regret it," I whispered. "Because it will make Miguel's life better to have you in his life. Every single day. He will know you. Really know you."

"I wish he could." Alejandro stared at me. His dark eyes were liquid and deep. "I wish I could tell you…"

I held my breath. "Yes?"

His face suddenly turned cold, like a statue. He looked away. "Forget it."

I exhaled, wishing I hadn't said so much.

He drove the car off the main road, then took a smaller one, then turned on a private lane that was smaller still, nothing but a ribbon twisting across the broad-swept lands. Alejandro stopped briefly at a tall iron gate, then entered a code into the electronic keypad. We proceeded inside the estate, which looked so endless and wide, I wondered how anyone had wrapped a fence around it, and if the fence was visible from space, like the Great Wall of China.

Then I saw the castle, high on a distant hill, and I sucked in my breath. It was like a fairy-tale castle, rising with ramparts of stone and turrets stretching into the sky.

"Is that…?" I breathed.

"Sí," Alejandro said quietly. "My home. The Castillo de Rohares. The home of the Dukes of Alzacar for four hundred years."

It took another fifteen minutes to climb the hill, past the groves of olive trees and orange trees. When we reached the castle at last, past the ramparts into a courtyard surrounding a stone fountain, he stopped the car at the grand entrance on the circular driveway. He turned off the engine, and I could hear the bodyguards climbing out of the SUV behind us, talking noisily about lunch, slamming doors. But as I started to turn for the passenger-side door, Alejandro grabbed my wrist. I turned to face him, and he dropped my arm.

"I am sorry I hurt you, Lena. When I left you last summer, when I refused to return any of your phone calls—I did that for good reason. At least—" his jaw tightened "—it seemed like good reason."

"No, I get it," I said. "You didn't want me to love you."

"No. That's not it at all." He lifted his dark eyes to mine. "I didn't leave because you loved me. I left because I was falling in love with you."

CHAPTER SIX

I STARED AT him in shock.

"What?" I breathed.

A hard knock banged against the car window behind me, making me jump. Turning my head, I saw a plump smiling woman, standing on the driveway outside, dressed in an apron and holding a spoon. She waved at us merrily. I saw the bodyguards greeting her with obvious affection as they went into the grand stone entrance of the castle.

"Another housekeeper?" I said faintly.

"My grandmother," he said.

"Your—" I whirled to face him, but he had already opened his door and was getting out of the car, gently lifting Miguel out of his baby seat. Nervously, I got out of the car, too, wondering what the dowager Duchess of Alzacar would make of me.

"Come in, come in," she said to the bodyguards, shooing them inside. She kept switching from English to Spanish as if she couldn't quite make up her mind. "Knowing Alejandro, I'm sure you didn't stop for any lunch, so everything is ready if you'll just go straight to the banqueting hall…"

"Abuela," Alejandro said, smiling, "I'd like you to meet my son. His name is Miguel."

"Miguel?" she gasped, looking from him to Alejandro.

He blinked with a slight frown, shaking his head. "And this is my new wife. Lena."

"I'm so happy to meet you." Smoothing one hand over her apron, she turned to me with a warm smile, lifting the wooden spoon high, like a benign domestic fairy about to grant a really good wish. "And your sweet baby! I can hardly wait to…" Her eyes suddenly narrowed. "Your new what?"

Coming over to me, Alejandro put his free arm around my shoulders. "My wife."

She lowered her spoon and looked me over, from my long hair to my soft white blouse with the Peter Pan collar, to my slim-cut jeans and ballet flats. I braced myself for criticism.

Instead, she beamed at me, spreading her arms wide.

"Oh, my dear," she cried, "welcome to the family. Welcome to your new home!"

And she threw her arms around me in a big, fierce, welcoming hug.

Shocked, I stiffened. Then I patted her awkwardly on the back.

"But I'm being silly," she said, drawing back, wiping her eyes with her brightly colored apron.

"My name is Maurine. But please call me Abuela, if you like, as Alejandro does. Or Grandma. Or Nana. Whatever. I'm just so happy you're here!"

"Thank you," I said, unsure how to handle such immediate warmth and kindness.

"But you—" she whirled on her grandson with a scowl "—you should have known better than to elope!"

Alejandro looked abashed. It was a funny, boy-ish expression on his masculine face. "We would have waited and had a proper wedding," he said, rubbing his neck sheepishly, "but Abuela, it happened so quickly...."

"Huh. Don't think you're getting off that easy. We'll talk about it later. Now—" her plump face softened as her eyes lit up "—let me hold that baby."

Ten minutes later, Maurine was giving me a speed tour of the castle, on the way to the dining hall. "The foundations of Rohares date from the times of the sultan," she said happily. "But most of the building dates from the early seventeenth century. It was bombed in the war, then when we came back we had no money and it fell into dis-repair." She looked sad, then brightened, smiling up at her grandson. "But Alejandro made his fortune in Madrid, then restored every part of it, made Rohares better than it had ever been before! And here's where we'll have lunch...."

I stopped in the huge doorway of an enormous dining hall that looked as if it came from the late

Renaissance, complete with soaring frescoed ceilings, suits of armor beside the ancient tapestries and a stone fireplace tall enough to fit a person inside. And at the center of the huge, gymnasium-size room, there was a long wooden dining table, large enough to seat forty or fifty people, and groaning beneath the weight of the luncheon spread, flower arrangements, and place settings carefully designed with fine china and the brightest decor.

My mouth dropped as I stared at it.

"Cold and drafty, *sí?*" Alejandro said smugly, grabbing a marinated green olive and piece of cheese off the platter on the table. "Just as you said."

"I've never seen anything like this," I breathed. "And the food…"

He gave a low chuckle. "Abuela believes food is love."

"I can see that," I said faintly, staring up at his face.

I left because I was falling in love with you.

My knees were still weak at what he'd said in the car. It was so far from everything I'd ever imagined, I couldn't believe I'd heard him right. "Alejandro…"

"Abuela can be bossy about it, but she loves nothing more than taking care of people, along with her garden and home." He grinned, shaking his head ruefully. "She now has an unlimited budget, a clear schedule—now she's given up her charity work—and infinite time. When it comes to the domestic arts, she is unstoppable."

"Amazing." I looked at him hesitantly. "But Alejandro…"

"Yes?"

"Did you mean what you said?"

His dark eyes met mine. He knew what I was talking about. "Don't be afraid. As you said—much has changed in this past year."

I hadn't realized I'd been holding my breath, but at that, I exhaled, like air fizzing out of a tire. "You're right," I said, keeping my voice steady. "Everything is different now."

"The past is past. Now we are partners, parents to our son."

"Exactly." I looked away. The bodyguards, apparently accustomed to being fed lunch like this by the dowager duchess, were already at the table, filling their plates and murmuring their appreciation.

Maurine suddenly reappeared in the solid-oak doorway, holding Miguel with one hand, a small card in the other. Going to the table, she snatched a card off a place setting, then replaced it with the new card. Turning back, she patted the chair, beaming at me. "You're to sit here, dear."

"Oh. Thank you, Maurine."

Smiling, she looked at Miguel in her arms, and started another peekaboo game. She'd been lost in baby joy from the instant she'd picked him up in her arms, and the love appeared to be mutual. I watched, smiling, as Maurine hid her face with her hand, before revealing it so Miguel could reach out to bat her nose triumphantly, leaving them both in hopeless squeals of laughter. Alejandro watched them, too.

"Thank you," he said quietly.

"For what?"

His dark eyes met mine. "For coming to Spain like you promised."

"Oh." My cheeks flooded with shame to remember how I'd initially refused. "It's, um, nothing."

He turned away, watching his grandmother play with his son. "It's everything to me."

My blush deepened, then I sighed. "I was wrong to fight it," I admitted.

"You? Wrong?" Alejandro shook his head. "Impossible."

I scowled at his teasing tone. "Yes, wrong. I'm woman enough to admit it. After all, Maurine is Miguel's family, too." I looked around the huge banqueting hall, filled with antiques that seemed hundreds of years old. I had to crane my head back to see the wood-timbered ceiling, with its faded paintings of the ducal coat of arms. "And this is his legacy," I said softly. "This will all belong to him someday…."

Alejandro was no longer smiling.

"Yes," he said. "It will."

For some reason I didn't understand, the lightness of the mood had fled. I frowned.

He abruptly held out his arm. "Let's have lunch, shall we?"

Even through his long-sleeved shirt, I could feel the warmth of his arm. The strength of it. From the end of the long table, I saw the bodyguards looking at us, saw one of them nudge the other with a sly grin. To outward appearance, we must have looked like goofy-in-love newlyweds.

Alejandro pulled out the chair Maurine had chosen for me, waited, then after I sat down, he pushed it in and sat beside me.

Looking down at the table, I saw three different plates of different sizes stacked on top of each other in alternating colors. At the top of the place setting, there was a homemade paper flower of red-and-purple tissue paper, very similar to the paper flowers my mother had made for me when I was young. Beside it was a card that held a small hand-written name, with elegant black-ink calligraphy.

The Duchess of Alzacar
my darling new granddaughter

Looking at it, a lump rose in my throat. "Look what she wrote."

Alejandro looked at the card, and smiled. "Yes."

"She's already accepted me in the family. Just like that?"

"Just like that." He made me a plate with a little of everything, and poured me a glass of sparkling water, then red wine.

"Wine for lunch?" I said doubtfully.

"It's from my vineyard by the coast. You should try it."

"All right," I sighed. I took a sip, then said in amazement, "It's delicious."

"You sound surprised."

"Is there anything you're not good at?" I said a little sulkily. He smiled.

Then the smile fled from his handsome face. His dark eyes turned hollow, even bleak.

"Keeping promises," he said.

The blow was so sudden and unexpected that it felt like an anvil hitting the softest part of my belly. The moment I'd let my defenses down, he'd spoken with such unprovoked cruelty it took my breath away. Reminding me.

Did you lie to me in the past? Or will you lie to me in the future?

Take your pick.

"Oh," I breathed, dropping my fork with a clang against the twenty-four-karat-gold-rimmed china plate.

He'd done me a favor reminding me, I told myself savagely. I couldn't start believing the pretense. I couldn't start thinking we were actually a family. That we were actually in love. I couldn't surrender!

And yet…

"Are you enjoying yourself, dear?" I looked up to see Maurine smiling down at me from the other side of the table, with chubby Miguel still smiling in her arms. "I hope you see something you like!"

"I do," I replied automatically, then realized to my horror that the exact moment I'd spoken the words I'd been looking at Alejandro. Quickly, I looked down at my plate. "What's this?" I asked, looking at one of the dishes, some kind of meat with leeks and carrots.

"*Pato a la Sevillana,* a specialty of the area. Slow-cooked duck roasted in sherry and vegetables."

I took a bite. It was delicious. "And this?"

"*Rabo de toro.* Another classic dish of Andalucía. Vegetables, slowly braised with sherry and bay leaf."

Bull's tail? I tasted it. Not bad. I tried the fresh papayas and mangoes, the *albóndigas,* the fried-potato-and-ham *croquetas.* I smiled. "*Delicioso!*"

"*Muy bien,*" Maurine sighed happily, then turned on her grandson, tossing her chic, white hair. "Though *you* don't deserve lunch. I should let you get fast food at a drive-through in Seville!" She hitched her great-grandbaby higher on her hip against her pinafore apron. "I cannot believe you got married without inviting me to the wedding! My only family! After I waited thirty-five years to see you get married! After the way you used to make me bite my nails over those wretched skinny, self-centered women you used to cavort with!"

"At least I didn't marry one of them, eh, Abuela? Do I not get credit for that?"

"Yes," she sighed. "On that, you did well."

The two of them smiled at each other, and I had the sudden image of what it must have been like for him to be raised by Maurine in this enormous castle. Alejandro had lost his parents even younger than I'd lost mine. My father had died of a stroke, my mother six months later of illness. But Alejandro had lost both parents in a car crash when he was only twelve. He'd also lost his best friend, Miguel, whom he'd thought of as a brother, and even their housekeeper.

My smile suddenly faltered. All this time, I'd moaned and whimpered so much about my own difficult childhood. But Alejandro had barely hinted aloud about his. A very masculine reticence, but enough to make me writhe with shame. No wonder Alejandro had been so determined that our Miguel, his only child, should come back to Spain, his home, and meet his grandmother, his only family, who'd raised him and loved him.

Even though she didn't seem to be one hundred percent loving him right now.

"But still." His grandmother's chin was wobbling. "All I asked was that you let me attend the wedding. It was my one and only chance to see you get married and I…"

"It was the worst wedding ever," I heard myself blurt out.

Both of them turned to face me. She looked amazed. He looked faintly strangled, as if he were afraid of what I might say next.

"It was just the two of us—" I shook my head "—along with the priest and some stranger as witness. There was no cake. No flowers. You didn't miss anything, Maurine!"

"Call me Abuela, dear," she said faintly. Her gaze softened as she looked at me. Whatever anger she was now lavishing on Alejandro clearly did not extend to me. She blinked with a frown, tilting her head. "You didn't have any flowers? Not one?"

"It's not entirely his fault," I said apologetically. "We felt we should get married immediately, without too much fuss, because of..." I glanced at our baby in her arms.

"Ah." A look of understanding filled her eyes. "Yes, of course."

"The legal part is done, but Alejandro was just saying on the drive that he wished we could have a reception, a party of some kind, to introduce me to his neighbors and friends. I mean, he did tell a few people in Madrid that we were engaged—" I looked at Alejandro beneath my lashes "—but that's not the same as celebrating with neighbors and family."

"No, it's not," she said thoughtfully.

Taking a bite of juicy ripe papaya, I sighed. "But we just don't know what to do. I mean, Alejandro is so busy with his company, and of course I have my hands full with Miguel. I wouldn't have a clue how to organize a party anyway, not a big one. So we were thinking we could maybe hire a party planner, maybe from Madrid...."

"A *party planner!*" Maurine gasped indignantly. "My new granddaughter—and my great-grandson, this little angel—introduced to all my neighbors and friends with some dreary, chic party arranged by a paid *Madrileño!*" She put a dramatic hand over her fulsome chest. "I would turn over in my grave!"

Alejandro's eyes met mine. His lips quirked as he said, "But Abuela, you're not dead."

"You're right, I'm not," she snapped. "Which is why *I* will be planning your wedding reception. Oh, there's no time to waste." Turning away with Miguel still in her arms, she hurried from the dining hall, calling, "María! Carmen! Josefa! Hurry! We have a new project—the most important party I've ever done!"

I turned back to my lunch, only to find Alejandro looking at me. He said in a low voice, "Why did you do that?"

The intense way he was looking at me made me feel nervous and fluttery inside. "Do what?"

"You could have told her the real reason for our quick marriage. That I forced you to marry me, against your will. That I threatened a custody battle."

"Oh." Awkwardly, I looked back at my plate. I took another bite of the *Pato a la Sevillana*. He just waited. Finally, I said in a small voice, "I didn't want to tell her that."

Alejandro came closer, the hard edges of his jaw

and cheekbones leaving shadows across his face. "Why?"

My cheeks felt hot. I couldn't meet his eyes.

"Were you trying to protect her?" He was so close now that I could almost feel the heat through his black tailored shirt. My gaze remained down, resting on his shirt just below his ribcage. Just below his heart. His voice was so quiet I could barely hear as he said, "Or were you trying to protect me?"

"You," I whispered.

The only noise in the cavernous dining hall was the distant murmured conversation of the bodyguards sitting at the far end of the table, the clink of silverware against china, the thunk of wineglasses against the wood.

Alejandro leaned forward, his elbow against the long oak table, bringing his face very close to mine. It was almost painful to be that close to so much masculine beauty. Unwillingly, my eyes traced the hard slant of his cheekbones, the rough edge of his jawline. His darkly intent eyes.

And his sensual mouth. That most of all. I watched, unable to look away, as his lips moved to shape a single word.

"Why?"

I swallowed, sweeping my hand to indicate the elaborate decorations and luncheon spread down the long table.

"She loves you. And you love her." I shook my

head and blurted out, "All this time I've been moaning about my family in London. I feel so stupid for complaining about my childhood—while all the time, you yourself—"

He put his hand on my cheek. "It doesn't matter now."

Our eyes locked. I caught my breath, feeling the warmth of his fingertips brushing my skin. Feeling how much, deep inside, I wanted him to touch me. On my cheek. Down my neck. Everywhere. Unwillingly, I licked my lips.

But I couldn't give in. I couldn't surrender. If I ever gave him my body, as I'd done the year before, my heart would follow. And I didn't think my shattered heart could survive when he betrayed me as he inevitably would—hadn't he told me as much himself?

Is there anything you're not good at?

Keeping promises.

I pulled back, suddenly desperate to get away from the dangerous energy sizzling between us.

"You love each other. You're a family." My voice trembled, betraying me. "I want you to be happy."

He suddenly leaned forward, his eyes dark.

"What would make me happy," he said huskily, "is having you in my bed. Right now."

I sucked in my breath. My body trembled.

"No," I whispered.

His dark eyes met mine. "We both know how this will end."

He was right. *He was right.*

"Thank Maurine for me…." Setting down my silverware, I stumbled to my feet, tossing my napkin over my half-empty plate. "I'm done…."

And I ran.

Tears blurred my eyes as I fled the dining hall, into the shadowy hallway. I dodged antique chests and an old suit of armor, only to run straight into Maurine.

"My dear, whatever is the matter?" she said, looking astonished.

"I just need some—some fresh air," I choked out.

"Of course." Looking bewildered, with my baby still smiling and happy in her arms, she pointed to a door down the hall. "That leads to the gardens…."

I ran down the dark hallway, beneath the cool, thick stone walls of the *castillo.* Flinging open the door, I found myself beneath the bright, hot Spanish sun and the softly waving palm trees. I kept going, almost blindly—wanting only to be away from the castle. From the man who owned it.

Just as he now owned me.

But he would not own my heart, I vowed to myself, wiping my eyes. Not my heart and not my body…no matter how he might tempt me otherwise. I couldn't give in. I couldn't….

I ran down the stone path, past green hedges and huge oak trees with soft, full greenery, past a pond and a picturesque gazebo in an English-style garden, past something that looked like a hedge maze straight out of *Alice in Wonderland*. Choking out a sob, I abruptly stopped. I found myself in a rose garden, surrounded by a profusion of colorful blooms, gentle yellow, soft pink, innocent white and a blaze of red like heart's blood.

"Lena."

His voice was low behind me. Shocked, I whirled around.

"How did you…?"

Alejandro stood in front of me, dark and tall and powerful. Colorful roses and the primal green of the garden hemmed us in on every side, like a riotous jungle. "I know this garden. It's been my home since I was a child."

The sun left a frost of golden light against his dark hair, like a halo, tracing down the length of his body, his tanned, olive-toned skin, his sharp cheekbones, his hard-muscled body that moved with such sensual grace.

"I won't sleep with you," I breathed. "I won't!"

His cruel, sensual lips curved.

"We both know you will." I watched, mesmerized, as the words caused his tongue to flick against the edges of his lips, into the warm, dark honey of his mouth. I remembered how it had felt when he'd kissed me last night. My lips still felt bruised, from the sweet remnants of that fire. "You want me. As I want you."

"I won't let you take me because I am *conve-*

nient." I shook my head fiercely. "You can't have me now, Alejandro!"

He came closer, towering above me, our bodies so near they almost touched.

"Can't I?" he said huskily.

I stared up at him, shivering. Sunshine shimmered in the greenery around Alejandro, making the flowers gleam like colorful lights, the roses like tumbled scarlet against the deep forest green, the leaves and thorns and tangling vines.

Reaching out, he stroked a long tendril of my hair. "I wanted you from the moment I saw you in the hallways of that London mansion, watching me with such longing in your eyes." He lifted his gaze. "I wanted you then. I want you now. And I will have you."

His dark eyes were like deep pools, illuminated by streaks of amber in the sunlight. The kind of eyes that make you lose your breath, the kind a woman could drown in.

The kind of eyes that could make a woman forget a whole lifetime of grief and everything she should have learned from it.

He wanted me. The thought was like a flower. Like one of those beautiful, hardy, deeply poisonous oleander flowers I'd seen growing along the Spanish highway.

He wanted me.

"We are married now," he said.

"For Miguel's sake."

"*Sí*. We married for the sake of our son." He followed me, his powerful body intent, with his dark hair and his dark clothes, like a stalking panther. "But that is not why I want you in my bed."

"But I can't trust you—"

He straightened, his face dangerous. "Why do you think that?"

"You said you lied to me and will lie again. You said you're no good at keeping promises...."

Alejandro looked away. "That was about...something else." He looked back at me. "I will always keep my promises to you."

"But how can I believe that?" I whispered, my heart running like a scared deer.

"Because it's true." He moved closer, running his hand down my long, loose hair, down my back. I shivered beneath the soft, seductive touch. Lifting his hand, he stroked my cheek as he whispered, "Be with me. Be my wife."

My whole body trembled, leaning toward him.

"And if you still think you can't trust me..." His fingers gently stroked my cheeks, lifting my chin as he said softly, "Trust this."

Lowering his head, he pressed his lips against mine. I felt his warmth, his power, the strength of his body. I closed my eyes, lost, dizzy with desire. When he finally pulled away, I stared up at him, trembling.

"Please," I choked out. I lifted my gaze to his.

Please don't make me love you. "Please don't make me want you…."

He rubbed the pads of his thumbs along my swollen lower lip, and gave me a smile that was breathtaking in its masculine triumph. "Too late."

In the distance, I heard Maurine calling from the castle. I twisted my head, listening, and so did he.

Alejandro suddenly cupped my face in his hands. His eyes were dark. Merciless. "Tonight," he whispered. "You will be in my bed. Tonight…" He ran his fingertips down my shoulders, cupping my breasts. I gave a soft gasp, and he returned a sensual smile. "You will be my wife."

CHAPTER SEVEN

TONIGHT, YOU WILL be in my bed.

Tonight, you will be my wife.

The day raced by. I could not hold the hours back. The clock was ticking and when night fell, I knew he would take me, if not against my will, then at least against my heart.

The dinner table was busy and crowded and happy, because apparently Maurine, the daughter of American-Basque sheep ranchers, had gotten into the habit of eating with her entire household staff, many of whom lived in cottages on the edge of the Rohares estate, and their wives and children were always welcome, as well. Freshly made breads, fruit and cheese were spread across the table in a feast that also included meats, stews and seafood paella, and all kinds of desserts, *tortas* to *galletas*.

"You should see it on holidays," Maurine said to me with a smile, when she saw my eyes widen at the crowd that completely filled all the chairs at the table in the dining hall. "Then, everyone invites their extended families as well, and they come from all over Andalucía."

"Where on earth do they sit?"

Maurine's smile lifted to a grin. "We have to bring all the tables out of the attic and extra rooms, and bring in every antique chair we've got, and the old benches and chests."

"Nice," I murmured. I exhaled. "This place is amazing."

"Because of Alejandro." She looked a few places down the table, to where he was holding court with our baby son in his lap, introducing him to the families of household staff. The women were clustered around him, as if to offer obeisance to a visiting pasha. "He is my whole world. I owe him everything."

"I bet he'd say he owes everything to you. And looking at all this—" I looked at the food, at the decorations, at the care taken with all the details "—I'd have to agree."

"Oh, no." She shook her head vehemently. "If not for him, I never would have survived the aftermath of that car crash, when I lost my whole family...."

"I'm so sorry," I murmured. "I heard about that. Losing your son and daughter-in-law, and even the housekeeper and her son.... I can't imagine how awful. But Alejandro lived."

"That's right. Yes." Shuddering, she closed her eyes. "He saved me. I can still see him in the hospital, his little, injured face covered with bandages, his eyes so bright. Bones in his face had been broken, and he'd never look the same, but he was worried about me, not himself. 'It'll be all right, Abuela,' he told me. 'I'm your family now.'" She blinked fast, her eyes sparkling with tears. "He gave me something to live for, when I wanted to die. And more." She shook her head. "He saved this castle. Even at twelve years old, he was determined to win back our family's lost fortune. He knew he could do it. And he wasn't afraid."

"No." Alejandro wasn't afraid of anything. And he always got what he wanted. I shivered, remembering the dark promise in his eyes in the garden. *Tonight, you will be in my bed. Tonight, you will be my wife...* . I pushed the memory away. "How did he build a fortune out of nothing?"

"He went to Madrid at seventeen," Maurine said. "Worked eighteen-hour days, three different jobs. He took all the money he earned and poured it into risky investments that somehow paid off. He wasn't afraid to gamble. Or work. It just goes to show that nobility is in the heart," she said softly, almost as if she were talking to herself, "not the blood."

I snorted. "What are you talking about? He's the son of a duke. It doesn't get more noble than that."

Maurine abruptly focused her gaze on me. "Of course. That's what I meant. He's noble by birth."

Was she confused, or was she just confusing me? "Did people give you a hard time because of your background? I mean—" I shook my head awkwardly "—Alejandro said you grew up in the U.S., the daughter of sheep ranchers…"

"Shepherds, actually," she said, with a twinkle in her eye.

"Exactly. You were a regular girl—then you married a duke." I paused, trying to form the right words. "Did all the other aristocrats treat you badly? Did they call you a gold digger?"

"Me? No." She blinked, and her expression abruptly changed. "Oh, my dear. Is that what's been happening to you?"

I felt the color drain from my cheeks. "No, I…"

"Oh, you poor child." Her plump, wrinkled face was sympathetic, her blue eyes kind. She reached over and patted my hand. "Don't worry. You'll triumph over all the ugly, silly words that people can say. Alejandro loves you. And you love him. That's what matters."

Now my cheeks went hot. "Uh…"

"And I'm so happy you're part of our family." She gave my hand a little squeeze, then chuckled. "I was a little worried. You should have seen the women he dated before you. He didn't bring a single one home. For good reason. He knew I'd skewer them."

"I'm the first woman he ever brought home?" I said faintly.

She nodded. Her gaze became shadowed as she looked at Alejandro farther down the table. "I was starting to think he'd never let any woman into his heart. That he'd never let anyone know who he truly is." She gave me a sudden sharp look. "But you know. Don't you?"

I furrowed my brow. Was she talking about a biblical knowing? Otherwise I didn't really understand. "Um, yes?"

She stared at me, then releasing my hand, abruptly turned away. "How did you like the rose garden?"

I shivered in spite of myself. "It is…very beautiful," I managed. "Like paradise. But what were you saying about Alejandro…?"

Maurine's eyes shadowed. She bit her lip. "I can't believe you don't know. But if you don't, he has to be the one to…"

"Querida," I heard Alejandro say behind me. "It is time for bed."

Seriously? He was announcing this in front of his grandmother and the whole table? I turned with a scowl, then saw him holding up our sleepy-eyed son. Oh. He meant Miguel. With dinner served so late in Spain, it *was* past our baby's bedtime, and he was yawning in Alejandro's arms, causing dimples in his fat little cheeks. "Right." I held out my arms. "I need to give him a bath first…."

But Alejandro shook his head. He wasn't letting me escape so easily. "I'll help you. It's time I learned to do these things as well, don't you think?"

The gleam in his black eyes told me he knew I was scrambling to think of a way to avoid being alone with him tonight. Wondering if I could find a door with a lock. Surely there had to be one in this castle, with its choice of approximately five million rooms. I shook my head with an awkward laugh. "*You* don't want to learn how to give a baby his bath and put him to bed, Your Excellency!"

He snorted at that last bit. "A man needs to know how to take care of his own son." He lifted a dark eyebrow. "Don't you agree?"

"Yes," I grumbled.

"Such a good father," Maurine sighed.

I narrowed my eyes, then gave him a smile. "I'll show you how to change his diaper, too," I said sweetly.

He gave me a crooked grin. *"Excelente."*

A moment later, we were walking down the dark hallways, the noise of the happy dinner party receding behind us, beneath the thick inner walls of the castle.

"This way," he said, placing his fingertips innocently on the base of my spine to guide me. I trembled.

Tonight, you will be in my bed.

Tonight, you will be my wife.

"Our bedroom is in the new wing...."

"New wing?"

"This castle might have been home to this family for four hundred years, but antiques are—how shall I say this?—not my style."

Going up another flight of stairs, still holding our baby protectively with his muscled arm, he pushed open the door at the end of that hall. I followed him inside, and saw an enormous, high-ceilinged room with floor-to-ceiling windows overlooking a balcony. Modern, masculine, stark. With only one real piece of furniture.

An enormous bed.

I stopped. "But where's the crib?"

"I've had the room next door turned into a nursery." To my relief, Alejandro didn't even glance at the big bed, but just kept walking straight into the connecting door that led to the nursery, and its ensuite bathroom.

The bathroom connected to the nursery was as severe and cold as the master bedroom had been, all white marble and gleaming chrome. But it did have an amazing view. Wide windows overlooked the dark vistas of his estate, lit only by moonlight and distant twinkling lights on the horizon.

He stopped, frowning at the marble bathtub. "On second thought, I don't think this is going to work," he said tersely, looking from the enormous tub to the baby in his arms. "He's too small. We need to get a special baby-size tub...."

It was endearing, really, to see how worried he was. "Tomorrow, if you like, we can go get one. For today, it's no problem." Smiling, I took Miguel in my arms. "Since he can't sit up on his own yet, we'll just hold him up. And be careful." Leaning over, I turned on the water. "Having an extra pair of hands will help."

His eyes met mine. "So you don't…mind that I'm helping you?"

"No," I said softly, "I'm glad."

His expression changed. He started to speak, then turned away, sticking his hand in the water. When the temperature was Goldilocks-acceptable—neither too hot nor too cold—he plugged the drain so the bathtub could fill.

Sitting the baby on the marble counter, I started to pull off his clothes and the clean diaper beneath. "Can you grab his baby shampoo? It's in my bag. Oh." I turned. "It's still in the car—"

With a grin, Alejandro held up the baby shampoo from a nearby drawer, along with a white, fluffy towel. "You mean this?"

"Oh," I said. My cheeks went hot. "It was nice of your staff to unpack everything for me, but…"

"But?"

"It's just strange to have someone going through my stuff."

"You'll get used to it. You'll never have to lift a finger again, unless you want to. Especially with Abuela to oversee everything. She enjoys cooking, cleaning, shopping…" He paused, suddenly looking uncertain. "That is, if you wish that."

I lifted my eyebrows. "If I?"

Alejandro came closer to me.

"You are the duchess now," he said. "As far as the *castillo* is concerned, your rule is now law."

My cheeks went hot. I licked my lips, tried to

laugh as I sat on the edge of the bathtub and checked the water with my elbow. "So you mean I could fire everyone, throw out your tenants, buy Maurine a condo in Barcelona, get rid of all the furniture and paint the walls pink?"

But he didn't laugh.

"If you like," he said in a low voice. "Though I'd prefer we keep the staff and tenants. If you decided otherwise, I would need to take care of them some other way."

"Give them all houses and jobs in Madrid?"

"Something like that."

This kind of thinking surprised me. Most of the high-powered CEO types I'd seen in New York and London seemed to constantly need to resole their expensive shoes, due to the wear caused by stepping on all the little people. I looked at Alejandro curiously. "You really feel responsible for them, don't you?"

"Of course. They—" Tightening his jaw, he looked away. "They're my people."

"Oh." I bit my lip. "Maybe you're not entirely the bastard I thought you were."

"But I am," he said in a low voice. He lifted his gaze to mine. "I can't change who I am."

Something about the expression of the chiseled lines of his handsome face made me feel all confused and jumbled inside. For a moment, the only sound between us was the water running into the bathtub, and the soft yawns of our baby.

"All right, fine. The staff can stay." I sighed. "It would probably be easier to just get rid of me, then."

His lips quirked upward. "Never. Sorry."

"Miguel is your responsibility. Not me," I pointed out. "You don't have to worry about me. I'm not… one of your people." I looked away. "I can support myself. Just so you know."

"I do know. I've seen your paintings."

I stiffened. Edward had often patronized my *little hobby.* "What is that supposed to mean?"

"Isn't it obvious? I think you're talented," he said softly. He pointed toward the nursery. "Or didn't you notice?"

Frowning, I went to the door. And I sucked in my breath as I looked around the dark nursery, at the paintings lining the walls.

"You brought them," I whispered. "All the paintings from Mexico…all the pictures I did of Miguel since he was born."

"I wanted them here. With him." He looked at me. "With us."

A shiver went through me from deep inside.

"You are welcome to paint, or do any work you want," he said gravely, "but only if it nourishes your soul. And any money you make is exclusively your own."

"But that's not right. I don't expect you to support me, to support all of us—"

"That is my job," he said firmly, "to financially

support you and Miguel and, God willing, other children."

Other children!

I swallowed, breathing hard. It was as if he were offering me everything I'd never dreamed I could ask for. After growing up an only child, an orphan, I'd always secretly yearned to have a large family. Now Alejandro didn't just want to be a father for Miguel. He wasn't offering just financial stability for us both. He wanted to give me more children, too.

And create those children inside me....

No! I had to get ahold of myself. No matter how Alejandro looked at me in the shadows, or how the husky sound of his voice made me tremble. No matter if he seemed to be offering me my dreams. Without love, without honesty, *it wouldn't work.*

I shook my head. "You don't need to do these things out of duty."

"Not duty." His hand cupped my cheek. "It is my honor. And more." His eyes met mine as he said huskily, "It is my pleasure."

My cheeks flamed with heat. Sparks of need crackled down my body from that single point of contact. My lips went dry, and tension coiled hot, deep inside.

Nervously, I pulled away, looking down at the enormous marble bathtub. "Water's ready."

I carried Miguel to the tub, and Alejandro was suddenly beside me, rolling up his long sleeves to reveal his powerful forearms, dusted with dark hair. "Allow me."

Together, we propped him up to sit in the few inches of water. Alejandro held him upright as I lathered up Miguel's soft, wispy dark hair. The baby was already yawning as we toweled him off, and got him into his blue footsie pajamas decorated with baby animals. He was half-asleep as I took him into the nursery, to cuddle him in a rocking chair and feed him before bed. Alejandro sat beside us in a cushioned window seat. His face was in silhouette as he watched us, with the wide view of the moon-swept valley and the distant lights of Seville.

I cuddled our baby close, until his eyes were heavy and his mouth fell off the nipple, though his plump mouth still pursed, drinking imaginary milk as he slept sweet baby dreams.

I finally rose to my feet.

"Can I put him to bed?" Alejandro said. "At least try…."

"Sure," I said softly. I handed him the burping cloth, then the fuzzy cuddle blanket. "But you'll need to burp him first."

"Um…I'm not so sure that's a…"

"You'll be fine." I lifted a sleepy Miguel against his shoulder, over the burping cloth, and showed him how to gently pat his small back. Hesitantly, Alejandro followed suit, until our baby came up with a huge burp, before he softly sighed, and his eyes became heavy again.

Alejandro flashed me a look of triumph. "Ha!"

Seeing him that way, this handsome, ruthless, broad-shouldered man holding his tiny sleeping son—our son—my heart twisted. I smiled, and hoped the dim light of the nursery wouldn't let him see how I was fighting tears.

Against everything I'd once believed, everything I'd once feared, Alejandro was an amazing father. I knew he would take care of Miguel and love him and always be there to catch him if he fell.

"Now what?" he whispered.

"Tuck him into the crib, on his back," I answered over the lump in my throat.

Alejandro moved slowly, careful not to wake Miguel, careful to hold his head. He looked as if he were sweating bullets, like a man under the pressure of disarming a nuclear weapon, as he gently set our baby down into his crib. Leaning over beside him, I placed Miguel's favorite baby blanket, the fuzzy one decorated with elephants, softly by his cheek.

For a long moment, we stood over the crib, watching our son slumber, listening to his quiet, even breathing. Then Alejandro lifted his head to look at me.

Our eyes locked. And what I saw in his face left me shivering beneath the open weight of his hunger. Wordlessly, he pulled me from the room, closing the door behind us.

We were alone. In his bedroom.

I stared at him, my heart pounding. "You have to know—what happened in the garden today was a mistake."

"Sí," he agreed. "It was."

He was taking it a lot better than I'd thought he would. I exhaled. "So we won't…"

My voice trailed off as, for the first time, I realized someone had been in this bedroom while we'd been bathing Miguel. My eyes went wide.

A fire now crackled in the fireplace. Candles glowed from the marble mantle. And…no, surely it couldn't be…

Going toward the king-size bed at the center of the room, I picked up one of the scarlet, fragrant petals that had been scattered over the white bedspread.

"Rose petals?" I said dumbly. Turning, I held it up. "I don't understand…."

He gave a low, sensual smile. "Don't you?"

I exhaled. "You arranged this."

"Yes."

"But you just agreed that our kiss was a mistake—"

"It shouldn't have happened in the garden. Or the kiss in the coatroom in Madrid, either. I wanted you. I lost control. That was the mistake." Coming close to me, he shook his head. "But this won't be."

"Don't look at me like that," I whispered.

"Like what?"

"Like…" I licked my lips. "Like it's all you can do to keep yourself from ripping off my clothes and sliding me beneath you…"

"Because, *querida,*" he said, cupping my face, "it is. I've dreamed of you for so long…."

"You dreamed of me?" I breathed, remembering all the nights I'd yearned for him, in hot dreams that had made me ache, only to wake up bereft and cold in the morning.

"Yes. But tonight, *querida,* tonight," he whispered, lowering his head toward mine, "my dreams come true. Not for duty. Not for convenience. But for pleasure. For need." He slowly traced his hand down the side of my body. "There's been no one for me since you, Lena. Did you know that? No other woman I've wanted in my bed. Just you. And now you are mine at last—as I am yours…."

As the fire crackled in the fireplace, I saw the shadows of red and orange move across the hard edges and planes of his handsome, saturnine face.

"It can't be true."

He pulled me into his arms.

"Tonight," he said softly, "will be the first night of forever."

Trembling, I looked up into his dark eyes. I tried to think of something, anything, to send him away from me. I tried to make my body move away, to run. But it was no longer obeying me. My body knew what it wanted. What it had always wanted.

I felt his hands tighten on my back, over the fabric of my blouse, as he pulled me close.

And he lowered his head to mine. I felt the warmth of his breath against my skin. A hard, reckless shiver went up and down my body. Of need. Of desire so great it made me shake.

Because what I wanted now, though beautiful as flowers, could poison my soul, and kill my heart. Just like the oleander...

"Please," I breathed as I felt the roughness of his jawline brush against my cheek. It was all I could do, to keep from leaning into him, kissing him, pulling him hard and tight against me. I wanted him so badly, I could almost have wept from it.

He traced his fingertip very gently from my earlobe, along my cheek, to my full, aching lower lip. "Please?"

"Please..." I tried to remember what I wanted. *Please kiss me. Please don't.*

But he didn't give me time to gather my senses. Lowering his mouth to my ear, he whispered, "You are mine. Forever and always. My pleasure. My duchess. My wife. My lover..."

"No," I whispered. "I can't be...."

"I forgot." He drew back, his eyebrows an amused slash over his heavy-lidded eyes. "You said you do not want me."

"I don't," I said, praying he would believe such a lie.

"I see." He ran his hand down the bare skin to my throat. "So you feel nothing when I do this…."

Trembling, I shook my head.

"And this…" His large hand cupped my breast over my blouse, the tip of his thumb rubbing over my nipple, which pebbled, aching and taut beneath the fabric.

I couldn't speak. I looked up at him, my lips parted, my heart pounding.

"Give in. To me."

"But I don't love you," I choked out, but what that really meant was *Don't make me love you.*

"I do not ask for your heart. But your body—*sí.* Tonight…your body will be mine."

And he lowered his mouth to mine.

His lips were gentle, even tender. One touch, and I was proved a liar. Of course I wanted him. Of course I did.

I sighed, as his kiss deepened, became demanding, hungry. My arms wrapped around his shoulders, pulling him close.

He slowly lowered me back against the enormous bed covered with rose petals. I gloried in the heavy weight of his body over mine, pressing me deep into the soft mattress.

He pulled off my blouse, kissing down my body as each opened button revealed more of my skin. He lifted me against him, to pull off my shirt. I felt the warmth of his fingertips trailing down my naked arms, down my back. With expert precision, he unlatched my bra with a single flick of his fingers, and my breasts hung free, full and heavy and aching for his touch.

I heard the hoarseness of his breath as he pushed me back against the bed. Cupping my breasts with his hands, he nuzzled between them, lowering his head to one taut nipple, then the other, pulling it gently into his mouth as I gasped with pleasure.

"Wait," I choked out. "I want to feel you—"

Reaching for his shirt, I yanked it hard from his body. I was definitely not as careful as he'd been about the buttons. At least one ripped off entirely and scattered noisily against the floor in my desperation to feel the warmth of his skin. I exhaled when I could at last run my hands over his naked chest, feeling his hard sculpted muscles beneath the light dusting of dark hair. A low groan came from his lips, and he fell against me on the bed, ravishing my lips with his own.

Ohhhh… Deeper, deeper. The pleasure of his tongue against mine, his lips hard and so sweet, made me burn all over, made me lose my mind.…

He kissed slowly down my bare skin, working his way to my belly button, which he flicked with his tongue. Unbuttoning my jeans, he rolled them with my panties down my hips, peeling the fabric inch by inch down my legs, kissing and licking and nibbling as he went, until I was naked and gasping for breath.

He kissed the hollow of my foot, then gently pushed my legs wide. From the base of the bed, he looked up at me, spread-eagled across the bed, naked for his pleasure. I quivered with need. If he tried to leave me now—my lips parted. In that moment, I would have done anything—begged, even—to get him to stay.

But no begging was necessary. With a low growl, he removed his own trousers and then fell hard and naked upon me. I felt the length of him, like steel, pressing between my legs. Looking up at his face in the flickering shadows of the firelight, I realized that he wasn't in nearly as much control of himself as I'd imagined. In fact, he was barely keeping himself in check.

"You don't have to hold back," I choked out, pulling him down against me, my hips lifting of their own volition against his. "Please…"

And this time, there was no question what I wanted. But he would not let me control him or set the pace. Shrugging off my grasp, he slid down my body, then parted my legs with his shoulders at my knees. I felt the heat of his breath against my inner thighs. I gasped, reaching my hands out to grip the white comforter beneath me.

Pressing his large hands against my thighs, he spread me wide. He lowered his head and took a long, languorous taste.

My hips bucked beneath his tongue. The pleasure was almost too much to bear. I tried to move away. But he held me fast. He stroked me, licked me, leaving me wet and in the agony of almost unbearable pleasure. His sensual tongue flicked against my taut core, and I held my breath, tilting my head back, my eyes rolling back in my head as I lifted higher, and tighter.

The moment before I would have exploded, he pulled back. I whimpered. I heard his low laugh as he changed position, returning his mouth to where it had been, but pressing his hands beneath my backside to hold me hard against him. Spreading his mouth wide, he worked me with his tongue, going wide, then deep, then wide again. I felt his tongue thrust inside me, and cried out. My back arched against the mattress as he forced me to accept the pleasure, and as he proved to me, against my will, how much more of it my body could endure.

With a single ragged breath, I lifted higher, and higher, but again, just as I was about to explode, he lifted his mouth. He smiled down at me.

By this point I was starting to turn to a mindless mess, somewhere between blubbering and wanting to resort to physical violence, because I knew he was teasing me, forcing me to soar, to coast, then soar higher still.

Abruptly, he lifted my legs to wrap around his tight, trim hips. Rose petals flew up from the bed as he moved me, the flowers leaving a sensual, heady fragrance as they fell back to earth, sliding first against his body, then mine. I felt him pressing hard and stiff and huge between my legs. I exhaled, pressing my fingers into his back, nearly weeping with need.

Again, he started to pull away, but this time, I wouldn't let him go. My fingernails dug into the skin of his back, and I gave a low growl. *"Bien, querida,"* he panted. *"Bien."*

He positioned his hips, and in one rough movement, he shoved himself inside me, hard and thick and enormous, ramming himself to the hilt. That very first thrust made me explode from the inside out. I saw stars as waves of bliss shook through me. I heard a rising animal cry and realized to my shame that it came from my mouth. I fell back against the soft mattress, as if from a far distance, landing a limp heap on his bed.

He froze, still deep inside me in that first thrust.

"You can go on…" I panted, trying to catch my breath. "I already…"

"More," he said, eyeing my face hungrily. "Do it again."

Again? Was he crazy? I shook my head. "I can't…"

"Again," he said grimly.

He slowly pushed inside me, this time letting me feel every inch. He made me stretch for him, as I felt him deep inside. It felt good. But he was holding himself back for no reason. I knew there was no way I could…

Drawing back, he slowly filled me again, and then again. Gripping my shoulders tight with his hands, he rode me. To my amazement, a new tension began to build deep inside me. Different this time. Even deeper. With a gasp, I wrapped my hands around him, feeling the clench and unclench of the muscled cheeks of his backside, feeling the sweat on his skin as he fiercely held himself in check.

His thrusts became rougher as he rode me harder, faster, our sweaty naked bodies sliding against each other. He held my shoulders tight enough to bruise, as he pounded me hard, hard, hard. Deep, deep, deep. My back started to arch again. Seeing that, he sucked in his breath and lowered his lips to mine, kissing me. I felt the flick of his tongue against mine as he rammed into me so deep, and that was it—the brutality and force and lust shook me into an explosion so great I screamed into his mouth.

His self-control evaporated. With a low guttural growl, he shoved into me one last time, and with a gasp and groan, he spent himself inside me.

He collapsed, his body heavy over mine on the bed.

It took long moments for me to return back to earth. When I did, my eyes flew open.

"We forgot to use a condom," I blurted out. I expected him to look horrified. He did not.

"I forgot nothing." He gave me a heavy-lidded smile. "I want to get you pregnant, Lena."

Shock went through me as I stared at him with wide eyes. "But we…"

"I will fill you with my child, *mi esposa*. Try to fight me if you must," he whispered, then his smile lifted to a grin. "It is always a pleasure to battle with you."

CHAPTER EIGHT

SUNSHINE WAS SPILLING from the windows, across our naked, intertwined bodies spread across the bed, the white cotton sheets twisted and tangled at our feet. My first thought when I woke was to think it all had been a dream. Then I saw Alejandro, still sleeping in my arms, a soft smile on his chiseled face.

I caught my breath. My heart beat faster, in a rhythm like music, because joy—pleasure—everything I'd ever wanted had all come true at once.

Slowly, Alejandro opened his eyes, and his smile widened. His expression was open, and young, and he, too, seemed to be shining with happiness. *"Buenos días,"* he whispered, leaning forward to kiss me tenderly on the forehead, *"mi corazon."*

"Good morning." I blushed, looking away, feeling oddly shy.

Reaching out, he lifted my chin and kissed me, until all thoughts of shyness disappeared beneath the mutual hunger building anew between us.

How was it possible? We'd made love three times

last night—three times!—and yet he was still brand new. I gloried in his touch, in the feel of his naked, hard-muscled body against mine, his arms holding me as if I were truly the precious names he'd called me. *My pleasure, my duchess, my wife. My lover.*

And now something more. Something new he'd called me for the first time.

My heart...

We made love once more, hot, hard and fast—and good thing about that last bit, because thirty seconds after we'd both collapsed in a sweaty, gasping heap on top of each other, I heard an indignant cry from the nursery.

We looked at each other and laughed.

"I'll get him," I said, starting to rise from the bed.

"No." He put his hand on my shoulder, pressing me back against the soft sheets, and rose from the bed, pulling on a white terry-cloth robe over his hard-muscled body. "You got up last time. Relax. Go take a shower. Take your time."

I came out, hot and clean and pink-cheeked and happy. I got dressed in a soft pink shirt and skirt, and fed the baby as my husband had a shower in his turn.

This was just as I'd always dreamed. No. It was better. Just the three of us...

For now.

My hand slowly fell on my belly. *I want to fill you with my child.* Was I afraid? Yes. But did I also want, desperately want, another baby? Also yes.

So much had changed since the last time I was pregnant. Instead of being a fearful fugitive, I was married now. Settled. With a home.

Would it be so wrong to just let myself be happy? Alejandro was a good father. He was proving to be a good husband. He wanted to take care of me forever. He wanted us to be a family. And the way he made love to me... I shuddered at the memory of ecstasy.

Would it be so forbidden, so foolish, to trust my husband with my heart?

If only I knew the lie he was telling me, or had told, or would tell. He said he'd been faithful to me for a year, that he'd never be disloyal.

Of course, that could be the lie....

My lips pressed together, and I grimly pushed the thought away. I told myself that, since he'd shared so much of his body, surely he'd soon find it irresistible to share the secrets of his heart. And then I forced myself not to think about it.

Denial is a beautiful thing. A woman in love can be very good at focusing on the rose and ignoring the thorn—at least until it draws blood. Over breakfast, I kept smiling at Alejandro over my plate of eggs and *jamón,* my coffee diluted with tons of cream and sugar. And instead of treating me like a lovesick fool, as I no doubt looked like, Alejandro, the dark, dangerous, ruthless duke, did the unthinkable.

He kept smiling back.

"I'd like to take you around the estate today," he said, sipping his black coffee and reading the morning newspaper, "to meet my tenants."

"What?" I nearly dropped the baby rattle I'd been holding out for Miguel, who was sitting in my lap. Chortling, the baby grabbed it in his fat little fist and triumphantly began to shake. "I thought I'd meet them at the wedding reception."

"Abuela told me it will take her two months to plan the reception. We cannot wait that long." His eyes met mine. He seemed to sense my fear, because he gave me an encouraging smile. "You are my wife. It is right that I introduce you to the tenants on the estate. That is the merest good manners."

"But..."

"Besides. Knowing Abuela, the reception will be a lavish affair, to impress acquaintances and friends. I want the first introduction to be private. Personal." He paused. "Many of them have been farming this land for generations. They might have heard rumors. They might think that having a baby first, and getting married second, is a little..."

"Modern?" I supplied.

"Yes. Modern. I don't want them to wonder if this is a real marriage, or if we'll stand the test of time."

"Will we?" I whispered.

"We will," he said seriously, looking straight into my eyes. "And I want them to have no doubt you are here to stay." Leaning forward, he took my hand in his own. "I want them to think well of you, as I do." He looked at me. "Will you meet them?"

Having Alejandro look at me with his deep dark eyes, and hold my hand, and ask me something, in his husky voice, there was no possibility of resistance. No matter how the thought of trying to impress a bunch of strangers and convince them I would make an excellent *duquesa* filled me with dread. What if they thought I wasn't good enough? What if they had such deep doubts, Alejandro changed his mind about me and decided to find some other wife more worthy? "All right," I said hesitantly. "If you think it truly necessary."

"I do." Alejandro's eyes softened as he looked at our baby. "I'd like Miguel to come, as well. Because he is their future. And they are his."

I bit my lip, trying my best not to look nervous. "Right. Four hundred years on this land, right? So it's in Miguel's blood."

"Something like that." Alejandro put down his napkin and rose to his feet. "We'll see the Widow Ramirez first. She was my governess, once."

The thought warmed my heart. "She taught you as a child?"

"Both me and the...housekeeper's son."

"You mean Miguel," I said softly. "Your friend."

"Yes. We played together as children, studied together, fought. It didn't matter that one of us was a future duke and the other just the housekeeper's son. We studied the same subjects, lived in the same house. We both loved Abuela. We were friends. Until Miguel died that day."

"And you survived," I said gently, touching his shoulder.

"Yes. I survived." He turned away. "I'll get the keys."

I finished my breakfast and my orange juice. When Alejandro returned, he said, "Señora Ramirez is no longer as sharp as she used to be, but she still has a lot of influence with the other tenants."

"No pressure," I muttered, my heart suddenly cold with fear. I looked down at my pink shirt and floppy cotton skirt. "Maybe I should change."

He barely glanced at me. "You're fine."

"I want them to like me…."

Alejandro laughed. "Fancy clothes won't make them like you. In fact, if you showed up in a de-signer dress and five-inch stiletto heels, they'd like you *less.* The farmers respect honesty, hard work and kindness when it's called for. Bluntness when it's not." His dark eyes gleamed. "You should get along just fine."

"Oh, all right," I sighed, sure he was wrong.

A half hour later, the three of us were in his es-tate vehicle, a black, open-air Jeep, headed over a dirt road that crossed the wide fields and hills be-longing to the Castillo de Rohares.

The Widow Ramirez's house was a snug little cottage on the edge of the estate, where she grew organic peaches and persimmons, aubergines and artichokes, and raised goats that produced milk and cheese. Frail and wizened, barely as tall as my shoulder, when she answered her door she looked at me with critical, beady eyes. But by the end of the visit, she was smiling and pushing more of her homemade butter cookies toward me.

"Eat, eat," she pleaded. "You must keep up your strength if you are to give your husband more children."

I felt Alejandro looking at me, and blushed.

"*Gracias,* Pilar," he said, putting his hands on my shoulders. "We wish for more children very much."

"Of course you do," she said, pouring him tea. "I know it was always your desire to have a larger family, growing up so lonely, up in that huge castle, with your older sister off working in Granada. And your mother," she sniffed, "working night and day, when she wasn't distracted by the duke...."

"Sister? What sister? Alejandro is an only child," I added, frowning up at him. "Aren't you?"

He cleared his throat, glancing at his old governess. "You're confused, Pilar," he said gently. "You're thinking of Miguel. Not me."

Her rheumy eyes focused on him. Then she nearly jumped in her chair. "Yes. Yes, of course. That was Miguel. You are El Duque." She abruptly held out a plate to me. "*¿Más galletas?*"

"Yes, please."

She beamed at me. "It makes me so happy you

like my cookies. Alejandro—" she looked at him severely "—barely ate one."

He laughed. "I had three."

"Hardly any," she sniffed. She smiled at me. "You should take the example of your wife, and eat four or more."

"Gracias," I said happily, and took another one, buttery and flaky and sweet. "I will need this recipe."

"I'll be delighted to send it to you!"

Shortly afterward, as we rose to leave, Alejandro hugged the widow's small frame gently and looked at her with real love. "Take care of yourself, Pilar. We'll see you soon."

"You, too, M—Alejandro." Shaking her head with a wry smile, she reached up and patted his cheek, then looked down and kissed the top of our baby's head. Looking among the three of us, she said, "I'm so happy for you, my dear. How it's all turned out. You deserve a happy life."

Leaving her cottage, we got back into his open Jeep, tucking Miguel into the baby seat in the backseat. As we drove across the bumpy road, I exhaled in pure relief. Closing my eyes, I turned my face up to the warm morning sun, feeling happy that I'd somehow—I had no idea how—passed the first test. Instead of her tossing me out, she'd fed me cookies. And I'd pretty much eaten all of them. What can I say? They were delicious. I really did need that recipe.

Smiling, I turned to look at my husband. "She was nice."

"I'm glad you think so." He was looking at me with a strange expression, as if he wanted to say something. I frowned, and I parted my lips to ask what he was thinking. Before I could, he looked away.

"We'll visit the Delgado family next."

For the rest of the day, as my confidence built, I spoke with all of the tenants on his estate. They seemed relieved and happy that I spoke Spanish, though they took pleasure in teasing me mercilessly about my accent. They adored the baby, and all of them praised my new husband to me, even when he was out of earshot. One after another, they told me stories of his noble character, his good heart.

"The land was neglected, and El Duque brought it back from the brink...."

"My roof was falling apart, but El Duque helped me fix it...."

"When the crop died, I thought I would have to leave. But El Duque gave me a loan, enough for seed and animals. He saved us, and he himself was only eighteen...."

"He gave my son a job in Madrid, when there were no jobs to be had. José would have left for Argentina." The old woman wiped her eyes. "El Duque kept my son here in Spain, and I'm so grateful. I'll never forget...."

By the time we visited the last house in early eve-

ning, I was no longer even nervous. I was relaxed,
holding our baby, laughing and chatting with the
farmers, complimenting them on their well-cared-
for fields and animals, complimenting their wives
on their delicious *tartas*. And seeing how they admired Alejandro, how they treated him with such
respect. His people did love him.

And by extension, I realized, they were willing to
love me, for his sake. And for the sake of our child.

On the drive back home over the dusty road,
back to the castle at the top of the hill, we didn't
speak in the open-air Jeep. Miguel was sleeping in
the back. Finally, I smiled at Alejandro. "That went
well, don't you think?"

"Yes," he said shortly.

What could he possibly be mad about now? Biting my lip, I looked at the passing scenery. I was already starting to love Spain, especially Andalucía.
The air was warm, dusty from our tires on the dirt
road. The sun was starting to fade to the west, leaving a soft golden glow across the fields. I felt the
warm breeze against my skin, the air scented by
honeysuckle and bougainvillea and the jacaranda
trees in bloom.

But Alejandro didn't say a word. He pulled the
truck in front of the garage. Getting out, he opened
my door. When I stepped out of the Jeep, he pulled
me into his arms. I looked up at him, biting my lip.
"Alejandro, didn't I do—all right?"

"All right?" he said huskily. I saw the warmth in

his deep brown eyes. They held the same glow as the soft Andalucían morning. "I am proud of you beyond words, *mi corazon*. You made them love you. As…"

He cut himself off, but as I looked up at his face, my heart started to pound. "They loved me for your sake."

"No." He shook his head. "They loved you only for yourself. Your warmth, your smile, your…" Reaching down, he stroked my cheek. Something seemed to stretch tight between us, making me hold my breath. His hand trailed down my hair, down my back. "Come upstairs with me," he whispered. "Right now…"

"But dinner…"

He lowered his head to mine in a deep, passionate kiss, taut and tender, slow and sweet. I clutched his shoulders, lost in his embrace.

Miguel gave a plaintive whine from the back of the Jeep, and Alejandro released me with a rueful laugh. "But Abuela will be expecting us for dinner."

"Yes." I shook my head with a snort. We'd been fed at literally every house we visited. "I won't be able to eat a bite. I'm not the least bit hungry."

"Funny. I'm starving." He gave me a dark look that made my body burn, and I knew he wasn't talking about food. He sighed grumpily. "But you're right. Dinner has been arranged. We wouldn't want to disappoint Abuela…."

"No. We wouldn't." I took our baby out of the

truck, and we went upstairs to give Miguel his bath. Alejandro left to dress for dinner tonight, as Maurine had requested. I fed our baby, cuddling him in the rocking chair as he drifted off to sleep, plump and adorable in his footsie pajamas, holding his soft blanket against his cheek. I finally tucked him into his crib, then went to the master suite next door.

I felt dusty from the road, and was tempted to take a shower, but feared that would make me late, which would be rude. Especially since Maurine had insisted tonight's dinner was special somehow. So I just brushed out my hair and put on a long slinky dress and high heels. She'd asked us to dress up for dinner tonight, though what made tonight different from the other nights, I had no idea. I put on some red lipstick and looked at myself in the mirror. I looked so different, I thought. I barely recognized myself. I tossed my hair, seeing the bold new gleam in my eye—and liking it.

Smiling, I went downstairs. But as I walked down the sweeping stairs, voices echoed from the shadows of the stairwell below.

"You should tell her the truth." Maurine's voice was uncharacteristically sharp.

"No," Alejandro answered coldly.

"She's your wife—"

"She cannot know. Not yet. Perhaps not ever. I don't know if I can trust her."

"But this is your life we're talking about!"

"Not just my life. Also yours. And Miguel's. She could destroy us all if she—"

Then they looked up and saw me. I shaped my mouth into a bright smile, as if I hadn't heard anything, as if my heart wasn't pounding.

"You look spectacular, *mi esposa,*" Alejandro murmured, and held out his arm. He was dressed in a dark tailored shirt and trousers. "May I escort you to dinner?"

I nodded. But as we walked down the hallway toward the banqueting hall, the happiness that had been building inside me all day had suddenly gone *pfffft* like a balloon.

What was he hiding?

It was growing harder to push the question from my mind. Even denial will carry you only so far. My recent happiness suddenly felt like a house of cards waiting to fall.

I'd felt such incandescent joy, being in his arms last night. Being by his side today, meeting his neighbors and the people who mattered to him. Being introduced, with pride, as his wife.

Every moment I spent with him, I was falling deeper and deeper into an emotion I'd sworn I'd never feel for him again. Especially since I knew he was lying to my face. I was walking straight into heartbreak, only this time, I'd have no one to blame but myself.

Abruptly, I stopped in the middle of the hallway. He frowned down at me. "What, *querida?*"

I looked at him, my heart aching. "I need to know what you're hiding from me."

Setting his jaw, he shook his head.

"I wish I'd never told you," he said harshly. Dropping my hand, he looked at me with cold eyes. "Should we spend dinner apart?"

He was ruthlessly ending the conversation. Swallowing back tears, I shook my head. He held out his arm again.

We walked, the only sound our footsteps against the flagstones. "I wonder why Maurine insisted that we dress up for dinner tonight," I said over the awkward silence. "I just saw her wearing an old cardigan and jeans…."

We entered the banqueting hall, and my voice cut off.

It was completely empty of other people. The only light came from the blazing fire in the enormous stone fireplace. Tall tapered candles lit the table. Beneath the high, timbered ceilings, the shadows and fire made the room breathlessly romantic.

I blinked, bewildered. "This is why Maurine wanted us to dress for dinner…?" Then Alejandro gave me a sensual smile, and it all clicked into place. "You arranged this," I breathed.

He shrugged. "I spoke with her before we left this morning, and she agreed newlyweds need time alone."

"But what about dinner for everyone else?"

"They already ate." He came closer, his dark eyes

intent. "And I'm glad," he said huskily. "I want you to myself."

I stared at him, still conflicted about the way he'd coldly cut off my earlier question. Going to the table, he poured us each a glass of red wine that sparkled like a ruby in the firelight.

"Manzanilla wine. From my vineyard."

As we sat next to each other at the end of the long table, near the fire, I felt my anger starting to be melted by his nearness. The dinner was probably delicious, but I ate mechanically, barely tasting it. Alejandro moved his chair closer. He did not try to touch me. He started asking me questions, asking what I thought of Spain, how I liked the estate, how I liked the baby's nursery. He asked me how I'd first started painting.

"My father taught me," I said softly. "He always wanted to be an artist. But once he got married and had a family, he had to try to earn a living...." I gave a rueful laugh. "He was never good at earning money. But we loved him, just as he was."

Alejandro leaned forward, his elbow on the table, his chin resting on his hand, listening to every word. He focused his attention on me, as if nothing and no one else existed.

I knew how this worked. I'd seen it before. And yet I still could not resist. With every breath I felt him seducing me, drawing me in closer. Against my will, my heart started to warm.

The enormous banqueting hall, usually chilly

inside the castle even on a hot summer day, was growing increasingly hot. I found myself leaning forward, asking him questions in my turn, and all the while wishing he would kiss me, and hating myself for wanting it. Finally, I could bear it no longer.

"Why can't you tell me your secret?"

"Put it from your mind," he said harshly. "Or go."

"Fine," I said tearfully. I stood, turning away.

He grabbed me by the wrist.

Slowly, Alejandro rose from the chair, his body grazing mine as he fully stood, towering over me. My head tilted back to look at his face. He was bigger than me, stronger by far. But it wasn't his strength that overwhelmed me, but the stark vulnerability I suddenly saw in his hard, handsome face.

"This is all you need to know," he whispered.

He pushed me against the edge of the stone fireplace, holding my wrists above me, kissing my lips, my throat. Closing my eyes, I tilted back my head as waves of desire crashed over me.

"I want you, Lena," he whispered, his voice husky, his lips brushing my earlobe. *"Te deseo."*

I shivered. Then remembered why I was mad at him and tried to pull away. "I—I am dusty and sweaty from the road." I gave a casual laugh that no one would believe, least of all me. "I rushed downstairs because I didn't want to be late." He continued to kiss my face, and I closed my eyes, breathing, "But I should…really…go take a bath…."

"Bien," he purred. "I'll join you."

My eyes flew open. "A shower, I mean, not a bath," I stammered. "There's not much room in the shower for two…."

He ran his hands down my back, holding me against him. "Just enough."

He kissed me, and beneath the sensuality of his embrace, I sighed, and my lips parted. My body melted into his, my soft curves pressing into his hard angles as if his body had been made for mine.

Lifting me into his arms as if I weighed nothing at all, he carried me upstairs to our private, luxurious bathroom, where he gently set me on my feet. His dark eyes never left mine as he slowly pulled off my dress, then my bra, then my panties.

When I was completely naked in front of him, he wrenched me hard against him and kissed me deeply, hungrily. I desperately began to unbutton his shirt, then his trousers, until he, too, was naked.

Pulling away, he turned on the water in the shower. I glanced back longingly at the bed, but it was in the next room and seemed a million miles away. He kissed me again, and I gasped against his lips, his naked body hard against mine. Steam lifted from the hot water of the shower, making the luxurious bathroom of white marble and silver a magical, otherworldly place of ice and snow.

Except for the heat. Every inch of me felt warm, bursting with fire.

Alejandro pulled me into the shower. He pushed me away from him firmly, and I whimpered.

"Patience," he said, and I could almost hear his smile. He was still in control. Unlike me...

With agonizing slowness, he washed me in the shower, tangling shampoo in my hair, rubbing soap over my body, scrubbing every inch of me. I felt him stroke my full, naked breasts, my waist, my hips, the soft hair between my legs. I closed my eyes, swaying on my feet. I felt hot and unsteady as he caressed my hair, down my earlobes, my neck. I left handprints in the glass wall of the shower, against the white steam.

Turning me around to face him, he ran his hands down my breasts, over my belly, over my hips and thighs. Hot shooting streams of water poured over us both.

And he knelt before me. Gently parting my thighs, he pressed his face between my legs.

I gasped. His lips were tender and sensual and warm. His tongue slid against me, inside me, the merest breath of a stroke, hot and wet beneath the warm water.

I closed my eyes, pressing my hands against the glass wall behind me.

His hands slid around me, holding me firmly against his mouth. He teased me with the tip of his tongue, soft and light against the most sensitive part of me, then spread me wide and lapped me, until I tossed back my head, slapping my long wet hair against the glass as I shook all over. The hot, steamy water poured over us both as I felt his hands—his tongue—slide over my wet, pink skin.

For an intoxicating eternity, he teased me, bringing me almost to an explosion of pleasure beneath the steamy pulse of the shower, then backing away the very second before I would have exploded into bliss. It might have been seconds or hours, that he seduced me with this sweet torment....

When my need was too much to bear, and I was shaking so hard I could barely breathe with desire, Alejandro turned me around, pressing me against the glass, my bottom resting against his hard, thick length.

"You're mine," he growled in my ear. "Say it."

"I'm yours," I breathed, pressing my arms against the glass.

"Again."

"I'm yours!"

"Forever."

"Forever," I whispered.

He thrust inside me roughly, deep and hard, and I gasped.

I forgot everything in the overwhelming pleasure of having him inside me. *Pleasure* was not a big enough word for it. I melted, lost myself, found myself, until he exploded inside me, and I soared.

Afterward, both of us were panting and spent, and he abruptly turned off the water. He opened the shower door and toweled me off. Without a word, he lifted me in his arms and carried me to our enormous bed. Looking back, I saw the trail of water he'd left across his stark floor.

Clinging to my husband's naked chest as he carried me, I felt as if I were in another time or place. I wondered dreamily about other lovers who'd done this, hundreds of years ago, in this very castle, when the sultan ruled.

Setting me down naked on our bed, he looked down at me. I smiled up at him, blinking tears of emotion, of anger and joy all mixed up together.

Climbing beside me, he held me, kissing my temple tenderly. Our bodies intertwined, his wet skin sliding against mine. My hand stroked the hardness of his chest, laced with dark hair. He held me tight. My eyes were heavy, and started to close.

I'd told him the truth in the shower.

I was his.

Now and forever.

Because I love him....

The realization hit like a bolt of lightning, causing my eyes to fly open.

I was in love with him, and there was something he was keeping from me. A reason he was lying. A secret he thought would hurt me.

I was in love with my husband.

But if I knew the secret he hid from me, would that love be destroyed?

CHAPTER NINE

THE NEXT FEW weeks fled by in a blur. We spent our days doing the work of the estate, talking to tenants and managing the house. I started painting in the garden in the morning, and played with our baby on the floor of Alejandro's home office as he worked on the computer and spoke on the phone to employees around the world.

"I begrudge them every hour," he told me, stroking my cheek. "I would rather spend it with you."

My heart sang as the birds did, flying free through the lush green trees, across the wide blue Spanish sky. But eventually, Alejandro had to go on a business trip. "Madrid?" I pouted.

He laughed. "Granada."

"Isn't that where the Alhambra is?" I said eagerly, picturing the famous Moorish castle. "I'll come with you!"

He shook his head. "It will be a one-day trip, there and back. Very boring. Stay here with Miguel. Paint. Enjoy your day." He kissed my temple and said huskily, "I'll be back before bedtime."

Then he kissed me *adios* until my toes curled.

But after he'd gone, all the fears and shadows came back crashing around me, without Alejandro's warmth and strength to hide behind.

Was he really going to do business in Granada, as he'd said? Or was he there for some other reason?

Was this his lie?

Don't think about it, I ordered my trembling heart, but it was impossible, now that I loved him.

I feared knowing the truth.

I feared never knowing it.

"Dear?" I heard Maurine's tremulous voice. "I wonder if I could ask you a favor?"

"Of course," I said, desperate for distraction.

She smiled at me. "You are such a talented artist. I love the paintings you've done of my roses. You are the only one who's ever done them justice." As I blushed, she continued, "Alejandro's birthday is next month. Would you do a portrait of me and Miguel, in the rose garden…?"

"I'd love to!" I exclaimed, my mind immediately filled with painting materials, size and composition. I went into Seville for supplies, and by late afternoon, after Miguel's nap, the three of us were outside. I propped up an easel in front of where they sat on a bench, surrounded by greenery and red, yellow and pink roses.

The warm Spanish sun filtered golden light over the garden as I painted the portrait of the dowager

Duchess of Alzacar and her great-grandbaby, the future duke.

Maurine's lovely white hair was like a soft cloud around her twinkling eyes and smiling face. I drew her outline in loose strokes. That was easy, compared with the challenge of the wiggling, giggling baby in her lap. But I'd painted and drawn my son so many times over the past six months, I knew his chubby face by heart. I could have done it blindfolded.

I smiled to myself, picturing how happy Alejandro would be at the gift, reaching up to adjust the floppy pink hat I was wearing to keep the sunlight out of my eyes. Maurine chattered nonstop, while entertaining the baby in her lap. She told me how she'd first fallen in love with her husband, who'd had a title, "though it seemed useless enough, with no hope of returning to Spain, with the political situation," and absolutely no money or marketable skills. "It's so much easier to know how to work when you've been raised to it. My husband had spent his adult life sleeping in the spare rooms of rich friends from his Eton days."

"Sounds like my father. He wanted to work, but didn't know how."

"It's the upbringing, I think. Even when we finally returned to Spain, with the Navaro fortune lost, Rodrigo had no idea how to pay for the upkeep of this castle. It's not like the old days, when a duke could simply demand peasants give him tribute." She gave a soft laugh. "He was desperate to keep the title and the land, for the sake of his family's history. I loved him, so I did my best to help." She looked away, blinking fast. "I sold oranges from the orchard and gave castle tours. Sadly, our son was no better with money—the earning of it, I mean, not the spending of it. By the time Alejandro became duke, the roof of the castle was caving in, we were mortgaged to the hilt, and I was beginning to think I'd spend my elderly years begging on the streets, or selling oranges at street corners."

I laughed. "As if Alejandro would ever allow that." I smiled, remembering his bossy ways when he'd informed me that taking financial care of us was his job. "He, at least, had no trouble figuring out how to make money."

"No." She smiled, playing patty-cake with the baby. "But of course, his background is so different. He didn't have an overbearing father constantly telling him how an aristocrat was supposed to behave. The small silver lining of having no father at all, I suppose...."

"No father?" Frowning, I lifted the brush off the canvas. I looked around the easel. "But Alejandro's father was the duke. Your son."

Maurine looked up at me sharply, her face oddly pale. "Oh, yes. Of course."

I gave a laugh. "Is the sun getting to you, Maurine?"

"I'm an old woman. I get confused." Her blue eyes suddenly wouldn't meet mine. "But you're right. I think I've been in the sun too long."

She rose to her feet, still holding Miguel, who looked happy to be moving at last after so long sitting still. "I'm a little tired. I'll have the staff bring you some lemonade. And maybe look for Alejandro's hairbrush. Yes, his hairbrush…"

She left the rose garden without waiting for a reply. I stared after her, frowning. What did lemonade have to do with Alejandro's hairbrush?

"I thought she would never leave."

With a gasp, I whirled around. The paintbrush fell from my limp hand, landing with a soft thud into the grass.

Edward St. Cyr stood in the rose garden, near the thick hedge on the edge of the forest. Brambles had ripped the sleeves of his dark tailored jacket.

"Edward," I breathed. "What are you doing here?"

He stopped five feet in front of me, looking down at me. His eyes were stark against his tanned face as he gazed at me hungrily. "You have no idea how I've wanted to see your face."

He reached out a hand, but I stumbled backward, my long skirt dragging against the grass. Holding my floppy pink hat against my head, I glanced uneasily to the left and right.

Having him here, in Maurine's rose garden—in

Alejandro's castle—felt all kinds of wrong. Like finding a deadly snake amid the lush flowers. "How did you get in here?"

His lips twisted. "It wasn't easy."

"I told you I never wanted to see you again!" I narrowed my eyes. "You must get out of here! Alejandro will kill you if he finds you here!"

"Ah, but he's gone, isn't he?"

I sucked in my breath.

"And as for your precious duke..." A low, guttural curse came from Edward's lips. "I know you don't want him." He looked contemptuously around the lush, sunlit garden, to the stone walls of the castle just beyond the perfectly trimmed green hedges. "I've come to save you from this...prison."

"It's not a prison," I retorted. "It's my home! And Alejandro is no jailer. I..." I licked my lips, then whispered aloud, "I love him."

Edward's eyes narrowed, and his lips twisted downward, giving him an expression that was hard, even cruel.

"He seduced you, didn't he?" He took another step toward me, and I again backed away, knocking over the easel behind me. I gulped as Edward slowly looked me over, from my hat to my long cotton skirt covered with an artist's long smock. "He's got to you." He straightened, and this time his contemptuous glance was just for me, all for me. "You fell for his lines *again*."

I took a deep breath.

"I love him," I said quietly. "In a way I never loved you—and I never will."

His hands tightened at his sides.

"The charming Duque de Alzacar. Beloved by all." His lip curled. "Of course you're faithful to him. But is he faithful to you?"

I drew myself up coldly. "Of course."

"Are you sure?" He lifted a dark eyebrow. "You know, you must know, about the woman he visits in Granada?"

My lips parted. "Woman?"

"Ah," Edward said, smiling. "You didn't know. They have dinner together. Often. He bought her a tavern in the Albaicín district. Sometimes he even plays his guitar there. Singing old Spanish love songs. In front of everyone."

My mouth went dry.

Alejandro hadn't played his guitar for me. Not once.

Licking my lips, I croaked, "There are all kinds of reasons for…"

Edward moved in for the kill. "Sometimes he stays the night in the residence above her tavern. But sometimes," he said softly, "he just goes for a quick visit. For the day." His lips curled. "A bit of love in the afternoon."

The chill turned to ice. I desperately tried to think of a reasonable explanation for why Alejandro hadn't wanted me to come with him today.

I'll come with you!

It will be a one-day trip, there and back. Very boring. Stay here with Miguel.

It was the nightmare I'd imagined when I'd refused to marry Alejandro. Except this was a million times worse.

Because I'd let myself love him.

"Lying to your face." Edward came closer. "He has no shame. He thinks, in his arrogance, that he can have you, as well. He's out enjoying himself—keeping you prisoner…."

"I'm not a prisoner," I choked out.

He lifted a condescending eyebrow. "No?" He slowly looked around the rose garden. "I could make him pay," he whispered. "I could make him regret."

I gasped—not in fear, but in fury. "If you dare hurt him, I'll…"

"*Hurt* him?" His blue eyes suddenly blazed. "*He* is the one you are worried about? Where was his concern for *you* when he left your heart in ashes?" He took another step toward me, his expression changing as he reached toward me almost wistfully. "Where is your love for me, for saving you…?"

I turned away, stepping back out of his reach. My voice was very cold. "I appreciated your friendship—until the moment I realized you had no time for my baby."

"Lena, you can't…"

"If you touch me, I'll scream. And Alejandro will come running...."

Edward moved closer.

"He's not here, though, is he?"

This time, the expression in his face scared me. For a moment, I stared at him, heart pounding. But as I opened my mouth to scream, like a miracle, I heard Alejandro's voice from the other side of the garden.

"Lena? Are you out here?"

I nearly wept with relief.

"I'm here!" I shouted. "I'm here, Alejandro! In the rose garden!"

Shaking, I turned back to face Edward, but he was already gone, melted back into the forest.

"And don't ever come back," I whispered aloud. I prayed I'd never see him again. But I still heard his ugly words.

You know, you must know, about the woman he visits in Granada?

He was *lying,* I told myself. Alejandro told me he'd be loyal, that he'd been faithful for the past year, wanting only me....

But then, I remembered, he'd also told me he was a liar.

When I saw my husband's strong, powerful body push through the trees to me, I nearly wept.

"Querida," Alejandro murmured, kissing my forehead as he pulled me into his arms. "I came back

early. I couldn't bear to be away for…but what's this?" He drew back, his handsome face the picture of concern. "You're shaking."

"It's nothing," I said. My teeth chattered. "M-my easel fell."

"Ah." He smiled at me, his dark eyes warm. "Let me take care of that."

"Don't look at the painting!" I cried. "It's supposed to be a surprise. For your birthday."

Good-naturedly covering his eyes, he handed me the canvas. "I didn't see a thing."

I took the painting, slightly smeared from the fall and half-finished, with Maurine and Miguel looking like ghosts. And I wished I'd covered my ears and not heard a thing when Edward had told me about the woman in Granada.

"It has occurred to me," Alejandro murmured a week later, leaning over the sofa where I sat feeding Miguel, "that we never had a honeymoon."

"Honeymoon?" I said, twisting my head to look back at him. I shook my head. "You mean, without Miguel?"

"Don't worry." He brushed the back of my neck with his fingertips, making me shiver. "I'm not thinking Tahiti. That will have to wait. But a single night, just a two-hour drive away, surely you could manage that?"

I hesitated. "I don't know…"

"I promise you'll enjoy it." He stroked my hair, then gently kissed the crook of my neck, the edge between my shoulder and my neck. My shiver turned harder. "We will get a nice hotel. Go out for dinner. I'm thinking Granada...."

"Granada?" I stared at him, and the color must have drained from my cheeks, because he frowned.

"I thought you wanted to see the Alhambra."

I'd dreamed of seeing the famous Moorish castle since I was a child. But I'd spent the past week guarding my heart. Trying to stay distant and cold. Trying not to think about what I didn't want to know. Granada was the last place on earth I wanted to go.

Or was it?

"Maybe," I said.

He smiled, really smiled, for the first time in a week. Since I'd started keeping my distance, even when we were as close as a man and woman could be. "Is that a yes?" He tilted his head, looking over me slowly with a sensual, heavy-lidded gaze. "I'd be happy to spend time persuading you...."

My body immediately clamored for him to persuade me, hot and sweet and long. But sex wasn't our problem. We made love every night. Physically, we were closer than ever.

Emotionally, the weight of secrets had caused an ocean between us.

You know, you must know, about the woman he visits in Granada?

My smile faded. Like my courage. I shook my head. "On second thought…forget it."

"Why?" His eyes narrowed, and he moved around the sofa with lightning speed. He cupped my face, looking down at me fiercely. "I am trying to make it up to you!"

"What?" I breathed, searching his gaze. "What are you trying to make up for, Alejandro?"

"Whatever has made you so angry at me." His fingertips tightened infinitesimally. "I want you to look at me like you used to."

"And I want to trust you," I choked out, "like I used to."

He stared at me. He'd never heard that tone from me before. "When I was in Granada…"

I held my breath.

He continued, "You were alone with my grandmother. Did she…" He hesitated. "Did she say something?"

"Did she tell me your secret, you mean?" I said bitterly. "No. She is loyal to you."

He abruptly released me and rose from the sofa, his face hard. "Enough. We are taking a one-night honeymoon. You will come with me. You will have a good time."

I lifted my chin defiantly. "Is that a command, Your Excellency?"

"Take it as you wish." He glared back at me, his

eyes cold. "I will tell the staff to pack your things immediately."

The drive to Granada was short, especially after Alejandro stepped on the gas of his yellow Lamborghini. But with just the two of us trapped in the small space, it still took far too long. The tension between us was boiling, about to explode.

I forced myself to look at the guidebook he'd bought me about Granada. I tried to distract myself with its history. To choke back my frustration, my hurt, my rage. Because if I let out my feelings, I feared our marriage would end, and so would any chance at happiness. Forever.

I desperately wanted to ask him about the woman.

I desperately was afraid of the answer.

Alejandro did not speak to me. He drove us to a small hotel, a *parador* amidst the gardens of the Alhambra itself, in a building that was once a fifteenth-century convent, and a royal chapel to the kings of Spain, and before that, a palace and mosque of the Moorish emirs. Once there, he seemed angry at everyone. He glowered at the hotel staff. The moment we were alone in the simple, starkly furnished bedroom, he turned on me, and pressed me to the large four-poster bed in a ruthless, unyielding embrace.

All the women's magazines tell you to do one thing. To have self-esteem. To turn away from any man you cannot completely trust. Especially one who has broken your heart before. They say the past predicts the future.

I knew all this, but when I felt his hand stroke my cheek, the sweet satin stroke of his touch sent liquid fire through my veins. I saw the dark gleam of his eyes as he slowly lowered his head to mine, and I could not resist.

He kissed me, and I felt my heart explode in my chest. Felt my taped-together soul shatter again into a million pieces, even tinier than before, in infinite chiming shards that I would never be able to put together again.

I had to ask him. I had to be brave enough to ask, and be brave enough to listen to his answer— whether he answered with words, or with silence.

I suddenly realized this might be the very last time we'd ever make love....

"Maravillosa," Alejandro whispered against my skin. As he pulled off my clothes, as I pulled off his, as I kissed him, tasting the salt of his skin, I knew that even amid the pleasure, I was tasting the salt of my own tears.

I loved him.

So much.

And I knew—I'd always known, really—how this would someday end.

Through my tears, I kissed him back desperately, letting him pull me into the whirlwind of mingled anguish and pleasure.

But when the heat between us was satisfied, coldness was all that was left. Both of us still naked, he held me against him on the bed. His voice was low.

"Why do you not look at me like you used to? What has changed? What do you—know?"

I looked at him. His face shimmered through my tears.

"Edward came to see me last week. At Rohares."

"What!" he exploded, sitting up.

I held his hand. "I didn't ask him to come. He snuck in. I only spoke with him for a moment. He wanted me to run away with him. When I refused, he told me...you had a woman here. In Granada. That you visited her. That you bought her a tavern. That you even sing to her...."

For a long moment, we stared at each other in the slanted bars of sunlight coming through the window blinds. I could almost hear the pounding of my heart.

Then Alejandro's lip slowly curled.

"I will kill him," he said, and with cold menace, started to rise from the bed.

"No!" Grabbing his arm, I looked up at him pleadingly. "It's not about Edward anymore. It's about us. You and me." I swallowed, blinking fast as I whispered, "Do you love her?"

He looked down at me.

"Yes," he said dully.

My lips parted in a silent, heartsick gasp. Numbly, I let him go.

"So that is your big secret. The thing I expected from the beginning." I tried to laugh, wiping my eyes. "How very boring."

"It's not like that." Sitting on the edge of the bed, he scowled at me. "You think so little of my loyalty, even after all the time we've spent together?"

"But you said you love her," I whispered. "You've never said that to me. Not once."

I heard his intake of breath. "It's not like that," he repeated, setting his jaw. "Theresa is not my mistress."

"Then what?" I choked out. "What secret could you possibly be keeping, that would hurt me worse than that?"

"I protect the people I love. At any cost." His voice was bleak. I looked at him sharply, and saw the vulnerability in his eyes. The yearning. He took a deep, shuddering breath. "How I wish I could tell you everything."

Our eyes locked. Held. I opened my lips to plead—

He shook his head and rose to his feet. The yearning in his expression shuttered. His face returned to the handsome mask I knew so well—powerful, ruthless and cold.

"Come," he said. "Our time is short."

After a silent luncheon on the lovely terrace of

the *parador,* we walked through the gardens of the Alhambra, with their flowers and trees and wide lush pools. As beautiful and varied and wide as they were, they didn't hold a candle to the gardens of Rohares, in my opinion. Though perhaps I was biased. Because the castle had become my home.

Alejandro held my hand tightly as we walked. I didn't even try to resist. The truth was I wanted the comfort of his hand. It felt warm and strong in mine. Was it wrong of me to still want to believe? To trust him?

Yes. I was a fool. Any of the women's magazines would have called me an idiot for not already being on my way to a lawyer's office. And yet…

We met a guide who took us on a private tour. We walked through the graceful arcades of the Alhambra complex, through the lush terraces with their views of Granada in the valley below, past the blue pools hedged by myrtle, reflecting the wide blue sky. But in spite of the fact that I'd dreamed of visiting the Alhambra all my life, I barely noticed the beauty. As we walked through cavernous rooms, decorated with tile and geometric patterns and arabesques of Arabic calligraphy in plaster, beneath jaw-dropping ceilings soaring high above, of the sun and stars, my mind was scrambling, trying to put the clues together.

Why would Alejandro need to protect Maurine and Miguel? What could the secret be?

We had our picture taken together in the famous stone Court of the Lions, from the fourteenth century.

"No," the guide laughed. "You are newlyweds. Stand closer."

And so Alejandro put his arm around me. I looked up at his face, and again, I saw the yearning in his eyes. The yearning that matched my own.

"¡Perfecto! Now you look like lovers!"

As we left the Alhambra, I turned back to look at it one last time. It had been neglected over the years, vandalized, nearly blown up by Napoleon's soldiers. But after all that, it stood tall and proud over Granada. Unbowed. Unbroken. And so beautiful now. So loved.

"We don't need to see any more," I whispered over the ache in my throat.

"You're here. See it all." Silently, Alejandro drove us down the mountain to the city. We visited the Capilla Real, the royal chapel, getting special permission for a private tour that took us immediately past the long line of tourists outside, past the gypsies begging on the streets and musicians busking along the crowded edges.

In the dark, quiet interior of the enormous stone chapel, I saw the tomb of Ferdinand and Isabella, who together had practically ruled the medieval world in their day, even before they'd sent Columbus in ships to the New World. Together, they'd finally ended seven hundred years of Moorish rule, laying siege to Granada and driving the last sultan, called Boabdil, from the city.

It was said that the reason he gave up without a fight was to prevent the destruction of his beloved Alhambra. And so he spent the rest of his life mocked, and in poverty, a sultan without a throne....

Alejandro came to stand beside me in the cool shadows of the royal crypt. "What are you thinking?"

I looked at him. "How loving the wrong thing—or the wrong person—can ruin your life," I whispered.

"*Sí,*" he said quietly. He turned away. "Come. This place leaves me cold."

Outside the echoes of the shadow-filled chapel, we were hit by the brilliant Spanish sunlight, the noise of tourists laughing and talking, the distant sound of music. Life.

"Enough history," Alejandro said, shaking his head ruefully. "There's an ice-cream shop down the street, the most famous in Granada. The American first lady visited here recently and said it was the best ice cream in all of Spain...."

But I wasn't listening. I was too busy trying to think things through. Eating the ice-cream cone some time later as we walked, I looked at Alejandro sideways beneath my lashes. He was so handsome, so dark-haired and broad-shouldered. The man of my dreams, come to life.

What was the secret? What was it he couldn't tell me, for fear of endangering his grandmother and his son?

We walked through the narrow streets of Granada, and I bought some chocolates and a garden ornament for Maurine, and a small stuffed toy for Miguel, plus a wooden sword and shield he wouldn't be able to play with for at least a year.

I couldn't stop thinking of that last sultan, Boabdil, who'd sacrificed everything, his honor, his fortune, his pride, rather than see the palace he loved blown up into ash.

What would I sacrifice for love?

What would you?

Love me? Alejandro's words floated back to me. *You do not even know me.*

Maybe he'd been right. A year ago, maybe I'd just fallen for his power, his wealth, his influence. His beauty.

But now, as I looked at his face, I loved him for who he really was. The man who took care of everyone. Who was willing to sacrifice himself for those he cared about. As a father. A grandson. A neighbor. A boss.

A husband.

My heart caught in my chest. What was I missing?

Twilight was falling when Alejandro suggested

we go out for dinner and drinks. "A…friend of mine owns a restaurant in the Albaicín district."

I looked at him sharply. He nodded.

"Yes," he said quietly, watching me in the deepening dusk. "I want you to meet her."

I was shaking when we walked up the cobblestoned alleys of the Albaicín, the old Moorish quarter on the hillside beneath the Alhambra. We reached a prosperous-looking tavern, filled with people and music. I froze.

"Come on," Alejandro said gently. "It'll be all right." Pulling me inside, he brought me through the crowds to the bar, where he was greeted eagerly by the other patrons.

"Are you going to play tonight, *señor?*"

With a slight smile, he shook his head. "Where is Theresa?"

The man motioned toward the end of the bar with his glass of sangria. With a quick nod, Alejandro pulled me down toward a dark-haired woman.

"Theresa," he said, kissing her on each cheek.

"Alejandro," she exclaimed, returning the embrace. "I didn't expect you so soon!"

I stared at the woman. She wasn't what I'd expected. She had dark eyes and a round, friendly face, and she seemed at least ten years older than Alejandro. She smiled as she turned to me. "And this must be your wife." A big smile lit up her face. "Your Lena?"

My lips parted. *His* Lena?

"*Sí.*" Alejandro put his arm around me. "My Lena."

"I'm so happy to meet you at last!" she said with clear delight. "I told him he had to bring you here. Wait until you hear him play!"

"Play?" I echoed, looking at him.

He blushed. I swear he did. "Yes. I play a little guitar sometimes. No one cares I'm a duke here. They only care how well I play the guitar...."

"Are you that good?"

"Let him show you." Theresa gave me a wink. "Drink orders always go up thirty percent when you sing, Alejandro." She turned to me with a smile. "Go grab a table, if you can find one.... And what will you have?"

"Bourbon," he said. "Rocks."

"Right. Lena?"

"Something light...sangria?"

She chuckled. "Light?"

"Isn't it mostly juice with a bit of red wine?"

She gave a hearty guffaw and glanced at Alejandro affectionately. "Innocent little thing, isn't she?"

"Very," he said quietly.

She sighed, looking back at me, she suggested, "I'll make you a *tinto de verano*. Dash of wine, sugar and a little lime with sparkling water. Trust me. It won't go to your head."

She was right. The delicious concoction was a

mixture of tart and sweet and bubbles, with lemon and limes floating beside the ice. I had one glass, then another, then a third, then looked down at my empty plate and realized I'd ordered and eaten a whole plate of dinner without paying the slightest attention.

"What time is it?" My head was swimming. I put my hands to my temples. "She said this drink wouldn't go to my head," I said accusingly.

Alejandro gave a low laugh. "It wouldn't, but you had four of them."

"Four?" I looked with amazement at my empty glass. "They just taste so light. The most delicious wine cooler ever invented."

"You should stop."

I looked at him brazenly. "You should tell me who you really are."

Time suddenly stood still.

"Don't you know?" he said hoarsely. "Haven't you guessed?"

"Don't tell me you're already having your first fight." Theresa was holding out a guitar. "Fix it, *pequeño*. Play."

"*Sí!*" the people around us clamored, pounding on their tables. "Play!"

Alejandro shook his head. "We're leaving."

But I didn't want to leave. I wanted to see what everyone else apparently already knew. The other side of my husband. The one he'd never let me see. "Will you play?" I whispered. "For me?"

He whirled to look at me. Then he gave a slow nod. "For you, *mi amor*." He slowly took the guitar in his hand, and there was a burst of cheers and applause. "This is just for you."

Walking across the crowded tavern, past all the tables to the tiny stage, Alejandro sat on a stool. With his guitar in his lap, he said simply into the microphone, "This is for my bride. The mother of my child." He looked at me. "The woman I love."

My lips parted in a silent gasp.

Could he have said…

Surely he couldn't have said…

How strong were those *tinto de verano* drinks anyway?

Exhaling, Alejandro strummed his guitar, and in a low, husky voice began to sing. It sounded very old, and Spanish. He was a good musician, I thought in amazement, really good, far better than any tycoon-slash-duke had a right to be. The music was so heartbreaking and pure that at first, I didn't bother to listen to the words.

Then I did.

Alejandro stared at me from across the room, and sang about a young peasant boy who'd dared to put on the clothes of a prince. He'd gone through life as an imposter, until he died heartbroken, wishing he could see, just one last time, the peasant girl he'd left behind.

Love me? My whole body flashed hot, then cold as his words took on new significance. *You do not even know me.*

I dimly heard the whispers hissing through the room. "That's the Duke of Alzacar—and she must be his new wife—they're obviously in love…." But I just listened to the music, and suddenly, it all fell into place.

Maurine's shaky words. *If not for him, I never would have survived the aftermath of that car crash, when I lost my whole family…. I can still see him in the hospital, his little injured face covered with bandages, his eyes so bright…. He was worried about me, not himself. "It'll be all right, Abuela," he told me. "I'm your family now."*

Pilar's voice. *I know it was always your desire to have a larger family, growing up so lonely, up in that huge castle, with your older sister off working in Granada. And your mother working night and day, when she wasn't distracted by the duke….*

I couldn't breathe. I felt as if I was choking. The walls of the tavern were pressing in. Rising unsteadily to my feet, I pushed through the tables and headed for the door. I saw Theresa's surprised face as I flung it open and headed outside.

In the quiet night, in the empty, cobblestoned alley, I fell back against the rough stone wall and looked up at the moonlight, shaking. I jumped when I heard the slam of the door behind me.

"So now you understand," Alejandro said quietly behind me.

"You're not the duke at all," I choked out, hardly able to believe it even as I said it. "The real Alejandro died in that crash, didn't he? Along with his parents. And your mother—the housekeeper."

"I had to do it." The only sign of emotion was the slight tightening of his jaw, the low tone of his voice. "Maurine had lost everything. And I loved her. Growing up in the castle, she'd always treated me like a grandson. And on that terrible day, the day of the crash, she lost everyone. When she came to see me at the hospital, she seemed to have aged ten years. She was so alone. I couldn't leave her to die in the dilapidated castle, with no one to take care of her...." Swallowing, he looked down at the cobblestoned street. Moonlight left a trail of silver on his dark silhouette as he said quietly, "So I told Maurine I would be her family from now on. Her grandson."

"How is it possible no one knew?"

"Alejandro and I looked very much alike. We were the same age, same build. And after the accident, my face was injured. We used that to explain the difference. Not that anyone asked. People had long since stopped coming to the castle. The duke and his family had chased most of the tenants away by harassing them over rents. Even their old society friends shunned them, since they were always asking to borrow money. Alejandro's parents felt ashamed of how far they'd fallen. Just not ashamed enough to work for something better." He looked up. "My mother was the only servant left, and she hadn't been paid in a year." Taking a deep breath, he said simply, "When Abuela claimed I was her grandson, and pawned the last of her jewelry to pay the transfer-of-title fees, no one questioned it."

"But a few people knew."

He nodded. "Pilar, our governess." He glanced at the restaurant door. "My older sister. Theresa."

My lips parted. "Your sister?"

"Half sister. She's eight years older. She was working in Granada when the accident happened. She rushed to the hospital as soon as she heard, but Abuela convinced her to keep the secret. They have all kept it. Because they love me. And they love Abuela." He looked away. "As I grew older, it felt wrong, stealing Alejandro's title and name. I promised myself that I would never marry, never have a child. The family line, and the family lie, would end with me. I convinced myself that was redemption."

I stared at him, tears now falling down my cheeks in the moonlight. "That was why you said you're no good at keeping promises," I whispered. "Because you had a child. And then you married me. I thought…" I shook my head. "I thought you meant you could never keep your promises of fidelity…."

"That I would cheat on you?" he said incredulously. He came closer, his face blazing with emotion as he reached out to cup my cheek. "From the moment we met, you've been the only woman I wanted. Even for the year we were apart—there was no one else for me. No one."

"But…when I told you I loved you…"

He gave a low, humorless laugh. He shook his head. "You really don't understand, do you? When I promised myself I'd never marry or have a child, I made sure I would keep that promise by only allowing myself to date women like Claudie…cold, sophisticated, heartless women I'd never be tempted to love. You were different. You were the woman I could not resist," he said softly. "You made me break every promise I'd made to myself. I wanted to tell you everything. Where you were concerned, I had no self-control."

I stared up at him, my lips parted.

"When I heard you were pregnant with my child, I was desperate to find you. But once I did, and we were wed, I suddenly knew I'd never be able to tell you the truth. At first, because I was afraid you'd use the information to blackmail me, and try to take my son away. Then because I owed it to Miguel. You were so proud our son would someday be a duke…."

"I never cared about that!" I said fiercely. "All I care about is you. And Miguel…" I looked up at him with an intake of breath. "Your real name is Miguel."

He gave me a wicked grin. "You can see why I didn't mind our son's name."

My knees shook, because my world was spinning. "But after we were married—surely then you knew you could trust me?"

"You have such an honest heart." He sobered. "I didn't want you to have the burden."

"Burden? Are you kidding?" I gave a laugh that was giddy, almost hysterical. "If you knew what I'd imagined…"

"It's worse than you think." His face had turned deadly serious. "My grandmother and I both broke laws with our lies. We could be charged with fraud and possibly sent to prison. For myself, I would have been willing to take the risk, to tell you the truth. But Maurine…" He looked down. "I was afraid to take the risk, for her sake. The idea of her in jail…"

A sudden noise down the quiet street, perhaps a cat knocking over a trash can in a nearby alley, caused us both to jump. I looked at him.

"You can trust me. No one will ever know." I swallowed and whispered. "Did you really mean what you said in the tavern?"

"The song?"

"That you—" I blushed a little "—actually— love me?"

His eyes went wide. Then, with a low laugh, he pulled me in his arms.

"Oh, *querida*. I have loved you from almost the first moment we met. Your sweetness, your nobility, your honesty."

"I was so afraid…. I believed all the wrong things…."

Alejandro wrapped his hands around mine. "And now you hold my heart, my life, in your hands," he said quietly. "You have the power to take Miguel from me, to go back to Mexico, to walk away." He lifted his dark gaze to mine in the moonlight. "You own me completely. What will you do?"

"What will I do?" I whispered, tears in my eyes. Putting my arms around him, I pulled him close and pressed my forehead against his heart. "I will love you, Alejandro. Forever."

CHAPTER TEN

WE ROSE FOR a late breakfast the next morning, after a night in our hotel room with much giggling and even more lovemaking. As eager as I was to see our baby after a whole night away from him, I was also lingering, enjoying every last moment of this brief, perfect honeymoon.

No one would ever be able to part us again.

"I think," Alejandro said thoughtfully as we left the hotel, "that was the best honeymoon I've ever had."

"Best and only," I said.

"No, surely not only. Our marriage will be nothing but one long honeymoon," he said huskily, then to prove it, he kissed me. The kiss soon became so intense and deep that Alejandro muttered something about renting the room for another night, and started to pull me back toward the hotel.

"But we can't!" I protested with a laugh. "Miguel…"

"All right," he grumbled, then his eyes smoldered. "But I'm taking you back to our bedroom as fast as the car will go."

But at my request, we returned to Rohares the long way. He took me to the spot where legend said Boabdil, the last sultan of Spain, took his very last look at Granada, after he was forced to cede it to Spanish King Ferdinand and Queen Isabella.

"Oh, no. I left the guidebook at the hotel," I said sadly, then brightened. "But I left my name in it. Hopefully they'll find it and call."

"A guidebook? Get another one!"

"It's a souvenir," I whispered, "of the happiest night of my life."

He kissed me, then standing on the hill, we looked back at Granada. "They say Boabdil wept when he looked his last upon his city," I said wistfully. "And his mother mocked his tears. She sneered that he was weeping like a woman for what he could not fight for as a man. Can you believe that?"

"People can say hurtful things to those they love," Alejandro said quietly. "Especially when they're backed into a corner and their own hearts are breaking."

As we drove back home, I suddenly realized Alejandro was right. I thought of all my anguished years feeling lonely in London, wishing hopelessly for my grandmother, my uncle and Claudie to love me. But they could not, because they did not know how. Instead, they'd relentlessly pursued the wrong things, luxury and status and appearance. They'd never known that the only way to gain happiness was not only to follow your heart, but to give it away.

Leaning over, Alejandro took my hand. Bringing it to his lips, he fervently kissed it. My eyes blurred with tears as I smiled at him, thinking how lucky I was.

And that was the moment I forgave my family for not loving me. Sometimes, I thought, you have to make your own family.

Blushing, I said shyly, "So what do I call you now?"

He looked at me. "I've grown fond of Alejandro. I'll let my son keep Miguel." He turned away, facing the road. His hands tightened on the steering wheel. "After we get back, I'm going to talk to a lawyer. I'll see if there's any way to renounce the title without causing risk to Maurine." He looked at me. "But it seems so much to ask of you."

"What?"

"Would you be heartbroken to give up the title of duchess—and know Miguel would never be a duke?"

"Are you kidding?" I gave a low laugh. "I'm happy to give it up. Do you really think I'm duchess material?"

He looked at me seriously. "Yes, *mi amor.* Yes."

"I'm happy as your wife," I whispered. "However that may be." And he squeezed my hand in his.

When we arrived at Rohares Castle, we hugged our baby and Maurine, who immediately started telling us every small detail of their extremely uneventful night, which mostly involved patty-cake and Miguel dozing as his great-grandmother read him Washington Irving's *Tales of the Alhambra*. "So Miguel felt part of the experience, too. It seemed appropriate...."

"Like his name," I said. Smiling, I glanced back at Alejandro. "It turns out I named him after his father."

With an intake of breath, Maurine looked between us. Then she gave a whoop of joy. "Took you long enough," she cried, then hugged us, telling us we were silly to be so emotional as she wiped her own eyes. "So. I, too, have news. The best news of all." Maurine looked between us, beaming. "While the two of you were on your honeymoon, I did something with your hairbrush...."

The house phone rang loudly from across the great room. Wondering if it might be the hotel calling about my guidebook, I said hurriedly, "Just a minute." Rushing across the room, I answered breathlessly, "Hello?"

"Don't say my name."

Edward?! I gritted my teeth and rasped, "I'm hanging up now."

"If you do, you'll be sorry."

Something about the cool confidence of his voice made me hesitate. "Why?"

"Because I know."

"What?"

"Everything."

A chill went down my spine. I tried to bluff. "Everything about what?"

"About your husband. And the lie he told twenty-three years ago."

The chill turned to ice. "I don't know what you're talking about."

He snorted, then said quietly, "I followed you to Granada. I was in the shadows on the street. When you came out alone from the restaurant, I was going to comfort you. Then your husband followed you out. And gave me all the ammunition I would ever need to destroy him. And that so-called grandmother of his."

Turning, I stared wide-eyed at Alejandro and Maurine across the great hall, where they were laughing together. I gripped the phone. "What do you want?"

"What I've always wanted. You."

"I don't love you—"

"Yes. I know. You love him. So if you want to protect him, this choice should be easy for you. I'm waiting in a car at the castle gate. Call the guard. Tell him to let me in."

"If I tell Alejandro how you're trying to blackmail me, he will kill you."

"I'm sure you're right. Which is why you won't tell him."

"You don't understand! That's not just an expression. He will literally kill you!"

"Let him try," he said flatly. "Tell him, if that's how you want this to go. I'm not afraid. I have nothing to lose." He paused. "Do you?"

I shuddered, trembling, afraid that Alejandro would really kill him, and he'd end up in jail not just for fraud, but for murder. "What do you want me to do?"

His voice was smooth and slick. "Tell him you've changed your mind about your marriage. Tell him you only wanted him when you thought he was a real duke, but now...you're in love with me."

Horror filled my heart. "He'll never believe it—"

"He *will*. That's what frightens you." He gave a low laugh. "Tell him you're going to spend tonight with me, and your lawyers will be in touch about divorce—and custody. That bit about custody is just for you, by the way. I'll let your baby live with us. Doesn't that show how much I care?"

"You never cared about me," I whispered. "If you did, you couldn't do this."

"I took care of you. I saved you. I earned you. Not him."

"I'm a human soul—not some trophy to be won!"

"You should be mine," he said coldly. "Let him watch you leave with me. Make him believe I'm the one you want. And I'll forget what I know. Do it for his sake. And the old woman's."

"Edward, please..."

"Three minutes. Then I'm calling a press conference."

"And he'll kill you!"

"Then Navaro will be in jail for the rest of his life. And your kid will have no father. Or great-grandmother. Make your choice. You say you really love them? Prove it."

The line clicked off.

My whole body shook as I hung up.

"Who was it?" Alejandro said behind me.

"N-nothing. I mean, no one."

"Which is it? Is something wrong?" His eyes were sharp. Of course he knew something was wrong. He saw right through me. Saw my anguished heart.

So how could I break his—with a lie?

And yet—how could I not?

Wide-eyed, I looked across the great hall toward Maurine, who at her age would likely never come back from the shock of a scandal and trial for fraud, much less being sent to prison. I looked at my sweet baby in his baby swing, who would endure the experience I'd feared most—being surrounded by paparazzi—before he lost his father. And Alejandro. I looked at him, hardly able to breathe. If he really did attack Edward as I feared…

I remembered the look in his eyes in Granada when I'd told him that Edward had visited me. I remembered the cold menace in his face.

I will kill him.

"Lena?" Alejandro frowned, coming closer. "Who was on the phone?"

The phone suddenly rang again. I picked it up.

"Your Excellency?" It was the security guard at the gate. "There's an Edward St. Cyr here. He has no appointment. Should I let him inside?"

I took a deep breath.

"Let him in," I said faintly, then hung up the phone. I picked up my handbag. I walked slowly toward my family, feeling as if I was going to die.

But I would die for them. I looked at those three beloved faces, in this beautiful old castle I'd already come to love. My family. My home. Would I do it? To save them?

Yes.

"Where are you going?" Alejandro said.

"I'm sorry." My teeth were chattering. My words were faint. "Our marriage is over. I'll be back to-morrow. So we can discuss c-custody...."

I stopped at the door. Alejandro was staring at me with open-mouthed shock. I was trembling so hard it was all I could do not to black out.

But it was the only way to save him. To save all of them.

I was the one who'd allowed Edward into our lives. I was the one who should pay for that. Not them.

But as I looked into Alejandro's face, I knew that he, too, would suffer. Squeezing my eyes shut, I turned away.

"Edward's come for me," I choked out. "I'm leaving with him now. We both know it never would have worked out with us, Alejandro. Not for long…"

"What are you saying?" he breathed, searching my gaze. "I don't believe you!"

"I'll be back with a lawyer—tomorrow…." My voice ended on a sob. Whirling around, I fled for the door. Outside, I saw Edward waiting in an expensive SUV. The windows were all rolled down, the engine still running. Sobbing, I climbed in beside him. He gave me a triumphant, cruel smile.

"Wise choice," he said coldly. "Very smart."

"I don't feel smart," I whispered, hating myself, hating this choice already, wanting to do nothing more than jump out of the vehicle. And suddenly, that's just what I needed to do. "No. NO. I can't do this—"

Reaching over me, Edward put on my seat belt. It felt like a restraint.

"You'll soon be free of his influence," he said softly, reaching toward me. "I promise you."

I shuddered at his touch. "Don't!"

With a low laugh, he put down his hand. "Have it your way. I am a patient man…."

But as he turned the steering wheel and started to drive down the circular courtyard, Alejandro was suddenly there, standing ahead of us, blocking the way to the road.

He wasn't looking at Edward. He was looking only at me. I saw his lips form my name.

"Make him believe you love me," Edward growled in a low voice. "Make him believe."

I licked my lips. I looked at Alejandro's stark face. The anguish in his dark eyes.

And I couldn't go through with it.

"I can't." My voice trembled as I started fumbling with my seat belt. "I can't do this. Let me out of here!"

"Too late," Edward said grimly, holding on to the latch as I tried to fight him.

Alejandro saw us struggling through the front window. Hands clenched at his sides, he started walking toward the SUV, now staring at Edward with narrowed eyes, his powerful warrior's body threatening his murder.

Edward's mouth twisted as their eyes met. He glared back, the same expression of murder in his face.

They both intended to kill or be killed today.

Over me.

With a low, cruel growl, Edward stomped on the gas, increasing speed as he drove the SUV straight at Alejandro, who was unprotected and alone in the castle courtyard.

But my husband didn't turn and run. He didn't back down. Instead, he started running straight at the car—as if a man could play chicken against seven thousand pounds of steel!

I screamed. Grabbing the steering wheel, I twisted it hard to the left. Veering off balance, Edward's SUV crashed into the stone fountain and twisted, then flew, high into the air.

As if in slow motion, I felt us fly up, up, up, at the same time we flipped in sickening circles, around and around. We hit the ground with a bone-jarring crunch and rolled down the long hill, all the way down. Then, with a shudder and metallic groan, the SUV was still.

I wasn't dead. I was upside down, held into the passenger seat by the taut seat belt that had knocked the air out of me, leaving a streak of pain where it crossed my chest.

Panting, I looked over at the driver's seat. It was empty. Edward was gone.

"Lena!" Alejandro cried. A moment later, my door was wrenched open, and suddenly he was there. He yanked open the seat belt, and caught me in his strong arms as I fell.

Cradling me desperately, my husband sank to the ground, still holding me against his chest. He ran his hands over my body, found no life-ending injury and exhaled, holding me tight against him, rocking me in his lap. "Oh, my love," he choked out. "You're safe. You're safe. For a moment I thought…" He looked at me fiercely. "Don't ever do that to me again!"

"I'm sorry," I wept, pressing my head against his chest. "He learned the truth and said if I didn't come with him, he would ruin your life and Maurine's and even Miguel's. I couldn't risk you going to jail for the rest of your life—"

"I'd rather be sent to jail for a million years," he said hoarsely, "than lose you." I felt his body trembling beneath me. Reaching up in amazement, I brushed away a single tear trailing down his tanned, hard-edged cheek.

Pressing my forehead to his, I whispered, "Thank you for not letting me go."

He cupped my face, looked me straight in the eyes. "Never. We are forever…."

A low growl made us both turn.

"You'll be sorry." We turned to see Edward collapsed on the grass, where he'd been flung from the vehicle, across the hill. "Both of you," he panted, "will be sorry."

Alejandro's hands tightened on me. I looked up at him in terror. "Don't kill him. It's not worth it. Remember you promised you'd never leave me…."

"Kill him?" He looked at me incredulously. "Why should I? Look at him…."

For the first time, I noticed the odd way Edward's arms and legs were stretched out in unnatural directions on the grass. But even his body wasn't as contorted as his face.

"I'll tell the world," Edward panted, "how you all committed fraud. I'll ruin your lives—both of you—the old woman and that baby, too…."

Alejandro glared at Edward, parting his lips to answer. But someone else beat him to it.

"Calm down, dear. You're acting crazy."

Maurine stepped calmly between us on the hill. She peered down at Edward benignly, as if about to offer him cookies at a party, and the upside-down SUV behind us, with its crushed steel doors and a wheel still spinning, was just a decoration, like fairy lights or balloons. "Whatever you think is wrong, Alejandro is my grandson."

Edward gave a hard laugh. "It's a lie." He coughed. "I'll prove it when I get the court order for a blood test...."

"You know, I always wondered." She smiled, then looked at Alejandro, who was still on the ground, holding me protectively in his lap. She gave a brisk nod. "I was about to tell you, before all the fuss broke out. The hairbrush. You're my grandson, Alejandro. Really and truly. The grandson of my heart." She gave us a broad, self-satisfied smile. "Also a grandson of a DNA test."

I felt Alejandro jump. His face was pale.

"What...?" he breathed.

"The silly secret was just causing such a problem between you two." She looked between us severely. "And the way you were botching things. It just was ridiculous. Honestly, I'd always wondered why your mother stayed on as housekeeper for all those years, even when my son wasn't paying her. And then there was that family resemblance.... Anyway. It never mattered to me one way or the other. Until it started to interfere with your happiness." She grinned. "So I took your hairbrush and had a DNA test. You are my grandson, Alejandro. By heart, as you always were. But also by blood."

"No!" Edward screamed. Then he was suddenly quiet. I think he had fainted from pain.

Rather vengefully, I hoped he had. Although I didn't want him to die, of course. I didn't. Really, I didn't.

Alejandro's eyes were wide. "Is this true, Abuela?"

She nodded. "Remain the Duke of Alzacar, and if anyone wants to check if you are my grandson, let them." She looked at him and said quietly, "There is no one left in the family to inherit, if not you. No one you're cheating of his rightful due. And let me tell you something more. You're the finest duke of them all."

I saw him blinking suspiciously fast. He rose to his feet, helping me to rise, as well. He hugged his grandmother, then pulled me into the embrace. When we finally pulled away, I wiped my eyes, then glanced over at Edward, still unconscious.

"We should call an ambulance, do you think?"

"I can see him breathing," Maurine said with a dismissive wave of her hand. "He's fine." She sighed. "But I'll call." She glanced at Alejandro. "And I expect the *policía* will want to come, as well.…"

She went toward the castle, and Alejandro looked at me.

"She's right. We have only a few moments before the police arrive," he said quietly. "A choice must be made."

"So make it," I said, trusting whatever he'd decide.

He clawed back his hair. "I am tired of secrets. Tired of lies." He turned to me. "I never want another secret to shadow the light between us."

I nodded, unable to speak over the lump in my throat.

"So." He smiled at me, blinking fast, then gave a decisive nod. He walked over to Edward, who was still unconscious, his legs stretched out at a painful angle. He put his fingertips to the other man's neck, then straightened.

"Is he—dead?" I said. Not hopefully. Really.

He shook his head. "His pulse is strong. He will recover."

"Too bad," I said.

Alejandro looked at me in amazement. Coming back, he wrapped his arms around me. "It's not like you to be bloodthirsty, *mi amor*," he murmured.

"I can be dangerous—" I reached up my hand to caress his cheek "—when it comes to protecting those I love."

"Yes." The corners of his sensual mouth quirked. Then his expression became serious. "But are you brave enough to face what lies ahead? There will be scandal. Or worse. Though perhaps I can protect Maurine…."

"How?"

"I will say that she was distraught over her family's death, and that I tricked her into believing I was her grandson."

"Oh, she won't like that at all."

"No," he agreed. He looked at me, emotion in his dark eyes. "Can you bear it, Lena? The storm that might come? Miguel will lose his legacy...."

"You're wrong." I put my hand on his cheek. My eyes were watery. "His legacy is more than some title. It's doing the right thing, even when it's hard."

"And love," Alejandro whispered, pressing my hands together as he kissed them fervently. "Loving for all your life, with all your heart."

"It's family, always and forever." Looking up at my husband, I smiled through my tears. "And whatever may come—our forever has already begun."

There are all kinds of ways to make a family.

Some ways are big, such as the way Maurine took in an orphaned twelve-year-old boy and insisted on claiming him as her grandson.

Some ways are small, such as when I sent an invitation to my wedding reception to my cousin Claudie.

Autumn had arrived at Rohares Castle, and with it harvest season for our tenants. The summer heat had subsided, leaving a gorgeous swath of vivid colors, of morning mists and early twilight, full of excuses to sip oceans of hot tea with milk in the morning and go to bed early with my husband with a bottle of ruby-red wine. Every night, we lit a fire in the fireplace—and in our bed. And that fire, as months passed, seemed only to get bigger and brighter.

Just that morning, Maurine had caught us kissing in the breakfast room. She'd laughed. "I don't think the honeymoon will really ever end for you two," she said affectionately. Then the doorbell rang, and she'd hurried from the room with a desperate cry: "The florist! Finally!" And we were alone.

I'd given Alejandro a sensual smile.

"Could I interest you in a little more honeymoon?" I said, batting my eyes coyly, to which my husband whispered, "All day, every day," before he kissed me senseless, then picked me up like a Neanderthal and carried me upstairs, back to bed.

Now, the crowded banqueting hall was lit up for evening, bedecked gloriously in autumn flowers in the most beautiful wedding reception I'd ever imagined. Across the crowds of our guests, I caught Alejandro's eye. He smiled back at me hungrily, as if it had been a year since he'd last taken me to bed, instead of just a few hours. His hot glance almost made me forget we were surrounded by family and friends.

"I told you he would be your husband," a voice crowed behind me. "I always can tell!"

"You were right." Turning, I smiled at Dolores, my neighbor from San Miguel de Allende who'd been whisked here from Mexico for the reception.

She'd been equal parts impressed and triumphant when Alejandro had sent a private jet to collect her.

I'd sent Mr. Corgan, Mrs. Morris and Hildy a first-class ticket here from London. They were still working for Claudie. "But she's mellowed a great deal since she became Mrs. Crosby," the butler informed me. "He's rich, and that has made her very happy."

But I could see that for myself. Claudie had arrived at my door swathed in fur, with her brand-new husband at her side.

"I'm going to give you your inheritance back," was the first thing she announced to me. "David said it's the right thing to do. And besides—" she grinned "—we can afford it."

Same old Claudie, I thought. And yet not exactly the same. "Thank you," I said in surprise. I paused, then smiled. "Donate it to charity. Introduce me to your husband?"

She beamed. "I'd love to."

David Crosby was fat, short and bald, but he was indeed very rich, a king of Wall Street. They looked totally wrong together. Until you saw the way they looked at each other.

Claudie told me they'd met through a matchmaking service just for rich people.

"Trophy wives for billionaires?" I guessed.

"After all, Lena," she sniffed, "not everyone can manage to randomly fall pregnant by the love of their lives."

"No, indeed," I said.

"And I'm so happy…" she said wistfully, and I thought that she, too, must have been very lonely in London.

"I'm happy for you, truly," I said, and impulsively hugged her. My cousin stiffened, then let me hug her. I was encouraged. We weren't exactly best friends, but it was a start. And after all, we *were* family.…

Pulling away, she wiped her eyes. "At least you dress better now. Your style used to make me physically ill."

Distant family, thankfully.

But Alejandro and I were surrounded by people who cared about us. I looked around at all the people who were here, celebrating our marriage. Thinking with relief about the one who was not.

I still woke up in a cold sweat occasionally, thinking how I'd almost lost everything by getting into Edward St. Cyr's SUV that day.

Edward, sadly, had lived.

Oops, did I say that out loud?

Yes, he lived. From what I'd heard, he'd had an easier time than he deserved. A punctured lung and five broken bones. When the ambulance and police arrived, he'd refused to press charges against anyone, or even talk about the accident. But as he'd been lifted into the ambulance, our eyes had met, and he'd coldly and silently turned his face to the wall. He was done with me. A fact that left me profoundly grateful.

I tried to wish him well, because he had once been my friend.

Okay, but seriously. He'd tried to run over my husband with his Range Rover. That's not the kind of thing I could ever forgive, or forget. So mostly I just tried not to think of it.

Because we had so many other things to be grateful for. As I stood in the banqueting hall of our castle, wearing flowers in my hair and a blue silk gown, I caught Alejandro's eyes across the crowd. And I suddenly didn't see all the princes and farmers, starlets and secretaries, or the happy mix of our neighbors and friends. I didn't see the champagne, or the amazing food, or the flowers hung joyously across the rafters amid a profusion of music and laughter. When I met my husband's gaze, I shivered, and no one else existed.

Alejandro had contacted a lawyer and confessed everything. With the lawyer's advice, he'd thrown himself on the mercy of the court. As Maurine's DNA test had proved, he was the duke's heir, and his only heir at that, and so the group of nobles who oversaw this type of thing decided to allow him to keep his title. He'd also kept the name. Apparently the combination of money and being a direct blood descendant made a big difference. Suddenly, no one was using the word *fraud*.

The scandal was intense, though. For weeks, our

castle had been under siege, with crowds of reporters shaking our gates, clamoring for a picture or an interview. But since no one on the estate or in the nearby town would talk, even the scandal died eventually, especially when the Hollywood star I'd seen at Alejandro's party in Madrid had been discovered naked, drunk and belligerent at the base of the Eiffel Tower. Bless her heart. The paparazzi eventually melted away, as our story was old news. Just in time for our reception today, too.

Tomorrow was Alejandro's birthday. His *real* birthday. I would give him the painting of Miguel and Maurine, and show him the brand-new photo album I'd begun for our family. On the back page, I'd tucked in a picture of a sonogram. We were going to have another baby sometime next summer, when the jacaranda trees were in bloom.

I could hardly wait to give Alejandro his gift....

I heard a clank of silverware against crystal. "Everyone. Could I have your attention?" Looking up, I saw Alejandro holding up his champagne glass. "I'd like to thank all our family and friends for coming today...."

"Any time you want to send your private jet," someone shouted.

"Or first-class tickets!"

"Or help me pave my garden path—how's Wednesday?"

There was scattered laughter, and a few tipsy cheers.

Alejandro grinned. "I'd also like to thank my grandmother for doing such a wonderful job designing this party...."

"Darn straight," Maurine said stoutly, holding our smiling baby in her arms. Miguel, though barefoot as he did not like shoes, was suitably dressed in a baby tuxedo.

"I'd like to thank our baby son for sleeping so well at night...."

Darn straight, I echoed, but didn't say aloud.

"But most of all—" Alejandro's dark eyes glowed with tenderness that took my breath away as he looked at me "—I'd like to thank my beautiful wife. Lena. You gave me the family I never dreamed I could have. Just waking up in your arms every morning is a heaven beyond what any mortal man should deserve. But I will spend the rest of my life trying." He held up the flute. "To family. Forever."

"Family forever," everyone cried, with the greatest cheer of all.

"Thank you," I said to them. I blinked fast, smiling with tears in my eyes. "I love you all." I looked at my husband. "Especially you."

Coming through the crowd, Alejandro took me in his arms, and kissed me soundly in front of everyone. And I kissed him back. Oh, boy, you bet I did.

It was crazy. Just a year ago, I'd been so scared and alone. I'd hated Alejandro. I'd thought I would remain a single mother forever.

The disastrous night we were married in Madrid,

Alejandro said sometimes fate chooses better for us than we can choose for ourselves. But I think there's more to it.

It's not just fate. You create your own future, step by step, by being brave. By doing the right thing. By telling the truth. By trying your best.

By reaching for the man you love, and giving him the chance to reach back, pull you into his arms and finally show you the man he really is inside—the powerful, infuriating, sexy, compassionate man whom no one else will ever truly know.

Love, like trust, is earned. It is kept, day by day, night by night, as we reveal to each other who we were. Who we are. And most of all, who we hope to be.

* * * * *

Pulaski County Public Library
121 South Riverside Drive
Winamac, Indiana 46996

W9-CGU-407

Dr. Aubrey Andelin on:

REVIVING FADED LOVE

"When a man has lost the love he formerly felt for his wife, I say, if he will apply the teachings of this book—*if he will be a man*—he can cause her to blossom into her full womanhood, to regain lost charms so that he can love her as he once did."

MASCULINITY

"The supreme quality of manhood is the strength of a noble character."

TRUE FULFILLMENT

"A man's greatest fulfillment does not come through recognition, honors, money, security, material goods or sex. It comes in being a *man*."

DR. AUBREY ANDELIN's wide and varied background has given him unusual insights into the role of the male, especially as he serves as a husband and father in today's society. He and his wife, Helen, are the parents of eight children and have achieved success and harmony in family life. Mrs. Andelin is the author of *Fascinating Womanhood* and *All About Raising Children*, both available from Bantam Books.

Bantam Books by Helen Andelin

ALL ABOUT RAISING CHILDREN
FASCINATING WOMANHOOD

QUALITY PURCHASES

Companies, professional groups, churches, clubs and other
organizations may qualify for special terms when ordering 24 or
more copies of this title. For information, contact the Direct
Response Department, Bantam Books, 666 Fifth Avenue, New
York, N.Y. 10103. Phone (212) 765-6500.

MAN OF
STEEL AND VELVET

Aubrey P. Andelin

BANTAM BOOKS
TORONTO · NEW YORK · LONDON · SYDNEY

*This low-priced Bantam Book
has been completely reset in a type face
designed for easy reading, and was printed
from new plates. It contains the complete
text of the original hard-cover edition.*
NOT ONE WORD HAS BEEN OMITTED.

MAN OF STEEL AND VELVET

*A Bantam Book / published by arrangement with
Pacific Press Santa Barbara*

PRINTING HISTORY

*Pacific Press Santa Barbara edition published September 1982
12 printings through October 1982
Bantam edition / July 1983*

*All rights reserved.
Copyright © 1972 by Aubrey P. Andelin.
Cover photo copyright © 1983 by Anthony Loew.
This book may not be reproduced in whole or in part, by
mimeograph or any other means, without permission.
For information address: Pacific Press Santa Barbara,
P. O. Box 219, Pierce City, Missouri 65723.*

ISBN 0-553-23363-7

Published simultaneously in the United States and Canada

---

*Bantam Books are published by Bantam Books, Inc. Its trademark, consisting of the
words "Bantam Books" and the portrayal of a rooster, is Registered in U.S. Patent
and Trademark Office and in other countries. Marca Registrada. Bantam Books,
Inc., 666 Fifth Avenue, New York, New York 10103.*

PRINTED IN THE UNITED STATES OF AMERICA

O   0 9 8 7 6 5 4 3 2

Dedicated to my wife, Helen, a truly fascinating woman who provided me with the encouragement to proceed with this work.

WHEN A MAN'S A MAN

"There is a land where a man, to live, must be a man. It is a land of granite and marble and porphyry and gold—and a man's strength must be as the strength of the primeval hills. It is a land of oaks and cedars and pine—and a man's mental grace must be as the grace of the untamed trees. It is a land of far-arched and unstained skies, where the wind sweeps free and untainted, and the atmosphere is the atmosphere of those places that remain as God made them—and a man's soul must be as the unstained skies, the unburdened wind and the untainted atmosphere. It is a land of wide mesas, of wild rolling pastures and broad, untilled valley meadows—and a man's freedom must be that freedom which is not bounded by the fences of a too weak and timid conventionalism.

"In this land every man is—by divine right—his own king; he is his own jury, his own counsel, his own judge, and—if it must be—his own executioner. . . . in this land a man, to live, must be a man."

—Harold Bell Wright

The above is quoted from the book *When A Man's A Man,* in which is described the vigorous breed of men necessary to endure life in the early western United States. Although this tough breed of men is no longer necessary in order to exist, we do still need real men if we are to achieve a world worth living in. Our present times are more complex and demanding than in the past. "Wild pastures and untilled valley meadows" are not our challenge today, but some of the greatest challenges of history are before us. Our time demands excellent men more than ever before.

CONTENTS

INTRODUCTION

This is a book which teaches men to be men. In attempting to do this, I recognize at the onset that I am likely to encounter a great resistance. No man I ever met would concede that he is not already a man, or that he has lost a significant part of his masculinity. His very nature demands a respect for the masculine in him. So fundamental is this that to suggest a loss of manliness is perhaps the greatest affront that can be made to him. Yet, the sad truth is, speaking generally, men are no longer men. This fact becomes all too obvious when the average man is measured against the undeniable criteria which will be presented in this book.

American men received a stinging insult from British psychiatrist Dr. Joshua Bierer, who described them as a "bunch of weak-kneed, lily-livered sissies." In a previous survey made in 1964, he thought women were at fault, declaring American women to be domineering. "Before, I thought that the women wanted to rule the country. I changed that opinion. Women are *compelled* to take over, not *fighting* to take over," he continued. "I thought the men who attended some seminars I spoke at with their wives would shoot me for my remarks—but instead they all agreed with me. It's still the fatherless society. The husbands are not husbands. All the women are crying out for a strong man and he's just not there," he said.

Throughout our society we find men who are weak, spoiled,

pampered, spineless for the most part, lacking moral, physical or mental strength or all three. There are men who fail to take their position as head of the household, who allow women and children to push them around, not wishing to accept the responsibility which is rightfully their own. Some in fact blatantly encourage their wives to assume this burden. Many of our so-called jokes center around the idea of the wife "wearing the pants" in the family. Her husband is facetiously portrayed as a bungler, inept and incompetent to understand or control his family.

To a great extent men have failed to assume the responsibility of providing "bread for their tables." Women must come to the rescue. Every day millions of them leave their households to assist men in earning the living. The "working mother" is becoming more the rule than the exception. The deterioration and loss of effectiveness in so many homes is in great part a consequence of the neglect resulting from the mother deserting her post—a situation she often laments but can do nothing about.

Lack of chivalry is apparent on every hand. Women, of necessity, must take care of themselves. They change their own tires, wash the automobiles, mow the lawn, repair the furnace, paint the house and lift heavy objects. Where are the men waiting to offer masculine assistance to the gentler sex?

In addition to failing at home, men are failing to measure up in society. We are in a period of crisis where it is likely that the great inheritances we enjoy from the labors and sacrifices of generations past may be lost. Freedom is in jeopardy. It is a time of turmoil, strife, and numerous problems. Our only hope is for men to rise to their feet as real men. But where are the heroes of today? Where is the man who will proclaim, "Give me liberty or give me death!"? Where are men willing to sacrifice time and energy to rescue a dwindling society?

SOCIAL PROBLEMS CAUSED BY LACK OF MANLINESS

The general lack of manliness is producing far-reaching social problems. The man who fails to stand up as the head of the family creates trouble in his home. There is a lack of order. The weak-kneed father also creates the "dominant mother," for someone must add substance to the family life . . . someone must determine policy and make decisions. Often urgent demands make it necessary for the wife to step into the leadership role when her husband fails to do so.

Such default in leadership causes great unhappiness and frustration to women. If she must be the "man of the family," she is not free to function as a woman, to devote her time and thought to making a success of her equally demanding duties as a wife and mother. Her lack of a strong man to rule over her, something she has every right to expect, may cause severe emotional reactions in her. She tends to become insecure and sometimes desperate.

Children of a recessive father also suffer as innocent victims. They are made to feel insecure due to lack of firmness and decisiveness. Children who grow up in a home where the father does not command obedience for his word, *learn disobedience*. They learn that they do not have to yield to authority. When turned out into the world, they are likely to be the rebellious youth as we know them today. They are the troublemakers on campus, the lawbreakers and delinquents of society.

The man who allows and encourages his wife to work outside her home creates further social problems. She must divide her interests between her work and family. Since her work is usually more demanding, the children and home life suffer. She cannot serve two masters. Her neglect of home life results in lack of love, attention, and development of the children as well as her failure to serve as the understanding wife.

Homosexuality is another social problem caused by lack of manliness. As the father fails to portray a strong male image in the home, there is a *blurring of roles* between mother and father, and the real distinction between male and female becomes obscure. Both boys and girls fail to find a definite sex image with which to identify. Because of this, the girls fail to grow strongly feminine and the boys fail to grow strongly masculine, further contributing to the tendency of "unisex." If men are truly men and women women, this contrast will keep the sexes attracted to one another and reduce the tendency to the unwholesome and destructive perversion of homosexuality.

Still another social ill attributed in part to the weakness of men is the women's liberation movement. Had men been strongly masculine, devoted to the care of women and children, holding women in high regard with an appreciation for their role in the home, giving to it the respect and honor which it deserves, it is unlikely that so many women would want to desert this position. As it is, many women feel themselves to be "second class citizens," the victims of an oppressive male population who have taken to themselves the jobs that are exciting and fulfilling. They want to be "liberated" from their traditional female duties. Had men helped women to feel the importance of their work, women would have been happy to serve in the home, considering it an opportunity for fulfillment, and would hold men as well as themselves in high regard.

And last, when a man is weak or in any way fails to measure up as a man, women and children lose respect for him. This in turn can weaken their relationship, leading to marriage problems and a gap between parent and child.

These serious social problems illustrate the urgent need for immediate action. Truly, there has never been a time of greater urgency when men and women must understand how best they can contribute to the well-being of themselves and society. It appears that if we do not produce a generation of real men immediately, our entire civilization as we know it may soon be lost. In peril are our most sacred and cherished institutions . . . marriage, family life, freedom of country . . . the very foundations of organized society and religion.

THE NEED

Our crucial times require men of strong minds, kind hearts, and willing hands, men who find joy in labor, men of courage, honor and strong opinions, clear minds and high goals . . . men who are not afraid of great responsibility, men who can become dedicated to a task and will surrender their own selfish desires and pursuits to a life of service, men whose word is as good as their bond.

But along with this fiber of steel there must be a gentle nature. We need men who can appreciate a sunrise or a sunset, men who love their families with passion and honor, men who adore womanhood, yet dislike weakness or coyness. We need men with compassion, sensitive to the needs of the less fortunate, men who are tender with their wives and children, men who have developed an ability to love.

This book outlines the way to become such a man. It is the way to a man's greatest fulfillment. Fulfillment does not come, as many suppose, by recognition, honors, money, security, material goods or sexual fulfillment. Although these attainments contribute greatly to a man's feeling of well-being, his greatest fulfillment comes in being a man.

This goal is attainable, regardless of one's station in life, through the application of definite and unfailing principles. One is not limited by the restrictions which usually accompany so-called success.

This book will teach you how to understand women, their feminine nature and peculiarities, and how to build a beautiful relationship and an enduring marriage. It will teach you how to stand at the head of your household, gaining the utmost respect from wife and children. It will teach you how to succeed as a man in your work, in your community, and to fulfill your duties as an integral part of society.

Among other things you will learn:

1. What it means to be a man.
2. How to understand women.
3. What it is that women appreciate in men.
4. What it is that brings security to women and children.
5. How to handle a woman when she "tries to take over."
6. How to handle children in a way to win their hearts.
7. The role of man as a divine calling.
8. How to handle difficult situations which arise in marriage.
9. The fulfillment every man is seeking.
10. Why some successes cannot be sustained.

MAN OF
STEEL AND VELVET

I
THE IDEAL MAN

The ideal man as I see him, is a man of "STEEL and VELVET." This term I have borrowed from Carl Sandburg who used it to describe Abraham Lincoln. I know of no other expression which so adequately portrays the perfection of manhood.

THE IDEAL MAN

STEEL   VELVET

THE STEEL

The ideal man has the strength, endurance, and temperance of fine steel. He is a composite of many sterling qualities. Foremost among them is his willingness to *assume masculine burdens,* to "earn his bread by the sweat of his face," and thus properly provide for himself and family. He is a man who *takes pride in this masculine responsibility.* He delights in this opportunity to prove his manhood, and serves with enthusiasm and honor. He does not face his duties sullenly, as though there were no escape, nor does he lean upon society for sustenance. When his problems become difficult, he takes pride in trying to solve them himself. Only in emergencies does he look to others for solutions.

In no way does he shirk the responsibility to protect and provide for his wife and family. He is happy to shoulder this obligation, not only for his moral responsibility to do so, but for the feeling of manliness it gives him. If placed in a position where he cannot function in this important capacity, he is most uncomfortable.

This feeling of responsibility to his family provides substance to the faith which his wife places in him when she leaves the security of her parents' home to make her way with him. She must rely upon his sense of duty to provide for her, to shield her from the harshness of the world, to provide strength in her new experience.

Not only does he assume responsibility for himself and family, but he is also a *"builder of society."* He recognizes the world's urgent needs and, with a sense of social responsibility, contributes his measure to making the world a better place. He is not afraid of great responsibility, even when it requires time, toil, and personal sacrifice. All this he does because of his feeling of moral obligation to others, and he does so without complaint.

A man of steel is a *masculine man.* He is aggressive, determined, decisive, and independent. He learns efficiency in the affairs of a man's world, demanding quotas of himself in reaching an objective. He is competent in a task, fearless and courageous in the face of difficulty, and master of a situation. He has deep convictions and steadfastly holds to these convictions. He sets high goals for himself . . . goals which require dedication and patience. He is not afraid of strain and diligence. He rejects softness and timidity. When he has made a decision based upon the best of his judgment, he is unbendable as a piece of steel. These qualities of masculinity set him apart from women and children and weaker members of his own sex.

A man of steel has a *sterling character.* He remains steadfast to his convictions even under pressure. He is a man of honor and integrity. He is fair, just and honest in his dealings, possessing moral courage and self dignity and all of those diamond traits which make up a strong character. He becomes master of himself through a conscious effort to incorporate the virtues of strong character in his life. When subjected to pressures, he stands firm.

In addition to all of this, he has achieved a feeling of *confidence* and peace within which comes from his personal victory over himself. And physically, the man of steel has a *body of strength and skill.*

THE VELVET

The velvet qualities include a man's gentleness, his tenderness, kindness, generosity, and patience. He is devoted to the care and protection of women and children. He understands and respects their gentle nature and recognizes it as a complement to his manliness. He is chivalrous, attentive and respectful to the gentler sex and has an ability to love with tenderness. He has, in addition, an enthusiastic and youthful attitude of optimism which defies the press of years. Humility is also a part of the velvet, subduing the masculine ego as his rough nature is refined.

In considering the function of the steel and velvet traits combined, they may be compared to a large, tall building. The steel qualities relate to the sturdy framework of steel and concrete which ties the structure steadfastly together and anchors it to its foundation. Without this strong inner framework, the building would not hold nor function under the pressures of its use and outside forces. The velvet relates to the building's decor, its art forms, its landscape and interior finishing which add softness and beauty to the otherwise stark and stern mass of steel and stone.

When properly blended, these traits of steel and velvet compose the ideal man, a masterpiece of creation and the greatest contribution to the well-being of society. The attributes characterized as steel are the framework of his being, demonstrating a steadfastness in purpose born of the self-respect a man feels when he is true to himself . . . when the quality of his life is such that he can live comfortably with himself as his own best friend. This produces confidence analogous to the strength of a bar of steel which is thoroughly refined and tested. When the velvet qualities are added, a masterpiece results. That firmness which otherwise might appear harsh is softened. It is not unlike the large, heavy hands which have been trained to play the violin. Such hands carry the raw strength to crush the instrument in a moment, but there is no danger of such a thing, as the gentle strokes used in bringing forth the beautiful music demonstrate a softness and appreciation for the artistic. Both the steel and velvet are necessary to produce a great character. There has never been a truly great man on the earth who was not a possessor of both.

MEN WHO ARE STEEL ONLY

Throughout history men who have had certain very strong *steel* traits have left their mark upon the world, but . . . lacking character, refinement, tenderness and other velvet characteristics, they have not been great men. Such are the great military geniuses and political leaders such as Napoleon, Caesar, Hitler, Mussolini, and scores of others. The eminence these men achieved was not done without some merit. It must be recognized that each possessed qualities which inspired confidence and trust—these are some of the qualities of steel. These men provided a forceful leadership, an assurance of protection of the right and interests of their people (so they promised), doing so in a manner of strong confidence. The virtues of an upright character were largely missing as also the glaring lack of nearly all the qualities of velvet. Yet support was given them because of strong leadership and confidence.

Although the strong show of certain steel qualities was sufficient to establish them in power and win support of millions, yet this was insufficient to sustain them for an extended time. The lack of character, principally, and the crudeness and coarseness of their lives was self-defeating. Instead of being numbered among the great, they are classified as enemies to mankind.

MEN WHO ARE VELVET ONLY

There are scores of men throughout history who have been "velvet" men. Although they do not stand out as enemies to society, they do not stand out for anything else. They become non-entities, being remembered for nothing of note. Not being real men, their softness does not build a better world, either in their family circle or in society.

JESUS CHRIST

Only such men as achieve a balance of the steel and velvet stand securely on an unshakable pedestal. At the apex of this relatively small group of individuals stands Jesus Christ, who was the epitome of all that was good and strong. In no area was He lacking. A study of His life reveals an intriguing demonstration of the steel and velvet. Never did He lose sight of His responsibility to complete "the work he was sent to do." He maintained His devotion to it until the end when He said, "It is finished." He was a leader of men, women, and children—true to His convictions until death. He had the moral courage to introduce ideals and standards which were in conflict with popular teachings of His day. He dedicated His life to the service and salvation of others, lifting people to higher planes of thought and living. He was a builder of society. And He was a masculine man possessing courage, determination, fearlessness, decisive judgment, and aggressiveness. He was skilled and masterful in a difficult situation, never afraid to face the hardness of his enemies. Some artists over the centuries have pictured Him as thin, effeminate and physically weak and shy. Just the opposite is the case. He had a strong body, sufficient to drive the money changers from the temple and adequate to perform strenuous masculine tasks.

His character was spotless, built on the highest of moral principles and standards of perfection. He was eager and enthusiastic about life, promising, "I am come that ye may have life and that ye may have it more abundantly." Yet with all of His strength and courage, there was about Him a gentleness that drew to Him women and children. Women wept at His feet and children surrounded Him. With all this He had humility. Though He was worshipped as perfect, He denied His goodness, saying, "There is none good but the Father." Yet with this humility there was a self-dignity about Him which commanded respect. As He stood before the judgment of the high courts, He bore His false accusations valiantly and faced the scoffing multitudes with superb dignity.

ABRAHAM LINCOLN

Christ stands alone and none can be compared to Him. However, in a modest way other great men have left a mark that will not be forgotten. Such is Abraham Lincoln, who was described by Carl Sandburg as possessing qualities of steel and velvet. Note the following quoted from his writings:

"Not often in the story of mankind does a man arrive on earth who is both steel and velvet, who is as hard as a rock and as soft as drifting fog, who holds in his heart and mind the paradox of terrible storm and peace unspeakable and perfect.

"During the four years he was President, he at times, especially in the first three months, took to himself the powers of a dictator; he commanded the most powerful armies till then assembled in modern warfare; he enforced conscription of soldiers for the first time in American history; under imperative necessity he abolished the right of habeas corpus; he directed politically and spiritually the wild, massive, turbulent forces let loose in civil war. He argued and pleaded for compensated emancipation of the slaves . . . failing to get action, as chief executive having war powers, he issued the paper by which he declared the slaves to be free under 'military necessity.' In the end nearly four billion dollars worth of property was taken away from those who were legal owners of it—property confiscated, wiped out as by fire and turned to ashes." Such actions as these are a clear demonstration of the steel qualities of Lincoln.

And of his gentle traits, Sandburg says:

"In the mixed shame and blame of the immense wrongs of two crashing civilizations, often with nothing to say, he said nothing, slept not at all and on occasions was seen to weep in a way that made weeping appropriate, decent, majestic. An Indiana man at the White House heard him say, 'Voorhees, don't it seem strange to you that I, who could never so much as cut off the head of a chicken, should be elected or selected, into the midst of all this blood?'" Mark Van Doren tells us, "To me, Lincoln seems, in some ways, the most interesting man who ever lived. He was gentle, but this gentleness was combined with a terrific toughness, an iron strength."

The greatness of his character is revealed by the way people revered him at his death. As Carl Sandburg describes it: "In the time of the April lilacs, in the year 1865, on his death, the casket with his body was carried north and west a thousand miles; and the

American people wept as never before; bells sobbed; cities wore crepe; people stood in tears with hats off as the railroad burial car paused in the leading cities of seven states." Such is the greatness of a man who has the strength of steel and the gentleness of velvet.

That this combination of the steel and velvet in men has always been admirable is evident throughout history. Some have won public acclaim by steel virtues alone, but the true heroes, those men who have won the hearts of people and stood out as great among their fellowmen, have always been the combination of steel and velvet. And it has always taken both to win the hearts of women.

In no way does a man need steel and velvet more than in the manner in which he handles women and children. It is the combination of both strength and gentleness that makes women surrender their lives to a man, giving him unconditional love and devotion.

PETRUCHIO

For a perfect example of the use of steel and velvet in dealing with women, let me refer you to the character of Petruchio in William Shakespeare's "The Taming of the Shrew." Although fiction, the character of Petruchio is accurate as it relates to real life.

Petruchio was a strong, rough, and unyielding man who was looking for a wife, in haste. He approached Katherina, the daughter of a wealthy man. Katherina was beautiful and young, but a real shrew. She was sharp-tongued, unruly and defiant. No one, not even her own father, could subdue her. But Petruchio, intrigued by the challenge of her unruly nature, as well as being tempted by her wealth and wishing to find a wife in haste, approached her with gentleness:

Bonny Kate, and sometimes Kate the curst;
But, Kate, the prettiest Kate in Christendom;
Kate of Kate-Hall, my super-dainty Kate,
For dainties are all Kates; and therefore, Kate,
Take this of me, Kate of my consolation;
Hearing thy mildness prais'd in every town,
Thy virtues spoke of and, thy beauty sounded,—
Yet not so deeply as to thee belongs,—
Myself am mov'd to woo thee for myself.

Each time she snapped back at him he ignored it and called her, "sweet Kate, gentle Kate." And finally he won her and wed her. And then his firmness, his steel, came to light on their wedding day: The father had prepared a wedding feast, but Petruchio announced that he and Katherina would take their leave. To which Katherina said:

> Do what thou cans't, I will not go today,
> No, nor tomorrow, nor till I please myself.
> The door is open sir, there lies your way;
> You may be jogging whiles your boots are green.
> For me I'll not be gone till I please myself.

And then, as she marched forward to the bridal dinner, he pulled her back:

> They shall go forward, Kate at thy command.
> But for my bonny Kate she must with me.
> Nay, look not big, nor stamp, nor stare, nor fret;
> I will be master of what is mine own.

And to the others, he said:

> She is my goods, my chattels; she is my house,
> My household stuff, my field, my barn,
> My horse, my ox, my ass, my any thing;
> And here she stands, touch her whoever dare;
> I'll bring my action on the proudest he
> That stops my way in Padua, Gumio,
> Draw forth thy weapon, we're beset with thieves;
> Rescue thy mistress, if thou be a man.
> Fear not, sweet wench; they shall not touch thee, Kate;
> I'll buckler thee against a million.

There are some in modern times that would vehemently oppose such possession of womanhood, terms such as chattels or goods. But the story, true to life nevertheless, brought out the best, not the worst, in Kate. His firm masculine leadership over her, combined with gentleness, won her heart devotedly. In the final scene she valiantly defends the man's position as master of the woman:

Thy husband is thy lord, thy life, thy keeper,
Thy head, thy sovereign; one that cares for thee,
And for thy maintenance commits his body
To painful labor both by sea and land,
To watch the night in storms, the day in cold,
Whilst thou liest warm at home, secure and safe;
And craves no other tribute at thy hands
But love, fair looks and true obedience;
Too little payment for so great a debt.
Such duty as the subject owes the prince
Even such a woman oweth to her husband;
And when she is forward, peevish, sullen, sour,
And not obedient to his honest will,
What is she but a foul contending rebel,
And graceless traitor to her loving lord?
I am ashamed that women are so simple
To offer war where they should kneel for peace;
Or seek for rule, supremacy or sway,
When they are bound to serve, love, and obey.
Why are our bodies soft and weak and smooth,
Unapt to toil and trouble in the world,
But that our soft conditions and our hearts
Should well agree with our external parts?
In token of which duty, if he pleases,
My hand is ready, may it do him ease.

LANCELOT

Another example of steel and velvet is in the character of
Lancelot in the legend of King Arthur. It is important, though, to
first make clear that the movie version of the story is not correct.
Lancelot and Guinevere did not have an illicit affair. They did love
each other, but it was "from afar," withholding any affection or
demonstration of their love.

Lancelot was unanimously regarded as the strongest, bravest,
most admired knight in the kingdom. With almost superhuman
strength he won against all his opponents in the tournaments of the
knights. But it was not until he revealed his *velvet side*, his
tenderness and concern for his fellow knight, that he won the heart
of Queen Guinevere and the undivided respect of his countrymen.
After defeating his fellow knight in battle, his heavy masculine

body bent over the dying knight and he prayed with fervor and kindness of spirit for the suffering man to return to life. This concern for his fellowman, this gentleness of velvet, combined with his proven strength and manliness, made him, in the eyes of the Queen, the "perfect man."

It must be remembered that not all great men are recorded in the pages of history. There are many, perhaps thousands, who have been both "steel and velvet" who are unknown to the world. They are men who have valiantly served their families, standing strong and firm as the leader of women and children. They have faithfully earned their bread "by the sweat of their face," and have been men in every sense of the word. Although they have not won acclaim in the eyes of the world in general, they have nevertheless been real men. Their existence only proves that every man has within his own world the possibility of being a man of steel and velvet by growing as a man.

The blending of the steel and velvet, then, becomes the objective of this study. First, to learn the essential ingredients of each. Second, to learn how they may be achieved on a personal basis. These are not opposing forces, as good and evil, but are complementary qualities which should be developed to the utmost. Only when the steel and velvet are adequately developed together does a man become truly great. A deficiency in either category will result in inevitable difficulty.

MAINTAINING INDIVIDUALITY

In teaching fundamentals of truth which serve as precepts for all men to live by, one may suppose that we are trying to make men alike . . . as carbon copies of one another. This is not so. The fact is only too obvious that the human personality is created with distinct individuality which makes it unique, separating each person from all others. The identity of personality should always be preserved.

But it is well to recognize that certain fundamentals serve as guides. The qualities which we describe as being steel and velvet serve as an aspiration to all men. They are deep running fundamentals which know no distinction, are not altered by age, personality, or background. They do not destroy the uniqueness of the individual. They enhance the man, helping him to become his better self.

Below is a chart of "The Ideal Man" divided as "steel and velvet." Also listed are six qualities of each which will be taught throughout this book. This guide, if understood and applied in daily living, will aid men to advance to a more perfect manhood.

THE IDEAL MAN

STEEL

VELVET

1. Guide, protector and provider
2. Builder of society
3. Masculinity
4. Character
5. Confidence
6. Health

1. Understands women
2. Gentleness
3. Attentiveness
4. Youthfulness
5. Humility
6. Refinement

STEEL:
Makes women and children feel secure. Arouses admiration of all. Makes women feel womanly.

VELVET:
Promotes good human relations among all people. Awakens love in women and children.

Together they bring a man peace, happiness and fulfillment

PART I
THE STEEL

II
MAN'S BASIC ROLE

A man's most important responsibility in life is to be the *guide*, *protector* and *provider* for his wife and children. This role is not merely a result of custom or tradition, but is of divine origin.

There is sufficient proof in the Holy Scriptures that man is designated as the undisputed head of the family. In the beginning when God created the man and the woman and placed them in the world to subdue it, He said to the woman, "Thy desire shall be to thy husband, and he shall rule over thee." (Gen. 3:16) Many years later the Apostle Paul reaffirmed this principle when he said, "The husband is the head of the wife, even as Christ is the head of the church . . . therefore, as the church is subject unto Christ, so let the wives be to their own husbands in everything." (Eph. 5:23) He also told women to "reverence" their husbands. (Eph. 5:33) Peter, the apostle, also supported this principle by saying, "Ye wives, be in subjection to your own husbands." (I Peter 3:1)

That the man is born to *protect* women and children is apparent when considering his body build which is larger, stronger, and has greater endurance than the woman's. The woman was made for a different purpose, has a body build that is delicate and sometimes fragile, but blessed with the function of bearing children.

Proof that man was commissioned to *provide the living* is supported in the beginning when the Lord gave instructions for man and woman to live by. To the man he said, "In the sweat of thy face shalt thy eat bread." (Gen. 3:19) This command was not

15

given to the woman, but to the man. Although she was given to him as a "helpmeet" and sometimes worked in the fields with him, it was not her direct responsibility.

The role of the man as the guide, protector and provider is his first and foremost responsibility. No other duty can compare to it. Urgent, of course, is his additional responsibility outside the home as the builder of society wherein he assists in solving difficult social problems to ease the burdens of other people. But these things are secondary to his obligation in the home. His usefulness in the world is realized principally as he builds a happy home and marriage and produces well-adjusted, useful children. These are his greatest contributions to the well-being of society.

WHEN A MAN FAILS IN HIS ROLE

A failure in the home, on the other hand, is a man's greatest failure. If he fails in marriage, if he fails with his children, if his home is troubled or divided by divorce, or if his children are unruly, wayward or irresponsible, he has failed in his most fundamental duties as a man. No success in life can compensate for this failure in the home. He may have achieved great things in the world of men, he may be a man of science, industry or government and have made notable contributions, but what can atone for his failure in the home? He is principally responsible for its success or failure.

The home is the most basic unit of society. The strength of a country lies in the home and the security and happiness of the family. It is difficult, if not impossible, for either the man, the woman or the children to give much of value to the world if their home is troubled. The troubled home affects the man in his work, the woman in her homemaking, and the children in their personal development. The man stands as the head of the household, the shepherd of the flock; and only when he functions successfully in this calling is his house in order. And only when his house is in order can the community and thus the nation function as it should.

WHEN HE SUCCEEDS

On the positive side, when a man functions well as the guide, protector, and provider, when his home is ruled with firmness and kindness, love and good leadership, with the security and comforts that are necessary, and when his children develop into happy, well-adjusted citizens, then has he made his most notable contribution to the world. Other contributions may be added, and they are important, but they are secondary to the success of his family.

It has been said that one sign of a man's success is demonstrated when he walks up the path leading to his home and his children run with eagerness to greet him, and his wife, smiling, lovingly greets him at the door. This is a man's greatest success and therefore his greatest achievement.

THE WOMAN'S ROLE

The woman's basic role is to be the *wife, mother,* and *homemaker.* Her role as the wife is indicated by the following: When God made the man he said, "It is not good for man to be alone. I will make a helpmeet for him." And thus she was given to him to be a wife, a supporting companion, his encouragement, and sometimes even his strength. Her position as a mother was established when God blessed her with the function of bearing children.

A woman's household responsibilities are clearly defined in the description of a virtuous woman in the Book of Proverbs (Ch. 31): "She seeketh wool and flax and worketh willingly with her hands . . . she bringeth her food from afar . . . she giveth meat to her household, she planteth a vineyard . . . she is not afraid of the snow for her household are clothed with scarlet . . . she looketh well to the ways of her household and eateth not the bread of idleness."

Besides her domestic role, a woman needs to give benevolent service outside the home. She has a certain debt to society to make the world a better place, as does man. But in her case, it is a feminine service, such as helping the poor, serving in the church or community, assisting in youth problems, etc. Giving such a service enriches her life and makes her a better wife and mother. But at no time should this role supersede her duties in the home. Her first and sacred obligation is to her family, to serve them as the wife, mother and homemaker.

THE COMPLEMENTARY PARTNERSHIP

In the ideal home the man's and woman's duties are distinctly divided. There is little overlapping except in emergencies. Not only does this follow divine command, but also logic and reason. Every group of beings must be organized to avoid chaos. This consists of delegating duties to each member, making each accountable for his assignments. A family is a small organization and thus must also follow this pattern.

The joining of these roles forms a complementary partnership. Neither the man nor the woman is superior. Both are indispensable and of equal importance. But as we see so plainly there is a difference of responsibility. Longfellow compares the partnership of a man and woman in the following way:

As unto the bow the cord is,
    So unto man is woman;
Tho' she bends him,
    She obeys him,
Tho' she draws him,
    Yet she follows;
Useless each without the other.

from "Hiawatha"
by Henry W. Longfellow

This partnership has also been compared to a lock and key that joined together form a perfectly functioning unit. Each has a different function, yet each is necessary. Neither is superior. One is useless without the other.

CAPABILITIES OF EACH TO FUNCTION IN ROLES

When God blessed man with the responsibility to guide, protect and provide for his family, he also blessed him with the temperament and capability to function in this role. He was given the capacity to shoulder heavy responsibility, to endure the stresses and strains of the marketplace, to struggle with difficulty, to work long hours, to battle with problems in his complex world and to make weighty decisions. Although his burdens may become heavy, and discouragement enter in, he has the basic nature to function in this masculine role. He has but to turn to God for sustenance . . . for guidance and for additional strength to fulfill his destiny. God has given him this responsiblity and will also bless him with the capacity to fulfill it.

The man was not created, however, with the capacity to function as a woman. He does not have the basic temperament to assume the monotonous and trivial tasks of the household, to tend the children, do the wash and cook the meals. He may do well with woman's work in an emergency and may have a deep appreciation for the service she renders, but he does not thrive on her responsibility.

The woman, on the other hand, was blessed with the temperament to cope with the problems and responsibilities of the feminine world. Although delicate in body build, she has great endurance in her own sphere. She can spend sleepless nights tending a crying baby or caring for a sick child. She can struggle with demanding tasks, all of which seem to need doing at the same time. She is patient with trivia and endless meals which come three times a day throughout the year. A feminine woman not only copes with such problems, but she thrives on them.

But as a man is not so adaptable to feminine tasks, neither was the woman designed to be a man, to be a carpenter, bricklayer or auto mechanic. She was not made to build her own shelter, fix the roof or repair the furnace, or to worry about finances or make weighty decisions and thus to lead the family. She was not made to be a business executive, a leader of industry, a scientist or a politician. She was made to be a wife and mother. Here is where she functions best. Many women do, of course, take on masculine responsibility . . . especially when their husbands fail in this respect. But when they do so they lose some of their essential womanliness. When a woman rises to a position of leadership in the business world, she must develop masculine capacity, but this she does at the expense of her femininity. She must, in fact, subdue her gentle nature if she is to do a man's work.

It is a fundamental fact that men and women differ temperamentally, psychologically, physically, socially and in capacity to do a specific job. Although they are equal in intelligence, their intelligence is not on identical subjects. They do not think alike, have the same perspectives, nor do they react in the same way to a given circumstance. They worry about different things, and they worry differently. Men and women do not have the same capacity in a specific job. One has only to live for a short time in this life to observe these differences. But this is an important part of the divine plan for men and women. Each was given the capacity to function best in the specific male and female role.

MARRIAGE

The security of the partnership of the man and the woman lies in binding them together in marriage. Only then will each have the incentive to do his best and build an enduring family life together. Any other arrangement, whether it be an assumption, oral agreement or other, is not sufficient to endure for any period of time. It does not provide sufficient incentive to make a whole-hearted effort towards a high goal and overcome the obstacles and problems along the way.

The most important reason for matrimony, however, is that "Marriage is ordained of God." From the beginning it has been a sacred institution. "What God hath joined together, let no man put asunder" implies that it is part of the heavenly plan. This seems reason enough to respect the institution of marriage.

In spite of the sanctity of marriage there is a threatening trend today to do away with it. Many young people are afraid of marriage, hesitating to step into its binding obligations. This fear is undoubtedly due to the many marriage failures of the past few generations, the mounting divorce rate, and the trouble observed even in those marriages which remain together. Although we can sympathize with these fears of marriage, it must be recognized that the solution lies in correcting the problems that have existed in the troubled marriage, rather than rejecting marriage altogether.

David V. Haws, chairman of the department of psychiatry at the Country General Hospital, Phoenix, Arizona, has said, "Marriage, imperfect as it is, is still the best solution we have to keep the family intact and make a man responsible for the children he has procreated."

The most important way a man can contribute to the security and happiness of his marriage is to successfully live his masculine role. This means, in review, that he rule his household with firmness, kindness, and love . . . that he provide an adequate living, that he protect his wife and children and in every way serve as a man. In addition, if he will learn to understand women and children, and contribute to their needs, he will achieve a happy marriage on a high scale.

TRENDS OPPOSING MALE AND FEMALE ROLES

There is a worldwide trend to do away with the traditional male and female roles and achieve equality between the sexes. The goal is to eliminate any differences in responsibility so that they share all duties together. It is suggested that a man and wife share equally in making decisions, in earning the living, and in housekeeping and care of the children. There is a total rejection of traditional male and female roles with the claim "they are no longer useful to society."

Known as "Women's Lib," this movement, initiated by a group of women who have become dissatisfied with the woman's traditional role in the home, is attempting to reshape the thinking of both sexes. They consider homemaking a second-rate job and advocate that women move into the man's world on an equal basis.

They view their own work in the feminine world as confining and isolating and limiting to their personal development. They say, "While our husbands have the freedom and opportunity to be out in the working world, experiencing new people, new ideas, and perhaps the creative joy of seeing the world change for the better, we are at home in the isolated household with no one to talk to but little children." They claim they are a shadow to their husbands and a servant to their children. They would like to be freed from "the shackles of male supremacy." In total, they want "liberation" from their mundane existence and would like to share in the world's "more interesting work."

These women are ignoring some fundamental principles. They fail to realize that happiness and fulfillment come only as people give of themselves to the world in service and duty in that work which is important to be done. No work anywhere is more important than caring for children and doing other domestic duties which keep the homefires burning. This work naturally falls to the women and can best be done by them. It is a sacred responsibility. For a woman to desert her post is a serious dereliction of duty. It makes just as much sense for a man to say, "I'm tired of earning the living. I want to find something more exciting and less demanding."

In the woman's sphere there is a record of failure. Our generation is one of divorce, troubled homes and rebellious children, as well as many related social problems. Women must return to their homes and serve there. Women are thinking too much of what they "want to do" rather than of what they "ought to do."

Only when men and women willingly assume the responsibilities they were born to do, when they devote themselves to making a success of them and lose themselves in this great responsibility, forgetting about their own selfish desires, will they find happiness and will we have a better world. It is primarily the duty of the man to fulfill his responsibility as a man and encourage his wife and daughters to be competent and happy in female duties.

Advocates of the "share alike" philosophy demonstrate an unusual lack of insight into human behavior as they ignore completely the serious social problems which arise from this blurring of the male and female roles. Countless children grow up in environment where the distinction of the sexes is so obscure that no clear-cut example exists for them to follow. Many homes lack definitive leadership, and the very differences that should be emphasized are purposely minimized as men act like women and woman act like men. This in turn can lead to underdevelopment of the child to his own sex and in some cases to homosexuality.

HARM IN WOMEN'S LIB

In review we can say that equality of the sexes leads to a blurring of roles in the home, giving no distinct male or female image for children to follow. In addition, the woman is encouraged to desert her post where she should be serving devotedly. The greatest harm comes to the children as they are deprived of a mother's undivided interest. When a mother works *by choice* outside the home, doubts are cast in the children's minds as to their mother's love and interest in their welfare and happiness.

Besides the harm that comes to the children, there is a distinct harm which comes to both the man and the woman. With the emphasis on equality, the man does not assume the full masculine role. He is robbed of his opportunity for personal development . . . those experiences that develop his masculinity. The woman also is harmed in a different way. As she divides her life between two worlds, she takes on masculine attitudes and abilities and loses some of her femininity. Neither the man nor the woman develop to their full potential, nor does either experience real fulfillment.

HOW YOUNG MEN FACE THE MASCULINE ROLE

Many young men are fearful of stepping into the responsibilities of marriage and family life. It is common for some to postpone marriage for this reason. Usually only the emotion of intense love will cause a young man to overcome his fears and step into marriage.

Even after marriage many men have severe adjustments to the load they have assumed. They are suddenly faced with an additional dependent, a household to run, furnishings, the prospect of children, etc. Before, they were relatively free of responsibility. This adjustment is natural and deserves understanding. But always there is the assurance that the step of marriage and family life is a desirable one . . . one that will lead to personal development and happiness and peace within if one is successful in this important step. Those who reject this responsibility without just cause, demonstrate a weakness of character and sacrifice the opportunity to grow as a man. Growth comes through adversity and difficulties—not through the pursuit of the "easy life."

THE SECOND MILE

The secret of gaining satisfaction and fulfillment in this important role is in going the "second mile." This instruction was given by the Savior when He said, "If any man compel thee to go one mile, go with him twain." There is in this simple statement a key to mastery over a situation. Let us refer to Jewish history at that time to understand its true meaning.

When his instruction was given, Israel was ruled by the Roman government. Common among the Roman soldiers was the practice of oppressing the Jews with such things as forcing them to carry a burden or a pack for some distance. In this instance, Jesus instructed them to be willing to carry it twice as far as they were compelled. He recognized a fundamental principle . . . that the only way to take the burden out of work is an abundant willingness to do more than is required.

Going the "second mile" is the way a man lightens his burdens and learns to enjoy his responsibility as a man. A half-hearted effort nets nothing in satisfaction. As one devotes himself to his family, going beyond the call of duty to be as completely responsible as possible, he experiences satisfying fulfillment.

Another great principle of truth was given when Jesus said, "He who loseth his life for my sake shall surely find it." As one loses himself in the responsibilities that are his, forgetting about his personal or selfish desires, devoting himself to making a success of the calling God has given him, he finds himself.

PRIDE IN RESPONSIBILITY

Equally important is that a man take pride in his many manly responsibilities. These duties, he realizes, are his alone. He does not lean on his wife or children or others in his famliy; not does he expect society to support him. The job is his. A masculine man takes pride in his God-given responsibility.

If his burdens become heavy, he does not run away from them or turn to others for assistance. He looks to himself for solutions. He may have to reorganize his life, re-evaluate his situation and possibly eliminate unnecessary obligations which have been placed upon him. He may have to move to a less expensive residence, or cut down the family budget, or make other sacrifices. But he independently solves his problems as best he can and then carries on. This is what it means to have pride in one's masculine responsibility.

This does not suggest that there will not be emergencies when one *must* turn to others, when it is impossible to independently solve the problems. But only when no other avenue of solution within himself is available does he turn to others for help.

FULFILLMENT IN MASCULINE ROLE

Inborn within man is a desire for personal fulfillment. This can be defined as a feeling of satisfaction a man has regarding himself, or a pride in his own life.

This fulfillment is gained principally by:
1. Proving one's worth. This may be done by reaching objectives, overcoming obstacles and exercising unique talents and abilities.
2. Making a worthy contribution to society.
3. Character development. This means becoming a more worthy person.

Fulfillment may come from many avenues—any avenue which

requires talents and abilities and produces worthwhile achievements. The successful artist, writer, scientist, politician, etc., receive a measure of fulfillment for worthy contributions in their fields, as will any man engaged in work which is beneficial to mankind. This is an important area of man's fulfillment.

His greatest fulfillment, however, lies within his family role as the guide, protector and provider. As he works patiently and diligently to provide comforts for his family, he develops unselfishness. Overcoming obstacles and solving problems develop character and refine the spirit. His leadership over his flock develops this masculine trait more fully, and as he stands at the head of the family he must be a shining example for them to follow. He must subdue his weaknesses and take on strengths. He has incentives which were unknown to him before marriage. Marriage is his greatest field for personal development.

As a man reaches high objectives in family life, he attains the greatest rewards life can offer. His children are his kingdom—his wife his queen. As his children become young adults, he enters the best period of all. He begins to enjoy the "fruits of his labors" as he delights in the company of his mature children. The beautiful relationship he has built with his wife is the center of his joy.

Proof that his home is the center of a man's fulfillment is evident in viewing a man who has failed to make a success of family life. His children will be a heartache to him, and his marriage may have left scars of defeat. The most fundamental area for his fulfullment has not been fruitful. He may have achieved his goals outside his home and may be honored among his associates, but this success does not compensate for his failure in the home. His happiness is as an empty shell and his fulfillment robbed of its full measure.

WHEN MEN FAIL IN THEIR WORK

During middle age many men who have not reached the measure of success they have been seeking begin to realize their sad situation that the work they had devoted themselves to these many years has not amounted to much. They may say, "I have missed the boat. What I have been doing has not really paid off. I'm getting older, and if I don't do something exciting and different now, it will be too late." They are concerned over

advancing age and loss of physical strength. Many such men turn
to the world of pleasure for fulfillment, seeking before it is too late
some measure of life's enjoyment. Others may make a last
desperate attempt to amount to something, to win the appreciation
of their fellows. Regrettably, may turn to other women and a life
of degradation.

But if a man has reared a successful family, he need not fall into
this pitfall of thinking. His family is his achievement—his
children the richest fruits of a successful life, and his joy the love,
respect and devotion of a wonderful wife. God did not command
that man be on the pinnacle of success in his work. He
commanded only that he earn his bread by the sweat of his face.
This he may have done devotedly, but may now fail to realize its
accomplishment. He can find satisfaction by focusing on this part
if he has done it well.

Married children continue to need counsel, strength and
encouragement. A man is a father as long as he has children. All
home ties are strengthened through these conscientious efforts,
and one enjoys a deepening feeling of joy.

But regardless of a man's need for fulfillment, let us keep in
mind that there are certain areas in which we *must* serve. A man
has a God-given responsibility to his family to be their guide,
protector and provider, and as he loses himself in this important
responsibility, not thinking of reward, fulfillment will naturally
follow.

REWARDS TO OTHERS

In addition to the personal fulfillment that comes to a man as he
succeeds in family life, grest rewards come to all members. As he
faithfully fulfills his role, offering firm leadership to all, his wife
and children enjoy security. This is an essential ingredient to their
happiness. A woman's security does not lie in money her husband
earns. She finds it in *him* as a responsible and dependable man.

As a man rightfully takes over the duties of his calling, this
leaves the woman free to be a woman, to concentrate on making
her career in the home successful. Because she has a man to lean
on, and is not responsible for earning the living or doing the
"man's work," she can devote herself to the feminine arts and
building a happy family life. This in turn brings her fulfillment.
Because her husband is a man, she is more of a woman.

Together they build a happy home and make their most worthy contribution to the well-being of society. This is the greatest service that can be rendered. The gift of wonderful children and a happy home is priceless!

III
MAN, THE GUIDE

Again we must emphasize that man is the divinely appointed "head of the family." Society did not assign him this position. It was God who placed him at the head when he said to Eve, "Thy desire shall be to thy husband and he shall rule over thee." (Gen. 3:16)

The leadership position is one of trust for which man is accountable to God. It is not a position that one may decide he does not want . . . nor can he pass it to another whom he may consider better qualified. To allow others to forcefully steal his leadership demonstrates gross weakness of character and lack of obedience to principle. There is no way a man can neglect this calling with clear conscience. To turn aside from this sacred responsibility is a serious dereliction of duty in the eyes of God.

There are some people in modern times who dislike the God-given plan for family leadership. They feel it places too great a burden on the man or is unfair to the woman. There is an effort to do away with the patriarchy, substituting instead, "equality of leadership" between man and woman. What such advocates fail to realize is that God's plan is *not* one which burdens, frustrates, or deprives the individual. It is one with blessings attached . . . the most ideal plan for the family to live by in attaining order, unity and peace. In addition, it provides the greatest opportunity for both men and women to develop as individuals. As the man assumes leadership, he grows as a man. As the woman is relieved of this position, she becomes more of a woman. She is free to concentrate fully on the responsibilities in *her* sphere.

LOGIC OF MAN BEING THE HEAD

Not only is leadership of the family of divine origin, it follows logic and reason. No organization can function without a responsible head. We observe this immediately in government, business, social groups, military, etc. There must be someone to direct activities, to initiate action. There must be someone ultimately upon whom responsibility and decisions rest. Without a head, disorder and chaos result.

A family is a small social group of intelligent beings and therefore must be organized with a leader. Policy and rules must be established. Decisions must be made daily, and sometimes at the moment. These are not necessarily momentous decisions, but may be as simple as "May Larry take the car tonight?" Suppose husband and wife disagree? When the wife yields to the man, order results.

Some will ask, "Why must the man lead? Why not the woman?" The reply to this is also very logical. The man is the bread-winner and protector. If he is to succeed in this role, he must have the power of decision. For example, he may be having difficulty making his income cover expenses. He may feel a change of jobs, perhaps a move to another city, is necessary in the solution of the problem. He must be free to make such a choice and move his family to a new location. If his wife is the leader, she may choose to remain in their present location. This would be unjust to the man. It is logical that the role of the provider and leader belong inseparably together.

LEADER NOT A SUPERIOR PERSON

A man as the leader may be in a superior *position* but this does not suggest that he is a superior person. He is merely functioning in an office or calling. The wife honors her husband's *position* or *authority* as the leader and gives it the obedience and respect deserving a leader.

For example, a commander of a naval fleet may be in a superior position over his fellow officers, but this does not mean he is in any way a superior person. He is merely filling an *office* or *duty*. Those who honor him or yield to his authority are giving obedience due a superior *officer*, not a superior *man*. This is a matter of law and order.

And neither is the man's position as leader of more importance than the woman's supporting role. Both are equally important! Yet they are different in position. The man's duty is to lead; the woman's, to follow.

DUTIES OF THE GUIDE

The duties of the guide are: 1) To determine the policies, rules and laws for the family to follow. 2) To make decisions in guiding the family.

The father has the right to establish rules of conduct, expenditure of money, laws of the household, religious affiliation of the children, educational planning, etc. He has the right to make decisions concerning the family, those decisions related to his role as the guide, protector and provider.

The father may wish to *delegate some of his authority* to his wife, especially in affairs of the household and matters concerning the children. She is closer to them than he is, in their day to day activities, so he will naturally leave many things up to her, and not be concerned about them. But he maintains the right to "step in" when necessary or when important to do so.

Or the father may turn to his wife to *seek her viewpoint* in matters of family planning or decisions. She may be his counselor and offer wisdom and valuable advice. Her perspective may be an all-important one. But the power to determine is his, even if in opposition to hers.

The father may also wish to consult with the *children*, by calling them together in a family council meeting. He may carefully listen to even the smallest child, regard his feelings and consider his viewpoint. But the responsibility of decision is ultimately his. He stands as the shepherd of the flock. His decision should be honored and respected by all members of the family, even when they do not agree with him. They are not honoring *him* so much as they are honoring his *office* as the guide, or his right to lead.

EVERY MAN A LEADER

Every man must be a leader. He may not be a leader in industry, government, or even a local men's organization, but if he is married he will be a leader of a family. The importance of this position in the home cannot be overestimated. The home is the most basic unit in our society. How it functions to meet human needs directly affects all other institutions to which we belong. The man's conduct as "head of the family" will, for better or for worse, affect all society. This crucial organization, then, *the family*, needs prime leadership, the man offering all of the qualifications necessary to function successfully in guiding the family safely and securely.

THE IDEAL LEADER

The ideal leader assumes the position as head of the family as a sacred responsibility. He takes pride in this masculine role, does not set it aside or turn it over to others. He has a keen feeling of responsibility for his place as leader, realizing that it is one of his most important functions in life. He serves patiently, with dedication and devotion.

He is a leader of steel and velvet. He has those steel qualities which accompany great leadership—firmness, decisive judgment, courage, steadfastness, and a keen sense of justice.

He rules over his flock with firmness. He does not allow others to dictate, to steal his leadership, to push him around or pressure him into things against his own judgment. He does not appease or make concessions. He fearlessly follows the dictates of his own convictions. But in his firmness he is always fair.

In making *decisions* he is always *careful*. If he does not have sufficient knowledge upon which to base a wise decision, he will carefully attain that knowledge. He will seek the counsel of his family members when necessary to get their ideas. But once he has made a decision based upon the best of his judgment, he will have the *courage of his convictions*, the steadfastness to follow through. He may make mistakes, but allows for those mistakes. He has the *confidence* that his judgment is usually sound. Because he has confidence in himself, others believe in him and follow him readily.

The ideal leader will also have *velvet* qualities. He has a *kindly consideration* for those he is leading, a *tender-heartedness* for the desires of others, *unselfishness* and a *willingness to sacrifice* his own pleasures for members of his family. Any leader must be unselfish if he is to be great.

But along with his velvet tenderness, a great leader must be a little *hard-hearted* at times. He must have the toughness of steel in following through on what he considers a "right decision," even if it means bitter disappointment to those he is leading. This unalterable courage of his convictions is the supreme quality of leadership that brings "order to a household."

A great leader has *humility*. He is not too proud to listen to the counsel of his family members and, in fact, seeks their opinions when he feels the need to do so. If one of them is right and he is wrong, he is humble enough to admit it. He realizes that, being human, he has limitations, that others may contribute immeasurably to his leadership role, especially his wife.

With this combination of qualities—firmness, courage, decisive judgment, and justice, and the velvet traits of tenderness, consideration, and humility—a man is equipped to offer excellent leadership to his family, to bring order and peace to his household—the perfect situation in which to establish an ideal home and rear well-adjusted, happy children.

EVERY MAN HAS CAPABILITIES TO LEAD

Since men were born with the sacred responsibility to create a family and appointed to be their leader, they were also born with capabilities to lead. It is a religious truth, that the Lord God gives no commandment to His people without also giving them the means to carry it out. Therefore, since God blessed the man with the leadership of the family, He also blessed him with the capacity to lead.

A man has the physical, emotional, and temperamental makeup to lead. Consider his physical structure. Is he not superior in strength and capacity to those he leads? Although it is not likely he will have to force a family member, yet he has the capacity to do so and can overpower them when necessary. This realization should keep him from being afraid to face up to any member of his family.

Emotionally he is equipped for the burden of leadership. He has the fortitude to make weighty decisions. Sometimes he must, within a few hours, make a decision that may affect his family for a lifetime. Based upon a few facts and the best of judgment, he hurriedly draws conclusions and comes to a decision. Such risk is frightening to women, and sometimes they would find it impossible to reach a decision in such a short time. But men have the ability to make such a determination. They have the emotional stamina to take the strain.

Men also have the temperament for decisions. A man is inclined to be decisive . . . to be able to size up a situation rather quickly. He is not apt to waver for long. A woman, on the other hand, is different, is inclined to fluctuate, and sometimes postpones a decision because of its difficulty. A man is not apt to become frustrated with the continual demand of decision-making as he has an inborn temperament to cope with such matters.

If a man finds that he is lacking in any of these qualities, it may be due to the background of his childhood. Growing up under the leadership of a weak father or a dominating mother may have caused a lack of development. These traits may be recessive in him and therefore appear to be nonexistent.

If for any reason a man feels that he does not measure up in his role as the leader, he can rest assured that he *does* possess the inate qualities to lead. He has but to turn to God for a realization of these virtues. If he will exercise faith in himself, in God, and will seek divine assistance in his problems, he will grow to succeed in leadership.

FAILURES OF MEN

The American male, more than any man in the world, is a failure in regard to leadership of his family. Referring again to the statement of Dr. Joshua Bierer, "It's the fatherless society. All the women are crying out for a strong man and he's just not there." Let's review some of the failures of American men:

1. *First is the man who fails to assume his position as leader:* He does not lead. He does not determine family policy, make plans, set down laws or issue commands or make decisions. The family is like a ship without a captain, tossed in a tumultuous sea. If the family is to be led, the wife must do so . . . occasionally children must. The husband sits back without concern. He has defected and his responsibility goes to another. His attention is on other things. He is irresponsible.

2. *Second is the man who allows his wife and children to push him around:* He may wish to lead, but because of weakness or fear he allows his family to dictate. He is a "pushover," a "jellyfish." He follows the course of least resistance. Instead of claiming his position, he cowers at the demands of others. There are a few men who are actually afraid of their wives, even with fear of bodily harm. The "pushover" is a miserable failure in his masculine position. He feels he should lead, but does not have enough backbone to make a fair attempt.

3. *Third is the man who succumbs to pressure of women and children:* This man is no jellyfish. He exerts himself to lead, but due to insufficient strength and firmness he "gives in" to the pressure of his family, against his own convictions. Pressuring of the family may take the form of harping, needling, "bugging," convincing, moral pressure, weeping, whining, wailing, and other means to get their way. Or they may go so far as to make demands, issuing ultimatums with a threat of consequences.

Some men succumb to pressure because they are "busy" or preoccupied with other important matters. They feel they do not have time to "wrestle" with the problem. It seems easier to "give in" and keep peace than to hold firm to the position of leader. They do not give their responsibility of leadership the top priority it deserves.

Other men grow *weary* from pressures. They are like the judge in the scriptural parable of the "importuning widow" who became weary of the widow's requests night and day and so gave in to her wishes. The man may believe that he should stand firm, but due to constant harping he relinquishes rights and prerogatives which should be sacred to him.

I was once in the company of a man who had two teen-age daughters who were guilty of this practice of "harping." The father had bought a horse for the girls which was to be delivered to their ranch several days hence. But the girls urged the father to borrow the farmer's truck and take the horse immediately. They pleaded and begged, as they had done in the past for other things. The man, embarrassed and torn in his feelings, turned to me for advice. "Tell them 'No,' in no uncertain terms," I said, "and stick to your guns." Supported by my courage, he faced the girls with a firm "no." They were in tears and coaxed continually until we were in the car and well on the way home. They sat in total silence for awhile, then began mumbling to themselves and looking harshly at their father. Such a denial was new to them and a severe adjustment. They were used to having their way. They had thought before that "it pays to plead," but for the first time, they felt the weight of their father's words. If he kept up this firm sort of leadership, his girls would soon learn that "pressure is of no avail," and they would be smart enough to stop.

4. *The fourth failure of men is to compromise:* In this case the man does not give in completely. He stands his ground to a degree, but makes concessions, or appeases in one way or another. This weakness is a mark of a poor leader and one which will lead to future trouble. Leaders of nations have been guilty of this unwise practice in settling international affairs, but by so doing they have weakened their own position. Compromising is never considered good practice in leadership.

Men must become aware that, although it is wise to listen to family members, to consider their ideas, to accept good suggestions, it is never good leadership to "give in" *against one's own better judgment.* A mark of great leadership, on the other hand, is to stand firm to one's own convictions, regardless of the feelings of others. This is not only a leader's right; it is his obligation.

5. *Fifth is the man who allows his wife to steal his leadership:* In this case the wife does not "pressure" her husband. She *usurps* his authority. She is a dominating woman by nature and therefore tries to "take over" the leadership of the family. Her husband may wish to lead, but she overpowers him. She makes the decisions, determines family policy, makes plans without his sanction, etc. The children turn to her for consent.

Or if she is more subtle in her domination of her husband, she offers endless suggestions, gives advice and counsel for him to follow, always telling him what to do and when to do it. In either case she is out of place, and the man who will allow his wife to hold the reins in the family is also to blame and has failed in his leadership role. He must, if he is a man, overpower her and regain his position as head of the household.

6. *Sixth is the man who fails to "make his leadership stick" or to command obedience from his family members.* In this case the man may give instructions or commands to his wife (or children), but she does not obey. She may feel that her opinion is as good as his, that she does not have to follow his word but can do as she pleases. The children also follow this pattern of disobedience, for they have learned it from their mother. The man who allows this conduct, who fails to stand firm and command honor to his word, has failed as a leader.

In some cases the wife (or child) does not willfully disobey, but has a struggle within herself in an effort to follow his counsel. She believes his word should be law and has a desire to follow his command, but her own selfish desires overcome her and she also disobeys. If the man allows this action in his wife and children, he has failed once again to command respect for his leadership position.

7.   *The seventh failure of men in leadership is lack of velvet:* This is an opposite problem. The man may rule with strength and firmness of steel, but he lacks a gentle consideration for those he leads. When simple requests are made, they are brushed aside. When heartfelt desires are expressed, they are denied. When a family member pleads for consideration, the man is without compassion. Filled with selfishness, he is not willing to be inconvenienced or to make the necessary sacrifices for their benefit.

When a family member has been disobedient, he is severe in his judgment, harsh in his punishment. Such men rule their households as tyrants and fail in one of the most important qualities of great leadership. A man *must* rule with kindness, consideration, justice, mercy, love, and unselfishness, if he is to succeed with his family. The prime quality that gives velvet to leadership is *unselfishness*. A man must have both the firmness of steel and the softness of velvet to rule his family properly.

8.   *The eighth failure of man is due to a "weak" ego:* This problem is so subtle that men themselves seldom realize this fault. In this case the man often says "no" to a request, when he would prefer to say "yes." He does this *just to show his authority.* Or he may resist a well-thought-out idea or suggestion from his family. Here, again, he does this to prove his authority. His habit of saying "no" is due to a weak ego. He feels a need to prove himself as a man—especially as a leader—and saying "no" to his family is one means of doing so. This increases his ego.

What he fails to realize is that he does not have to say "no" to his family "just to show his authority." There are numerous opportunities to say "no" when there are legitimate reasons for doing so. As the man learns to be firm, decisive, and to have the courage of his convictions, he will command unwavering respect from his family, and *this* will bolster his ego in a wholesome way.

A man with a wholesome ego does not have to resort to saying "no" just to show his authority. Instead, his conduct is like the following: If a family member makes a request or suggestion, based upon wisdom or good sense, and if the idea seems sound to him, he will say, "That sounds like a good idea. Let's try it." He does not take advantage of his leadership position to bolster his ego. He feels no need to say "no" when he means "yes." He does not use family leadership as a proving ground for his self worth.

9. *The ninth failure is due to an oversized ego:* In this case the man has a feeling of *superiority* over those he leads. This is not a superiority of *position,* but a superiority of total worth. He may feel more intelligent, more gifted, capable and otherwise qualified than his family members. Therefore, he resists their advice, ideas, and suggestions. He lacks the humility to listen to them, does not seek their counsel, and therefore divides his family from himself. Strange as it may seem, and probably confusing to him, his superior image does not command the respect of his family. Instead, it arouses contempt. Only a man who is humble in his position, who recognizes his limitations, realizing that he is not infallible, is a great leader.

THE VALUE OF HUMILITY IN LEADERSHIP

A mature, well-educated father, with years of experience and the advantage of age may well learn valuable things from his children, if he has the humility to listen. Children are sometimes wizards when it comes to ideas. The story is told of a truck driver who wedged his truck inside an overpass. He called on the city for expert advice in extracting the vehicle. Every possibility was considered (so they thought), until a young boy came to the scene and said, "Why not let out some of the air from the tires?"— something they had not thought of. Such contributions of youth should keep men humble.

Wives, too, have tremendous ideas when heard. Yet, a man who suffers from an oversized ego may feel it humiliating to "listen to his wife." I once heard a woman give some sound suggestions to her husband in the presence of another man. Her husband said, "Don't listen to her; she doesn't know anything." And, although it is not in harmony with family order and good leadership for a wife to dominate, or to offer too many suggestions, or give pushy advice, it does pay to listen to her and consider her thoughts. Such is the mark of a humble leader.

CAUSES OF MEN'S FAILURES

It is helpful to discover the major causes of men's failures to lead. They can be listed as follows:

1. *Lack of Knowledge:* There has been a lack of knowledge in America of the basic principle that a man should lead. It has not been clearly understood that the man's sacred responsibility is to stand at the head of his family. Instead of a clearcut knowledge of this principle, there has been a mistaken idea that the man and woman should lead equally, both having equal voice and power of decision in the family. Some have felt it unfair for the man to be in the superior position and the woman to follow. In modern times this has been called "male supremacy."

2. *Lack of Conviction:* When a knowledge of this divine principle of the man's leadership has been taught, it may not have been taught in a way that a man understands it or can comprehend its tremendous importance. The knowledge may not have been supported by the Holy Scriptures, which can lead to a conviction of its truth. Whatever the failure, there are many men who, although they do understand at least in part that they should lead, lack the conviction to apply its principle in daily living.

3. *Lack of Self-Discipline:* A man may have the basic knowledge and conviction but lack the self-discipline to apply it to life's experiences. Due to weakness in his character, lack of self-control, he allows women and children to dominate or pressure him, or he may fail to offer the gentle velvet needed in leadership. He may know that he must be unselfish and kind, but due to an uncontrolled temper is harsh and self-centered and unforgiving. In either case the man fails due to lack of self-discipline.

Men's failure to lead is not the fault of women and children, although their weaknesses may contribute somewhat to the problem or at least make it more difficult. The blame lies with the man. The role is his and he must take it, hold on to it at any cost. It is a sacred calling, and he should feel a great responsibility to follow through.

To blame a child or the wife for his failure is like blaming a child for his undisciplined, obstreperous and offensive conduct. The real blame lies with the parent for his inability to discipline the youth.

The trend to weak leadership in the home and lack of "velvet" has been going on for several generations now in America and has led to some widespread and disastrous social problems, described as follows:

SOCIAL PROBLEMS CAUSED BY POOR LEADERSHIP OF MEN

As has been already stated in the introduction, the general lack of manliness has led to many social problems. But I wish to reemphasize these problems here, and particularly in regard to man's lack of firm leadership.

1. *The Dominating Woman:* The dominating woman has become one of our major social problems, leading to a multitude of related problems. To sum it up, "When you have a society of dominating women, you have a society of unhappy, insecure women. You also have an equal number of frustrated, unfulfilled men. This, in turn, affects their relationship and brings trouble into marriage and the home."

The reason for the unhappiness of men and women, as the woman dominates, can be explained. In taking over the leadership of the family, a woman acquires certain *masculine* characteristics which accompany leadership. She learns to be aggressive, decisive, efficient, and competent in the leadership position. One day she comes to the rude awakening that she has lost some of her feminine charm. This is as important to her as masculinity is to a man. The hurt is doubly compounded when she realizes that through default her husband has brought this upon her. As she loses her femininity, her husband's feelings for her are adversely affected. He may appreciate her and love her, but he regards her as less of a woman than he once did. The tender, protective feelings he had for her in the early days of marriage are gone. Such a loss causes the deepest of pains.

As the husband defects in his leadership to his wife, as he allows her to take over the reins of the family, he tends to lose the masculine characteristics of leadership. He is less aggressive, less dominant, less decisive. He is less of a man. This frustrates him and causes him to feel unfulfilled. His wife loses a certain respect for him as she detects this loss of manliness; so her love for him is also affected. This cannot help but cause a weakening of their relationship and thus affect the entire home scene.

It would be unfair to place all responsibility for the dominating woman on the man. Women themselves have taken initiative beyond justification to dominate the household. Some have usurped authority, trampled on men's rights, pressured and demanded their way. But in spite of women's aggressiveness to lead, men are principally to blame. With a strong man, the dominating woman does not exist. Women take over as men allow them to. The resonsibility to retain his position as leader is his, and this he must do at all costs.

2. *Trouble in the Home:* The home where the father's word is not law is a home of trouble and discord, chaos and confusion, affecting all members of the family. These troubles are subsequently poured out upon society where everyone pays a penalty for the neglect of the father who fails to be the shepherd of his flock.

3. *Youth Rebellion:* Children who grow up in the home of a weak father who has not commanded respect for his word or obedience to his instructions, children who have been permitted to follow their own desires and inclinations in contradiction to their father's will, are following a pattern of rebellion in the home. When such children are mature and are turned out into the world, it is natural for them to follow this same pattern of rebellion. They rebel against authority, established customs, and accepted principles and standards. These are the young lawbreakers, guilty of crime and delinquency. These are the young rebels on campus who will not comply with the rules. These are the youth who are seeking to experiment with the "new morality" and other forbidden practices. They are rejecting refinement, culture, and the disciplined life. These young rebels are the products of rebellious homes.

Young rebels are sometimes produced by an *overly strict* father, who lacks the velvet of leadership. Such men do not respect the rights of children and unjustly demand or deny too much of them. Because of such unfair leadership, children may rebel against the teachings of their father. He has failed to win them to his way of life.

4. *Homosexuality:* Recent social studies reveal that the growing problem of homosexuality is often the result of the home where a strong "father image" does not exist. There is a "blurring of the roles" between the father and mother. The father does not stand out as strongly masculine nor the mother as strongly feminine. Children in such an environment lack a sex image to identify with and therefore do not develop as strongly masculine

or feminine. This may cause serious trouble later, resulting in practices of homosexuality and lesbianism.

5. *Women's Lib:* Underlying the complaints of this movement is a dislike if not an open hostility and hatred towards men. At least a portion of this discontent is aimed directly at man's failure in leadership. Women are crying to be "liberated from the shackles of male supremacy" and eventually desire to eliminate the patriarchy which honors the man as the decision-making head of the family.

In thinking of men's guilt as it relates to the feminine rebellion, one observes that the "lack of velvet" in dealing with them is probably the main cause. Had men been more considerate of women, more unselfish and fair in their dominion over them, there would have been no need for women to seek freedom from such leadership. Women would have enjoyed the security of a strong leadership because it was tempered with gentleness and thoughtfulness.

* * *

We have viewed the weakness of men's leadership and have observed there to be a lack of both steel and velvet. We have also observed the many social problems which occur when the father is not a proper head of his house. Let us now turn attention to the principles involved in good leadership and how they may be applied in daily living.

IV
HOW TO LEAD
WOMEN AND CHILDREN

There are some fundamental principles which, if understood and followed, will aid immeasurably in leading women and children. Such leadership is frequently difficult and exasperating in the extreme. In this field of leadership a man is tested as in no other, for the relationships are far more intimate and often fraught with emotion. But if a man will study and apply the 17 principles outlined below, he will find his task much easier, and he will grow in a way that will greatly surprise himself and those he leads.

1. *Take hold of the reins and keep them:* A man must first assume the mantle of leadership, taking responsibility for making the major decisions, for directing family members, for delegating authority and dividing responsibility. In this way the household is put in order.

Many women do not realize the obligation they have to follow their husbands, that his leadership is not self-assumed, but is divinely appointed. They must be taught this principle and understand the sacred responsibility the husband has and the magnitude of his calling. His position should be respected, his word honored, and obedience given to his instructions. This a man must teach his family to win their wholehearted support.

It would be ideal if parents would teach their sons and daughters this order of God at an early age that they might understand these

42

principles as a guide to establishing their own homes later on. First the sons would learn that they must prepare themselves for leadership, and the daughters would learn to yield to this leadership and to encourage it in the man. If these principles are clearly understood before marriage, it is likely that more thought would be given to mate selection than seems to exist in most cases. In every way the father must seek to clearly and unwaveringly establish himself as the undisputed leader and not deviate from this position.

2. *Teach the way of life:* If a man is to be the guide for his family, it is essential that he teach them principles to live by, standards and ideals which will serve as guides throughout their lives. He can sit at the bedside of his little children and teach them concerning the origin of man, how he was created in the image of God, the purpose of life on earth and man's destiny after death. They can be taught their responsibilities as children of God and principles to follow in becoming better persons. If a man is unsure of himself in these basic beliefs, he can seek God through prayer and search the Scriptures seeking a revelation of truth as a guide.

One very fine means of instructing family members is the holding of a family home evening once each week. During this evening the father should instruct his family, giving them guiding principles to guide their lives. The children will have a chance to ask questions and make comments. Mother will also contribute valuable ideas. This brings a family close together. Recreation and fun may be added to make the evening more interesting.

3. *Provide a sense of direction:* There are always numerous uncertainties facing us. Indecision and unrest exist, plans fluctuate, change, or hang in a state of flux. Problems are often unresolved. These situations are not too difficult if the father always provides a sense of direction. This means presenting a positive side to the family . . . giving them something to hold on to.

During times of unrest or uncertainty, a man must reassure his family that he is giving careful thought to the future, that plans are being considered and the problems will eventually be resolved. People need something to hang their hopes on, whether the dream is vague or specific. A man's thought for the future, his effort to conceive some type of plan, provides security for his family even if the plan is somewhat vague. He is their captain. When they are tossed about, as at sea, he needs to chart the course and indicate the destination.

Some men hesitate to reveal plans even at times of great indecision, fearing that, should they not materialize, the family would suffer too much disappointment. Perhaps he fears that, should he feel it unwise to proceed, he would have a moral obligation to go ahead anyway. Perhaps he fears that confidence in him will be shaken. This may be true if the plan is outlined in specifics and great enthusiasm has been built up. But if a man will keep to generalities, emphasizing desire and hope and avoiding binding commitments, he will bring a feeling of security to his household and provide a sense of direction.

4. *Display confidence:* A good leader of any group displays confidence in himself. He speaks with a self-assured voice, appears to know where he is going, trusts his judgment, and is not plagued with doubts and fears. Because he appears confident in himself, it is easy for others to follow. People naturally trust a self-assured leader, whereas it is difficult to give full support to one who lacks this quality.

Now, most men are not as confident as they need to be. They suffer from self-doubt, fears and complexes of all kinds. But even if this is the case, it is important that they *give the impression* of confidence. They must hide their fears and put on a brave front for the sake of their followers.

For example, take a man who has suffered financial defeat. He may not know where his next meal is coming from or where to turn for solutions to his problems. His heart may be filled with tremendous doubts and fears, but he hides his shaky feelings from his wife and little children, lest they suffer fear also. He puts on a brave front and presents a confident picture to his family.

Even great military generals who lead thousands of men in courageous battles, suffer inwardly from fears. A famous general in World War II, noted for his courage in battle, admitted that he always felt fear in the face of danger. But his men never knew this. He displayed a confident side to them, and this gave strength to his men. They trusted him and followed him with confidence.

5. *Seek knowledge:* A good leader may be confident, but he is also *humble*. He realizes his limitations, that he does not know *all* about *everything*. He therefore seeks knowledge from reliable sources before making plans, decisions, or solving problems. If he is considering a move to a new community, he does not rely upon his own limited knowledge. Instead, he goes to the community and checks out the facts. He investigates the schools, housing, business opportunities, weather, the people, and its special

problems. He opens his eyes and takes a good, honest look and disregards emotion or whims. Or, if he is a young man planning a future occupation, he finds out facts. What will the responsibility really be like? He does not rely upon merely what people say it will be like. Or if he is considering a change of jobs, he finds out what his daily responsibilities will be, his potential, his problems or limitations, the pay, etc. What he does not already know, he finds out and does so very thoroughly. He does not trust to luck, an impression, or the opinion of others. He gains true knowledge—an accurate picture.

He may also wish to gain the advice of others. This is sometimes very good. In the business world, men frequently pay a high fee for the advice of consultants, advisors, and counselors and feel that the money is well spent. But in seeking the advice of others, it is essential to choose a person who is knowledgeable on the subject and not a novice. It is especially important that you not seek advice from just anyone. Such advice may be worse than none. In general, it is best to "avoid opinions of others as you would a plague." Seek only the advice of those whom you can trust, people with knowledge and wisdom on the subject. If in doubt about a person's qualifications, it is best to rely upon your *own* judgment, for you have a more accurate perspective of your circumstances than anyone else.

After you have gained knowledge and competent advice, carefully weigh out the facts, *considering your own viewpoint.* Then make a determination based upon the best of your own judgment. Do not trust completely in the knowledge or advice of others. Remember that you may still know more and have better judgment than they. Also, God may be guiding you in a direction that seems illogical in the face of the facts. It is best to heed strong feelings and follow your own convictions.

If you find that you lack important knowledge upon which to base a decision or plan and do not know where to turn for the necessary information, remember that you can always turn to God for answers. He will give to you in full measure whatever you need to know. The Savior taught, "If any man ask for bread, will his father give him a stone?" And in the book of James, "If any man lack wisdom, let him ask of God who giveth to all men liberally and upbraideth not. But let him ask in *faith*, nothing wavering."

6. *Consult family members:* In matters which concern the family, it is usually wise to consult the family members for their

viewpoint. There may be some exceptions to this rule, where it may be best not to bring them into a situation. For example, if the father is considering a change in his business, a change which will affect their future, and if the reasons for this change are too complex or too difficult to comprehend, it may be better not to talk with them about it. But in most cases the family *will* comprehend and not only deserve to be consulted but can serve as a valuable aid to the father in making a wise decision.

The wife especially should be consulted, for she is usually a man's most loyal friend. The wife has a perspective that no one else in a man's life has. She is closer to his objectives and his problems than others, yet not so close as he is. Her perspective is more accurate where his may be distorted and exaggerated. She stands back a little from the situation, thus making her viewpoint valuable. Women may be limited in knowledge of facts, but they are inclined to have valuable insight. Voltaire has said, "All the reasoning of men is not worth one sentiment of women." And Christine Rossetti commented, "Men work and think, but women feel." Women can be fountains of wisdom. But it is to be remembered that hers is not to be considered the dominant voice. The man need only consider her viewpoint and then follow his own convictions.

Children also should be consulted, for they have interesting and valuable viewpoints also and should never be underestimated. They will appreciate being a part of family planning and will be more cooperative and willing to sacrifice for objectives. It will, in fact, bring father and children closer together if he invites their ideas.

The best arrangement for the father to consult with his family is to hold first a private meeting with his wife in which they discuss family plans, problems, and decisions. In this meeting they can work towards a unity of feeling. This can be followed by a *family counsel* to which all of the family is invited. In this meeting matters of importance are presented, and each of the children is invited to express himself. No one is excluded just because he did not volunteer. Each person is asked for his ideas. At the end of the meeting the father assures the family that he appreciates their ideas and will weigh them out carefully, but will have to hold the right of final decision based upon his own judgment.

The "husband-wife" meeting and the family counsel may be held when the need arises, or as a routine, once a week. It can be held in connection with the family home evening, mentioned previously, or at a separate time. If it is held as routine, it has many benefits. If the father does not have matters to discuss, the wife and children will, and it will assist the father in bringing greater harmony into his family.

7. *Be decisive:* The dictionary defines the word decisive as "having the power or quality of deciding." A decisive man is able to gather facts and draw conclusions quickly and come to a firm decision without difficulty. Indecisiveness is to fluctuate or vacillate. There is a hesitancy to come to a firm decision even after all the facts are known and considered. Or there is a tendency to postpone the decision. Or, if the decision is reached, it is never quite final. One always has to reconsider.

Indecision brings great pain to a family. A leader who has this fault is handicapped, and his job becomes an onerous one. Decisiveness, on the other hand, helps a family immeasurably. It is like adding grease to the wheels. There are many decisions to be made in a family, almost daily. Some are of momentous importance, some are small; but all must be faced in one way or another. For a leader to be decisive is a wonderful asset.

This trait can be cultivated. One must force himself to draw conclusions quickly and firmly. But before doing so he should make a careful study of all the facts. It is necessary to take some risk, and one will have to realize that this is an integral part of the matter. Most indecisiveness is caused by fear . . . the fear of making mistakes. This problem will be discussed in the following point.

8. *Allow for mistakes:* Fear of humiliation is a strong deterrent in decision making. This fear can be minimized by facing life realistically and allowing for "human error."

Every man will make his share of errors in judgment. Not all decisions will be wise, not all plans fruitful. Success is never assured nor can results of a given decision and course ever be accurately measured beforehand. Therefore, a man must be willing to face this fact and allow for mistakes, not worrying about the consequences. If he has followed the principles of good leadership, being careful to gain adequate knowledge, and considered the viewpoints of his family, he will avoid an unnecessary number of mistakes.

As far as the wife is concerned, she is less concerned as to the outcome of a decision, as a general rule, than she is to the attitude of confidence of the leader. Women tend to be very understanding and in the face of defeat will extend great understanding and sympathy. They do, in fact, enjoy playing this part of the understanding angel in a man's moment of real need. Women do not tend to criticize a man for his failures and mistakes so much as they *admire* him for his courage to venture out, take risks, and do the things he believes in.

9. *Win their support:* Even though it is not always necessary, it is wise for a leader to win the support of his family in his plans and decisions. If they do not agree, try to explain your point of view with great patience, especially to your wife. Tell her you need her support, you value her opinion, but you are sure she will understand that if you are to lead you cannot do so unless you follow your own convictions. Emphasize that her support is invaluable to you. Try to sell her on your ideas so she will be in harmony with you. If this is not possible, at least try to win her support to "your right to lead." Remind her that you alone are responsible for the leadership of the family—the decisions and their outcome.

Don't try to win her support by pressuring her or ridiculing her ideas. If you do, she may feel an obligation to support you, but this is not the kind of support that will strengthen your position.

If a man does not make an effort to win his family's support and willfully goes against their wishes, they may have the impression that he does not consider their feelings of any worth. They will then feel more opposed than before to his actions. This makes for trouble in the leadership position, for the man stands alone in his decision.

But, if support is gained, it may prove invaluable to you later on. Should disappointments arise and plans fail to materialize as you had planned, you will be comforted to know that your wife, although she may not have agreed fully, did give approval and support to your decision. You will not be alone in your problems. You will not need to apologize for failure, and she will have no reason to point out your mistakes.

10. *Keep reasons confidential:* When announcing plans and decisions to your family, it is not always necessary to explain your reasons for coming to a decision. Sometimes it is an advantage if you keep them confidential, especially if the reasons are difficult to explain or may arouse questions in the minds of the family. *Your decision may be sound but your reasons may seem wrong or illogical.* This may cause others to question your judgment or present opposition to the course you have taken.

Often, a man is impelled to lead, not by logic or sound

judgment, but by inspiration, perception, or even hunches. In these cases he may not know the reasons for his actions. The reasons may appear illogical, even to him. Any attempt to explain reasons may seem futile. One can, however, always explain the truth—that he has a *conviction* that his objectives are wise. He can win his family's support to his convictions, even if he cannot sell them on his reasons. This is all that is necessary, as people like to follow a self-assured leader.

God does not always reveal His reasons to us. We must learn to trust in Him. We are instructed in the Book of Proverbs: "Trust in the Lord with all thine heart, and *lean not to thine own understanding*. In all thy ways acknowledge Him and He shall direct thy paths." God's path is always right, but His purposes may seem illogical to us. We may not be able to comprehend the full meaning of His divine plan. So He conceals His reasons from us and teaches us again and again to trust in Him. And such it is with any leader. His followers must learn to trust in him in many situations.

11. *Consistency and follow-through:* When a man has conceived an idea or plan, has given it careful thought, laid definite plans based upon his best judgment and set an objective, the time comes to move ahead towards the goal. A good leader does not turn back at some point along the way unless an unforeseen emergency arises.

Let's take an example: Suppose a man desires to take his family on an extended trip which will not only be a wonderful adventure but will have great educational value. He gives the idea careful thought. He convinces himself that the idea is not only feasible but is sound. He announces his plans to his family, and they excitedly start making preparations. They build up to a high peak of enthusiasm and set a definite objective.

As the date of departure nears, there are several human weaknesses in men which may arise to destroy such plans. The first is the tendency to "lose heart." If the object is high, it may begin to seem exceedingly difficult. A man may ask himself a dozen times why he ever conceived such a "wild idea." There appear to be many problems, and the goal may seem beyond reach. This new view of an objective is much like the view one takes of a majestic mountain. Seen from a distance, it does not seem like such a great task to climb it. As one approaches, however, and finally reaches the base, the mountain seems much higher than at first thought. It now seems almost insurmountable.

This same experience can be felt in objectives. From a distance they appear easy, but near at hand one loses courage. The perspective is greatly altered.

The second human tendency which destroys plans is *"self-doubt."* One may have a marvelous idea, but because he conceived it himself, a man may begin to doubt his own judgment, remembering mistakes in the past and fearing a repetition. He will begin to question the soundness of his judgment and feel the plan is not worthwhile or worth the sacrifice.

The tendency to become "sidetracked" is another hazard to the fulfillment of such plans. One may have had every intention of following through in the beginning, but has now become very involved with other things which seem to take precedence. He is now too busy to go. He may have taken on extra responsibility which he feels he cannot neglect. Important as the plans seemed when he laid them, they seem unimportant when placed beside his present interests and responsibilities. These are not unforeseen emergencies, but self-assumed obligations. Justified as he may feel to cancel plans, his weakness is revealed in that he did not put a high enough value on his plans to keep himself free to conclude them. These three tendencies are weaknesses and should be overcome.

The lack of follow-through on the part of the father can have a disheartening effect on the family. Not only is there a loss of enriching experiences that could just as well have been had, but the family suffers a certain lack of security, especially if it happens frequently. They will come to lack trust in the father's word. When new plans are presented, there will be doubt concerning the outcome. The family will lack faith that the plans will materialize, and a certain disillusionment will set in. Considering these problems which arise in the minds of family members, it appears that it would be better to follow through with objectives even though it may not be quite so prudent as originally thought.

Unforeseen circumstances do arise, of course, which make plans unwise. But the amazing fact is that women and children readily adjust to emergencies. They undertand these situations. But they do not understand or make adjustments easily when there is no justifiable reason for "turning back." They suffer disillusionment in the face of this retreat action.

There is a certain honor, justice, and fair play for a leader to follow through with plans, not only for the benefit of those he leads but for what it does for the man himself. He feels true to himself and develops a feeling of courage and honor. It is a mark of good character. And it develops trust and devotion in women and children.

12. *Listen to their ideas and suggestions:* A part of the real velvet in leadership is to listen to the family when they come to you with ideas and suggestions. Especially is it important to listen to your wife, as she is in a secondary position in leadership and carries some of the responsibility. I am not referring to those times when the father *seeks out* their viewpoints, as already explained. I am referring to "unsolicited voices."

A man may resist listening to his family's suggestions. He may consider it an affront to his authority. He may expect women and children to remain silent at all times, unless asked. Or it may seem a little humiliating to listen to them when he expects that he should know all the answers himself. It can even cause him to feel a little unmanly to listen, especially to women. Or, if he *is* kind enough to listen, he may do so impatiently, giving the impression that he is in a hurry or feels imposed upon.

A wise leader will listen and carefully consider other viewpoints. Valuable ideas come from many sources. It is not only wise to listen, but a leader has an obligation to do so. Although he is in a superior position as the leader, they who are led have a *right to be heard*. They do not have the right of decision, but they have a right to a voice in matters which concern them. A leader has an obligation to consider other viewpoints, even if they are in opposition to his own. When a family member comes to the father with a suggestion, the father can deal wisely with him as follows:

a) Stop all activities and give your full attention. If this is not possible, make an appointment for a time free of interruptions. Then give your undivided attention.

b) Listen carefully. If you are not in agreement, withhold your opposition. Do not present negative thoughts at this time. To do so shows great inconsideration for his right to speak and your responsibility to consider his thinking.

c) Be understanding. Express sympathy for his ideas. More than anything else a person wants to be heard and considered. This is more important than to have his ideas materialize.

d) Tell him that you will *think about it* and will give it careful consideration. Do this although the answer may be so evident to you immediately that you have no doubt about it. This shows courtesy and kind consideration of feelings. He will feel that he has a voice and that his ideas will be considered. There is always the possibility that that which seemed so clear to you immediately will be altered as you consider more facts. On the other hand, if you give a fast answer or quickly toss the suggestions aside, it displays thoughtlessness, perhaps arrogance. If the matter is of vital importance, tell him that you will seek the Lord in prayer for guidance.

e) After you have carefully weighed the suggestion, if the idea is sound, be humble enough to admit it. Express appreciation. If the idea is unsound, point out why in a manner that is kind and firm. In doing this, be very sympathetic with the opposing viewpoint. Do not belittle ideas or regard them as unimportant. Show respect for others' thinking but explain that you must follow your own convictions even if they are in opposition. Sometimes your reasons may be difficult to analyze or for others to understand. In such cases, explain that you do not have a good feeling about it and feel responsible to follow your deep convictions.

13. *Listening to requests and special desires:* Much the same procedure is followed as when listening to differing suggestions. After you have listened and had time to consider it carefully, if the requests seem reasonable, give consent. Do not be afraid of spoiling them, especially your wife. It develops her femininity and gentle side. She will feel more loved and therefore more loving. And with children, although it is unwise to provide them with an overabundance of material things, they can be granted many little concessions which are absolutely harmless. For example, my little girl once asked her mother if she could wear her new dress to bed. Sensing how much it would mean, her mother said "yes." This child is an adult now and has never forgotten this unusual concession. The more ridiculous the request, the more children seem to appreciate it.

If the request is not justified, if it is selfish or unwise, make your refusal gently. Again, show sympathy for feelings. If the desire is right but you cannot possibly grant it at present, then express your deep regret that you cannot and state your desire to give it if you could.

Let them know that there is nothing you would rather do than give things to those you really love. Your attitude in giving, your willingness to give, is more important than the gift itself and just as much proof of your love.

Whatever you do, never ignore or disregard a request, however insignificant it may seem to you. Very often a little boy will request a sailboat or some other item which may seem of no consequence to his father, but to him it means everything. His heartfelt desire needs to be recognized. A man might think he would like something else just as much and, because it may be easier to obtain, might supply a substitute. If it is not wise or possible to have what he wants immediately, he must somehow be taught patience to wait. Perhaps some sacrifices may have to be made. This sympathy and understanding of the father may mean more than the toy itself. *Whatever our children ask, they should have a listening ear and sympathy and consideration for their desires.* The Savior taught, "If your children ask for bread, do you give them a stone?" A cold denial of a heartfelt desire can make a woman or a child feel that you have given them a "stone."

14. *Listening to problems:* As their leader, your family will confront you with many problems, great and small. Some are of major importance and must have careful consideration. Solutions should be sought or pointed out wherever possible. But all problems, great or small, should be listened to and considered. The wife especially needs her husband's help with her problems, for she is dependent upon him. He holds the power of decision.

With small problems and especially with children, it may be only sympathy they need. They need to know that someone understands. They do not always need or *want* solutions. For example, if Johnny is shunned at school, it may be difficult to find real solutions. Nor is this necessarily what he needs or wants. He wants your sympathy for his problem. He needs to know that you are with him, that he is not alone. Often children will resist attempted solutions since what they really want is understanding. You can be assured that if either wife or children resist your solutions, you are failing to give what they really want . . . sympathy.

This is not to suggest, as in the case of Johnny, that you should not also point out methods of dealing with the situation. Perhaps he must make improvements in himself. And although these may not be the full solution, they teach a person how to cope with problems. Even this should be preceded by a sincere sympathy for the problem itself.

Never use negative means of minimizing a problem. For example, never say, "I had it far worse," or "Others have a harder time than you," or "You should be thankful for what you have." These remarks make a person feel foolish or ashamed for bringing the problem to your attention. They will regard you as being critical and lacking in sympathy. A positive means of minimizing a problem, however, is this: "You have lived through more difficult things than this." This makes a person feel heroic and is a recognition of the faith you have in him.

15. *Listening to objections, complaints, and dissenting voices:* A difficult time in leadership is in dealing with objections and complaints. No one really likes this unpleasant task, so it is easy to minimize or turn aside from the problem. Sometimes the complaint is in opposition to your plans and decisions. This is a time when a man is most apt to become irritated and resist listening, feeling that his judgment is being questioned. He may be upset or even furious to have an opposing view presented when he has settled his mind and concluded things in another direction.

A man who is unwilling to listen to a dissenting voice is not equipped to lead. He does not have to yield—he only needs to listen and consider. To do so is a most valuable aid in promoting good family relations. Right or wrong, they have a right to speak.

In ancient India kings held what was called a "dunbar court." These sessions were held almost daily at which time opportunity was given for the subjects to present themselves before the king to voice suggestions, criticism, or complaints. These courts were highly successful and promoted good relations. It will do the same for a father who is willing to listen.

It is important to stress that a leader need not heed all complaints. Without the knowledge he obtains from listening, how is he equipped to pass judgment? It is difficult to be sympathetic with someone who is bringing forth a criticism, but, such is one of the tests a real leader must face. He will not immediately take a defensive attitude or point out others' mistakes nor make them feel foolish or ashamed for voicing their complaints. Instead, he will be patient and sympathetic and attempt to view the problem from their point of view. Such is a good demonstration of respect for human rights and dignity.

16. *Hold to your convictions:* The supreme quality of leadership is for one to be able to hold firmly to his convictions. With all the velvet suggested—kindness, patience, consideration for ideas

and feelings of the dissenting voices—a good leader will hold fast to his convictions. He will follow the dictates of his own conscience and have the courage to follow his own judgment even in the face of opposition from those he loves. He will not be moved by pleas or tender feelings. If necessary, he is willing to bring bitter disappointment to his family in his obligation to his own feelings of what is right and wise. This quality is compared to the strength of fine steel that may bend slightly but will not yield to pressure. It is a trait of greatness among men. It makes for peace, order, and harmony in the home. And it brings security to women and children.

It is interesting to know what this quality in a man does for a woman. Although she loves the velvet in him, she needs his steel. This is her security in him. She may seek to rule, she may try to dominate, *but always she loves only her master.* This explains why a woman will sometimes stay with a tyrant when one would think she has every reason to leave him. He may be hard and sometimes even cruel, but she sticks to him like glue because his firmness brings security to her life.

Weak men, on the other hand, often lose their women. The man who can be dominated and pushed around does not earn respect from his wife and robs her of a deep need for security. In spite of a million kindnesses he does for her, years of sacrifice and devotion, she cannot tolerate her life with him.

A man I have known for many years married a girl of ambition and drive for worldly possessions. She had dreams of special accomplishments for her husband and in her mind had him fitting a different role from that which he had for himself. Although this was probably the greatest difficulty, it was compounded immeasurably by the fact that he would continually give in to her pressures . . . whims as well as deeper feelings.

Going against his better judgment, he would go into debt for things she "just had to have." Always there was the thought that she would be satisfied if she could have these things that meant so much. It became a matter of continual appeasement.

This man was a good worker, a reasonable provider, and true to his wife in every respect. His moral standards were above reproach. He was the epitome of kindness and long-suffering, being temperate in manner. He dedicated his life to looking after his family, always sublimating his own interests to theirs.

The consequences were that the *more he gave in, the greater was her disrespect for him.* Although the couple were "religious," with high standards, her feelings for him degenerated into a near contempt. The natural kindness and tenderness which was so typical of his character and which was actually so admired by many of his friends was, ironically, the quality which destroyed his marriage. Always compromising to avoid a showdown, being willing to give in rather than face her demands or unpleasantness, was finally the thing which brought on the ultimate failure. After twenty-five years of marriage, they went their separate ways.

Children also benefit from their father's firmness. They cannot respect a father they can push around. He does not provide security. They may as well be put out in the world by themselves, making their own decisions. He is not a guide they can rely upon. They only feel security when they have a father who will not yield to pressure. In divorce courts, children will almost invariably choose the parent who has been the most firm with them.

Women and children are *entitled* to firm leadership. They do not understand this need themselves. This explains why they so often try to dominate and pressure to get their way. In reality they are testing to see if the firmness they need is really there. They will love you more, respect you more, and feel far more secure if you will not yield against your better judgment.

17. *Seek God through prayer in your leadership position:*
When we realize the great responsibility that is ours as leaders of a family, a role that extends for a lifetime, and when we become aware of human rights and needs, the necessity for us to discern wisdom from foolishness, good judgment from poor, and the great consequence of our decisions, it becomes apparent that the role is beyond our capacity without the daily help of God. Without His help the risks are too great—with His help success is assured. If you will seek the Lord in daily prayer, naming specific needs and problems, placing your trust in Him, He will aid you and sustain you in the great calling which He has placed upon you.

UNDERSTANDING THE WOMAN'S
SUBORDINATE ROLE

A woman is very much in a subordinate position to her husband. The man leads, the woman follows. He holds the right of decision, the final say in everything. She is dependent upon him for all she has, for every freedom, every consideration, for everything she does and every place she goes. He holds the reins in the family.

And yet she shares equally the responsibility of the family. She shares the same sacred responsibility for its success, is a partner in its problems and burdens. She has a desire, probably even greater than her husband's, for a happy home and successful children. Yet, to accomplish her goals, she is dependent upon her husband . . . upon his decisions, his wisdom and judgment. She is at his mercy for justice, fair play, and understanding of her human needs and desires. Hers is a case of responsibility without final authority. She does not have control over her own life. In a way it is similar to the problem of our early American forefathers who had "taxation without representation."

It is vital that a man understand and appreciate this subordinate position. Suppose, if you can, that you were partially responsible for the success of a large industry. You have a deep desire for its success, feel keenly its problems, and search for solutions. But you have a president that rules over you. To a great extent your hands are tied. Everything you hope to accomplish, every goal or objective, is directly dependent upon him. You are at his mercy. Your only hope lies in his unselfish consideration—his appreciation of your ideas and feelings.

A woman has such goals as these. She wants a happy home and children. There are numerous things she believes are necessary to accomplish these goals. She wants a smooth-running home with conveniences and beauty—a home that will serve the family well. She wants good health and opportunities for the children and many, many more things that make a happy home. She also has deep human needs and rights herself. Filling these needs is an integral part of the home. And yet, she is at the mercy of her husband to accomplish these goals and needs. She is dependent upon his understanding, his unselfishness and kindly consideration of her. She is dependent upon his cooperation in reaching her objectives. He holds power over her, over everything she holds near and dear. Every desire of her heart is tied to him and his rule over her.

When a woman marries, she puts her faith and trust in her husband. She gives up her freedom and moves into his camp. When he denies her what is rightly hers, serious things can happen in the marriage. Love is apt to disappear altogether, for love will soon vanish when selfishness and inconsideration enter in. Strange things also happen when a woman is denied human rights. For example:

Suppose a wife orders a new type of linoleum or floor covering for her kitchen. She immediately realizes that it is a poor choice. Her husband says it is fine and that she will get used to it. But as the months roll on, she finds it more and more difficult to live with. An attempt to explain to her husband is futile. He may even raise his voice and tell her that will be the end of the matter.

When a woman's rights are so easily put down, she may resort to strange behavior. She may develop a desire to move to a new community. (He would never consider a move to a different house in the same city. There would be no justification.) As her desire grows, she hints of it to him—he ignores it. Finally, she develops asthma, or some other reason develops where a move is necessary.

The same strange action may be noted in other situations wherein a woman may find herself trapped. She may want a doorway cut between the master bedroom and the hallway so she can hear her children at night. She may want a fireplace in the living room or some other desire that a man cannot understand. She may have made a mistake in selecting paint, furniture, drapes, tile, or carpeting, which she finds difficulty in living with. She tells herself again and again that it is of no consequence, but she finds herself continually disturbed by it and frustrated in being unable to make changes since her husband is unwilling.

It is well to recognize the effect of color and design on human beings. The problems created by lack of harmony in our daily environment are marked and cannot be ignored. They are not whims of the imagination. These are real problems, and strange and unpredictable behavior occurs when one is trapped in such a situation.

A woman is not always honest in her dealings with her husband. She cannot be. This is because of her subordinate position. Often she must say "no" when she means "yes." She may concoct false reasons for her action, untrue justification for her desires. A man, she may reason, will never understand. She has no power to meet her needs.

A wise leader can change all of this nonsense. If he will understand her subordinate position, he can end his problems and hers. He certainly does not have to give in against his judgment, but he can learn to be as fair with her as he is with himself. When a man makes a mistake what does he do? He changes things. If he buys a new car he does not like, he turns it in on another model.

He may consult his wife, but, holding the power of decision, he can make the change. Not so with a woman. She must go through official channels. She is utterly dependent upon her husband for changes.

When a man understands the sensitive position his wife occupies and her vulnerability to neglect and abuse when he is insensitive or selfish, he can appreciate why she reacts as she often does. The hard and embittered attitude of some women crying for "liberation" can be understood.

In man's leadership of his family, it is plain to see that there are many things to be considered. Sound instructions need to be given, encouragement and understanding offered, human rights respected, and justice and mercy must be exercised. The responsibility is a great one, extending for a lifetime, for even when sons and daughters marry, they need their father's guidance. If he has given wise leadership in their youth, they will turn to him, naturally, for further guidance along life's paths. But this responsibility, great as it is, it is not beyond the capacity of man to do, and to do it well. He need only apply the principles of good leadership, as have been outlined, and seek divine guidance in his calling.

PRINCIPLES OF GOOD LEADERSHIP

1. Assume the leadership responsibility as a sacred calling.
2. Instruct family in good principles to live by.
3. Provide a sense of direction.
4. Display confidence.
5. Seek knowledge before making plans and decisions.
6. Consult family members for their viewpoint and feelings.
7. Be decisive.
8. Allow for your mistakes.
9. Win their support.
10. Sometimes keep reasons confidential.
11. Be consistent—follow through.
12. Listen to family ideas and suggestions.
13. Listen to and consider requests and desires.
14. Listen to problems, offer solutions or sympathy.
15. Listen to objections, complaints, and dissenting voices.
16. Hold to your convictions.
    a. Don't be pushed around.

      b. Don't be pressured against your better judgment.
      c. Don't compromise.
      d. Have the courage of your convictions.
17. Seek God through prayer.

V
MAN THE PROTECTOR

A part of the male responsibility in life is to protect women and children, especially members of one's own family. As has been stated, this masculine role is God-assigned, and to aid him in his role as the protector, man was created with a body which is physically stronger, with greater endurance than the woman's. God also placed within him a natural courage that women do not have and implanted in his nature an instinct to defend and shield from harm those who need such care.

The role of the protector is more than a responsibility—it is an opportunity to grow as a man. In serving the gentler sex and protecting the weakness of children in shielding them from the hardness and difficulties of life, a man naturally develops his strength and manliness. To be robbed of this opportunity to protect and shelter is to be robbed of manly growth.

Yet it must be recognized that the opportunities to protect the family are not the same as they have always been. For example, in the early days of American life, families needed protection from Indians, snakes, and wild beasts. The elements had to be subdued. Often men had to build their shelters with their own hands and cut their supply of wood as protection against winter's cold. Demanding necessity required a man to protect his family; otherwise they would perish. As was quoted from "When a Man's a Man" in the introduction of this book, "in this land a man, to live, must be a man." Although opportunities to protect the family today are less demanding and different in many respects, there is still a need for protection in some very vital ways. Women and children need men to protect them from the *dangers, strenuous work,* and *difficulties of life.*

PROTECTIONS FROM DANGERS

Women and children need protection in a particular way concerning three types of dangers—sexual assault, evil influences which corrupt the mind and spirit, and the hard elements of life:

1. *Sexual assault:* Ours is a dangerous world with many evils on all sides. Drugs, alcohol, immorality and other corruptive vices create callousness in men and encourage evil designs. The danger of sexual assault and along with it the threat to life itself is greater than at any time in history. Not only should masculine protection be offered, it should be insisted upon.

Women and children should not be permitted to go places alone at night or to enter questionable environments or be escorted by persons not entirely trustworthy. Girls should not be permitted to hitchhike. Those who do risk their chastity and their very lives. The fact that they put themselves at the mercy of the motorist shows a lack of awareness of these dangers, which further proves their need for masculine protection.

Women sometimes willfully go their way unprotected in the world, but do not let this deceive you. They do so out of a strong disposition to accomplish a goal or task. Although women may appear to be independent and even resist the protection of men, they love for men to insist upon protecting them. I have known women who have resisted a man's protection, but smile with admiration when he insists.

2. *Evil influences:* Our families also need to be carefully guarded against unwholesome influences which would corrupt mind and spirit. Trash movies, indecent literature, and unwholesome company as well as drugs, alcohol, immorality, and other corruptive evils are threats to women and children which could lead them to great mental and emotional harm. Especially do our children need to be protected from these evil influences, since they are often too young and innocent to comprehend the danger to themselves.

3. *The hard elements:* Women and children need protection from the hard elements of the world—the cold, the wind, the

rough terrain, heavy traffic, heavy equipment, lightning, thunder, and even dogs, spiders, and mice. It may seem strange to you that women need protection from such things as spiders and mice. The truth is that whether the woman actually needs this protection is not so important as the fact that she *thinks* she needs it. If her fear is apparent, if she is trembling at the sight of a shadow in the dark, her fear is just as real as if she were frightened by a tiger. It is comforting for her to have a man calm her fears and place himself as a barrier against the dangers.

PROTECTION FROM STRENUOUS OR MASCULINE WORK

The need persists for women and children to be protected from *strenuous work* which produces undue physical strain. Working with heavy equipment, lifting boxes, moving mattresses, hauling rocks, etc. are masculine chores and are difficult for most women. It is true they have the capacity for some of this work, but it is an assault on their femininity to have to do it. In preserving and protecting the delicate natures of women and children one enhances his masculinity. Because this is an acute problem we shall deal with it in more detail later in this chapter.

LACK OF PROTECTION TODAY

There is a noticeable lack of feminine protection today. Women are seen everywhere with no concern as to their safety. They take long distance trips alone and walk unguarded down dark streets. We find women doing all kinds of masculine work—lifting heavy bundles, fixing the plumbing, repairing the furnace, working with heavy equipment, and doing other difficult tasks.

Several years ago I had an experience which saddens me as I recall it. I rented a trailer from a man to do some light moving. When I returned the trailer, his wife was on duty. She was dressed in heavy work clothes, wore shoes which resembled army combat boots, and wore a man's cap. At first glance I thought she was a man. As I tried to unhitch the trailer, she moved in with a large wrench and said, "Here, let me take care of this." She was competent and knew just what to do. When it was unhitched, I started to push it to the spot it had to go, but she said, "Let me do that," and she pushed me aside.

I do not know whether her husband placed her in this position, allowed her to do it, or whether she willingly assumed this manly task, but I do know that if her husband were a real man, if he knew the meaning of chivalry and the need to preserve femininity as well as his own feeling of manliness, he would never have allowed her to take over this masculine work.

I recall another disturbing experience, this time in the Far East. To me the Oriental women have always represented something special in femininity. Their features are small and delicate, and they seem to be soft and dependent in nature. Traveling in Hong Kong I noticed a large construction job, apparently a multi-storied hotel. There was a line of several dozen women carrying mortar in a hod to the masons. To see these gentle little women bending their backs to carry a load such as this and in a masculine trade was enough to bring tears to the eyes. I am not analyzing the hard economics of life in China, or the responsibiliy the men had in this case. I can only say it seems pathetic that any of the lovely ladies of our world must so serve.

Certainly women are somewhat to blame themselves. Many of them have by choice taken over masculine responsibility. They have not respected themselves as women and are responsible for moving into the man's realm. But I do know that in a majority of cases men are to blame. Men sit back and allow women to lift heavy objects and struggle with many chores. The women may at first request manly assistance, but due to neglect, laziness, or lack of responsibility, the men do not take hold of their masculine duties. Women are forced to do the man's work in a great many cases because the men do not offer to, or sometimes even refuse to. To keep peace in the family, solve problems, and avoid friction, women quietly do the man's work themselves.

Children also are often unprotected. A young girl told me that when she was sixteen her parents sent her alone with strange people to travel to the East. She had never met them before, but to save money the parents paid these strangers for her transportation. In another instance a young girl was sent to a large city alone to find a job. She was only seventeen and arrived at the train station with no one to meet her. She had to find city transportation to a prearranged place she was to stay. She sought work by herself, solved her own problems, and fought her own way in life. One may rationalize and suggest that it is good for young people to meet such situations, but the dangers involved are too great.

Some children are allowed to do heavy work far beyond their capacity. Although it is developing for them to learn responsibility and do hard work, it should always be limited to the capacity of their years.

HARM IN THE LACK OF PROTECTION

Harm to the woman: Lack of protection greatly diminishes the femininity of women. As they take upon themselves masculine responsibility, brave the world, and assume burdens beyond their normal capacity, they acquire a certain masculine ability.

There are many women who have become quite competent in masculine tasks. They paint with skill, are adept at repairing a machine, and are able to lay cement. They fight their own battles and make their own way in life. But the important thing to note is that as they become competent in masculine labor, they tend to lose their womanliness.

Let me refer you again to the lady who unhitched the trailer for me. As she moved into the man's world, she did so at the expense of her femininity. She was trying to be of assistance to her husband, and helpful to me, but at what price? I could not regard her as a woman. She was repulsive and awkward in her dress. I had sympathy for her and even a feeling of heartfelt compassion, but I did not feel I was in the presence of true womanhood. And yet I could see that she could have been a real woman. She could have been feminine and charming.

As a woman is placed in her natural sphere, surrounded by the feminine tasks, as she moves about her domestic surroundings with her natural adaptability to her world, she is a delight to a man. Here is heaven's creature, born to be vastly different from man. She has a charm, probably unknown to herself when in her natural sphere. But this charm is lost, and what a loss it is, as she moves in the man's world.

Lack of protection can also cause a woman to develop a *resentful attitude* towards her husband. If she asks for his help and is ignored or refused, it can cause several feelings to occur. In the first place, it is an insult to her femininity to be refused masculine help. She may also feel it evidence that he does not care about her. And she cannot regard him as much of a man for refusing to do work which is rightly his. If, out of necessity, she must do the job herself, she will feel imposed upon and deserted. Such feelings join together to form a resentful attitude. Women desire and expect chivalry and protection from men. When they do not receive it, their feelings are naturally altered. They will probably not realize the cause of such feelings, but they will be felt nevertheless.

Harm to the man: The man also suffers a loss of masculinity. As he fails to do the man's work, he denies himself the feeling of manliness, one which could bring him great satisfaction. He loses one of his opportunities to grow as a man. In neglecting a duty that is rightly his, he can develop a negative attitude towards himself, a feeling of guilt for neglect of duty. It is a great principle of truth that unless we assume the burdens that are ours, we cannot attain a feeling of well-being and happiness.

Harm to the household: The man's failure to perform his household tasks is the cause of much discord in many homes. The subject of much discussion and even humor in the households of this country is the husband who disregards the leaky roof, the uncut lawn, or unwashed family car as he sits down to read the paper or watch T.V. As the wife patiently waits until Saturday, the man sneaks out of the house to play golf, fish, or play games with his men friends. Should he be surprised, then, if the wife, who first gently asked him, then patiently reminded him, has finally resorted to harping and nagging to get an essential household chore accomplished? She is not to blame; her husband has brought this upon her. He has produced a nagging wife through his neglect of duty. And this has brought discord into the home.

Harm to children: Children are greatly harmed by the lack of protection from dangers. When allowed to enter the dangers of the world unprotected, it may be true that they develop a self-reliance out of necessity. But this will occur at the expense of their feelings towards their father. His lack of protection is evidence to them of his lack of concern and therefore his lack of love. They do not feel treasured. One always protects that which is treasured. This disregard for them and their safety is painful to them.

If children are given strenuous work to do beyond their normal capacity, they may carry their burdens without complaint but not without injury to their feelings. Their attitude towards their parents will be adversely affected. They will interpret it as lack of love and concern. The greatest need children have from their parents is to be loved and treasured. Any evidence of a lack of love and concern can greatly harm the child. Studies among youngsters who are in serious trouble usually disclose a feeling of being unwanted, unloved, and misunderstood. Here is the so-called generation gap.

SUGGESTIONS FOR PROTECTING WOMEN FROM STRENUOUS OR MASCULINE WORK

Certain duties around the house are too strenuous for women, and therefore belong to the man. The man, however, is inclined to think that because the work is associated with the home, it falls into the wife's category. Or, if he has worked hard all day and brought home the paycheck, he may feel he has done his part. He may expect to do these jobs *if* he can find the time or *when* he feels like it, but does not have it in his mind as a direct responsibility. The fact is that someone must do the man's work. If it is beyond a woman's strength or ability or is of a masculine nature and therefore not proper for her, who is to do it? The man's masculine assistance is essential; yet not receiving this assistance is the source of discord in many families. The solutions, however, are simple, and a suggested outline is given here.

1. *Divide household responsibilities:*

   a) *Her work:* Cleaning the house, cooking, shopping, care of the children, sewing, washing, ironing, transporting children, etc.
   b) *Your regular home duties:* Cleaning the garage, doing the yard work, washing the car, keeping the house in general repair, changing the filter on the furnace, putting salt in the water softener, keeping house painted, etc.
   c) *Your occasional or emergency duties:* Moving furniture, repairing equipment, lifting in heavy groceries, building shelves, etc.

First, divide responsibilities so that they are clearly defined, and there will be no misunderstandings. Discuss it with your wife in detail and come to a mutual agreement on each duty. Some jobs can be done by either the man or the woman, such as transporting the children to music lessons or doing the grocery shopping. The important thing is to have a clear understanding about who is to assume the job.

2. *Getting your regular home duties done:* It is important to place these home duties in *proper priority* along with your other activities. They certainly do not take preference over regular employment, but they are in priority over sports and entertainment. This is likely a touchy spot for many men who feel this recreational activity and commitment with friends to be of prime importance. But consider it this way: A man who does not place these home responsibilities ahead of his own pleasures is not setting a proper example to his wife and children. He can hardly complain if his wife fails to have meals on time because she was visiting on the telephone, or his children fail to do their job because they were too busy playing.

Once you know what you must do, set a particular time during the week to do your work. Early morning is excellent as it is usually free of interruptions. You will find satisfaction in getting these jobs done quickly and regularly and will soon form the habit along with other responsibility in life.

In work such as yard work, painting, and cleaning the garage, children can be assigned the duty, or the job can be hired out to someone else. But the man should assume the responsibility to *follow through* and see that the job is completed and not expect his wife to worry about it. A major part of any responsibility is "seeing that it gets done." There is nothing so disheartening to a woman as to hear her husband say, "All right, children, get the weeds pulled and the yard cleaned up," and then leave it up to her to see that they do it. She might as well take over the responsibility herself.

If a woman has been used to worrying about a man's job, she may find it difficult to "let go" completely. She may remind her husband frequently to get the job done, a habit which can be very annoying to a man. The solution lies in his letting her know that he accepts the responsibility and that she is not to worry about it. He should tell her that whether he does it or neglects it is his concern and that in any case she is not to remind him or be concerned about it. This will be the means of his more completely feeling the responsibility and therefore getting the job done.

3. *Facing the occasional or emergency duties:* These are the jobs that are not on the regular schedule. They arise as emergencies, and one may not even be aware of them unless the wife points them out. They are a source of real contention in many

families, since the wife must ask her husband to do them, and it may appear that she is nagging.

When such requests are made, a man is usually not in the frame of mind to respond. He may be preoccupied with other things. They were not in his plans, and, not wanting to be bothered, he ignores them, hoping they will go away. Since they don't usually go away, he finds himself being reminded again and again, which only builds up the more resistance to doing them. Finally, the frustrated wife gives up, calls a repairman, or does the job herself. The trouble is that now she has a resentment towards her husband.

This painful problem can be resolved in the following ways:

a) Face the responsibility as yours, not hers. This is not a favor she is asking; you're part of the household, too.

b) Get the job done immediately and out of the way if possible.

c) If you cannot do it immediately, tell her you will do it, and add it to your notebook of home responsibility. Arrange a definite time to do it or hire it done.

d) Most important—let her know you have assumed the responsibility, you're concerned about it, and that she has no further worry about it.

When the job has been taken care of, don't act like you have done some big favor for your wife for which she is now indebted to you. She may appreciate it and offer gratitude, but the job was yours and should be regarded as such. Any job requiring masculine strength or ability belongs to the man and not the woman. It seems trite to have to dwell on such simple problems which have such simple solutions, but the sad fact is that they are a major source of friction in a home. A man who will willingly perform these duties will be greatly appreciated.

The joy of living is greatly increased when a home is kept in good repair. It is wiser to live in a smaller, less expensive home which is well cared for, painted, and in good condition than to live in more luxury where things tend to fall apart. A well kept house is basic to good living and a marvelous example to the children. Whether the house is humble or not is of no matter. In establishing these priorities, a man may have to adjust his values and use self-discipline, but it will greatly aid him in his overall responsibility as a man and bring harmony into the home.

4. *Preparation for home duties:* Some men are inadequately

prepared for their work in the home. Despite training in a specialized field in which they are highly educated and skilled, they may know little or nothing about repairing a toilet, planting a lawn, carpentry, or fixing a motor. No one likes to take on a job in which he feels incompetent, so one has no choice but to hire it done or learn the rudiments of handling it. Again, it is not the wife's responsibility to acquire this knowledge, so if a man doesn't know, he is expected to learn. Although one may find it easier to hire these chores done, there is satisfaction in learning how to solve many of the household maintenance problems. There are numerous emergencies from time to time when immediate outside help is not available. Family members at such times will look to the head of the family for solutions.

Fortunately much information is available to help us. Adult education sometimes offers courses in such subjects. The classes are given at a very modest fee. Books are available on all such subjects as well. Another good source are friends and acquaintances who are not so inept as we may be.

When acquiring knowledge, do not do so as if it were a hobby in which you are expected to have a natural interest. Accept it as a necessary responsibility just as you would learn to read or write, earn a living, or do anything which is a preparation for life. When a woman marries, if she does not know how to cook, sew or clean, she is expected to learn. If she does not know how to make beds, change a baby's diaper or clean a home, she is expected to learn and is considered a failure if she does not. When she acquires this knowledge, she does not do so as if it were a hobby to satisfy her own interests—she does so as a preparation for a major responsibility. Our responsibility is obvious.

One can acquire some competence in such duties without expecting himself to have the art of the professional or the skill of the tradesman. One need learn only enough to fulfill the essential needs. Of course there is a great deal more satisfaction if one learns to perform a job well.

In summarizing man's protection of women from strenuous or masculine work, keep in mind that one will solve his problems by first dividing responsibility at home, outlining those duties which are his and either doing them or seeing that they are done by others. When emergencies arise, we should willingly take care of them or assure our wives that we will as soon as possible. A man should always give his work at home proper priority and regard it as his responsibility, not his wife's. If he lacks knowledge or skill, he should learn so that he can fill this important need.

PROTECTION FROM DIFFICULTIES

Women and children need to be protected from certain difficulties of life. These include problems which require masculine fortitude to cope with, problems which otherwise would produce worry and strain beyond the capacity of women and children. They need to be protected from situations with troublesome people in which they may be insulted, imposed upon, pressured, taken unfair advantage of, or misused in any way. Women, especially, are inclined to be subjected to such misuse unless protected by a man.

For example, a relative or friend may impose unduly on a woman. Perhaps special favors or considerations are expected, and she is overpowered by these requests. Accommodating by nature, she may not have the strength to refuse or know how to deal forcefully with the matter. Or she may be pressured to take on burdens or responsibility which she may not want or have time for. Rather than to criticize her for taking on more than she can handle, help her to reduce her commitments and become uninvolved.

Another example is when a woman is pressured by a salesman to buy something she really does not want. Or he may extract a commitment from her to buy something on the time payment plan. Before she knows what she is doing she has signed on the dotted line and finds herself with a binding obligation she wished to avoid, and lacking the fortitude to do something about it. A man can come to her rescue and usually legally remove her commitment, since the law tends to be lenient towards a wife in these cases.

Special difficulties are such things as an accident with the car or financial entanglements. An overdrawn checking account, unbalanced budget, living beyond one's means and other financial difficulties can bring a woman to a painful predicament. She may have no one to look to but her husband to find her way out. What a comfort to her is the man who will show forth sympathy and lend a helping hand in seeking solutions. A foolish woman may need some counseling and even a severe lecture, but this should be withheld until the problem is solved.

Another difficulty occurs when a woman makes a purchase

covered by a warranty only to find the product inferior or in some way deficient. In attempting to recover the loss, she may confront an unreliable firm who offers excuses and willfully tries to avoid the obligation. She is in a situation where she is unable to bring them to terms. It is natural for her to turn to her husband, hoping his forceful nature will be sufficient to deal with the problem.

Tender women are also very much perplexed by harsh, open criticism. If the criticism is unjust and she is unable to defend herself, she will need assistance. These illustrate some of the difficulties women may find themselves in. Children, too, experience difficulties and need protection of adults, especially their father.

In summary, let us remember that women and children need protection in three ways:

1) Protection from dangers
2) Protection from strenuous or masculine work
3) Protection from difficulties

REWARDS OF CHIVALRY

In reviewing the role of the man as the protector, let me assure you that this service is greatly appreciated. Your wife and children may take for granted your role as the guide and provider of life's necessities, but when a man steps out to defend and shield those who are less able to do so for themselves, he becomes a hero in their eyes.

The story has been told for generations of how Sir Walter Raleigh placed his cloak over the mud for Queen Elizabeth to walk upon. So great was her appreciation that she made him a knight. Did she do as much for the soldiers who fought valiantly for her?

Women and children cannot forget the acts of chivalry from men. Such protection is in reality a "velvet" trait, but because it is dependent upon a man's strength, ability, and courage, we have studied it as a "steel" trait. Chivalry is, in fact, both steel and velvet which is why it is so appealing to women.

What it does for the man has already been explained as an opportunity to develop strong courage and forcefulness. It solves many problems in family life and brings love, peace, and harmony into the home.

VI
MAN THE PROVIDER

> In the sweat of thy face shalt
> thou eat bread, until thou
> return to the ground.   (Gen. 3:19)

We have already learned of the man's sacred responsibility to "rule the family" and to protect them from the hardness of life. His obligation to provide the living is just as sacred, for in the beginning God said, "In the sweat of thy face shalt thou eat bread, until thou return to the ground." We need to remember that this command was not given to the woman, but to the *man*. This he must do regardless of the struggle involved or the diversion of other interests that may be uppermost in his mind.

When God placed man in the world and gave him the divine command of earning his bread, he *cursed* the ground with noxious weeds, thorns and thistles. This action was not entirely punishment, however—it was also a blessing, for He said, "I have cursed the ground *for thy sake*." The thorns and thistles were given as opportunities to help him grow as a man. All of the struggles, burdens and difficulties that men face in earning the living are for a divine purpose and should be regarded as opportunities for personal growth.

There is a certain disregard in modern times for the sacred and traditional role of the man as the provider for the family. Efforts to change the law would remove the man's obligation to pay alimony in the event of divorce. The proposed laws place an equal burden on the woman for the support of the family. Modern *trends* also follow this pattern of thinking. Many feel that the man's role as sole provider is unfair, that it overtaxes the man and may be injurious to his health. They advocate a sharing of the burden of earning the living, with the wife taking equal responsibility. In return the man is expected to share the burden of housework and care of the children.

Some modern trends even go so far as to suggest that society share the burden of the living. When the man's load grows heavy, he is to turn to the government for assistance. It is suggested that all men draw an unearned income from the government, whether he needs it or not. This is a far removal from God's command and has led us away from the simple truth and established many false teachings and destructive practices.

Modern trends and laws do not establish correct principles. We must return to God for proof that the man is the divinely appointed provider for the family. Any failure on his part to do so is a serious neglect of duty. In the New Testament the Apostle Paul warned, "If any provide not for his own, he hath denied the faith and is worse than an infidel." (1 Tim. 5:8)

The responsibility to provide the living should be in top priority in a man's life—his first and foremost obligation. Often a man, on the contrary, will have a greater desire for personal fulfillment, to develop some talent or make some worthy contribution to the world or in some way "leave his footprints on the sands of time." Noble as these goals are and important as they may be, they are secondary to his responsibility to provide the living.

Not only is his a sacred responsibility—it is a *moral one*. Each man born into the world has a moral obligation to take care of himself, his wife and children. The man who does so is a gift to society. The man who does not, is a burden. Because of his failure, others must sacrifice to take care of the needs of his family—a responsibility that in reality belongs to him. In his failure to provide the simple necessities of life, he has failed as a man. He does not have strength, but weakness. Here is the most fundamental area where he must function in order to be a man. *The man who does not provide for his own is not a man.*

WHAT A MAN SHOULD PROVIDE

Simply stated, the man should provide the *necessities*. This means food, clothing, and a shelter—plus a few comforts and conveniences. Through all generations of time it has been recognized that when a man marries, his wife and children are entitled to his financial support. Failure to meet this obligation has been just cause for divorce, and even after the marriage separation, the man is still under financial obligation. Financial support and, along with this, "fidelity" have always been the two main conditions in marriage to which a woman is entitled. But, whether these laws remain in force or not, the moral and sacred obligation is just as binding—the need just as great.

It is important that the man provide a shelter separate and apart from anyone else. This is important for the sake of privacy and giving the wife the opportunity of making her house a home in her own way. Perhaps this is why a special instruction was given by God, immediately after he created the man: "Therefore shall a man leave his father and mother and cleave unto his wife." (Gen. 2:24) Under stress of circumstances there may be a tendency for a man to move his wife and children in with parents, to ease his burdens. Although there may be some justification for this temporarily, it is contrary to the divine plan and unfair to the wife if this situation extends for any time beyond a brief emergency.

Although a man has a sacred and binding obligation to provide the necessities, he is under no such obligation to provide the *luxuries*. Women and children are not entitled to ease and luxury, to style and elegance. The man's duty is not to provide a costly home, expensive furniture and decor. Concerning the education of his children, he does have some obligation to provide them with a basic education, but such a binding obligation does not extend to a higher education, music lessons, the arts and cultures. He may wish to provide these—and it may bring him much pleasure in doing so, but it is not his responsibility.

In providing a high standard of living, some men make near economic slaves of themselves with great disadvantage to themselves and to their families. Too often a man is so consumed with meeting ever-increasing demands placed upon him—not only by his family, but by himself, that he does not preserve himself for things of greater value. He has little time to give to his wife and children—time to teach them the great values of life, how to live, standards to follow—and time to build strong family ties.

A man also is entitled to some time for himself, for recreation, study, meditation, etc. And he has a need to be of service outside his own circle, a commitment to society, as we shall see later on in this writing. Church service is an important part of this as is civic responsibility. Men have talents which need to be shared, ability which could be developed to make the world a better place. *It is not right for a man to spend his entire time and energy to provide luxuries for his own family circle.*

MAN'S CAPACITY TO PROVIDE

Let us examine how God has prepared man to fulfill his responsibility to provide. His preparation includes physical, emotional, and temperamental make-ups.

A normal man who has adequately preserved the body God has given him is a perfect specimen for his work. He has a strong body which functions beautifully under normal strain. To see a man at his work, his muscles functioning in beautiful coordination, is to see the handiwork of God. He has great physical endurance, taking day-in and day-out toil which extends for a lifetime. He enjoys the flexing of muscles and the habit of work.

The man was blessed with the emotional make-up to endure the demands of his work—the stresses and strains of the marketplace, the roar of industry, the uncertainties of the crops in the field, and the financial challenges of the office. He can endure worry and has the capacity to overcome his obstacles, solve his problems, and thus succeed at his work.

He is competitive in temperament, a characteristic fitting him to gain his place in the working world. He is aggressive, decisive, and possesses all the qualities necessary in dealing with perplexing problems in a challenging world.

There are, of course, many men who succumb to the pressures of the working world. Statistics point out that the competitive business world is killing our men. Since the man's life expectancy is somewhat less than the female, his arduous life style is said to be destroying him.

In reality men do not die so much because of their work as because of other things. He may not have taken proper care of his health, may have filled his body with bad food, drugs, alcohol, tobacco, etc. Or, he may be suffering from frustration engendered in the relationship with his wife and children. They may be making demands of him, demands which are unjust and unreasonable. Further frustrations occur because he has not assumed his rightful place as leader. If his home life is filled with turmoil and unpleasantness, he will feel strain in his work.

Or he may be working too hard and too long in providing the luxuries for his family. This has taxed his body beyond its God-given capacity. His work has been blamed for killing him where in reality his "striving for luxuries" is doing so.

Any normal man, who has properly cared for his body and is in good health, has the capacity to provide the necessities of life for his family with reasonable ease. In addition he will have a reserve capacity, allowing for responsibility beyond his home as well as time for personal pursuits. God has blessed man with greater capacity than we sometimes suppose.

PRIDE IN HIS RESPONSIBILITY

There is a masculine pride in connection with a man's responsibility to provide the living which is inborn in a real man. He accepts his obligation with a willingness of spirit, regardless of the difficulties encountered. He is not a leaner; he is not looking for someone else to carry his burdens or to do what he is charged with doing. This natural instinct is not a vain weakness in men, but is implanted in them by God for a divine purpose—to assure that families will be adequately provided for.

For him there is satisfaction in knowing he has a niche to fill which is vital. He realizes that within his family, no one is so well suited to meet this need as himself, and he sees the benefit to himself and his family as he funtions in this important role. Security comes to all family members in seeing their leader struggle with difficulty, solve his problems, and cope with the challenging circumstances that confront him in earning the living. Confidence is focused on the individual rather than on material things, for they see that he is adaptable to the many unexpected and unpredictable events he may have to face.

A lady once told me that during the early years of her marriage her husband lost his job, as did many other men, when a financial recession struck their community. Many men were overcome with a defeated attitude. Her husband set out to find another job and would spend the entire day away, walking the streets, seeking interviews and doing everything conceivable to find a job.

Eventually he found work and during these years of recession made a living for his family. Family circumstances improved greatly later on, but this wife recalled these difficult years as the time when her husband really proved his adequacy as a responsible provider.

So great is the feeling of masculine pride with some men that they suffer real distress if they are unable to provide for their own. For example, a man of my acquaintance had been a good provider all of his married life until he had a serious illness which made him bedfast. His illness persisted for years with a gradual deterioration until it became apparent he would never work again. During this time his wife provided the living. She took care of the needs of the family and had his care to shoulder also.

This man of great pride suffered tremendously because of their reversal of roles. No justification for his predicament could ease the pain in seeing his frail and feminine wife have to shoulder the burden of earning the living. Great sadness overcame him day by day and he slipped, not only in body but in spirit.

Although this man may have failed in his inability to adjust to his circumstances, he is to be admired for his keen sense of responsibility. I am certain that when God placed pride in a man's heart, He did not intend that he never turn to others for assistance in times of emergency, or that there is any disgrace in accepting the benevolent kindness of those who really care about him—but I do feel that He intended that each man have pride in his manly role and not lean on others unless absolutely necessary.

FAILURES OF MEN TO PROVIDE

There is, unfortunately, a failure with some men to be responsible providers. This is illustrated in the pleading letter of a young woman who wrote:

"I cannot seem to accept one thing in my husband. He does not seem to care whether or not he provides for us. He was in the insurance business where he did very well, but quit because he wasn't happy in it. He now sells brushes which he says he likes, but only spends four hours a day doing it. Consequently we are desperate for money. We have been living with his parents for the past seven months and it doesn't even look hopeful that we might possibly have our own place to live. I am losing all respect for my husband and without respect there is not real love.

"My husband's parents tell me that he has never been a responsible person and that they were hopeful that our marriage would change this. They sympathize with me. What makes things worse is that I had to be very independent and responsible as a child and teenager; thus it is hard for me to unlearn these qualities. If my husband had these qualities, it would be easier for me to unlearn them."

Here is a man who has failed on several points. Not only does he fail to provide an adequate living with a home of his own, but he apparently is undisturbed by these unhappy circumstances. There is no evidence of remorse or suffering for this situation. No hope is offered that things will improve. Just because his former employment wasn't so much to his liking is not justification to leave it for a lesser job, no matter how much he enjoyed the new job. Whether a man likes his work may be important, but it is secondary to its being adequate in providing a living.

Another situation concerns a young couple with three small children. They were a beautiful pair, both handsome and intelligent. The husband had the misfortune of losing his job. He made an effort to find work but jobs for which he was trained were very difficult to find. In the process of deciding how to best solve his problems, he approached his wife with the suggestion that she find a job. He offered to remain at home and care for the children as he felt she likely could find employment sooner than himself.

His wife was shocked and crushed at this suggestion. In pouring forth her heartfelt feelings and seeking advice as to how she should react to his suggestion, several deep feelings were expressed: 1) She loved being with her children and cherished her time with them. She felt a duty to guide and train them and never dreamed of leaving this responsibility. To do so was a great personal sacrifice to her. 2) The husband's situation was not a desperate one. Several jobs were available but he wanted to wait for something more in line with his training. She felt this demonstrated a poor sense of values on his part. 3) She was suffering an emotional adjustment towards her husband—a disillusionment stemming from his failure to feel responsibility, his lack of manly pride in his duty to provide. Instead of lifting the burden, he was turning to her to do so. Her feeling of security in him was being threatened. The romantic feeling was disappearing. Many men fail to realize this strong emotional feeling in women, wherein they yearn to be protected by the man they love.

Take in contrast the case of another couple. This man had also lost his job. He was a highly skilled technician and also could not find work in line with his training. His circumstances were just as desperate. But instead of turning to his wife for the solution, he took a lesser job. The only job he could find was working as a farm laborer in the fields. This meager work was tiring and poor pay, but it solved his problems. Some would have said that this man "lacked pride" in humiliating himself to accept unskilled work. I say the opposite. He *had* genuine masculine pride in his responsibilities. He was willing to do whatever was necessary in order to fulfill an obligation that was his.

Many men are gross failures in that they lean on the state to provide for them when there is no justifiable reason. They may feign an illness or pretend to seek work, but fail deliberately to find it. Always there is a shirking of the responsibility to work. In deceit and weakness they force others to carry the burdens that God has given to them. They are not men, but leeches on society—lambs, doves, kittens, but not men of steel.

THE WORKING WIFE

Millions of working wives are in the marketplace. In reviewing the sacred principle of the man providing the living, it appears that we have gone far afield from God's command. There are certainly emergencies wherein a wife must work, but the majority of these cases are not so justified. Certainly there are also individual circumstances where the earning of money to provide the basic living is not the motive. Consider the following reasons given for the working wife:

1. *Easing financial burdens:* Often a woman will offer to work to ease her husband's load. He may be under such financial difficulty that she may fear for his health. She may prefer not to work but is willing as a sacrifice to ease his burdens. This is very noble and unselfish, but unless it is absolutely necessary her husband should decline her offer by saying, "No, I will not allow you to work." Women love such a firm refusal. In fact, there is nothing a feminine domestic woman will delight in more than not being allowed to work. It is something she will likely boast of to her friends with pride. Together they can solve their problems by reducing their standard of living and employing principles of thrift and resourcefulness and thus preserve the husband's right to be the sole provider.

A contrasting situation occurs when it is the husband's idea for his wife to work. He may not only suggest she do so, but urge her to, literally shoving her into the working world against her will. I know a husband and wife, both school teachers, where the wife has been urged to work over the years. Her husband allows her only three weeks off for a baby. Always his justification is that they need the extra money. Her working clearly seems to be his idea. Surely there must be alternatives to such heavy dependence upon her which deny her the right to serve in her own feminine world.

Studies indicate that the working wife may not actually earn as much as supposed when one considers the extra expense demanded by her working, such as extra clothing, transportation, baby care, etc.

2. *Working for luxuries:* In the majority of cases women work for additional luxuries or conveniences, whether they admit this truth to themselves or not. It may be that she has a drive to meet the standards of friends and is overly material-minded. If her husband tries to discourage her from working, he may be met with great resistance. But in this case as with any other when she is not justified in working, her husband should exercise his right to insist that she not work. She will probably resent it temporarily, but will one day come to see that she has lived a better life than the woman who works for luxuries. This man has a difficult situation to cope with, for he must inspire her with a greater sense of values. She must be brought to realize the value of her presence in the home. She should further understand that in protecting his wife a man is preserving his pride. Some women have never understood these fundamental principles.

It may not be the woman, but the man, who has the desire for luxuries and suggests that his wife work. I know a man who sent his wife out to work so he could have a cabin in the mountains. The next year he wanted a boat to go with it. He felt that they would never have any of these pleasures if his wife did not supplement his income. She complied, and perhaps they did receive great pleasure from these material things. But there is a price to pay for such a decision, as I will explain.

3. *A broadening experience and greater fulfillment:* This rationale is frequently used as justification for the woman working, both by herself and her husband. They may feel that she will be a more interesting and happy person if she leaves the confines of home where she may be quite bored to seek a career on

the outside. Some feel that home life and tending children limits a woman's development and that she needs to get out where she can utilize her talents, intelligence, and gifts for not only the betterment of the world but of herself. Although this may sound good on the surface, some fundamental principles of life are being ignored which cannot be disregarded without serious consequences, as I will point out.

HARM IN WOMEN WORKING

1. *Harm to the woman:* When a woman shares the burden of earning the living, she tends to lose some of her femininity. This is so because in her home a woman has her best opportunity to acquire the charm of her womanliness. As she develops love, patience, and the feminine arts and skills, she acquires a charm that makes her *distinctly different from a man.* But when she rejects this role for that of the man's world, she tends to lose this luster and charm of her femininity. Instead, she must take on certain masculine characteristics to succeed in the working world.

Another harm is this: When a woman divides herself between two worlds, it is difficult for her to succeed in either. In her world alone she has challenge enough to achieve the domestic excellence she desires. Here she is the understanding wife, the devoted mother and homemaker and gains great satisfaction from a job well done. This takes great effort. But as she divides her time and interests between two worlds, she is not likely to succeed in either.

Even if she rejects her home sphere and turns her heart and soul to the working world, she will have difficulty, for in many jobs she will have a natural disadvantage. She will not meet man's excellence in his world, but will always be secondary to him. So she wanders between two worlds, having rejected her own where she could have been superior and gained great satisfaction and chosen the man's where she will never be anything but a second rate man.

When a woman works because it is her husband's idea, an even greater harm can come to her. His suggestion that she work casts doubts in her mind as to his adequacy as a man. If he must lean on her, she will question his ability to solve his problems and face responsibility that is his. This can cause her to feel insecure.

Still another harm to consider is the woman's relationship to her employer, especially if he is a man. The wife is accustomed to looking to her husband as the director of her activities. When she finds herself taking orders from another man, it is an unnatural situation for her. She owes him a certrain obedience as her employer, and in countless hours of close contact she may find herself physically attracted to him. Seeing him at his best and perhaps as a more dynamic and effective leader than her husband, she makes comparisons unfavorable to her husband whose faults and failings she knows all too well.

If her employer happens to be calloused and does not regard her with the measure of dignity she deserves, he may require of her work that is beyond her capacity or otherwise negative to her best interests. Or if he is unwholesome he may take unfair advantage of her, being aggressive or even demanding of her. He may be insulting or otherwise offensive. Regardless of her situation in the working world, a woman is out of her natural sphere when she is taking direction from anyone other than her husband. A man with a keen sense of responsibility towards his wife finds such a situation very abrasive and will avoid it if possible.

2. *Harm to the man:* When a man is made aware of his inadequacy to provide for his family, his masculinity suffers. If he has a natural pride in his responsibility, he will be terribly humiliated to fail in this important obligation and may feel himself to be less of a man than he wants to be.

His feelings towards his wife may also suffer. An important principle to recognize is that masculine men have a protective feeling towards women—an inborn desire to protect and shelter them. In fact, a man's feeling of love and tenderness towards a woman is very closely tied to his desire to protect and shelter her. When she joins the working world, she proves she can make her way without him. This naturally diminishes his protective feelings.

The man himself may not realize the pride and tender feelings he is robbed of when his wife works, especially if she has done so for a long period of time. For example, I am reminded of wandering nomads in the desert who have never seen more water than barely enough to quench the thirst or scantily bathe themselves. To attempt to explain to them how it would be to live beside a lake where the sound of fresh water continually played upon the shore would be something they could not comprehend. A quart of water to the nomad might seem an abundance. A man, likewise, may fail to experience that great sense of well-being that can surge through him by realizing he has measured up in the most important role he has, or that tender feeling as he protects his family from hunger and want.

3.   *Harm to the children:* When a mother works due to a compelling emergency, children seem to adjust to the situation quite remarkably. They are able to comprehend circumstances and seldom hold them against their parents. They may suffer neglect which may be harmful, but will not suffer a lack of love or concern.

If, however, the mother works by choice, great harm can come to the child. When he realizes that she prefers to work instead of taking care of him, that she places her interests, or luxuries, as more important, he will be apt to interpret this as lack of love and concern for his welfare.

The children of working mothers usually suffer considerable neglect. Not in all cases, but in most. The woman who works must dedicate herself to her job, in order to succeed and to earn her pay. During the working hours her job has priority. At times it may be demanding. Her children are less demanding. They are naturally the ones that suffer.

4.   *Harm to society:* The trend for the mother to be out of the home is a pattern of living which has extended for many years in America, since the emergency of World War II took millions of women into factories. It has been during this time that we have developed some of our most threatening social problems— marriage problems, divorce, violence in the streets and on the campus, drug abuse, rebellion against social customs and moral standards. Many of these problems can be traced to homes of working mothers. The children fail to develop properly. Some never learn to read, or have personality problems, or develop into mental cases, or fail to find purpose or happiness from life. They turn from the ways of the parents and seek new ways.

Dr. David V. Haws, acting chairman of psychiatry, General Hospital in Phoenix, has said, "Mother must be returned to the home. The standard of living is a fictitious thing. It is a woman's primordial function to stay home and raise children. She should not join the hunt with men. A man, too, feels less of a man when his wife works. If you don't leave a family of decent kids behind, you have left nothing. The footprints we leave on the sands of time are soon blown away. Basic to the solution of adolescent problems of any generation is an intact home." The problem of the working wife cannot be ignored as a prime contributor to trouble in society.

PREPARATION FOR ROLE AS PROVIDER

In planning his life's work, a young man should first try to get a wide scope of the possibilities. Too often young men limit their consideration to the work they are familiar with—the professions, school training, or work their father or relatives engage in. Such a limited choice may exclude talents and interests that the young man may have hidden within him.

One very good means of getting a broad scope of job opportunities is a book put out annually, called *Educational Outlook*. This can be checked out of the library or purchased from book stores. This book lists every conceivable occupation open to men. It will no doubt present many which you have never even considered as possibilities. After you have carefully made a search of possibilities in which you may be interested, consider the following priorities:

1.   *Providing an adequate living:* First in consideration is that the work will provide an adequate living. It will be necessary to consider the future and the number of children you hope to have. You will have an obligation to provide them with the necessities, some comforts and conveniences, and to keep them from financial worry and distress. You alone will be responsible to meet these needs. You cannot trust to luck or circumstances to see you through.

There will be a temptation to place other things ahead of this priority. A man may greatly wish to exercise some talent or ability, or to engage in work which may be highly useful to society. Important as these altruistic aims are, if they will not earn an adequate living, they will not be proper goals to consider. There have been men in history who have been dedicated reformers who have devoted their lives to curing the ills of society while their own familes suffered hunger and want. Artists and musicians, also, have justified their efforts as a noble work while their families were greatly neglected. The man who is a man will assume his God-given role as a provider and place it as his first and foremost obligation in life.

In addition to the necessities and comforts, a man may *wish* to provide his family with more. He may wish to attain a standard of living beyond the necessities and to provide his children with opportunities, etc. If so, then these must be taken into consideration when planning his life's work, for he alone will be responsible.

2. *Ability to succeed:* Next, a man will need to consider his ability to succeed in a chosen field. Do you have the talent, adaptability, or capacity for the job? You may have to turn to professional counseling for assistance in answering these questions. There are departments in both high schools and universities that have this service.

It is very disturbing to function in a job where one has difficulty in performing it well. Better to direct yourself into a job where you can give an adequate service. You must, of course, consider your own personality. Are you satisfied with mediocrity or will you never be satisfied unless you reach the top of your field? If not, then do you have the capacity to reach the top?

3. *Work you enjoy:* Of important consideration is that you enjoy the work you have chosen. The entire family is benefited when the father is happy in his work, and the man will function far better in a job which brings him satisfaction. Men are created with different interests and therefore have the capacity to enjoy some type of work far more than others. Some men can so dislike their work that it can bring them misery. Sometimes a father has found himself in the "wrong field" in the midstream of life and has had to change, to the great disadvantage of his family and himself.

4. *Is the work a challenge to your ability or capacity:* A serious mistake that many young men make is to choose a field that is too easy. They may have capacity far beyond their chosen field and have therefore frustrated their personal development and limited their potential. It is always wise to choose a field even a little beyond one's own capacity, that growth may take place in reaching upward.

5. *Is the work conducive to good family life:* Questions to ask yourself are, "Will the hours be conducive to good family living? Will I have to be out of town frequently? Will my work require Sundays, the day I should devote to the spiritual welfare of my family? Will the work be demanding in such a way that it will interfere too far with my family life?"

Another point to consider is the location of your job. Will it be in the city or the country, a metropolitan area or a suburb? Although this need not be a determining factor necessarily, it is well to consider that children are helped immeasurably by being next to the beauties of nature. It helps them to develop a faith in God and will assist them in character development, especially if they have the opportunity to be next to the soil where they will have some responsibility for work themselves.

6. *Financial means for preparation:* Next to consider is your financial situation and if you have the means for the education necessary. Some of the professions are very costly and beyond possibility for most young men without outside assistance. This will have to be considered along with your desire and adaptability.

7. *Service to humanity:* Consider the worth of the job itself and its usefulness to the world. It can be disheartening to a man to spend years of time and toil in a work that is of no real consequence. He may even be engaged in manufacturing things which are harmful to society rather than beneficial. This can plague a man's conscience and distress him so much that in middle age men have been known to develop a depressing feeling that life is passing them by. They search for some way to redeem themselves and often change jobs at a sacrifice of considerable money. A man's job should be important work, work upon which the success of the world depends. It need not be spectacular or revolutionary, but it needs to be essential. Participating in work that helps make the world a better place will bring a man a feeling of well-being, a feeling of contributing something to the world in addition to supporting his family.

VII
FAMILY FINANCES

Few families are free of anxieties and contentions in the matter of family finances. To some it is a matter of such major importance as to be an ever-festering sore, never healing and continually thwarting the happiness of the home. As a factor in marital breakup, it is one of the primary causes. Problems arising from debt, selfishness, unwise use of money, and conflict in values are sources of contention. Here are a few facts which, if recognized, will aid in the solutions to these problems:

THE MAN'S RESPONSIBILITIES

There are three major areas of responsibility that fall to the man in money matters:
  a)   To provide the money
  b)   To manage the money
  c)   To do the necessary worrying about the money

We emphasize continually that it is the man who should provide the income. Unfortunately many men think this is the full scope of their obligation. It is certainly a most important part, but by no means the total. What about the management of the money? Withoug wise direction, the money earned may not meet family needs.

As the *manager of finances,* the man will be expected to

manage the entire pay check. He will be responsible for house payments, car expense, insurance, taxes, medical bills, yard and house maintenance, and an allotment for his wife for household and personal use. He will be responsible for paying the bills, and if there is not enough money to cover these expenses, he will face this problem realistically. He will not expect his wife to take over this department. He will, of course, expect her to offer cooperation and to cut expenses when he requests, but the overall role in money management belongs to him.

In the ideal home the man will also do the necessary *worrying* about money. He will face the unpaid bills, insufficient funds, and creditors. If there is not enough money to cover expenses, this will be his concern. He will ponder over his problems, struggle with the difficulty, and seek solutions. If additional income must be secured, he will consider a second job. He will not allow his wife to do the worrying, but will protect her from it by *showing how concerned he is himself*. He will explain to her that he is giving careful thought to their problems, that he is greatly concerned, and that she is not to worry about it.

As the money manager, *a man must maintain his position as leader,* maintaining the power of decision in the family. Let me explain the importance of this: In solving financial problems, a man may have to make major changes—a change of jobs, move to another community, change to a less expensive residence, sell one car, or in other ways reduce the standard of living. To make these changes it is essential that he have power of decision, without resistance from his wife and children. If he is to make the living and to manage the money, he must maintain the power to solve his problems.

This makes it very clear why it is such a mistake to have the wife manage the money. She does not have the power of decision. She cannot make major changes to solve financial problems. It would be grossly unfair to expect a woman to manage the money unless she also has the power of decision. The role of the leader and money manager belong inseparably together.

THE WIFE'S RESPONSIBILITIES

The wife's responsibilities are decidedly different from a man's, but essential, and can often mean the difference between his success and failure.

a) To cooperate with her husband's plans and decisions in solving money problems or reaching financial goals
b) To provide a peaceful home atmosphere
c) To make a dollar stretch in the money allotted to her

1. *Cooperating with husband's plans:* The wife will be expected to cooperate with her husband in any changes he must make in solving their financial problems. If she can willingly accept a reduction in the standard of living, or can understand and accept major changes which will mean a sacrifice or an adjustment on her part, this will greatly assist her husband in his financial plans.

She is also expected to accept her husband's financial goals to "get ahead." The entire family may be expected to sacrifice things they need or want, but the wife will be the key in setting the proper attitude of complete cooperation. In fact, if the wife will not cooperate, will not willingly "go without," it is impossible for a man to reach a financial goal which requires sacrifice.

2. *Provide a peaceful home atmosphere:* The wife is to provide a home life relatively free of turmoil and disorder. When there is peace in the home, a man will be more successful in his work. And if he has financial problems, they will not be compounded by problems and pressures of home life. He will be able to think through his problems and reach solutions more easily.

3. *Making a dollar stretch:* The wife is often responsible for a man's financial success or downfall, according to how she manages the money allotted to her. We can make a comparison of two families with identical incomes and find that one is living in comfort and the other in poverty due to the wife's ability or inability to make the money stretch. A woman is expected to be economical, discriminating, and wise in the use of money, and thus greatly assists her husband in his financial obligations.

THE WIFE'S BUDGET

A prequisite to an understandable and workable relationship between husband and wife in handling money matters is the wife's budget, which should cover the following:

a) Food
b) Clothing for the family

c) Household expense
d) Her personal expense (clothing, cosmetics, etc.)
e) Miscellaneous family expense (muscic lessons, school supplies, etc.)

The budget should be based upon how much is needed and how much the man can afford. It should be sufficient to provide an *excess* if the wife is careful. This excess she should be allowed to keep as a reward for her thrift; she should not be accountable for it and should have full freedom to use it as she chooses. The wife's budget should be a definite amount to be paid on a specific day of each month or week without any need on her part to ask.

The basic dignity of many women has been offended by selfish or thoughtless husbands who do not realize that their wives are entitled to a portion of the family income for their own use. It is no wonder that eventually many of them are forced into the working world to preserve their self-respect.

In realizing the value of a budget, remember that the only money she has comes from you. She is dependent. She must ask or do without. Many women would rather go without than ask too often. Despite the fact that many states have community property laws based on the premise that half the husband's earnings belong to his wife, many wives feel reluctant to ask for a portion and feel the husband has full claim on the income he earns. It may be up to you to assure her that she is entitled to a fair portion of the family income. Be happy to share it with her. Make her feel comfortable about the situation and relieve any tendency to humiliation which she might feel.

PROBLEMS IN FAMILY FINANCES

There is a great deviation from the ideal I have just described which works to the detriment of many families. Let me name some of the mistakes in money matters:

1. *The working wife:* The wife who must share the burden of earning the living is leading a double life. She is not free to meet her financial part—to provide a peaceful home atmosphere and make a dollar stretch. She will, in fact, find that she must be more extravagant with money as she is more conservative with her time. She will not have the time to shop for bargains, to do the sewing, re-cover the sofa or cook economy meals. She is denied the

womanly satisfaction of thrift—of making something useful from very little. Instead of her contribution in making the dollar stretch, she shares in her husband's part—earning the living.

2. *Wife manages the money:* In millions of cases men come home at the end of the work week with a check which they hand over to their wives. They may ask for the return of a small amount for pocket money, but she is expected to manage the rest. She will pay the bills and meet all expenses. Being so involved, she will consequently do the worrying. If the money does not cover expenses, she will face the situation and struggle with it, weighing one value against another. If she finds solutions, she may come to her husband for his approval. He may not be that concerned. How can he be? He is too far removed from the problem. An actual case illustrates this point.

The husband gave full responsibility to his wife for the management of their money. As their family increased, she became more concerned than ever as she had great difficulty in covering all the expenses. While she was searching for a solution to her dilemma, her husband was offered a transfer to another city where his salary would be increased substantially. The job was tempting but the city was not. They were residing in a peaceful community where he was completely satisfied. Fishing in mountain streams was available nearby. The city to which he would be transferred was crowded and far removed from the streams and lakes he enjoyed so much. He rejected the job offer, much to the distress of his wife.

The problem in this case was that he was sufficiently removed from their financial difficulties as to feel no urgency, yet he held the power of decision. His wife, on the other hand, shouldered the burden of money management but was denied the power of decision. This unfair arrangement naturally leads to misunderstanding and recriminations.

Much harm results when a wife is placed in this position of disadvantage. The results are not dissimilar to those occurring when she moves into other areas of a man's responsibility. She loses part of her glow, her distinctive feminine nature, and is usually not as successful as he would be in the same capacity. This is logical, for she is functioning in a man's job for which she will likely not have an adaptation. If she is required to handle money matters that belong to her husband, she will find herself "wearing the pants." This is a very frustrating position for her, particularly if her nature is to want to be feminine.

We continually hear the argument that many women are better equipped to handle money than are some men. This is obviously true. But her talent is not going to be lost if she is second in command and has the responsibility for the household budget. I've seen many women who handle all family finances, and the results are never ideal. They may do a remarkable job so far as the money goes, but there is generally a conflict in the husband-wife relationship. She rightfully feels that he isn't fulfilling his responsibility, or perhaps she feels that he is incompetent. In either case it diminishes the feeling which should exist between them.

Many women suffer severe strain when given such responsibility. They experience nervousness, hypertension, and even sexual frigidity. Being more delicate in nature than men, they find themselves the victims of these negative reactions without understanding the cause. The strains of money management also tend to interfere with a woman's duties in the home and may result in complete demoralization.

I saw this happen to a family I knew quite well. The wife was managing the finances when the husband began to have serious difficulties in his business. The family was plagued with debts and heavy obligations which they could not meet. Knowing of these problems was bad enough for the wife, but she had to also face irate creditors and attempt to explain the difficulties in which her husband was embroiled. As this went on, her worries became so severe and all-encompassing that her children were neglected and her house was in disorder. She lost all interest in her home life. She had no spirit to give beyond the trying hours she spent in a hopeless situation that finally resulted in bankruptcy. This dire neglect at home was foreign to her nature, for she had formerly been a neat and organized housewife and dedicated mother.

3. *Husband fails to do the worrying:* Sometimes the husband fails to worry about financial problems, or at least appears not to be concerned. He may disregard the house payments or let bills accumulate. If they have debts, he may not be making any plans to get them paid. His wife will assume that he is not concerned about them. This brings her into the picture and causes anxiety. If he does not worry about the debt, she wonders how it will be paid. She may regard him as irresponsible and worry more over the man than the obligation. Her feeling of security is threatened not so much by the debt as by the man's lack of concern over it.

In reality the man may be greatly concerned over his situation and only trying to protect his wife from worry. What he does not realize is that as long as she is aware of their financial difficulties, his silence may be misinterpreted as a lack of concern. Her mind is put at rest only when she realizes that her husband is deeply concerned, that he is making plans to solve the problems, and she therefore has no need to concern herself.

The only way a woman can be completely protected from worry is to know nothing about the problem. This is seldom if ever advisable. She is certain to detect, either through circumstances or through his attitude, that there are problems. There is a further threat that through her husband's death or incapacity the entire burden would suddenly fall to her and she would be completely unprepared to cope with it. The safest rule is that she knows the truth and realizes her husband's feeling of responsibility for its solution.

4. *Wife's opposition to financial plans:* Great difficulty occurs when a wife will not go along with a man's effort to solve his financial problems. If he is cutting expenses or making major changes, she may resist his decisions. While this is extremely frustrating to him, it is well to recognize the wife's difficult situation. Unless she is made fully aware of the entire situation, she may find it very hard to understand why drastic reductions or changes are necessary. She is expected to trust his judgment in plans which may not seem justifiable to her.

If you are in such a situation as this, employ the principles of good leadership explained in a previous chapter:

a) Seek her viewpoint before plans are definite.
b) Consider her feelings and express a sympathy for those feelings.
c) Try to win her support—explain to her that you need her support.
d) Make certain that you are sufficiently convinced of the step you are recommending and that you will have the courage to follow through firmly.

If this action is taken, women will more readily make the adjustment. When they fully understand, they may be quite willing to make sacrifices beyond what you would expect.

5. *Extravagance and living beyond one's means:* Husband or wife or both may be guilty of this grievous fault. It is the cause of most of our financial troubles. Little difficulty would be faced

financially if families purchased only those things they could comfortably afford.

To solve this problem, a sound philosophy must be developed in which there is the definition and establishment of proper values. Material possessions, luxuries, comforts, and pleasures mean very little when weighed against the peace of mind one can know when he is living comfortably within his means. Great as may be the pleasure and joy of elegant furnishings, expensive art objects and fine clothing, these should not be valued more highly than the health or mental peace of the father who must provide these luxuries. There is no way to measure the happiness that is lost through the financial bondage people submit to in the allurement of extravagance. To follow a plan which frees one of this bondage is worth more than gold.

A major cause of extravagance is the desire to impress others. This is a useless effort. Friends of worth are not impressed by our homes and elegant furnishings. They are impressed only by our kindness, our character, and the worthiness of our lives. We may be trying to impress ourselves by thinking that our possessions are a measure of our worth. This self-deception is quickly dispelled in a moment's serious thinking when we realize we can comfortably live with ourselves only as we contribute something of value to our fellowmen.

Self-control is the answer to overcoming extravagance. This means a strict rule to avoid buying that which one cannot afford. Years ago I learned an excellent guide in wise buying: When considering a purchase, ask yourself these questions:

a) Do I need it?

b) Can I afford it?

c) Do I need something else more?

d) Can I get by without it?

This latter question is the supreme test, for if one thinks he needs it and can afford it but is willing to get by without it, he is developing a spirit of thrift which will overcome extravagance.

6. *The husband who is tight with money:* Many wives complain that they are living with a miser who will not allow sufficient money to even purchase adequate and wholesome food. The children are never allowed to go to the circus or for a pony ride. The little girls are denied hair ribbons and other things he could well afford but thinks are senseless expenditures. At the

same time he may be buying expensive cars and sports equipment. One man I know even purchased an airplane for his private use, while his wife was on a household budget so strict she could hardly get by.

One would suppose that such a man feels that his income is really his own and that the services of his wife count for nothing and that his children have no claim on him. Such selfishness usually brings on serious consequences, for no one can live under such despotic treatment.

We have reviewed many of the problems involved in family finances and pointed out solutions to help. The following suggestions are given to assist you in money management.

SUCCESS IN MONEY MANAGEMENT

To be wise in the use of money is of greater consequence than the ability to earn a larger income. Too frequently there is no correlation between the amount of money earned to one's competence as a family provider. A national magazine carried some case histories of various families in certain economic levels showing their incomes, budgets, and debts or savings. It was interesting and startling to note that some families with an income of $100,000 per year or more were on the brink of financial ruin. In one case professional counselors were called in by creditors to take over completely the income, allowing a limited amount to the earner of such a fabulous salary for pocket money.

A medical doctor of my acquaintance with an income of near $75,000 per year (he had earned this amount for several years) decided to return to a university some distance from his home for further training. He had to borrow money to make the trip and get settled.

Developing the wisdom to manage money wisely is an ability which can be learned. One has but to follow certain guidelines and rules. The following ideas are given as suggestions:

1. *Save money:* "A penny saved is a penny earned" is an old adage. From this, one might reason that $100 saved is $100 earned. Let's see. If one needs $100, there are two ways to get it: a) Earn it; or b) save it.

To have an additional $100 from earnings, a man will likely have to earn $130 or more, depending upon the amount that he pays in taxes and other deductions. If you save the $100, you will need to save only $100. Considering this, each dollar saved would be equivalent to $1.30 or more earned. It is as though you were earning interest by saving the money rather than working for it. Any investment that would pay such a high return would be considered phenomenal indeed. The old saying is not so true, for a penny saved might very well be as much as two pennies earned.

2. *Avoid a second car:* One of the heaviest drains on a budget is an automobile. Granted that in most cases one is a basic necessity, most families now have two or more. An automobile frequently results in a greater dollar drain than housing, a college education, or food requirements for a small family. Nothing depreciates quite so rapidly with such constant demands for operation and maintenance. Families have been known to solve critical financial problems by selling one car.

You may feel it impossible to get by with only one car. Financial advisors point out that in most cases it is easily possible. The second car is purchased mostly for occasional use—usually not for more than once or twice a week. The use of municipal busses, even a taxi, is far less expensive than owning a second car. Second cars also encourage other expenditures since they make a family more mobile.

3. *Preserve health:* This is another means of preserving wealth. Many years ago the highly respected financial advisor Roger Babson was asked, "What is the safest financial investment a man can make?" Mr. Babson, accustomed to offering advice about the stock market and other business investments, offered this surprising but valuable advice. "The safest financial investment a man can make is in his health."

When health is disregarded, when the body is neglected or abused with tobacco, alcohol, or other stimulants, not only will money be wasted on their purchases but on the breakdown of the body and disability which follows. When Mr. Babson gave this excellent advice, he recognized that the body is the machine whereby a man makes an adequate living. To preserve this ability to provide, one must also preserve the machine which makes this possible.

4. *Avoid time payments:* Almost anything now can be bought on "time payments"—furniture, automobiles, clothing, appliances, jewelry, and even vacations. With the exception of buying a home, time payments are almost always foolish, for two sound reasons:

a) If you cannot afford to pay the cash, you cannot afford the item.
b) High interest rates greatly increase the cost.

The high interest rates used to be somewhat obscured from the customer and thus many people were innocently led into unwise financial obligations. But now, strict regulations recently imposed inform the borrower of the actual rate of interest. We can see clearly the additional costs we are getting into. Avoiding this costly extra expense is one of the keys to sound money management. One financial counselor summed up rather succinctly his thoughts on time payments: "There are two kinds of people—those who don't understand interest and pay it, and those who do and collect it." And this is often the difference in principle that makes one man poor and another rich.

5. *Avoid borrowing money:* In addition to "time payments," men sometimes borrow from loan companies or individuals for a variety of reasons. Although it may be sound to borrow money for an education, or to increase one's business opportunities, most loans are painful mistakes. Those to avoid are—burrowing money to live on a higher plane, to go on a vacation, or to have conveniences, comforts or luxuries.

It is impossible to measure the anxiety, sleepless nights and heartache caused by debt. Money is so easy to spend and so difficult to save, especially for paying off debts. Ordinarily men do not worry so much about debt as women. The natures of men and women are so different. The nature of man is to struggle for his place in the world. He may even consider debt as a challenge, or a part of this struggle. He is not so security-minded as to let a good opportunity pass him by just because it involves borrowing money. But the woman is different. She looks to the man for security and protection—to provide a safe place in the world for her and her children. Debts stand as a serious threat to this feeling of security. Facing this fact, the man should carefully regard her feelings and avoid debt for her sake, if not his own.

One of the greatest disservices of our day is the bombardment of enticing advertising urging people to spend now and pay later. This concept is morally wrong and engenders habits which are destructive to sound and happy living. Nothing good is ever gained. Easing the burden now cannot possibly make it easier later—when you have to not only pay the debt but also the interest. I have known some men to make an iron-clad rule to "never borrow money unless in urgent emergency." It is a sound rule for a wise money manager.

These are only a few of the most fundamental rules in managing money wisely. Other things may be learned which will greatly aid a man in money management. The May 1970 issue of *Changing Times* issued a most instructive article titled "62 Ways to Beat the High Cost of Living." Invaluable aids were given in money use, covering such topics as financing, food, purchasing, vacations, furniture and automobile buying. One of the first recommendations was to cancel all charge accounts, destroy all credit cards, and go on a cash basis. It is not so difficult to earn an income sufficient to meet family needs if we know how to spend it to greatest advantage.

Of the utmost importance in money management is an abiding feeling of responsibility to pay one's bills on time and meet every financial obligation. If circumstances require an extension of time, one should face the problem immediately with the creditor and work out arrangements. It is easier to face an embarrassing situation such as this at the very outset.

INVESTMENTS

The purpose of this study is not to attempt a comprehensive analysis of such a complex subject, but merely to point out a few helpful guidelines which will assist you in averting some rather common problems.

A sound investment can ease the burden of making the living by providing a supplementary income. If a man works reasonably hard, is careful and saving with his money, he should be able to set aside some money each year for this purpose.

Some investments are very safe. Savings accounts are of this type and offer liquidity and provide an immediate return on your money. The interest rates are low, but if money is deposited regularly, it can prove to be an investment free of worry, bringing security and satisfaction to you and your family. Thrift is a virtue which produces rewards other than financial. As a guiding principle to live by, it is an aid to character growth and an enhancement to self-esteem.

Among the varying types of investments, there are those which are moderately safe but not liquid; others are very safe but tie one's money up for an extended period. It would take a special study to review the many types of investments available and the merits and demerits of each. I would like only to issue some special warnings.

Investments which show promise of high returns are invariably filled with great risk. Sometimes they turn out well; other times they are sad and shocking mistakes. There is a certain element of chance in investments which even the more knowledgeable men may not be able to accurately assess. With all the facts at their disposal to enlighten them, most investors discover that there are too many undetermined factors to make a clear, safe judgment. Therefore, the most shrewd businessmen acknowledge the risk attached to investments promising high return.

Unwise investments have caused bitter disappointment, a spirit of defeat and even suicide. Although some of the brave ones come out of the fray better men and gain a certain amount of valor in the financial battleground, it is not a road which is desirable or recommended as the good life.

No one can provide absolute rules to follow in making wise investments, but we can rely upon some definite guidelines which will free you of painful and distressing experiences:

1. *Never borrow money for investments:* It is not wise nor morally right to risk money that does not belong to you for use in speculation. Invest only money you already have or is surely committed to you.

2. *Never mortgage your home to secure money for investments:* Every family would be greatly benefited if they had a home free of mortgage. Although you may be forced to buy a home on the time payment plan, which is what virtually all families do, yet your obligation is to pay off the obligation and free the home from all encumbrances. Money for investment is not justification for mortgaging the family home—the return never justifies such a risk.

3. *Never invest more than half your savings in a risk venture:* This rule greatly diminishes the risk involved and disappointment should the investment fail to meet expectations. One must *believe* in any venture if he is persuaded to risk any amount at all. So the temptation may be overwhelming to invest all funds available in something one has confidence in.

4. *Risk only those funds which, if lost, would not disturb the normal routine of family life:* If you follow the above rules you will more easily gain the support of your wife. Women are usually very much afraid of investments and will tend to oppose anything which carries an element of risk. If you can assure her that the investment will not endanger her security, that funds are available to meet current obligations, she will likely have an open mind. Also, if you are a man who has proved his financial reliability by keeping bills paid and all obligations under strict control, her confidence will be much stronger. Beyond that she must realize that it is your prerogative to make investments which you think advisable and in the interests of the family.

Before committing himself to any investment, a wise man will again employ the principles of good leadership in first, consulting his wife; second, considering her viewpoint; and third, trying to win her support. She is not so likely to condemn an investment if she has been permitted to express her feelings beforehand. She bears a responsibility along with you, and should she be left a widow, would have to live with it.

It is surprising how many investments are made on hunches or questionable recommendations in a spirit of gambling. The least that can be said is to learn as much as possible before making the decision. Classes are available and good books as well as qualified men who have no selfish interest in your investment.

SUMMARY

We have talked at length of the man as the leader, protector, and provider. While much can be said in each of these categories, there is a strong correlation among them which tends to fuse them into a single function and responibility. A man cannot, for example, measure up to his full stature as a provider and ignore his duties as a leader and protector. Some men assume that if they provide adequately the physical needs of their dependents, they are accountable for no more. The folly of this assumption is revealed on all sides and particularly in the youth rebellion which is an outgrowth for the need for leadership and example.

Happiness is not to be found outside the acceptance and performance of one's duty. Certainly man's chief duty to himself and others is to learn to understand the nature of his responsibilities in these vital areas and become as effective as possible in their performance. The promise is a greater fulfillment than he has ever known.

VIII
MAN, THE BUILDER
OF SOCIETY

Beyond his role in the family, a man has an additional role to perform as the builder of society, to correct social ills, solve problems, and make improvements which will make the world a better place for all. Each man who lives has some obligation to give of himself to create a better world than has been before, to do something of benefit for those now living and generations to follow.

His most important contribution is achieved, of course, in building a happy home which is free of problems. If his marriage is intact, his children well-adjusted citizens—if the family members are all lifters in society and not leaners—he has not created problems for others to worry about. In his case it is not necessary for public agencies to be created to solve problems created by him and his family. When he has succeeded in this way, he can take on additional responsibiity to build society and touch in a beneficial way the lives of countless other people.

PROBLEMS OF SOCIETY

We have inherited a society which is a combination of marvelous advancements but gross weaknesses. We have conveniences for the home that surpass what royalty had in the past. Fine furnishings, floor coverings, washing machines and refrigerators as well as countless other technical achievements are a boon to mankind. We have a high degree of science and industry. Our highways are masterpieces, our buildings miracles of workmanship. But with all of our progress, human beings are in real trouble.

We have mental illness to surpass any time in history, divorce on the increase, troubled homes and youth problems. In varying degrees people suffer unhappiness, with uncertainty as to just how happiness can be attained. Many are stumbling along life's way without a knowledge of how to live.

There is a noticeable emphasis on materialism. Money and possessions are primary goals. Because of this, women are leaving the household to work for luxuries and conveniences and are setting aside those things of greater value.

Alcohol is numbing the minds of our nation's population so that it is impossible for them to be directed by conscience, or to think clearly through problems or discern correct principles. This has led to a weakening of standards. The most serious weakness is "immorality" (sex without marriage), which stands as the number one threat to destroy us. The greatest problem in our country is not poverty nor international strife, but *immorality*. We have only to look at the downfall of great nations to see the spiral downward when immorality is rampant.

Perhaps the most frightening problem in society is the loss of faith in government. Our country is not as it was when founded by brave and valiant men. Freedom is fast disappearing and being replaced by socialism. People are being brought into bondage through oppressive taxation and dependence on government.

We are becoming a "godless" society with religious principles being questioned and reverence for God being removed from our public schools and universities. Whereas our country was formerly a God-fearing nation, based upon the statement "In God We Trust," it is fast rejecting religion as a vital part of both government and country.

Besides these spiritual and moral issues, our physical environment is deteriorating. Although we have an abundant food supply, it is grown on deficient soil that has been robbed of vital elements and contaminated by pesticides and chemical fertilizers. Our food is not of the high and nutritious quality it was a few years ago. In addition, we have polluted our water systems and air. All of these things stand as a threat to the physical well-being of our population.

How great it would be if these problems did not exist, if we could build society in a positive way by the creation of fine literature, art and music, could build beautiful cities and parks. But these high goals may have to wait until we have rescued a dwindling society from disaster.

But we need not lose hope because of these critical problems. Faith must be implanted in the hearts and minds of men that with God's help mankind is bigger than the problems it faces. With the strength of many valiant men, miracles can be wrought and a better world than has existed in the past can be realized.

Each man, for his own peace of mind, must come to realize his personal responsibility to help solve the world's problems. He must develop a feeling of obligation to society, a consciousness of a debt that he owes to the world for the precious gift of life and for the inheritances he has received from the past. When we do not have this feeling of obligation, when we focus all of our energies on our own selfish goals, it creates an imbalance in the spirit of man that will invariably lead to emotional distress. This fact is recognized by Dr. Max Levine, M.D., a psychiatrist associated with the New York College, in the following statement:

"I speak not as a clergyman, but as psychiatrist. There cannot be emotional health in the absence of high moral standards and a sense of social responsibility."

This may explain in part the severe and widespread mental disorders we hear so much about. These are people who have not given of themselves to society. Because of their lack of concern for others and an inordinate self-interest, they suffer inwardly the turmoil which stems from neglect of duty.

SELFCENTEREDNESS OF MEN

Men are too consumed with their own problems, pleasures, and desires to be concerned about others. *Selfcenteredness* is the underlying fault in man's neglect of duty to his fellows. We shall consider examples of this widespread practice.

1. *Many men spend their spare time in pleasure and amusement* such as following sports events, hunting, fishing, camping, boating, riding motorcycles, visiting friends, and other pleasures. They may spend additional time polishing their guns or keeping

their sporting gear in order. And we must consider the many hours they worked to pay for their boats, trailers, camping equipment and motorcycles. Wholesome as these pleasures are and entitled to them as we may be, they consume a tremendous amount of time. If men are to assist in solving the world's problems, there must be some fair sharing of time with society.

2. *Most men waste a certain amount of time* in which no one is benefited—time spent loafing around, in idle talk on trivial matters, or attending movies of questionable worth, playing cards, and other useless pursuits. Many persons return from work and flop into a chair to be passively amused by whatever happens to be on T.V. Although we must recognize man's need for diversion from work, it seems that he should divide his time between activities which are a wholesome benefit to himself and to society.

3. *The disposition of most men is to live entirely for their own family and friends in their own little sphere:* A man of this disposition may appear to be an ideal citizen. His home may be in good repair and his yard neat and clean. He probably spends his weekends in gardening, lawn care, and keeping his cars polished. He provides his family with the material things they need and aside from an occasional parking ticket, he is never at odds with the law. He is not a burden to society, but neither is he building it. He is living for himself. His concern is for *his* home and *his* family. "I'm doing my share; let others do theirs" is his motto. His children may not have problems, but what about other children? Does he ever think of them? His is pretty much a sterile concern for anyone other than his own.

4. *Many men make a small contribution to society and feel they have done their part:* A man may occasionally make a small donation of $50.00 or so to a charity, thinking he has done his part. Or he may help a neighbor in difficulty or assist in a community project. These acts of consideration are of some merit, but much more is needed to make a dent in the world's problems. These small acts can hardly discharge a man's duty to his fellow men.

TYPE OF MEN NEEDED TO BUILD SOCIETY

The qualities of true greatness are required of men to build society in the most beneficial way and include these listed below:

1. *Men who can recognize needs:* First, we need men of *vision,* men who have a broad view of the world's problems, who can see the crying needs of the multitudes. They are capable of evaluating present conditions against an idealistic picture of what the world should be. And yet they have an *intimate perception,* can recognize the needs of a small child nearby, notice the downcast eyes of a teenager in trouble, and are sensitive to the needs of those who so closely surround them. They do not have to be told in which ways the world needs to be built—they are painfully aware of human needs.

2. *Men of compassion:* The world needs men of compassion, who are moved with deep emotion when viewing the aspirations and struggles of their fellowmen. They value human life, single or in the thousands. They are moved to action when they see people who are oppressed or discouraged. This was the quality of the Good Samaritan who, seeing his fellow man in trouble, came to his aid, a compassion sadly lacking in the priest and Levite who passed by on the other side. Compassion is the quality of velvet necessary in man to build society.

3. *Men of responsibility:* We need men who face responsibility when they see it. They do not turn away, imagining that someone else will be responsible. When the church calls for help, or the community, or when an important petition must be circulated, they respond to the call of duty and feel an obligation to help. They do not ask "do I want to do it," but "had I ought to do it?" They are not afraid of great responsibility; nor do they feel above the most menial tasks if they must be done for the benefit of mankind.

4. *Willingness to sacrifice:* With all responsibility, and especially *great* responsibility, there must be a willingness to sacrifice time, energy, comforts and pleasures to serve in some important capacity which is greatly needed. With any *great* responsibility there is always a *willingness to sacrifice.*

5. *Men of wisdom:* Society needs men of wisdom and knowledge, men who seek truth and who in their search have accumulated great treasures of knowledge to guide them so they have something worthwhile to contribute to the world and its problems. These men of truth have open minds and are willing to adjust their own thinking or preconceived ideas when they see the light of truth. They know the value of their wisdom and feel a responsibility to share it with others in a way that will be of benefit to them.

6.   *Men of determination:* Many of the problems of our world
are very challenging and discouraging. There have been many
men who have started out on paths that could have revolutionized
phases of our living and greatly benefited mankind, only to give
up somewhere along the way due to defeat or discouragement.
The world needs men who are *not quitters*, men who possess great
determination and have the drive to follow through on a difficult
job, regardless of the obstacles. Men of determination see *only the
object; the obstacles must give way.* They are unyielding,
uncompromising, when they have a noble objective as a goal.

7.   *Men of courage:* We need men who have both physical and
moral courage. Physical courage is the willingness to face dangers
and take risks, even the risk of life itself, for a worthy cause. This
was Patrick Henry's spirit of "Give me liberty or give me death."
We need men who are motivated, not for their own benefit alone,
but for others. The real heroes of time have not risked bodily harm
for some advantage to themselves alone, but for the benefit of
mankind. Such were our revolutionary forefathers who fought to
preserve liberty for all.

While it is stirring and inspiring to witness feats of physical
courage, probably there are many more opportunities for moral
courage when valor is required to defend a cause you know to be
right and which may be unpopular. The firmness and conviction to
stand alone if necessary in defense of those who cannot speak for
themselves in the face of a contrary sentiment, marks a person of
real courage. Moral courage is to do what is right, even in the face
of criticism, humiliation, or some disadvantage to ourselves.
Courageous men are not afraid to appear foolish in the eyes of
their fellowmen. They do what is right and let the consequences
follow.

HOW TO HELP BUILD SOCIETY

1.   *Preparation of self:* If we are to be of assistance to others,
it is first necessary to prepare ourselves, especially in the seven
basic ways just stressed. It will be important to gain knowledge
and wisdom so that we will be qualified to contribute something of
worth to the world. It is necessary to develop compassion and a
sensitive perception so that we will be able to recognize the needs
that surround us and help in a most beneficial way.

We must understand other people and realize that there are a multitude of circumstances peculiar to them alone and perhaps needs, which are particular for them. That person who has had the security of a congenial and happy home environment may find it difficult to appreciate the traumatic adjustments one might have who has never known such security. One who has enjoyed love and respect may not easily sympathize with one who has been deprived of such basic needs . . . who may have been rejected, criticized, and belittled during his developing years.

It is essential that we have a feeling of self-worth—a belief that we may be in some way of value to society. We must trust in our own innate ability and realize that as we grow in knowledge, we have the capacity to greatly alter for good some phases of living. This trust in self is beautifully described in the following words by Ella Wheeler Wilcox:

> Trust in thine own untired capacity,
> as thou wouldst trust in God Himself.
> Thy soul is but an emanation from the whole
> Thou doest not dream what forces lie in thee,
> Vast and unfathomed as the boundless sea.
> Thy silent mind o'er diamond caves may roll,
> Go, seek it, but let pilot will control
>   those passions, which thy favouring winds may be.
> No man shall place a limit in thy strength!
> Such triumphs that no mortal ever gained may yet
>   be thine.
> If thou wilt but believe in thy creator and thyself.
> At length some feet will tread all heights now unattained.
> Why not thine own? Press on! Achieve! Achieve!

God has endowed each one of us with a unique individuality and a capacity far beyond what most of us realize. If we but trust in this divine inheritance, we can serve in a way that may greatly alter the course of history. I am reminded of the lasting influences of Mohandas K. Gandhi upon his nation and the world. In his youth he was an ordinary young man with glaring weaknesses. No one could have guessed he could affect for good the lives of millions of people. And yet this young man with frail body and unimpressive voice had something great to give to the world. In his desire to serve and benefit mankind, his unique gifts came to light and he achieved a miracle by bringing the greatest nation of his time to its knees.

The secret of Gandhi's greatness was his *goodness*, his *deep conviction of God* and his *desire to serve humanity*. He also had a *pure motive* for serving mankind, not wishing to focus attention on himself or to win acclaim. His only desire was to benefit his people.

2.　*Observe what needs to be done:* As we develop a sensitive perception, we become aware of how best we can serve. But, generally speaking, society is built in two ways: solving difficult problems and advancing society in a positive way.

　　a) *Solving difficult problems:* These are divided in the following categories. Although they are interrelated, they can best be observed separately:

　　　(1) *Social problems:* These include marriage problems, divorce, youth problems, crime, drug abuse, alcohol, violence, race problems, and others.

　　　(2) *Mental and emotional health:* Many suffer from severe mental illness. The lesser forms are emotional turmoil, nervousness, uncertainties, insecurity, and unhappiness.

　　　(3) *Lack of morality or spirituality:* There is a general rejection of moral principles, God, and religion. Instead, we are troubled by immorality, dishonesty, pornography, and many other evil practices.

　　　(4) *World affairs:* This includes problems within our country and international problems.

　　　(5) *Health:* This includes depletion of food and soil and pollution of air, water, soil, and foods.

　　b) *Advancing society:* This includes advancements in industry, medicine, food production, education, the church, and in creative work such as music, art, design, architecture, literature, entertainment such as movies, T.V. and others.

3.　*Search for solutions:* When one considers the difficult problems facing society, he is apt to expend most of his energy complaining. There are more people than we need who are competent to list all of the ills we face. They can go through them one by one and with deep emotion enumerate the pains and grievances and threats to nearly everyone, leaving a feeling of despair and helplessness. It is safe to say that we are not so much in need of an elaboration of the problems as we are of some constructive solutions, even though the part we play may be a minor one.

These solutions can come from searching through information which has been written, which will provide a surer footing from which to approach a problem; or solutions can come from one's own perception and insight, perhaps based upon his own experience. When one searches his own mind for ideas, it is amazing the continual flow of new ideas that can come forth. Especially is this surprising in a society so sophisticated that one would think that all the answers would have already been given. Relating what one knows from his own particular viewpoint in solving a problem for someone else has resulted in some startling opportunities.

The greatest source of solutions is often the last to be tried. God, who is the fountainhead of truth and consequently knowledge, has said, "Seek and ye shall find. Knock and it shall be opened unto you. Ask and ye shall recieve." This is a definite and straightforward promise to all who will study God's word and ask in faith. If one's purpose is single to the end of doing good, the plea to God for insight will not be denied. Knowledge from God may come as something completely new to you, direct inspiration, or it may be a recollection of information already known.

4. *Avenues to serve:* Many men will be able to build society directly through their daily occupations. If they are engaged in work which is important to the world, they may well seek improvements in this phase of living. In fact, most of the major improvements of mankind have been accomplished along with a man's earning his daily bread. However, you may have some unique insight into a problem which is entirely out of your field of work. If so, you should be encouraged to follow your interest. You may be guided by a greater power than your own to make a contribution outside of your own work.

Whether a man serves in his work or aside from it, there must be a dedication beyond the desire for money. Horizons for human betterment extend beyond the "nine to five" commitment of most employment. In involves a state of mind which one adopts as a permanent part of his being. It becomes ingrained in his make-up until his desire to serve is not an obligation accepted because of duty, but rather because of desire.

And it is important to stress that society must be built in the right way. Some things which man has created have been detrimental to society. Not all technology or scientific changes have accrued to his benefit. We need those changes which will benefit the souls of men and help them find a better way of living. This is not necessarily the easier way, a more comfortable way, or luxurious way or convenient way—but a way that will make men happier because it is developing to them.

It is important to consider the power of example as a contribution to the welfare of mankind. The power of a single individual, such as Sir Winston Churchill during the war, can be phenomenal. When England and the free world were in deep gloom as totalitarianism was sweeping forth a mighty tidal wave, destroying every obstacle in its path, Sir Winston stood in the rubble of London with his fingers extended in the victory sign, promising his people that despite all hardships, they would "never surrender, never, never." Such uncompromising confidence fired a people to hope when all such hope should normally be gone.

No matter who we are, we are creating an influence which is felt by others. They may not even know us, but our respect for law, our attitude towards life, our enthusiasn or negativism are felt by others. We build or destroy society in our own way by how we live and think.

MOTIVES FOR BUILDING SOCIETY

There are two motives men have for public service: one is to win acclaim to themselves, and the other to benefit mankind. Let us consider these two motives:

1. *Desire for acclaim:* Inborn in every man is a desire for status or acclaim. This instinct is noticeable in all male members of the animal kingdom, from the lion, the bear, or sea walrus to the pecking order of the barnyard. There is always a jockeying for top position.

The human male possesses a noticeable desire to achieve honors and win positions of leadership and distinction. We find ourselves as participants or shouting observers at tournaments and contests to match skills for top honors. Sports of all kinds are big business where winning is the objective. In a vicarious way a man sees himself as the victor when "his team" or "his man" wins. So it is to be expected that men often direct their energies into activities to bring recognition, prestige and fame. They want to stand above other men and leave their footprints on the sands of time.

Reasonably controlled, this tendency is a virtue which gives impetus to a man in his work, providing him with that extra drive to succeed. Without it he is not quite the man he could be. Its complete absence leaves him something less than a man.

On the other hand, when the drive for acclaim reaches exaggerated proportions, when *it becomes the most important reason for reaching an objective, superseding things of greater value*, then it is an evil which is destructive to the man professing to do good. Similar to the lust for money, the drive for acclaim may spark negative traits causing one to lie, cheat, or steal and take unfair advantage of others, and all for his own advancement. He may push others aside in his lust for honors. He may go so far as to discredit another whom he considers a threat to his objectives. Because of his unrelenting thirst for recognition he may neglect his job and family and other responsibilities of great importance. Although his objective was intended to build society, on the route it destroys it.

2. *Desire to benefit mankind:* In contrast, consider the man who is building society solely for the benefit of mankind. He may be developing medical cures or advancing ideas to end erosion or pollution or writing a book which he hopes will bring about reforms of great significance. He may be a politician altruistically motivated to promote justice or a scientist dedicated to technological improvements to save time and ease life. Many men seek leadership in service clubs, the church, or public office to benefit others. Whatever his work, he has as a prime objective the benefiting of his fellowmen.

Such benevolence has many rewards. Such a man will be moved by love, compassion, concern, unselfishness, and a spirit of self-sacrifice for the benefit of mankind. He will not care who gets the credit for the achievement. If someone else comes along with an idea greater than his own, he steps aside and supports and applauds the other man's contribution. If someone beats him to the mark and reaches the same objective he sought sooner, he is happy that society is benefited sooner than he expected. If another is better qualified for a job than he, he supports that man who has the greatest talent.

Many inspiring examples of such dedication to public interest are before us. Men spend countless hours—sometimes their entire lives—in altruistic service with no thought for selfish acclaim. Frequently men work cooperatively to accomplish their objectives with greater speed and efficiency. No one really knows who came up with the genius—one or all of them. Who, for example, invented the jet engine? Who invented the automatic clothes washer? Who is really responsible that a few remarkable men have felt the elation of watching the earth to which they are tied revolve in a course completely independent of themselves as they watch from a vantage point on the moon? Countless men contributed their ideas, but we can be certain that the original ideas were not miserly kept secret by one who hoped to do honor to his name. The motive must certainly have been for the benefit of mankind.

> Remember: IT IS DIFFICULT TO MEASURE THE AMOUNT OF GOOD ONE CAN DO IF HE DOESN'T CARE WHO GETS THE CREDIT!

One of the revealing signs of a man who is moved by the right motive is that he does not focus attention upon himself or his work. He does not boast about his achievements or "sound a trumpet" before himself. He follows the precepts taught by the Savior.

> Take heed that ye do not your alms before men, to be seen of them: otherwise ye have no reward of your Father which is in heaven. Therefore when thou doest thine alms, do not sound a trumpet before thee, as the hypocrites do in the synagogues and in the streets, that they may have glory of men. Verily I say unto you, They have their reward. But when thou doest alms, let not thy left hand know what thy right hand doeth: That thine alms may be in secret: and thy Father which seeth in secret himself shall reward thee openly.

> Matt. 6:1-4

SHOULD WOMEN BE BUILDERS OF SOCIETY?

There are some who feel that women should build society in the same way that men do. One of our well-known politicians made a plea before the Senate for women to join forces with men in advancing society. He said, "One of the untapped resources of this country is woman power. We need them in science, medicine, engineering, politics, education—in all endeavors." Many young women are heeding such calls, feeling they have some great responsibility to give in these fields to make the world better. Women are needed to build society, but not in science and industry. Our deficiency is not a technological one. As I write these words, two astronauts are walking on the moon and returning scientific data to earth. Our scientific strides have been phenomenal and are going forth with such acceleration that we wonder if we are going to trip over overselves in the mad rush. We are not short of working personnel. The working week has been continually lessened until now we hear proposals that no one work over thirty hours per week, or that perhaps people be allowed as much as twenty-five weeks during the year as vacation. There is no conceivable way in which an assertion can be substantiated that we need more women in the working force to advance society there. There is sufficient male population to do so.

Women are greatly misled if they feel they will best achieve their duty to mankind by becoming a figure of renown in politics, science, and industry. Although they are capable of great public service, they can render no service of greater consequence than to establish an ideal home. Theirs is the prime opportunity to prevent and correct the great social evils *in the place most of them start*. There would be an absolute minimum of social problems if our homes were in order. Too much emphasis cannot be given in reminding our girls and women of their vital role in the well-being of society. The shaping of the lives of children is of such magnitude and consequence as to be incomprehensible—these values are realized not only here but extend into eternity.

If men cannot solve problems of government and industry, if we must lean on women for these responsibilities, then we have failed as men. Half of the population is male. There are plenty of men to produce the material necessities, but not enough women to be good mothers.

As with a man, however, there is an obligation upon a woman to give of herself in humanitarian service after she has fulfilled her responsibility in the home. Women are benevolent by nature and are greatly enriched by unselfishly giving of themselves to the church, the community, and to individuals who are in need. In the home, and by giving benevolent service, women greatly build society.

Women who choose not to marry are in a different category and are obviously free to give far more time to others. They are greatly needed in the world as school teachers, nurses, and secretaries, and to do other feminine work as well as benevolent service in assisting with social problems.

REWARDS

"Eye hath not seen nor ear heard, neither entered into the heart of man those things which God hath prepared for them that diligently serve Him." This reward is not withheld until we die and face our Maker, but is felt in good measure now. There is nothing that will bring peace to the soul in such abundance as to be in unselfish service of others. Jesus said, "Inasmuch as ye do it unto the least of these, my brethren, ye have done it unto me." This being the case, God rewards such honest efforts with His spirit immediately.

So often one discovers that those things to which he has directed most of his energies crumble as dust in the hands. Where he felt he was building a monument, he finds nothing, for his efforts have been selfishly directed. One who has given much of himself in the service of others will not find when he comes to die that he has not lived, or that he has lived in vain.

A man who will develop within himself a concern for others and proves this concern through constructive action brings benefits to his entire family. A woman's glory is in the success of her husband and the happiness of her children. Children are encouraged to greater strivings by the unselfishness and magnanimity of an exemplary father.

SUMMARY

The responsibility of building our better society rests primarily upon men. The function of women may well be more important, for it is they who shape the destiny of youth, establishing their aspirations and ideals. A woman is usually the motivation to a great man.

But it is the man who must take up the banner and move onto the stage and do something. Indicate by your attitude and actions that you expect a better world and are doing something to move it in that direction.

IX
MASCULINITY

So God created man in His own image; in the
image of God created He him; male and female
created He them."

Genesis 1:27

It is significant that we are created as either male or female.
Although we are all born into the world as God's children, we are
born as either a *male* child or a *female* child. Thus inherent
differences are placed in us to distinguish us from one another.
These differences are not only the obvious physical ones, but are
emotional and temperamental.

Masculinity is that part of a man which makes him so distinctly
different from a woman. By nature he is strong, firm, steadfast
and unyielding, whereas a woman by basic nature is soft and
yielding. As a man grows to be more masculine, these characteristics are more strongly solidified in his nature. As a woman
develops her femininity, she loses any traits of masculine firmness
or unyielding temperament. As we widen these differences
between men and women, a woman will grow more strongly
feminine as a man becomes more strongly masculine. This is one
instance where the development of separating differences works to
the advantage of both.

It is important to dispel any false ideas about masculinity. Some are inclined to think that the term means to be loud, bullheaded, hardhearted, and unemotional. These are not traits to describe masculinity as God intended man to be. What is true masculinity? Let's take a look.

THE MASCULINE TRAITS

That they may be more easily understood, we shall discuss the masculine traits under three main classifications: the physical traits, the masculine traits of character, and masculine ability.

1. *Physical traits:* A man may or may not be born with a large build, a deep-pitched voice, and a heavy beard. If he is, he can count it an advantage, but these characteristics by no means necessarily identify him as a fully masculine man. Of more significance are strong muscles which result from hard use or his physical energy or endurance which is derived from a well-trained body and spirit. A real man is made—he is not born.

Of more importance than his physical make-up is his *masculine manner*—his heavy gait, the firm and decisive use of his hands, the masculine stance, how he moves his head, and the tone of his voice. The masculine manner comes, not out of practice as an actor learns his lines, but is derived from an *inner attitude of manliness*. If he thinks like a man, he will surely carry himself as a man.

A friend I have known for many years is slight of build, being slightly over five feet tall. His frame is not sturdy, nor is he physically commanding. But he is a disciplined and educated man who has successfully served his family and community. He is easily recognizable as a manly man, even by those who barely know him. His bearing and self-confidence leave no doubt.

2. *Masculine traits of character:* Traits which are strongly masculine include aggressiveness, drive, decisiveness, firmness, determination, resoluteness, unyielding steadfastness, courage, fearlessness, independence, and competence and efficiency in the masculine world. These will be considered in some detail shortly.

3. *Masculine ability:* This may be defined as the *knowledge, skill,* and *ability* required in any masculine role, such as the ability to earn a living or the ability to perform a skillful work as a carpenter, bricklayer, plumber, office worker, financier, or medical doctor. It is exemplified in the leadership ability needed to guide the family or succeed in some phase of work. Or a man typifies

such ability by possessing the knowledge to build his own shelter, grow a garden, or otherwise protect his family from want. The skill may be inborn or acquired by education or specialized training. Masculine abilities are those adaptable to the man's role as the guide, protector and provider for the family and as the builder of society. These abilities are the means by which he solves his problems and reaches his objectives and fulfills his responsibilities.

Returning again to the *masculine traits of character,* it is well to devote some time to them for they are the least understood. The words have a definite meaning to all of us, but we shall now consider them as relating in a positive way to masculinity.

MASCULINE TRAITS OF CHARACTER

1. *Aggressiveness:* This is a self-asserting, pushing, or enterprising quality. The aggressor does not wait for things to come his way—he goes out to meet life, to get what he needs or wants, often in the face of opposition. This quality is of special value to the salesman or any man who is trying to reach the top of his field or advance in his work. He does not leave a stone unturned to achieve the objective he has set for himself. Used excessively, aggressiveness becomes a negative quality in that it may cause a man to push others aside for his own selfish interests; but when this extreme is avoided, aggressiveness is a force whereby worthy objectives can be reached.

The opposite of aggressiveness is lack of initiative in getting what you need or want. This quality is frequently found in the feminine woman who would rather "go without" than push too strongly for what she needs, deserves, or wants.

2. *Drive:* Those who possess "drive" have abundant energy for accomplishing their objectives. Drive seems to come not so much from the physical source as from the "spirit" which carries one on unrelentingly towards a goal. This quality is well described in the following verse:

THE CHAMPION

The average runner sprints
Until the breath in him is gone
But the champion has the iron will
That makes him "carry on."

For rest, the average runner begs
When limp his muscles grow
But the champion runs on leaden legs
His spirit makes him go.

The average man's complacent
When he does his best to score
But the champion does his best
And then he does a little more.

—Author unknown

Thomas A. Edison was a remarkable demonstration of drive in action. He was tireless in his objectives and took defeat as a further challenge. It is interesting to know that he claims his drive came from emotional self-mastery. The fact is well established that hard work does not drain off energy so much but emotional upheaval does, and can be so debilitating as to make physical exertion impossible under extreme conditions. Emotional health, then, is fundamental to the quality of "drive."

3. *Decisiveness:* This consists of the ability to make decisions. It is the power or quality of deciding *promptly and firmly*. A man with decisiveness is able to review facts and draw conclusions rather quickly and come to a firm decision without an undue struggle, without vacillating or wavering. He has a positive approach to his decisions. He may not always be right, but tends to use better judgment than does the man who wearies his mind by vacillating. Decisiveness does not necessarily imply sudden action, but does imply that after facts have been carefully weighed, a decision will be reached promptly.

Feminine women are inclined to lack decisiveness. When they make a decision, it is never quite final. They may change their minds a number of times. (Ask any building contractor who has built a custom home to order.) Or they will often postpone a decision, sometimes indefinitely, to avoid the struggle of vacillating over the matter. In women this quality seems to be attractive, but not so with men. Decisiveness is part of attractive manhood and inspires confidence.

4. *Firmness:* Firmness is the ability to remain constant, steady, or the same. The man of firmness is not easily moved or shaken from his convictions or decisions. He does not succumb to pressures of others when in his own mind he is confident he is

right. This is a most essential quality in leadership and for success.

This virtue is important for women also, especially in their dealings with their children and holding to ideals and principles. But truly feminine women are not so firm when it comes to activities away from home that do not involve moral issues. This seems to add to their womanliness rather than detract, as it does with a man.

5.   *Determination:* A man with determination is not easily swayed or moved off course. When subjected to pressures from individuals or circumstances, he is not deterred from his goals. This quality is essential to masculine leadership and to reaching objectives.

Christopher Columbus provides an outstanding example of a man with dogged determination to pursue a goal which he reasoned to be sound in the face of overwhelming opposition. Men serving under him were very much aware that a real man was in command.

This virtue should not be confused with "will power" or "self-mastery," qualities both men and women need in adhering to principles and standards. Women, in fact, tend to have self-control superior to men. But when it comes to determination which does not involve moral issues, a feminine woman tends to lack this quality.

6.   *Resoluteness:* This quality is similar to determination, only stronger, since it is characterized by a decided purpose. Moved by a strong conviction or objective, a man carries out his decisions with a steadiness which is unshaken. There is a *solemn will* attached to the quality of resoluteness, which suggests that the issue at stake is a moral one. This is a quality needed to carry a man to his objectives in the face of intense opposition or even defeat.

7.   *Unyielding steadfastness:* The man with this trait does not give up, quit, relinquish, or surrender under pressure of individuals or circumstances. In fact, the worth of this trait is fully realized only in the face of opposition. It is like the heavy mast of a ship whose strength is not realized until it is subjected to heavy winds at sea.

8.   *Courage:* Courage is a quality of mind which enables one to meet danger and difficulties with firmness and strength of spirit. The man with this quality will do what he believes in, in spite of the danger involved. The danger might be physical harm,

abandonment of friends, or loss of prestige. A courageous man has the strength of his convictions—will follow his own determination despite the risk of criticism or failure. He will not avoid an action because it may be fraught with problems or possible failure. If he believes it is wise and right, he will proceed. He is always carried along by his own convictions and objectives, which overcomes the fear of risk, defeat, or dangers. Cowardice is the opposite of courage.

9. *Fearlessness:* Similar to courage, fearlessness is more intense. A man of courage may have fears, but will follow his convictions in spite of his fears. The fearless man is free from fear. This may be the result of wide experience or may come because of a deep faith. Fear is, in fact, the opposite of faith, for where there is faith, fear vanishes.

10. *Independence:* We are all dependent upon one another and certainly upon God; yet independence is rightly considered a virtue wherein one is *relatively* uncontrolled by others. An independent man makes every effort to be self-sufficient in earning his livelihood. Only in the event of dire necessity would he rely on others for his sustenance. Such a man has the ability to solve his own problems and make his own way in life. Masculine men always possess this quality. Again, independence is lacking in feminine women who look to men as their means of support and for leadership. Lack of independence on a man's part suggests a quality of femininity which in a man is decidedly unbecoming.

11. *Competency and efficiency in the man's world:* I am speaking here of a man's efficiency in running his entire life, not just his occupation. I speak of efficiency in directing his family, in handling the money, and in making wise use of his time. I also refer to efficiency in any phase of his work or in solving problems in his masculine responsibilities as the guide, protector, provider, or the builder of society.

Women may be efficient, also, without being masculine. But this efficiency should be limited to their own sphere. They can and should be efficient in running a household, in the care and training of childen, etc. But when a woman moves into the man's sphere and develops efficiency there, she takes on masculine qualities.

The importance of this point cannot be emphasized too strongly. Some people vigorously reject this concept and suggest that I am saying women do not have the ability to be efficient in a man's world. Women certainly do have this ability, but remember that as they do, they tend towards masculinity.

For example, when a woman takes over the leadership of the family or management of the money, or steps into the man's world to assist in earning the living, she must acquire traits which are strongly masculine if she is to be successful in these jobs which are masculine jobs. These traits are very unattractive in women, which only verifies how admirable they are in men, since they are natural to his sex.

HOW TO DEVELOP MASCULINITY

1. *By serving as the guide, protector, and provider for his family:* The most effective way to develop masculinity is to function in the God-given role as the guide, protector, and provider of the family. If one accepts this role in good spirit and strives to his utmost to succeed in all three categories, masculine growth is inevitable. For example, as a man wholeheartedly accepts the position as patriarch or leader of his family, ruling with firmness and fairness, he will grow in the masculine qualities of leadership. He will acquire the traits of decisiveness and steadfastness and become that strong leader he has set himself to be. Should he, on the other hand, allow his wife to lead or, worse yet, insist that she lead through his own default, he will be denied this development and will actually retrogress, becoming less masculine than he was to begin with.

As one protects women and children, shielding them from the hardness and difficulties of life, he develops manly chivalry, courage, and valor. And as he strives diligently to provide an adequate living, facing problems and heavy responsibilities—as he overcomes these problems and meets the challenge—he takes on a quality of manliness that cannot be reached in any other way. When one truly understands this principle, it becomes clear that these male obligations or burdens are in reality opportunities which are highly desirable and essential to one's growth.

2. *By building society:* Further opportunities to develop masculinity and other desirable traits of steel come as a man projects himself beyond the interests of himself and his immediate dependents and becomes a builder of society. This occurred to Moses as he assumed the burden of the multitudes in bondage and led them out of Egypt. He grew in courage, steadfastness, and every other masculine quality needed to accomplish this almost

impossible task. Without this burden on his shoulders, he could never have grown into such a magnificent man.

Since Moses was already a member of the household of Pharaoh and in a position where succession to the position of pharaoh was a strong likelihood, one wonders why God did not allow natural events to take place and then instruct Moses to free the enslaved Israelites by decree. Rather, Moses was sorely tested and prepared through trials to increase in faith that he might become the man of strength that was required to not only lead the captives from bondage, but guide them for years to follow.

3. *By developing the masculine traits of character:* We have already learned of the masculine traits of character such as aggressiveness, determination, fearlessness, and many others. These can be acquired by an inner attitude of pride in being a man and by a conscious effort to put these traits to use in daily living. These traits may be already present, even in the young boy, but an awareness of them can help him grow in manliness.

4. *By increasing masculine skill and ability:* A man can gain further masculine development by increasing his skill or ability in any masculine field. This includes his own occupation or any masculine work such as building a shelter, pouring cement, planting a garden, repairing a car, fixing home equipment, repairing a roof, painting a house, repairing plumbing and other things. All of these skills help to develop the man. We see clearly that masculinity is developed by doing the work which naturally falls to us. These jobs are therefore a blessing, essential to our well-being and happiness. Why, then, do men so often resist?

5. *By developing his physical capacity:* In addition, a man grows in masculinity by developing his physical capacity. Physical work, exercise, and a well-nourished body result in the hardening of muscles, increased physical strength and endurance—a more perfect specimen of manhood. Proper nourishment and the avoidance of tobacco, alcohol, drugs, and other destructive products are positive ways to become more manly. It is ironic that many young men have been introduced to these pernicious habits that they may "prove that they are men," when actually just the opposite eventually takes place.

6. *By accentuating the differences between himself and women:* In developing masculinity, it is important to accentuate the DIFFERENCES between yourself and women. Avoid anything which is soft and yielding or otherwise feminine. Avoid hesitancy, vacillation, feminine mannerisms of speech and bodily

movement, or any characteristic which is identifiable as more to the nature of women.

A common feminine characteristic is to primp before the mirror, being conscious that every hair is in place. While no one will deny that good grooming is important, a preoccupation with the subject is unnatural to the masculine nature. Some men take an inordinate interest in clothes, considering cut, style and trends. They are concerned unduly as to how people react to their dress. They may wash, dry, and set their hair as is common to women. Their manners may be effeminate, i.e., use of the hands and manner of walk. These are some of the outer indications of a feminine nature that should be avoided.

7. *By setting challenging goals:* As a man accepts challenging goals, whether it is in connection with his work or otherwise, he brings to himself opportunities to enhance his masculinity. On the other hand, when he avoids the responsibility of high goals, seeking the easy route, he denies himself opportunities for personal development. The pursuit of easy things makes men weak, whereas the pursuit of challenging goals, great responsibility, and difficult paths strengthen a man's masculinity. This is not to say that a man does not deserve time for rest and relaxation, for these things renew the spirit and body; but it does mean that the general trend of man's life should be away from easy paths and towards the higher, more difficult goals. In this way he grows in manliness.

CHALLENGING GOALS, A MEANS OF DEVELOPING RESPONSIBILITY

So frequently men drift towards the jobs that are easiest to do. In school the "cinch" classes will have the heaviest enrollment, and those vocations and professions which require the least in effort will be the ones selected. All too frequently the effort and discipline required to reach a higher objective will not be exerted if something "acceptable" can be found which requires less energy.

Generally there is a point of compromise when parents, friends or family members will be satisfied; but the nobler self within may not be, for the effort has not been the best that could be given. The real man will prepare himself to do the thing which is difficult. In preparing for a vocation, the young man who is interested in being the most he can be will accept the strongest challenge available. It might require more years in training and more sacrifice to master more difficult subject matter. But to be true to himself he will reach for the upper limits of his ability.

Please note: This places no greater inherent value on any particular job. It is a matter of using one's available talents to the utmost, whatever category of work that finally puts him in.

Consider the conquests of some masculine men doing things which might appear ridiculous to the fainthearted. What, for example, drove Admiral Richard E. Byrd to explore the wastes of Antarctica? Whatever else may have justified the venture, certainly one great motivation for it, if not the dominating reason, was the desire to do a challenging, hazardous job. Not only those who go to such a wasteland experience this challenge, but those who vicariously participate as they view the movies and read of the dangerous exploits. People like to be part of something requiring courage.

What real merit can we say there is in climbing the sheer wall of El Capitan in Yosemite Park? Imagine the great risk involved, and what for? Whether there is any value or not in such an exploit is not the issue, but rather to illustrate a strong masculine trait to face a tremendous challenge and conquer it.

There is an abundance of challenge for every man. Most challenges are not so dramatic as these. But they may be more of a test of real manhood since they require the courage to carry on when acclaim or recognition is lacking. A wise man stated so well, "To do well that which is the common lot of all men is the truest greatness."

The philosophy of Henry David Thoreau is one of the most abused of our time. Writing something over a hundred years ago, he advocated a departure from materialism and a return to an uncomplicated life. Being a bachelor, he had a good less responsibility than otherwise, but his philosophy was not one of indolence. His time was methodically spent in study, research, meditation, and attention to earthy work sufficient to provide for himself. We must fight the tendency to succumb to the philosophy prevalent today to do the minimum. One decisively demonstrates his manhood by working at the peak of his capacity.

We have seen that in applying masculinity to the role of man, it is imperative to accept the role wholeheartedly and to demonstrate firmness in the pursuit of the tasks we face. These tasks are usually very ordinary, but their pursuit in a courageous manner is not ordinary.

SET SOME GOALS

Set some goals. Initially these might well be the development of something distinctively masculine, such as a program of physical fitness to harden the muscles. Perhaps it could be a project in the yard, basement or garage—some type of improvement, a job that your wife should not or cannot be expected to do.

Our highly specialized society has many drawbacks. Among them is the tendency to discourage the development of many masculine attributes which had to be used a generation or two back just to survive. When a man had to physically build the shelter his family was to occupy, when he obtained food through hunting and gardening, and when he had to supply the protection from danger in order to survive, the emphasis was clearly upon these important qualities. They were recognized as essential and appreciated. Unfortunately this definition is nearly unrecognizable in these days. The masculine traits will be seen in less obvious ways, but in ways no less important. But if emphasis can be placed upon the masculine by deliberately cultivating the outward manifestations, it will be an aid in enhancing the differences in the masculine and feminine with great benefit to both sexes.

WHAT MASCULINITY DOES

1. *For the woman:* A masculine man stirs the heart of a woman. In Cecil B. DeMille's version of "Samson and Delilah," the remark was made of Samson, "The man who can still the heart of a lion can stir the heart of a woman." When a man displays strength, courage, or any quality of manliness, women are naturally and deeply moved. This can be true of all women who observe him, not just the one who may be emotionally involved with him. As a woman who is strongly feminine and delicate inspires and moves men, so does a truly masculine man affect women.

It was Petruchio's masterfulness that tamed the shrew, Katrina, in Shakespeare's play and brought her lovingly to his feet. Wherever men are masterful, women succumb to this manly charm. Women may require more of men if they are to give them their love, but always they love only their master.

As a woman observes masculine qualities in a man, *admiration* for him is awakened. Every man desires to be admired, not for just himself as a person but for his manly qualities. This admiration can be given only as one serves in some manly capacity, for only then will there be anything to admire. For example, when a man sets forth on some daring adventure, or courageously pursues a difficult goal, those near will admire him. Or when he stands firm on a decision in the face of opposition, or takes off his coat to cover a shivering woman, she will be reminded of this chivalrous act and will have a feeling of admiration for him, as a man.

He may do other things less masculine in nature, such as helping with the dishes, shopping, helping a neighbor, or doing a thoughtful act for a child. These things are important and will awaken in a woman a feeling of respect and appreciation. But these are not acts which awaken the feelings of admiration of which I speak. This admiration that every man seeks can only be awakened when he serves in some manly capacity.

Important to remember also is that *manliness makes a woman feel womanly*. This is very important to her. In the presence of a strong, able and virile man, a woman feels, in contrast, delicate, soft and therefore womanly. This realization of her womanliness is one of the most pleasant sensations she can experience. She may therefore seek the company of such a man again and again for the renewing of this feeling. This is one of the dangers in marriage, for a husband who may lack these qualities of manliness makes it easier for his wife to succumb to the attentions of another man who seems to have them.

A woman can be quite unfeeling in the presence of ordinary men. If she is inclined to be slightly masculine in nature, most men will do nothing to affect her feelings. But when a strongly masculine man comes into her life, she suddenly feels like a woman. She may never have had this feeling before.

Women in the working world are sometimes subjected to this danger. Possibly her husband is not a particularly masculine man. As she enters the business world, she may acquire certain masculine traits. When she is brought into close association with a man who is strongly masculine, it can awaken a feeling of womanliness in her that is difficult for her to disregard. This problem can be lessened if she will return to her own feminine sphere where she can more fully develop her femininity. Then her own husband will be sufficient contrast to her femininity.

2. *For the man:* The feeling of being masculine is one of the most pleasant sensations a man can experience. It makes him feel like a man and thus sets him apart from women. This is one reason men strive so valiantly for high honors—not so much for the honor itself as for the realization of his powers exerted in attaining the goal. If he were given an undeserved honor, he would be denied the feeling of manly acomplishment. It is not being a champion a man glories in so much as the realization of his manly ability required to become one.

All men strive for fulfillment, but few realize just what it is or how it is gained. There is a mistaken idea that it comes as a result of money or acclaim. If these goals do bring fulfillment, it is because a man used his masculine abilities to attain them. Inherited wealth brings nothing in the way of fulfillment, nor does undeserved fame. This is a common reason why so many men of wealth and fame become desperately unhappy and commit suicide. Money and fame can, of course, bring fulfillment, but only as a man is a true man in attaining either. *Real fulfillment is a result of a man's growth as a man and his development of a noble character,* as we shall learn in the next chapter.

3. *Benefit to society:* When a man stands as the firm leader of a family, offering them the security of his strength and protection, and when his home is thus in order, society is immediately benefited. And when he also uses his masculine ability to help build society, his courage, drive, and determination have helped to make the world a better and safer place. Only men who have been really masculine men—brave, valiant and unwavering—have been our heroes and advanced mankind. These men are the building blocks of society. They are the real support of civilizations. Men who are weak, spoiled, pampered, spineless, soft and yielding have never done anything for the betterment of the world.

MASCULINE PRIDE, A SPECIAL PROBLEM

Men are proud that they are men. Unlike many women who turn deliberately from that which is feminine and seek a man's life in a world foreign to their sex, men tend to adhere more closely to that which is distinctly masculine. They may not be all that they could be, but like to think that they have the inherent qualities of manliness. Even a weak man will rise to defend his manhood when threatened.

Because of this, men are also proud of their special abilities, skills, achievements, muscular development, or any manly trait they have acquired through effort.

There are both benefits and hazards to this masculine pride. Inasmuch as pride is a part of his nature, we are assured that it serves a useful purpose. It is, however, a two-edged sword and can result in much pain and injury when permitted to dominate or when it is trampled on by some insensitive person.

Since the integrity and preservation of the family is essential to the well-ordered growth of all, God placed in man a keen pride in his responsibilities. Born in him is a desire to achieve something of merit, to be productive and a contributor to the welfare of others. A man has pride in his work and a desire to excel.

Since this is such an integral part of his being, anything which tends to depreciate his male ego usually encounters a vigorous, hostile or even uncontrolled reaction. As already indicated, even men who are effeminate hate to be told they have lost their virility. Others who do not bear this rather obvious mark highly resent any interference that they are deficient in any trait which is distinctively masculine. Although few men could qualify completely as being thoroughly masculine, to admit that they are anything less than a man would be unthinkable. With this built-in sensitivity, man has a very vulnerable spot which is frequently injured.

WOUNDED PRIDE

A man's pride can be seriously wounded by *ridicule, contempt, or criticism of his masculinity.* In the keen competition of the business world, men often belittle one another through cutting remarks and depreciating comments. Often this is an effort to build up one's own feeling of self-esteem. Sometimes a man's wife will unknowingly belittle his manliness by thoughtless comments, not knowing that she struck a raw nerve of male sensitivity.

One of the most common offenses is *indifference* towards masculinity. For example, a man may display great courage, or he may achieve a high honor worthy of great admiration from his associates, only to be pained by their indifference to his masculine accomplishment. He may have this same treatment at home where his wife ignores his achievements or at least fails to offer sufficient appreciation.

Men are often inconsiderate of one another and very callous about it. I read recently of a man who had lost his job as an engineer after more than twenty years' service with one company. Many engineers were unemployed in his area. When he went to the employment office for assistance, he was greeted with, "Boy, are you bad luck. I couldn't place you in a hundred years."

What could prompt such an insensitive remark? It is a direct affront to a man, suggesting how could he be so foolish as to find himself in a profession that wasn't needed (a few years earlier everyone was crying for engineers). Other unemployed men were told, "What's the matter with you? How can I ever place a man like you?" It is an inference that he doesn't have what it takes to hold a job. Such inhumanity defies understanding, especially when one contemplates the pride which is natural to man.

EFFECTS OF WOUNDED PRIDE

When a man's pride has been wounded, he experiences a cutting or humiliating sensation that can be painful to the emotions. If this happens frequently, he tends to build a *wall of reserve* around himself or to *go into his shell*. He becomes quiet, unapproachable and difficult to get next to. He may seem very natural and talkative on superficial subjects, but "clams up" if a conversation is too probing. Reserve can be a real problem in human relations since it cuts communications.

The reason a man builds this wall of reserve is because of fear—the fear that he may be met with further humiliation. He therefore withholds his thoughts and ideas because he does not wish to risk the pain of additional humiliation.

This wall of reserve is not a pleasant experience for a man, as you may already know. This is because men need and want to express themelves, to reveal their ideas and plans with the hope of winning approval and even admiration. But when a man has been humiliated over a period of time, he dare not reveal his thoughts for fear of further ridicule. Nothing but the absolute certainty that his ideas will be met with appreciation rather than ridicule or indifference will induce him to come out of his shell and express himself.

When pride has been wounded extensively and over a long

period of time, it can cause a *numbing effect* or a dulling of the senses. This is a *self-induced* numbness which a man can acquire unknowingly, to stand the pain of humiliation. The harm is this: Although it can reduce pain, it also reduces pleasure. In Dr. Edrita Fried's book *The Ego in Love and Sexuality*, she speaks of this numbing effect and its danger. "We pay dearly for the self-induced numbness, for while it relieves our pain, it also reduces our ability to experience pleasant emotions and to respond to pleasant stimulation. Unresponsiveness, like an indiscriminate scythe, mows down the flowers with the weeds."[1] The man no longer experiences the pain, but neither does he respond to the beauty of the sunset, the laughter of his children, or the love that his wife has to offer. This self-induced numbness can cause a man to become sexually impotent.

When a man's ideas have been squelched, his hurt pride can cause him to alter his life's plans or goals. He may lose heart in pursuing the goal he was planning with such dedication or give up the daring adventure he was so enthusiastic about. Much as he may wish to proceed, he does not want to risk the threat of further humiliation to his manly pride.

ELIMINATING HURT PRIDE

1. *Avoid belittling or humiliating other men:* In eliminating hurt pride, the first positive step one can take is to avoid inflicting wounds upon anyone else. The common practice of belittling is often made in humor without meaning harm. Although a man may not show evidence of humiliation, he may still suffer inner emotional pain. It is not safe to risk a cutting remark even though it is made in jest. If one wants to use someone as the butt of a joke, he should use himself. Many emotional problems would be relieved or eliminated if men would offer appreciation to one another rather than ridicule.

There is a temptation among men to cut one another down because of jealousy. Another tendency is to depreciate a man because it elevates one's own self-esteem. Another is because of a competitive feeling of wanting to rise above the other man. This striving for status is often responsible for the great amount of

[1] Dr. Edrita Fried, *The Ego in Love and Sexuality* (New York City: Grune and Stratton, Inc., 1960). Reprinted by permission of author.

belittling which occurs in the man's world. But these tendencies are rooted in human weakness and thus should be subdued.

2. *Heal the wounds of other men:* A second step in eliminating hurt pride is to *heal the wounds of others*. The parable is told in the Bible of the Good Samaritan who offered help to the wounded traveler on the road to Jericho. He dressed his wounds and took him to the inn for further care. The Good Samaritan is an example of how all men should serve one another.

In application of the parable in modern times, we cannot apply it too literally, since men are rarely beaten by robbers. But, there is another kind of wound inflicted sometimes as painful and destructive as the physical—the pain of hurt pride. If we are Good Samaritans, we need to heal the wounds of the afflicted by restoring self-esteem and offering appreciation and encouragement.

3. *By growing in manliness:* A third means of eliminating hurt pride is to grow in manliness. If you expect to always be appreciated as a man, it is essential that you do things worthy of that appreciation. Do things to be proud of! Eliminate softness and fearfulness and be a man! Build self-esteem within yourself. Then, when men attempt to cut you down, you will have an inner defense—a feeling of self-worth to protect you.

Men who are soft and weak are easy targets for belittling. Can they expect otherwise? If a man has not measured up as a man, he can hardly expect to be regarded as one. He must do things deserving of appreciation, if he is to avoid constant humiliation.

4. *By a sense of humor:* Another way of eliminating injured masculine pride is through a *sense of humor.* Often slighting remarks are made with no ill intent and should be received in the spirit given. Even serious accusations are tempered when one will come forth with a direct admission, even an exaggerated one such as, "You are right. I'm probably the most stupid guy in the office." The offender is disarmed immediately. Most people are not viciously anxious to offend. You can do them a favor as well as yourself through a sense of humor.

WHEN A MAN FACES FAILURE

1. *Face mistakes, failure and defeat with manliness:* The German author Goethe has said, "You cannot always be a hero but you can always be a man." Masculinity can be displayed just

as much in times of misfortune as in times of success. In fact,
times of trial offer an exceptional opportunity to prove manliness.
In defeat a man has the opportunity to display courage, idealism,
and an undefeated attitude—all masculine qualities of steel. He
may win more admiration in times of failure than in periods of
success, according to how he conducts himself.

Women are especially stirred to admiration when a man will
struggle in the face of serious obstacles or defeat. This is
illustrated in the case of a lawyer who had a good practice in an
eastern state, but for reasons of health was forced to move to a dry
climate. He came to California, but could not practice law as he
had not passed the bar there. Several months were required to do
the additional studying and prepare for the examination. In the
meantime he had to support his family, so he found employment in
a grocery store where he did heavy manual work. His wife
remarked that this was when she first really became aware of his
undefeated attitude. The manner in which he faced his problem
brought her more security and a greater feeling of admiration for
him than in periods when he enjoyed a prestigious law practice.

Men who are not manly in times of failure shrink from their
problems. They are filled with fear, complaints, and tend to blame
others for their situation. They do not awaken our admiration, but
rather cause disappointment for their lack of masculine fortitude.
Instead of revealing their weakness, if they would rise to the
occasion and show forth manly spirit, they would awaken
admiration instead of scorn. They would thus feel a new source of
strength and manly pride in having met defeat with valor.

2. *Acknowledge mistakes in times of failure:* Although it is
not necessary or even wise to acknowledge mistakes to everyone,
it is important to confess them to those closely involved,
especially your wife.

Because of a man's sensitive pride, he is extremely reluctant to
confess his mistakes to anyone, especially those who are near and
dear to him—his wife, in particular. The natural tendency is to
want her to see all the good points and none of the mistakes. When
defeat comes, a man tends to hide his mistakes, "sweep them
under the rug," or obscure them in any way he can. Frequently
blamed are unusual circumstances or "bad luck." This effort to
obscure failure is due to fear of humiliation. One cannot stand to
face the pain of humiliation in the eyes of those who mean so
much to him. But actually just the opposite is true. Acknowledg-

ing mistakes can actually relieve the pain of humiliation. Why is this so?

In the first place, acknowledging mistakes brings forth the virtue of humility, which is a *manifestation of strength rather than weakness*. One always appreciates a person who humbles himself in the face of defeat and objectively acknowledges his part in it. This trait of character brings forth admiration rather than scorn. When a man is met with this appreciative attitude, he is not going to feel the pain of humiliation, but will feel a pride in his manly strength of character.

In addition, confessing mistakes gives his associates a chance to be *forgiving,* if this is required. Especially is this important in the case of his wife. She will have the opportunity to bring forth her strength of character—her heroism. She will have the chance to overlook the mistake, to minimize it and to offer understanding and support in times of need. To deny her the opportunity to demonstate her own strength of character is to deny her a feeling of worth and satisfaction. Women love to heal wounds, to offer forgiveness, support and consolation in times of strife. Do not deny her this privilege.

Still another benefit from confessing failures is that your wife will be made fully aware of your mistakes. This will ease her mind so that she can forget about the matter. She will be assured that, if you have defined your mistakes to her, you have them clearly in your own mind and will not likely make the same mistakes in the future. But if you hide your failure or minimize it, she may have the impression that you are not aware of it and will be concerned that you may repeat the error. Consequently she may take it upon herself, for your sake, to inform you of your failures to save you from future trouble. This is doubly humiliating. To be so stupid that you do not realize your own mistakes and must be informed by your wife can be a painful experience.

If you obscure the truth of mistakes from your wife, she may tend to blame others for your failure. She may ponder the situation, feeling great injustices have been committed. This may cause her to take the initiative to put the wheels of justice into motion that recompense can be had. Women always have a natural inclination to justice—to make right a wrong. If her husband is actually the guilty one, her focus on the problem will eventually lead to the real truth which can be more humiliating than ever and may lead to entangling problems.

IS THERE MASCULINITY TODAY?

There is evidence of true masculinity today with some men. They are the strong men who are the builders of society, both in the home and in the world. They are the lifters who do more than their share without complaint. They are the men who meet every honest obligation and set a worthy example to their children—and to everyone else for that matter. They try to be what they hope everyone else will be. They are proud to be men, proud of their masculinity and are trying to develop it.

But it's unfortunately true that there is more of a lack of masculinity today than there is an abundance of it. This lack is at the root of more of our troubles than most men would care to admit. Many men are inclined to seek the soft and easy life. They shun responsibility or anything which is difficult. Their goals are easy goals. Their work is easy work. They want to be undisturbed, to rest, to "let George do it."

Men lean on women. They do not stand on their own feet, but expect the strength, initiative, mental fiber, and even physical work to be supplied by members of the feminine sex. They do not lead. They are wishy-washy and indecisive. They are easily pushed around by women and children and lacking in positive conviction.

There is a lack of chivalry. Men do not protect women nor add strength to their lives. They allow women to do the masculine chores and therefore fail in their own masculinity. Many men are effeminate in their mannerisms—the way they use their hands, walk, type of clothes, and interests.

There is a general lack of masculine skills and ability. Although a man may have a trade or profession by which he makes a living, he knows little else. He does not have the skill to solve his own problems.

The average man is not a builder of society. He is self-centered, not wanting to get involved in outside responsibility—a spirit of apathy. He may be up in arms over the sad state of affairs, but he does not want to do anything about it himself.

It must be emphasized that strong forces are operating which tend to deny the male responsibility as the guide, protector and provider and the builder of society, etc. A man of weakness might succumb to this philosophy, for in it his weakness is justified. Many women encourage it as they lean towards masculinity and seem to feel no conflict in this blurring of roles. Some openly resent their sex, envy men, and try to adopt their habits and functions.

There can be no argument in the fact that "God created man in his own image . . . male and female created he them." This creation was for a definite and eternal purpose wherein these separate identities are to be maintained and magnified.

In review, remember these salient points in developing masculinity:

HOW TO DEVELOP MASCULINITY

1. Assume masculine responsibility as the guide, protector and provider.
2. Help build society.
3. Develop masculine traits of character.
4. Develop masculine skills and ability.
5. Increase physical capacity.
6. Accentuate the differences between yourself and women.
7. Accept challenging goals.
8. Face mistakes, failure, and defeat with manliness.

X
CHARACTER

"What a piece of work is man! How noble in reason, how infinite in faculty! In form and moving how express and admirable! In action how like an angel! In appearance how like a god! The beauty of the world, the paragon of animals."

—William Shakespeare

The supreme quality of manhood is the strength of a noble character. A man may have the strength of masculinity which will add substance to his life, but it will never be of maximum worth unless refined by a *sterling character.* Harold Bell Wright recognized this when he described the man of the early West, "and a man's soul must be as the unstained skies, the unburdened wind and the untainted atmosphere." Shakespeare observed this when he depicts perfect manhood as being "in action like an angel, in appearance like a god." A noble character is the most important ingredient in making a man of steel.

Those qualities of character which relate to a man's *steel* side will be discussed in this chapter. There are others which are velvet traits—they will be discussed throughout the velvet part of this book. The steel traits which are most essential to strong character are the following:

SELF-MASTERY

"He who rules within himself and rules his passions, desires and fears is more than a king."

—Milton

The foundation of a noble character is self-mastery. It is the key to applying any virtue in which we may be lacking and will carry us to our greatest objective—becoming a perfect individual. *Self-mastery is the means whereby we apply knowledge of basic principles, overcome weakness, conquer appetites and passions, and devote ourselves to duty and reach our objectives.*

The goal of life is to become finer persons and eventually perfect things. The Savior taught, "Be ye therefore perfect, even as your Father which is in heaven is perfect." To reach this perfection we must acquire the virtues of love, patience, compassion, generosity, devotion to duty, and many other traits of real character. We will need to spend our time, money and energy in useful pursuits. It is essential that we properly nourish our bodies, to see that they have proper food, rest and exercise, so they will be perfect machines for our spirits. But, always there is an opposing force which pulls us downward away from these high goals. Inborn in us all is the tendency to evil. We are inclined to be carnal, sensual, lazy, irresponsible, selfish, and filled with fear. To overcome these weaknesses of flesh, we must employ the virtue of *self-mastery* and in so doing reach a higher plateau of character.

Self-mastery is the motivating force whereby we reach upward. Desire and willingness are not enough. Even knowledge and insight are not sufficient, nor is an emphasis on priority. Suppose, for example, that you would like to apply the knowledge of this book. You have the knowledge before you, and you may consider it highly important to your life. You may have a genuine desire and willingness, but unless supported by a strong will, little will be accomplished.

As further examples, a man may wish to improve his conversation, to guard against brutal frankness, bragging, or harsh criticism. Or he may wish to conquer the habit of over-eating, smoking, drinking, or other indulgences. He likely has sufficient knowledge to guide him, feeling it essential to his health or success, and has an intense desire and willingness to overcome these weaknesses. But without a will, he may go along forever with his same destructive habits.

Perhaps a man wishes to carry out a worthy objective or to more faithfully devote himself to duty. He may have every intention of follow-through and have a desire to do so, but unless supported by self-mastery, his tendencies to laziness, pleasure-seeking or fear may overcome his desire. No, not lack of knowledge, priorities, desire, willingness, or even lack of time are to blame for our failures to be better persons and do the things we need to do. It is our lack of self-mastery.

An interesting account is recorded in Scriptures of a rich young man who sincerely wanted to know what he should do to gain eternal life. He had made notable efforts to live a good life, could answer positively that he had kept the laws as he had been taught from his youth. Jesus, perceiving his principal weakness—a love of wealth—asked him to sell his goods and give to the poor and follow Him. Sorrowing, the young man turned aside, for an even greater weakness darkened his soul—the lack of self-mastery. Although he knew he should give up his riches, and very much desired eternal life, yet he could not rise above the selfishness and pride required to follow these instructions. His lack of will stood in the way of eternal blessings.

In modern teachings there is a certain "downgrading" of the virtue of self-mastery. Some say that it suppresses the emotions and that it is better for mental health to go along with natural impulses than to confront them with the opposition of one's will. Especially is this viewpoint applied to promiscuous sex. Some claim that denial of these urges will lead to frustration and emotional turmoil. Those who advance this false theory fail to realize that just the opposite is true, that it is not subduing impulses, *but SIN that leads to frustration and mental problems*. The goal of life is to have self-mastery over our natural impulses. The basis of true religion is to do that which is *counter* to human impulse—to love your enemies, to do good to those who hate you, and to pray for those who despitefully use you. The *natural* tendency is to hate our enemies and curse them that abuse us.

Other modern teachings say that although we must seek virtue, self-mastery is too difficult and that we must seek easier, more effective means of overcoming weakness. Self-mastery *is* difficult, and it is wise to use any means to make it easier. We can acquire knowledge that will help us understand the cause of our weakness and in this way assist us in overcoming it more easily.

Or we can adopt a positive habit to overcome a negative one or provide incentives, rewards, and reminders. But we must face the fact that we do not overcome weakness without strength—the strength of a strong will.

HOW TO GAIN SELF-MASTERY

Self-mastery may be gained in the following ways:
a) By training the will
b) By prayer
c) By fasting

1. *Training the will:* As one continually trains the will in small steps by employing the virtues of self-control, discipline and restraint, one grows in self-mastery. The training of the will is a deliberate action, or preparation in advance, rather than waiting for a great need to arise. When the will is trained by a continual effort in smaller steps, we become fortified. We are strengthened to meet temptation and weakness in emergencies which arise.

There are some effective means of training the will, such as the following:

a) *Do something you do not want to do* and do it regularly: It may be something unpleasant, like taking a cold shower every day or getting at a job you have been avoiding. The purpose is to train the will.

b) *Deprive yourself of something pleasant,* like not watching your favorite T.V. program, giving up your favorite dessert, not snacking between meals, giving up candy, soft drinks, coffee, smoking, drinking, or other habits. Although you may have other reasons for giving up these habits, in this case the primary purpose is to train the will.

c) *Demand definite quotas and performance of yourself,* such as arising at 4:30 each morning, getting a certain number of jobs done at a particular time, exercising a specific amount of time each day, outlining a definite program of responsibility and following through consistently. Do this deliberately to train the will.

d) *Do something difficult:* Set a goal for yourself that is not out of reach, but difficult. Pursuing a difficult goal will train the will, whereas seeking an easy goal does nothing for it. Or engage in work or responsibility that is difficult.

Children especially should be given difficult things to do if for no other reason than to train the will.

In each of these instances emphasis is upon training the will, otherwise one might be sidetracked. For example, one might determine to get out of bed a half hour early to do some extra studying, but unless training the will is kept in mind, one might rationalize that he can study at another time under conditions that are not so trying. Instead, he reminds himself that his objective is to train the will, reinforcing the thought by saying to himself, "I am doing this because it is difficult, and I will deliberately overcome the pull of the flesh in this way."

2. *Prayer:* To more completely gain self-mastery, it is necessary to seek the Lord's strength through prayer. If we are to reach upward, sufficient to conquer our passions, weaknesses and fears, or to reach high objectives, we will need a high degree of self-mastery. Such a goal can only be reached with the help of God.

Alcoholics Anonymous recognizes the need for God's help in overcoming the enslaving habit of alcoholism. They realize the futility of their problem without divine assistance. They must, in fact, acknowledge their helpless dependence upon God before they can make progress towards their goal.

I recall talking with a man who had been smoking for forty years and has successfully overcome this habit. He had tried again and again to quit, but was unsuccessful until he humbled himself and sought the Lord's help through prayer. "Then," he said, "God took away my desire to smoke."

High goals are often out of reach without God's help. The amount of self-discipline required to reach a high objective may be impossible without God to strengthen us, to give us mastery over the human weaknesses that so often deter us from goals.

3. *Fasting:* The most effective means of gaining self-mastery is by fasting. This is a religious practice consisting of abstaining from all food and drink (including water) for a period of at least twenty-four hours. During this time we humble ourselves before God in sincere prayer for his assistance. Fasting can be practiced in a time of urgency, when there is a particular need for self-control, or regularly as a means of gaining self-mastery. Fasting is a type of prayer, one in which we not only ask God for help, but demonstrate our intense desire by sacrifice of material needs.

Fasting with prayer is a powerful force in obtaining divine assistance. When one is willing to deprive himself of something he has every right to have, and to do it voluntarily and deliberately as an evidence of a sincere desire for heavenly favor, there is a power set loose that will work wonders.

Jesus Christ began his ministry by fasting. He did not attempt to shape the souls of other men until He first became master of himself. He left the crowded cities and went into the wilderness where He fasted for forty days and nights. His purpose was to overcome the powers of evil—to gain mastery over Himself. The Scriptures describe His trying experience in which He was sorely tempted by Satan who promised Him the satisfactions which all humans seek. By rejecting Satan He proved to Himself His mastery over evil. The means whereby He accomplished this self-mastery was a long period of fasting.

Self-mastery is the highest goal of a noble life. It was said of Jesus, "He put all things under His feet." And He promised us, "And to him that overcometh will I give the crown of life." And in the Book of Revelations we are promised the following: "To him that overcometh will I give to eat of the tree of life which is in the midst of the paradise of God." The rewards of both heaven and earth await those who attain self-mastery.

CHASTITY

Chastity means to be sexually pure, or to not indulge in sexual relations outside of marriage, or engage in immoral sexual practices. Those who lack this virtue—those who commit these unrighteous acts—are guilty of "sexual immorality" in the form of fornication, adultery, or homosexuality. Fornication is the act of having sexual relations when unmarried; adultery is the act of sexual relations by a married person with someone other than his own wife or husband; homosexuality is to have sexual attraction, feelings, or engage in sexual practices with one of the same sex.

Pernicious theories claim there is no harm in sexual immorality if these intimacies are practiced between two consenting adults who both receive satisfaction from it. They blame society for the feeling of guilt imposed upon them as a child would blame the waving branches of a tree for the wind. They are urging society to accept these evil practices to ease the pain of their outraged consciences and are ignoring the real harm that comes to themselves and to society because of promiscuous sex.

WHY BE CHASTE?

The first reason to be chaste is that it is a command of God. The ringing command "Thou shalt not commit adultery" was given to Moses for his people. This instruction was written in tablets of stone and reinforced in Scriptures many times. We read in 1 Cor. 6:9, "Know ye not that the unrighteous shall not inherit the kingdom of God? Be not deceived; neither fornicators, nor idolators, nor adulterers, nor effeminate, nor abusers of themselves with mankind."

Not only is chastity adhered to for reasons of obedience to God, but is for a divine purpose for the preservation of the individual and especially to avoid the destruction which inevitably comes to mankind when immortality is practiced generally. Sexual sin brings with it injury to the individual and is corruptive to society in the following ways:

HOW SEXUAL SIN CORRUPTS MANKIND

1. *Distraction and deviation:* Sexual sin is a great distraction to a man in his work and can cause him to deviate from his worthy goals or to neglect his duties. Since he focuses his interests and energies on immorality, he will neglect important phases of his life. This usually means neglect of his family, neglect of his work, and can lead to his downfall as a man.

2. *Conflict in spirit:* The spirit of God strives in every man to lead him to righteous paths. When a man commits immoral acts, he brings himself into conflict with God's spirit, or his own conscience, which produces a feeling of guilt. This guilt can cause emotional distress and mental health problems. Immorality also destroys the finer or more noble things about him which emanate from a good spirit.

3. *Loses the spirit of God:* It has been written in the Holy Scriptures, "He that looketh upon a woman to lust after her, or if any shall commit adultery in their hearts, they shall not have the Spirit, but shall deny the faith and shall fear." The spirit of God is greatly needed to guide a man to a successful life, to help him make wise decisions, lay sound plans, and use good judgment. When he loses the spirit of God, he is left to grope along life's paths with forces so bewildering and difficult that they defy

solution. This can bring on failure, both in his family and in his work.

4. *Eternal punishment:* Those who commit adultery "shall not inherit the Kingdom of God" as has already been pointed out in 1 Corinthians. They will also be due eternal punishment. The initial day of judgment, at the Second Coming of our Lord Christ, "will be a swift witness . . . against the adulterers and they shall be burned as stubble." (Mal. 3:5) Why God has placed such severe punishment on this particular sin may not be entirely clear to many, but in His noble purposes which are to bring about the happiness, development and eternal life of man, He follows undeviating principle.

5. *Downfall of nations:* The greatest threat of any country lies in immorality, and especially in sexual immorality. Like the columns of the temple of Gaza which Samson pulled down, causing the entire temple to collapse, so will immorality lead to the weakening and eventual destruction of an entire civilization. Sexual immorality was the principal cause of the disintegration of the Roman empire, Greece, Persia, Babylon, Sodom and Gomorrah, and many others. It is the greatest threat in America today as well as many other countries and supersedes all other problems. It does, in fact, create most of them. If for no other reason than love of country and love of life should we avoid immorality and run from it as the greatest enemy of mankind. It will tear from us all that is near and dear.

WHAT CHASTITY DOES FOR THE MAN

In addition to avoiding the pitfalls which would destroy him, chastity brings a man strength, both spiritual and physical. That individual who will garnish his life with virtue provides for himself an armor of protection which will help him to withstand other temptations. He will attain an inner strength of spirit which will help guide him to a more perfect life. In addition he will gain a bright countenance and a wholesome spirit which makes an evil-minded person uncomfortable in his presence.

The morally pure person has peace of mind—a freedom from fear that some long hidden skeleton in the closet will be uncovered, that he will cross paths with someone with the ammunition to blackmail or embarrass him. In teaching chastity to his children, he can do so with conviction and power.

A man who is sexually pure will prolong his sexual function and his health. Some have attempted to refute this fact and rationalize immorality with the claim that it is not healthful to suppress sexual desire. There is no competent study that can support such a thesis. Quite the contrary is true. Suppression and control of this strong desire brings forth strength and health of the individual and will prolong sexual function and satisfaction. One's sexual organs are not like muscles which must be flexed and used to avoid atrophy. Their function is enhanced under conditions of restraint, whereas promiscuity tends to debility.

It is well to note that one of the greatest frustrations of those who wildly and promiscuously vent their sexual passions is the loss of virility and a failure for sustained satisfaction. Bizarre aberrations are then indulged which not only fail to quench the fire but add to it. As with drunkenness and other serious vices, the end is sometimes self-destruction as one realizes that he has pursued a path which cannot provide the fulfullment sought. Next to the gift of life, the greatest gift to man is his opportunity to participate with diety in populating the earth. To make foul the fountain of life is a sin which is, in magnitude, next to murder.

OVERCOMING IMMORALITY

To suggest that a chaste life is unattainable is a ridiculous assumption. Many thousands of people attest by virtuous lives that they have achieved this goal. For one who has made the mistake of following an immoral course, his choice is to give it up and pursue a course that will produce lasting satisfactions. Few offenses are more difficult to overcome, and the strength given by God will be required to change the pattern. But an immoral life can be changed and the sins wiped out, if one's repentance is sincere and sustained. I say there is but one choice to make in such a situation. Any other choice than this will end in defeat and destruction of the soul. The steps to follow are:

1. *Recognize the sin:* The first step is to recognize the sin and its seriousness in the eyes of God, without an attempt to justify previous behavior. With a spirit of humility, determine to live a moral life.

2. *Approach God:* Come to God with humility, *acknowledging* your *guilt* with a *heartfelt sorrow* for your offense. Ask for *forgiveness* and *assistance* in living a moral life.

3. *Good works:* Get busy immediately on some completely unselfish project that will benefit someone in need. Give of yourself. This will provide additional strength in overcoming your problem.

HONESTY

We can best understand the principle of honesty by considering its opposite—dishonesty. The well-recognized forms of dishonesty are stealing, lying, and cheating. Men who claim character would not think of indulging in these forms of deceit, and yet these same men may still be guilty of dishonesty in the more obscure forms. They may, for example, obscure the truth, or give a false reason for their actions, or blame others for their own mistakes or weaknesses. They may make gross exaggerations or deliberately make a false accusation.

SOME FORMS OF DISHONESTY

One of the most common failings of men is to obscure the truth. Notorious exploitation has occurred in the rate of interest charges, especially to those unfamiliar with certain business terms. For example, a buyer may be told he is to pay 6% *add on* interest rate. He assumes that he is paying the borrowed money plus 6% interest which is added on. But the truth is obscured. *Add on* is an ambiguous or deceiving term. In reality, add on interest at 6% is about 12% simple interest. In other words, words are used which are technically not dishonest, but with intent to misrepresent, for they are not generally understood. This is a deliberate attempt to obscure the truth.

Another example is when unsuspecting or credulous investors are sold franchises where an unrealistic projection of profit is given or where all the hazards are not disclosed. The product may be insufficiently tested or may have inherent weaknesses in it. Vital data may be withheld, since it would be unfavorable to the seller.

Flagrant examples of dishonesty are observed in specialized services such as automobile repairing, electrical repairing, plumbing, and many others. Unnecessary work is done and parts installed which were not necessary, both of which are listed on the bill. There is no way the average man can detect this deceit.

Professional men are tempted to charge exhorbitant fees or charge a weighted price if the payer is an insurance company or a government agency. They charge "what the traffic will bear." "Others get theirs; I might as well get my share" is the justification.

REASONS WE ARE DISHONEST

Why do men who claim to be essentially honest engage in these more obscure forms of deceit? They are moved by the same basic reason that any man is dishonest, is driven to lie, cheat, or steal. The reasons have their roots in human weakness which are described here:

1. *Love of money and material goods:* This human weakness is the number one reason men rob banks, steal furniture and jewels. But it is also a reason behind the more obscure forms of dishonesty, such as those just described or other acts such as taking a small item from a store without paying for it, failure to return an overpayment, lying about a child's age to buy a ticket for half fare, buying goods wholesale under deceptive means, and lying to avoid paying income taxes. Some men have been known to switch price tags, to take lumber from a building lot, or help themselves to produce in the fields without paying for it. All of these acts have to do with money and material goods. Perhaps this is the reason the Apostle Paul made the statement "The love of money is the root of all evil"—in that it leads to so many forms of dishonesty and vice.

2. *Fear of criticism or humiliation:* This is the reason a person will cheat on a test—to avoid the humiliation of a failure. It is the reason we tend to blame someone else for our mistakes or grievous circumstances. I recall the experiences of a man who had always been quite well-to-do. Because of unusual circumstances, his business failed and he found himself in a humble situation. To save face in the eyes of his wife, he blamed someone else for his loss, a man who was entirely innocent. His wife became furious with the innocent man and caused trouble for both of them.

Fear of criticism is the reason we make excuses for our mistakes in an attempt to obscure the real truth. Always there is a fear that if the truth is known, it will put us in a bad light and invoke criticism. For example, a man may make a poor business investment. He may have known all of the facts when he entered the venture, but to save face with his fellows, he may say the seller deceived him, misrepresented the investment, or made promises which did not materialize. The real reason, which may have been poor judgment or even foolishness or greed, is obscured because of the fear of humiliation.

It is not necessary to reveal our mistakes to others. Certainly these errors in judgment are personal matters which we have every right to keep to ourselves. But it is an act of dishonesty to make false statements and accusations in an effort to "save face."

3. *Desire for acclaim, praise, or honor:* The desire for acclaim is strong in men as we have already learned. When a man desires a particular advancement or position, he may be tempted to defame a competitor's name by downgrading him falsely or accusing him unjustly. By depreciating the other man he may rid him from the competition and win the honor himself. Men will also copy someone else's work or claim someone's work as their own in an effort to win honor to themselves. This practice sometimes goes on in the school system. My little girl related the following experience: She had drawn a beautiful picture of a dragon. After school the little boy who sat next to her erased her name and wrote his own on the picture. When she confronted him with the matter, he said, "Oh, you can draw another. I had to do it to please the teacher and my mother."

If this practice is not stopped early in life, it can lead to a similar dishonesty in adult life. Often men will create original ideas or success patterns only to have them stolen by a competitor. In many cases these ideas cannot be protected by a patent. But it seems that although legal protection is not possible, there should be a moral integrity, a high degree of honesty which would prevent us from copying someone else's work or ideas if it will interfere or be competitive with their success or acclaim. Honesty and integrity are really beyond enforcement. To be strictly honest often requires the greatest soul-searching within.

Another form of dishonesty due to desire for acclaim is bragging or gross exaggerations with the intent of focusing attention on ourselves or impressing others. It is common for men to brag about their abilities or accomplishments and in so doing, "stretch the truth" in a way that will elevate themselves.

4. *Laziness:* Many people who would not think of stealing money or directly telling an obvious falsehood will steal just as

surely by failing to perform diligently and adequately on a paid job. While accepting pay for their time, they idle away sometimes hours each day in slothful and half-hearted effort. In a very real sense, what was once their own time is no longer theirs, for it has been purchased for a price. To idle it away while on a job is therefore stealing just as it would be to take money from the till.

5. *Drugs, alcohol, and other enslaving habits:* We must not fail to recognize the above motive for dishonesty, especially in modern times. The craving for drugs will drive a man to rob and steal, even at the risk of his own life, that his terrible urges may be satisfied. It is unfortunate that men who have already degraded themselves must further their downfall by stealing.

The reasons, then, for dishonest acts are principally a desire for money or possessions, fear of criticism or humiliation, desire for acclaim, laziness, and enslaving habits. If we can rid ourselves of these human weaknesses, we will find it easier to more consistently apply the virtue of honesty.

It is *the more obscure forms of dishonesty* the average man must constantly guard against, acts such as falsely blaming others, accusing, justifying, exaggerating, and concealing the truth. We should strive to be overly honest, if this is possible, that we may be assured of always being honest.

In the ideal man I am attempting to describe, honesty is not enforced through outside measures nor is it practiced through fear of detection or punishment. His integrity is not weighed out each night or at every critical period of testing. Honesty is an integral part of his being and comes automatically. Such a man is not governed by law so much as he is governed by his own conscience. The fear of violating his own integrity would provide the greatest deterrent to any act of dishonesty. His honesty provides for him strong guidelines of behavior which can be relied upon with certainty.

Karl G. Maeser illustrated this principle by suggesting that a truly honest man when placed in a confined area bounded by a chalk line, and giving his word that he would not go beyond that line, would be more solidly contained than a man locked behind steel bars supported by a ten-foot-thick stone wall, with no such promise.

Honesty is not only the strength of a good man's life, but is a principle of success which will help him in all of his activities— with his family, friends, and especially in his work. Dishonest men invoke principles which will surely be the means of their failure even in a material sense. However, the greatest reason for living an honest life is that it is a command of God, who said: "Thou shalt not steal, thou shalt not bear false witness."

DEPENDABILITY

Dependability means to follow through on a job, a responsibility, obligation, or promise. It means reliability, wherein full confidence can be placed in you to get a job done according to instructions, and at the time expected, and that you will not let other things interfere with the objective. The guide to acquiring this virtue is a simple one: *Do the thing you are obligated to do, at the time it needs to be done, whether you want to do it or not.* This requires self-discipline or the will to do it.

Dependability also means that you will keep your word, that you will do that which you have said you will do and not do that which you have promised not to do. It means that you will keep commitments, respect confidences you have said you would keep. It means that your word is as good as your bond, that it is sacred to you and can be solidly relied upon.

One often marvels at the simplicity and homeliness of the greatest virtues of mankind. Dependability is certainly one of them and one which is within the grasp of the most humble and least naturally endowed with talent. But its presence is rarely found. Instead, there is a great failure to follow through, with a rationalization of unforeseen circumstances, interruptions, demand, and other distractions that serve as excuses. There are, of course, legitimate emergencies whereby work must be interrupted, but most often laziness or a lack of feeling of responsibility is to blame. There are two general areas of a man's life wherein he must be dependable if he is to succeed. They are—on the job and in the family.

1. *On the job:* Other than basic integrity, the most fundamental quality for a man's success is dependability. It rates highes than talent, training, or experience. Talent is greatly appreciated in the working world but is of little value without dependability. Training and experience are valuable to qualify a man for a job, but are of little worth without dependability.

Who of us in selecting an employee would not rate dependability as one of the most essential qualifications? I once heard a man say, "Give me an untrained man who is dependable any day over a trained man who is undependable. I can train the dependable man and he will be a valuable employee, but I can do nothing with the undependable man."

2. *In the family:* Being dependable as a *provider* brings security to the family. The security of each family member lies more in the *dependability of the father* in earning a living than in the money itself. A father who may have inherited money or achieved it by some sudden, spectacular means may not provide a feeling of security to his family as much as a father who has consistently worked through the years and thus proved his dependability.

The father will also need to be dependable as the guide, to follow through with plans, promises, and family obligations when this is at all possible. This will build trust in his word, prove his dependability, and thus bring a certain amount of security to the family members.

Lack of dependability suggests a selfish attitude wherein one is likely to set aside a commitment, in order to follow a pursuit which is more convenient to himself or to his own liking. The interests of others may be deferred to grant attention to his own selfish interests. Dependability on the other hand suggests a concern and interest in other people.

Especially is it important to be dependable in the daily tasks and obligations which are the common lot of all mankind and which are often considered menial. In fact, to perform these tasks faithfully and well, without complaint, assuming his full share of responsibility, is an evidence of true greatness.

FAIRNESS OR JUSTICE

This means to strictly render that which is due, whether it be reward or punishment, and to do so with impartial or unbiased judgment. This subject can best be understood by first considering *unfairness* and *injustices*.

1. *Unfairness in giving pay or rewards:* We can observe injustices in a man's work where a miserly employer will fail to give a man what he justly deserves. He may extract everything he can from him and then pay just enough to meet the standards of the law. This type of man is guilty of injustice in his dealings with his fellowmen in that he has not rendered that which is justly due. Or a man can be unjust if he rewards a person with *more* than he

deserves. This can be especially true in a family where a father may feel generous towards his children and give them more than they deserve for a service rendered. If this happens frequently, it will give the child an unrealistic picture of life and the worth of his efforts, and is therefore unjust to him.

Unfairness can also be observed when we show *favoritism* in giving rewards for services rendered. For example, two men may render equal service and yet one may be rewarded with privileges, advancement, honor or pay to exceed the other man. This may be due to favoritism, or a special liking for the favored man. He may have a better personality, use better psychology, or be more friendly than the other man and thus wins special consideration that he does not deserve. To be guilty of favoritism is unfair. A just man will reward each man according to his deeds and is not swayed by superficial efforts.

This same favoritism can be observed at home between two children. In this case the father is partial to one child, often the oldest, youngest, or one he has a special liking for. He gives this child privileges or rewards which demonstrates unfairness towards his other children.

2. *Equating rewards:* There is a great tendency to reward two or more people equally whether they all deserve it or not. For example, one person may put forth special effort and be deserving of a reward, but in our kindly feeling towards all, we may make the mistake of rewarding them equally. In fact, to some, justice means equating. This is the attitude of a socialistic type of government that claims a high regard for all mankind by equating the wealth of the country. They ignore the principle of justice, in which men must be rewarded for their efforts and are injured, rather than helped, when they receive something for nothing.

There is sometimes a tendency for a man to equate rewards in his family where he loves all of his children the same and does not want to see any of them disappointed. I recall a painful example of equating in a family. One of the daughters wanted a chest. She saved her money for many months, denying herself entertainment and pleasures that she might have the cedar chest. When she bought it, her younger sister, seeing the chest, also wanted one very badly. But she had not been frugal with her money. She had spent it all on ice cream, candy, and pleasures. But her parents, in their desire to see both girls happy bought the other girl a similar chest. This was a great injustice to the daughter who had justly earned the cedar chest. The harm in rewarding the spendthrift and denying her the natural experience of disappointment is obvious. There are times when the only way a lesson can be learned is to suffer the consequences.

This same equating is often observed at birthday parties. The children engage in games and contests where a prize is offered the winner. But the hostess, in an effort to see that no one is disappointed, rewards each child with a prize. In so doing, she gives an incorrect picture of life. Children must be taught by experience that rewards are for those who earn them and that those who do not go without. They must learn to enjoy another person's success and to endure their own disappointment as a normal experience. Thus they will be given a more realistic picture of justice.

There is a great harm which comes from equating. It destroys incentive to earnestly strive for a goal which will bring personal rewards. Equate and you destroy incentive. This is the failure with socialistic types of government which take from the rich and give to the poor. They destroy a man's incentive to dedicate himself to a goal, to work long hours on a project far beyond the working hours in an effort to reach a high objective. One may feel that a righteous man would earnestly strive for worthy objectives without material rewards. But, when such a righteous man realizes that part of the money due him is used to give to another man who has not put forth effort, there is something within him that cries out "injustice."

In reviewing justice it is well to note that money and goods which are *inherited* are not in the same category as the injustices here described. Those who inherit wealth are not being paid for services. Inheritances are given as gifts, a tradition in which a father leaves his family that which he has accumulated, with the thought that they are to become stewards of family possessions. There may be problems attached to this tradition, but it is not considered injustice.

3. *Justice in rendering punishments:* Justice is to render punishments according to that which is due. Let us review circumstances. Suppose an employee has failed to follow instructions and thus has caused great difficulty for many people involved. He may have assembled some equipment wrong or failed to follow through on an important job. Or suppose a child has committed a bad deed or injured another child. In any case, how should the father or employer bring justice to bear?

First, he should make sure that the person involved understood instructions or what was expected of him; otherwise he could make an unfair judgment. Then, he should find out all of the facts involved. This may not be easy. Usually those giving details are so prejudiced in their own viewpoint that the story they give is highly colored. It may be given in a moment of high emotion or hurt or disappointment or hope.

After a man has found out all of the true facts, if this is possible, he should then free himself from any feeling of partiality or prejudice towards the guilty person; otherwise he will likely make an unfair judgment. He must also make certain that he has not expected too much, a performance beyond what a normal man can be expected to give. Or, in the case of a child, that he has not expected beyond the capacity of his years. He may have expected good behavior when he was tired or under stress. He may have expected scholastic achievement he probably would not produce himself under similar circumstances.

After a man has taken these four steps—1) he has made certain that the guilty person understood what was expected of him; 2) discovered all of the facts; 3) freed himself from partiality or prejudice; and 4) made certain he has not expected more than was fair—then he is prepared to make a fair judgment of the offense and determine just punishment.

The punishment may be only a stiff reprimand or it may be the denial of a privilege. He may assign extra work or responsibility or in some cases inflict physical punishment as is sometimes necessary with disobedient or impudent children. But whatever the punishment, justice requires payment for the deed. If a child steals something, even if it is of little monetary value, he should be required to return or replace the article and be reprimanded for violation of a serious principle. If a child is guilty of a civil offense where punishment of the law is required, he should take the full force of it. His parents should not step in and attempt to spare his punishment or in any way interfere with justice of the law.

When it is necessary to mete out severe punishment or a stern reprimand, it is always wise to follow up immediately with a demonstration of love or kindness towards the offender. If it is a child, he must know that you are not an opponent or enemy who wishes to do him harm, but are moved by love and concern for his welfare and personal development. Explain the principle of justice and that you are morally bound to exercise jurisdiction and punish when it is due. This principle also applies in dealing with employees.

There is a tendency for some men to be too firm and unrelenting in punishment, especially with children. This is often due to uncontrolled anger which causes a man to temporarily lose his judgment and become overly harsh. In this case, one must develop humility, allowing for human weaknesses. This will soften his spirit, and he will mete out punishment for the benefit of the offender rather than as an escape for his own anger.

The permissive attitude of so many men nowadays tends towards softness in discipline rather than firmness. This is occasionally seen in the working world where a man may think he is too busy to deal in complete justice with his employees. It may be difficult to discover the facts, or he may fear losing favor. If an employee is slothful or otherwise ineffective, a man may find it disagreeable to correct him and would rather dismiss him in as polite a way as possible rather than discipline him. A man who might otherwise be brought to more efficient and productive labor is denied the benefit of training which would be invaluable to him.

Because of love or tenderness, a man may be too soft in dealing with his children. Such emotional feelings tend to obscure the child's errors. When the child is involved in a conflict with other children, he is always innocent in his father's eyes. At school there is a tendency to blame the teacher or the other child when difficulties arise. Or if such a father does acknowledge his child's offense, he may overlook it or let him get off with a minimum of punishment. This softness can injure a child permanently and make him unprepared for the firm life ahead where society will deal justly with him in less favorable circumstances. It is the right of the child to be punished in justice for his offenses by someone who loves him.

Some may justify softness by calling it mercy. Because they do not understand this principle, they may feel they are obligated to be lenient in punishment, if not to forego it altogether. This may be right if the mistake was made in innocence, or if the offender is sincerely repentant, acknowledges his mistake and asks forgiveness. But this is not so often the case. Usually there is a justification for actions, a defense and tendency to blame others. If the offender does not show forth a sufficiently humble and repentant attitude, then justice must bring him to task. Mercy cannot rob justice, and there are many offenses for which one must make recompense even in the face of a sincerely repentant attitude. One can readily see that the leader of the family must acquire a keen sense of justice.

In review, I wish to restate the guidelines to rendering just punishments. They are:

1. Make certain the guilty person understood what was expected of him.
2. Discover all of the facts relating to the offense.
3. Free yourself of partiality or prejudice towards the guilty person.
4. Make certain that you have not expected more of him than is fair.
5. Make a fair judgment and render punishment due.
6. If your punishment must be severe or firm, follow up with kindness, love, and an explanation of your purpose in bringing justice to bear for his own benefit.

Especially in the home we see justice on trial. It is here that children first learn by personal experience. If the father has been just, they will be benefited; but if he has been unjust, they will be the first to detect it. Children have a very keen sense of justice which is why they are so sensitive about being treated fairly. The man who is firm but fair will serve his family well and gain the respect of those who associate with him.

UNSELFISHNESS

There is a natural tendency in man to be selfish, beginning in infancy. We observe this trait in tiny children who will take things away from one another without a tinge of conscience or cry to have their way in spite of inconveniences to others. In infants such behavior is not objectionable, for we understand their innocence. Children tend to outgrow this selfcenteredness quite readily, partly because of the teaching of their parents, but more because of their experience in the world. They soon realize that they must lose their selfishness if they are to get along in the world.

The problem is that most people lose only the amount of selfishness necessary to get along with others. They fail to grow beyond this point—to attain a high degree of unselfishness that is one of the principal goals of life. Instead, the main focus is upon their own lives and what is good for them. The point I wish to emphasize is this: Unselfishness leads to spiritual growth. In fact, *our spiritual growth is in direct proportion with our growth in unselfishness*. If we are growing to be more and more unselfish, then we are growing in spirit; but if we retain our selfcentered tendencies, then we fail to grow in spirit.

UNSELFISHNESS AND SPIRITUAL GROWTH

WHAT IS TRUE UNSELFISHNESS?

The following graph displays this truth:

Unselfishness is a willingness to give up one's own comfort or advantage for the benefit of someone else. There must be an element of *sacrifice* in a truly unselfish act. This means giving up some pleasure, comfort, material thing of value to you, or going to some trouble, risk, inconvenience, or out of your way for the benefit of someone else. There are some acts which are termed unselfish which in reality are not, such as giving away something you really do not want or need, doing something else which is little if any trouble, or giving a small donation to the church or poor. These may be acts of kindness, but they are not truly unselfish acts since they do not require sacrifice.

To grow in unselfishness, it is necessary to lose our self-centered tendencies. We must learn to think less of our own selves, our comforts and conveniences and advantages and think of others. Unselfishness takes place within the spirit of man and is not merely a superficial act of giving.

HOW A MAN'S WORLD ENCOURAGES SELFISHNESS

To a certain extent the man's world is one which encourages and cultivates selfishness. There is constantly before him his respon-sibilities to provide for his family. The demands are ever increasing and not wholly predictable. Despite careful planning the need for money is ever-pressing with the responsibility resting upon the head of the family. With the greater portion of his time allocated to earning the living, the emphasis in a man's life may be too strongly centered in his efort to acquire things for himself. The only way this problem can be relieved is to avoid a standard of living which is too high so that a man is somewhat relieved of the strain of earning the living and can cultivate a spirit of unselfishness for others.

Another phase of a man's life which encourages selfishness is the keen competition of the business world. One almost has to adopt the slogan "every man for himself" in order to succeed. With the great pressure and incentive to watch out for one's own interests, it requires a great deal of intellectual integrity to decide what may be selfish or not in business relationships.

I observed this lack of integrity in a man who was describing a scheme of raw land promotion to a group of prospective salesmen. He was at a high peak of enthusiasm as he described how they would be able to sell land which had cost only $300 an acre for as much as $4,000 per acre. When someone suggested that perhaps the deal was weighted too heavily in their favor with insufficient consideration for the buyer and his opportunity to profit from his purchase, his comment was, "It is obviously better for us than it is for them."

If we are to follow the principles of integrity, any business arrangement should be as nearly an equal arrangement as possible, considering costs, risks and effort that each contributes. It need not be a 50-50 deal, since both parties may not contribute the same, but for that which is contributed the chance for each to profit should be commensurate. Unless the deal is good for both parties, it is not good for either. This is not only a principle of integrity—it is a principle of success.

Sometimes we hear of legislators who feel it their duty to bring special advantages to the community they represent, regardless of the disadvantage other communities might sustain. While urging economy generally, for example, they may push for the continuance of a government project in their area which may not actually be productive enough to justify its existence. At the same time, they will oppose a similar project in another area with which they are not greatly concerned. Such an attitude is obviously hypocritical, for one will not apply to himself the same standards or criteria which he would apply to others. It is so easy to give "lip service" to a principle which is remote from us and expect others to do that which we cannot do ourselves. In this hyprocrisy we find the seeds of many of the social problems of our day.

The man who selfishly thinks of ways to enhance his own position can be sorely tempted to use any expedient means to do so regardless of the legality or ethics involved. Thus, his selfishness has driven him to other evils of character. A constriction takes place in his personality, a narrowness of viewpoint, diminishing his power to be effective. It is ironic that in his selfish drive for material things or advantage, a man sets in motion forces which make him less capable of attaining them than if he cared less about them. Thus the selfish man adopts traits which lead to failure, whereas the unselfish man applies principles which lead to success.

If a man is to be successful in the leadership of his family, it is essential that he rule with *unselfishness*. If he is not unselfish, if he only considers what is best for him, then his family will come to follow him only out of duty. But if he is unselfish, always considering what is best for all family members, with a willingness to sacrifice for their benefit, they will be able to put their trust in him.

A man should also unselfishly give of his *time* for the benefit of his family. Often a man will reason that when he has earned the living he has fulfilled his obligation to his family. He then spends the remainder of his time in his own interests and pleasures. The family may seldon see him, except at dinnertime and when it is necessary for him to be home.

True unselfishness means giving, not only of material goods, but time and energy for the benefit of others. This was the principle in the instruction given, "He who loseth his life for my sake, shall surely find it."

MORAL COURAGE

Moral courage is the courage to do that which is *morally right* or to follow correct principles at the risk of consequences. These consequences are usually the following:

1. Loss of money, or the opportunity for money.
2. Loss of prestige or acclaim.
3. Criticism or humiliation.
4. Loss of friends.
5. Loss of an advantage or position.
6. Physical harm.

One of the most common needs for moral courage is when we are faced with the possible loss of money if we attempt to do what is right. One example of this involves the tobacco industry. Recent studies provide sufficient proof that this industry is bringing sickness and premature death to millions of people. One would think this knowledge of the dangers of tobacco would impel the owners to close their factories immediately. But such would require a tremendous amount of moral courage—too much, apparently, when they consider the loss of revenue.

The liquor industry is bringing destruction *worse than death*—the degradation and spiritual downfall of millions. Producers of alcohol are well aware of the evils of drink. Alcoholics Anonymous is a continual reminder of the effort others are making to restore the damage brought on by alcohol. Yet, because of the tremendous amount of money involved, people in these industries do not have the moral courage to do what is right. The same can be said for the gambling casinos, the manufacturers of pornographic literature, obscene movies, or any industry which is destructive to mankind.

What about persons whose incomes are derived from the production and distribution of these damaging products, or who are employed in the gambling casinos? "At what point," they might ask, "am I personally responsible for injury to my fellow men? Am I such a small part of a great system that my individual responsibility is lost?" Greater moral courage may be required in this instance than in the first, where the ill effects are direct. Imagine for a moment the effect upon the world, if employees of all the manufacturers of vice had the moral courage to leave their work. Such a mass demonstration of integrity would indeed revolutionize the moral character of society. So it is not only the manufacturers of destructive products who are to blame—who lack moral courage—it is everyone involved in the distribution or service of them. Perhaps this should be extended to include otherwise legitimate businesses such as tradesmen who supply services to these industries. Are their hands entirely clean?

Persons in these industries must have feelings of guilt, for many of them attempt to clothe themselves with respectability by becoming associated with some worthy endeavor. Some of the gambling barons of Nevada give scholarships to students and aid to the blind. Shamefully, a number of states have legalized the lottery which saps millions of dollars from the weak with the excuse that the funds so obtained will go to education. (Shouldn't the aim of education itself encompass an effort to aid people in establishing sound moral values and habits?)

Moral courage is required in political life. One would suppose that men in politics would be thoroughly familiar with the Constitution, as it is the yardstick by which legislation should be considered. It is magnificent document designed to preserve the interests of everyone, with special emphasis upon the protection of the minority. Yet many politicians lack the moral courage to stand in defense of these principles of freedom if their prestige or job would be threatened by so doing.

It takes moral courage to defend a principle of truth when one's friends would be offended by such a stand. If one's neighbor operates a theater where undesirable movies are shown, it might be more convenient to let someone else initiate action to correct the evil. It is not always easy to remember that one should be on the side of "right" in every instance. One is reminded of the story of Abraham Lincoln where a friend remarked to him that the Lord must surely be on his side. The wise Mr. Lincoln replied, "I'm more concerned about being on His side than having Him on my side."

Inspiring examples of moral courage are contained in the Scriptures. We read in the thirty-ninth chapter of Genesis that after Joseph, who was sold into Egypt, had won favor with Potiphar and had been given full authority over his property and business, he was tempted by Potiphar's wife, who tried to seduce him. Rather than yield, he fled her presence, but not before she had torn his coat from him. With this as evidence, she blackmailed him and he was sent to prison. Despite this horrible injustice, he remained faithful and was, in time, able to redeem himself. He became the second man in authority in all Egypt, Pharaoh only being greater.

In ways great and small we are all given opportunity to display moral courage in our dedication to do what is right in the face of strong desire or pressure to compromise our principles.

SELF-DIGNITY

Self-dignity is a dignity of spirit. With this virtue we rise above unkind remarks, criticism, abuse, or any attempt to degrade or debase our character. Others may try to damage our reputation, but we maintain a kingly composure. This dignity of spirit is not something one superficially achieves by deciding he is going to respect himself, but arises from a genuine feeling of self-worth.

Men who are competing for position in the business world sometimes downgrade one another by spreading negative information about an opponent. This is done in the hope that he will be eliminated from the competition. When an innocent man becomes aware of this treachery, he is likely to become very angry and seek revenge. He may fight back with a vicious attitude, displaying character traits as negative as those of his defamer. If he does, he will lower himself in the eyes of his associates.

To attain self-dignity, it is necessary to restrain and control the emotions. It is also necessary to have a good character, including the traits listed in this chapter. For this reason, self-dignity was mentioned last. It becomes the crown which rests upon all the other virtues.

THE NEED FOR MEN OF CHARACTER

We desperately need men of character in our troubled times. They are needed in the affairs of the government, in the communications system, in industry, science, and in the business world. They are needed in all of the departments of education, at the printing press, in the fields, and in all endeavors. Men of character have always been the bulwarks of society. Honest men have been the builders of civilization, whereas men who are dishonest, unjust, and otherwise evil have destroyed it.

And what are men of character needed *for*? To advance science, technology, or to create inventions and useful ideas? Yes, but this is not the greatest need. We have made rapid progress in science and industry. *The urgent need is not to advance technology, but to advance spirituality.* Our greatest need is not to find a cure for cancer or an end to disease . . . "For we wrestle not against flesh and blood, but against principalities, against powers, against the rulers of darkness of this world, against spiritual wickedness in high places. Wherefore, take unto you the whole armor of God, that ye may be able to withstand in the evil day, and having done all, to stand." (Ephesians 6:12 and 13)

We need a *special kind of men* in our urgent times. Masculine men? Yes, those with great courage and determination. But this masculine nature must be refined by a noble purpose so that the motivating force of their life is for public good and not for selfish advancement. We need men with the virtues explained in this chapter—the kind of man described by J. G. Holland:

> God give us men. The time demands
> Strong minds, great hearts, true faith
>   and ready hands;
> Men whom the lust of office does not kill;
>   Men whom the spoils of office cannot buy;
> Men who possess opinions and a will;
>   Men who have honor, men who will not lie;
> Men who can stand before a demagogue
>   And damn his treacherous flatteries with-
>   out winking;
> Tall men, sun-crowned, who live above the fog
>   In public duty and in private thinking!
> For while they rabble with their thumb-worn
>   creeds,
> Their large professions and their little deeds,
> Mingle in selfish strife; lo! Freedom weeps!
> Wrong rules the land and waiting Justice sleeps.
>
> —J. G. Holland

HOW TO ATTAIN A NOBLE CHARACTER

Attaining a higher, more noble character is difficult for everyone. This is because we have natural tendencies to weakness and evil. Men are by nature carnal, sensual and devilish. There is an inborn selfishness is us, a striving for comfort and self-protection. Even within our family circle the tendency is to pour out our love and concern for our own—without too much thought for those outside. The focus is on us, on our own needs and desires. When we reach to higher heights, we are bound by our own selfishness; and when we seek to overcome the weaknesses of the flesh, the appetites and other indulgences, we must struggle against a carnal nature.

Only by turning to God can men reach a higher plateau of character. The strength which comes from God made David, the young shepherd boy, into a great and noble king. And it was he who so poetically declared the source of his strength: "The Lord is the strength of my life . . . The Lord is my rock and my fortress and my deliverer; my God, my strength, in whom I will trust; my buckler and the horn of my salvation and my high tower . . . Yes, though I walk through the valley of the shadow of death, I will fear no evil; for thou art with me: thy rod and thy staff they comfort me."

—Psalm 27:18, 23

REWARDS OF A WORTHY CHARACTER

The special reward to those who attain a worthy character is peace of mind or inner happiness. A most fundamental principle of truth is, "The good life promises the happy life." This is not necessarily a life free of problems, nor one of ease and comfort, but it is a life free of inner turmoil and emotional disturbances.

Spiritual growth means mental health. These two parallel one another. Only as we overcome, only as we lose selfcenteredness and self-indulgence and grow in the grace of a noble character can we gain peace of mind. This truth is supported in the most advanced knowledge of mental health. I would like to again refer to the statement by Dr. Max Levine, psychiatrist. "There cannot be mental health in the absence of high moral standards and a sense of social responsibility."

Another psychiatrist, Dr. Richard R. Parlour, has written: "Much of what has been called 'mental illness' by psychologists should more properly be called 'spiritual illness' or better, 'spiritual deficiency.' The aspect of personality predominantly influenced in the process of psychotherapy is the 'belief system' or in other words his religion . . . The field of clinical psychology, especially, is far closer to the field of religion than it has wanted to believe, and failure to see this kinship has hindered the development of clinical psychology."

And from the Book of Psalms come these inspiring words which remind us of the source of peace and happiness:

He who hath clean hands and a pure heart;
Who hath not lifted up his soul into vanity
Nor sworn deceitfully
He shall receive the blessings of the Lord.

—Psalm 24:4, 5

XI
SELF-CONFIDENCE

A self-confident man believes in his own ability or competency and does not have undue barriers or feelings of inadequacy. There is something appealing about a confident man's manner, the way he stands with head erect, chest up and legs slightly apart, or the way he walks with a positive assurance that he knows where he is going. Confident men use their hands with self-assured motions. There is an impressive tone in the voice which relays an abiding confidence within.

If a man has confidence in himself, it is easy for others to believe in him also. This fact makes confidence an essential quality in leadership, whether a man is leading an office force or a family. People will readily follow a self-assured leader who appears to know what he is doing and where he is going, whereas they are reluctant to put their full trust in a man who lacks this quality.

Lack of confidence afflicts most people. Many feel inadequate on their jobs and inferior to other men. They may want to reach a higher objective but lack the confidence to set out for the goal. Often there is something a man would very much like to do, and should do, but because of a feeling of inadequacy he puts the idea aside. And yet, confidence can be built by following the suggestions given here:

TAKE ON AN "AIR OF CONFIDENCE"

The first step to building confidence is to *take on an air of confidence* or, in other words, *act confident*. Walk with a firm step and speak with a steady, confident voice with head raised high. Give the impression to your associates that you know what you are doing and are qualified for the job at hand. Face your tasks with at least a pretended confidence. Hide any feelings of uncertainty or unpreparedness. For example, if you are called upon to speak, never apologize for your lack of ability or unpreparedness. Instead give the audience the impression of self-assurance. This very "air of confidence" will bring forth your better side and you will give a better performance than otherwise.

This positive "air of confidence" is sometimes necessary for the benefit and security of others and will more readily win their cooperation. I am thinking of a young mother who was left a widow with six dependent children. These children looked to her for strength and security to fill the gap left when their father died. She felt totally unprepared for the task, but she did not reveal this fearful side to her children. She acted confident that she could solve the problems and thus gave herself strength and her children as well. She found employment and was able to meet the needs of her family (with God's help).

In contrast, I think of a young man recently married who needed to find a job. This was not an easy thing to do, especially since he was lacking in experience and filled with doubt. To bolster himself he asked his bride to accompany him as he made application for work at several places. I sympathize with his lack of confidence, but had he put on an air of confidence, assuring his bride that he would manage to find work to solve their problems, and gone out to face the world with this attitude, he would have inspired confidence in himself and in her.

Many men are not nearly so confident as they would like to be or need to be, but they give the impression that they are. I have met some supposedly self-assured men who display great confidence in themselves, only to have them confess later that they suffer the same feelings of inadequacy that other men do. But, because of their display of confidence, those who surround them trust in them, cooperate in moving ahead to objectives, and somehow the man is able to bring forth positive qualities to meet the challenge before him.

As an example, consider the man who is leading a battalion of

men in battle. He may not feel prepared for his difficult
assignment. (Would any man?) The physical danger and the heavy
responsibility for the lives of his men tends to strike fear in him
and cause him to lack confidence in his ability to lead them safely
and adequately. But he does not show this self-doubt to his men.
He knows that they depend upon him for strength and assurance.
So he gives them the impression that he is confident. He probably
reasons, "I am not fully capable, but what man is under these
circumstances?" So he faces his challenge, and in a miraculous
way his confident attitude brings forth hidden ability and he is able
to meet the challenge of his situation more adequately than he
thought possible. His men are inspired and cooperate in reaching
the objectives before them.

This same attitude of confidence can be applied when a man is
leading a family. He may be painfully aware of his heavy
responsibility to lead his family safely and securely and wonder
how he will come forth with the talent and strength to do so. But
he does not reveal his uncertainties to his loved ones. Instead he
puts on "an air of confidence" and thus inspires them to put their
trust in him.

The "air of confidence" I have referred to is not to be
misunderstood for the negative quality of "hot air" displayed by
the man who resorts to bragging and exaggerations with the intent
to impress others. One can easily see through this phoniness and
overbearing demonstration of lack of conficence. An "air of
confidence" as used in a positive way may not require that
anything be said. It is rather a manner that a man assumes that
gives everyone around him the impression of confidence.

AVOID FAILURE PATTERNS

1. *At work:* In developing a feeling of confidence, it is
essential to avoid those things which tend to destroy confidence,
such as repeated failure at work. A man may drift from one job to
another, each time being unsuccessful. Instead of his work
building confidence, as it should, it destroys it. Each time he
meets with an additional failure his confidence is further under-
mined.

If a man has been unsuccessful in his work, the solution lies in
discovering his talents and locating a type of work where he can
adapt these talents. Every man has ability which will lead to

success if he will discover it and put it to work. However, discovering one's own ability may not be easy. In solving this problem it would be helpful to have an aptitude test.

There are many aptitude testing services available in this country in high schools, universities and some privately owned businesses. One very fine service is Bernard Haldane Career Seminars, 734 Fifteenth Street N.W., Washington, D.C. They also have offices in Los Angeles. This company has been successful in helping many misplaced men to locate themselves in positions where they are adaptable. Many men who have been unsuccessful in everything they have tried have become successful when relocated in jobs where they have an adaptation.

2. *In other activities:* Also avoid failure patterns in other activities outside of work, such as public speaking, sports, music, art, or other things which may require a special talent or ability.

It is obviously not expected that a man is going to be the "top runner" in everything he does, nor is this even desirable. Many of these activities are done purely for fun and not in a spirit of competition where achievement is to be measured. But if a man does engage in these activities with a desire to achieve, it will be undermining to his morale if he continually fails. It is certainly true that one improves with practice and should not give up merely because he is not good to begin with. But I wish to emphasize that, although each man has talents, *he invariably has limitations.* If a man wishes to excel in some activity, it is only prudent to concentrate on those things he can do well and thus build confidence, and avoid those things in which he can never be anything but mediocre.

I once knew a man who was determined to be a singer. He practiced many hours for several years and tried again and again to perform in public. Each time his performance was weak. I often wondered why he wanted so very much to be a singer. Perhaps in his youth a great singer had inspired him with this dream. But I also wondered about his misdirected energy and how it could have been used to develop a possible hidden talent within and thus bring him both satisfaction and confidence.

If I had a child who was not as keen academically as he should be, I would not encourage him to be a top student, unless this was his own desire. Instead, I would encourage him to be outstanding in wood work, mechanics, sports, or anything in which he could excel. As he succeeded in these fields, his confidence would expand and he would even be more apt to do better in his studies.

That student who appears to be dull may suffer merely from a lack of confidence, and when he realizes that he is gifted in other things, he may well move to the head of his class. Many failures are not the result of lack of ability, but lack of confidence. When we avoid failure patterns and concentrate on our abilities, confidence will grow, even in those areas we may have felt lacking.

AVOID PEOPLE WHO UNDERMINE CONFIDENCE

There are none of us so strong that we are not affected to some extent by the people we associate with. Hopefully our associates will be people of understanding and warmth, who will help us be the best that is in us. Unfortunately this is not always so. There are always people around who delight in tearing down other people or their work. Sometimes the most subtle tactics are used to depreciate. This may come from people who want to be our friends but have negative patterns in their thinking or flaws in their character which spread trouble everywhere they go. Sometimes it is out of jealousy that they downgrade another person, or the lofty feeling of self-importance that comes from being a critic. It is a human temptation to try to make ourselves look good by showing up the faults of others.

Avoid the associations with such people if at all possible. When you have sufficiently established confidence, you can cope with them on their own ground and put them in their place, but while confidence is growing, it is best to avoid their company. If you find that you cannot avoid them, face them head-on with your problem. Tell them that although you have weaknesses, you would prefer to be reminded of your strengths. Let them know that their remarks are destructive to your confidence and that you would rather have their help than their hindrance.

ALLOW FOR YOUR OWN MISTAKES

Frequently a man's own belittling or critical attitude towards himself undermines his confidence. The business man who loses money in a venture, the athlete who loses an important contest, the singer who hits a sour note, may feel unqualified for the work he is doing. The greater the aim for perfection, the more is a man inclined to be critical of his mistakes. This self-depreciation is the most destructive of all.

It is impossible to avoid mistakes in our lives. We are human beings, prone to error. We will not meet success on every turn, nor will we find it with every effort into which we put our best thought and skill. Our lives will be spotted with error and failure along the way. The cabinetmaker will make an error that will cost him a day's wages, and the athlete will do the same. He will not always win the game.

To maintain confidence we must allow for our mistakes and tell ourselves that a natural part of life is failure. The road to ultimate success is always strewn with failures. To expect perfection of ourselves is unrealistic. Fretting over mistakes can undermine our confidence and bring on additional failures. Allowing for mistakes, on the other hand, helps to maintain confidence and therefore encourages future success. *We must accept ourselves as human beings and allow in advance for our share of mistakes.*

OVERCOME INFERIORITY COMPLEXES

Often it is some deeply rooted feeling of inferiority which destroys a man's confidence. He may have native ability or skill equal to any other man, but because of some unfounded feeling of inferiority in his imagination he does not feel equal to other men. To overcome these barriers, it is important to understand them and how futile they really are. The following are some of the common ones men suffer:

1. *Complexes due to lack of money:* Ours is a materialistic culture which places tremendous emphasis on money and tends to equate it with the worthiness of the individual. If one accepts this concept, he would feel uncomfortable in the presence of one of greater wealth, since he would presume this person to be of more importance or worth and would not feel on an equal plane with him.

The truth is that people of wealth are not deserving of honor just because they have money. A person should be respected *for what he is*, rather than *what he has*. Like everyone else, people of wealth are both worthy and unworthy, depending upon their use of their means and the character they possess. Such a person should be respected for what he is, but not because of his possession of money.

Money is not an indication of superiority. Some inherit it or gain it by more fortunate circumstances than others or greater opportunity. Only in some cases is wealth due to a man's special talents, dedicated effort, or sacrifice. If this is the case, then this man can be admired for these positive traits, but not for the money itself. Another man who has put forth equal energy in another direction, but one which is less financially fruitful, is on an equal plane with him and need not feel inferior.

Sometimes our mistake is not in regarding the person with wealth as *superior,* but in fearing that he may consider us *inferior* due to our lack of money. This fear can cause a man to focus attention on himself and feel ashamed of his more moderate position in the other man's presence. He may hang his head, fail to look the other man in the eye, and act awkward and uneasy.

A revealing fact is that people with wealth are not inclined to regard those with less money as inferior due to their lack of wealth. They may, however, regard them as inferior due to other things, especially a lack of confidence in their presence. It is repulsive to see anyone devaluate himself in a sheepish manner due to lack of money. On the other hand, we greatly admire a man who, in spite of his poverty, will lift his head as high as the rich, look them in the eye, and meet them on equal ground. A man with such a wholesome self-respect is a greater man because he has achieved self-confidence without the support of money.

A person with a childhood background of poverty, who has been surrounded by people with more money, may have deeply rooted complexes, depending upon how his parents regarded their situation. If the parents were ashamed of their poverty, it is likely the child will be also. As he grows to adult life, he carries this feeling of inferiority with him. He may be a person of great intrinsic worth but may constantly depreciate himself due to his childhood feeling of inferiority. His only hope is in understanding that respect is derived from the worth of the individual and not from money.

The greatest danger is that people who feel that lack of money is reason to feel *inferior* will also feel that the acquisition of wealth will make them feel *superior.* Moved by this distorted viewpoint, they may direct all of their energies towards the accumulation of wealth, using any means to obtain it, that they might relieve their feelings of inferiority. But, like the gold at the end of the rainbow, the possession of wealth will never bring the feeling of self-worth they seek. Their feelings of inferiority can only be removed by disregarding money as a goal and developing those qualities of character which build self-worth.

2. *Complexes due to lack of education:* Nearly everyone has at least a moderate education. And yet some men feel inferior to others. A man with a moderate education may feel at ease around persons of similar status, but in the presence of more highly educated men he tends to feel inferior, especially if they have titles behind their names.

There is no justification for feeling inferior to a man because of his greater education. As with money, education does not necessarily make a man superior. He should be measured in terms of *what he is,* rather than what he knows. The mere acquisition of knowledge is not what counts, but how is is applied. That man who has trained and disciplined his mind is probably a better man for it. If so, he is deserving of praise. But even so, this need not make another man feel inferior. The less formally educated man may have a character as good or better, and will have areas of particular ability which are superior to others.

It is not likely that the man of letters will regard other men as inferiors. A truly educated man develops humility along with his advancement of knowledge. He learns very soon how little he knows in comparison to the vast store of knowledge which is available. He also knows, as a valuable part of his education, that every man has gifts and special qualities and also limitations. We are all both ignorant and learned, but on different subjects. Einstein was known to possess this humility along with his genuis. It was only in specialized learning that he was superior to other men. He was known to seek the advice of others on subjects he knew little about. If the highly educated do not regard men of lesser education as inferior, there is no reason for the less educated to so classify themselves.

3. *Complexes due to a lack of talent or accomplishment:* When we are around someone who has developed some great talent which makes our efforts seem commonplace, we tend to feel inferior. For example, suppose you are in the presence of an actor of great fame, of a famous sportsman, musician, artist, or public figure. You may have made a few strides to develop your gifts, but they are obscured by the unusual achievements of another.

Here, again, there is no reason to feel inferior just because of his accomplishment. He should be judged according to the kind of man he is, and not what he has achieved. He may actually be an inferior person to yourself. You may have put more energy into those things which make a worthy life than he has. If he is a talented person and also a fine individual, then he can be appreciated because of his overall worth.

We must appreciate, of course, that achievements of note usually come because of tremendous effort. Such a person often spends many years in his achievement. He has had periods of discouragement that the public knows nothing about. He has probably made many personal sacrifices for the sake of his talent. Few people realize the amount of dedicated effort which goes into the achievement of some men. We should always appreciate this effort as part of a worthy character. If the man has not measured up on all points, at least he cannot be counted as lazy. He is to be admired for his dedication and sacrifice to reach an objective.

With this thought in mind, you will likely conclude that your talent may not be so much less as perhaps your effort. Had you put forth a comparable amount of toil, sacrifice, and dedication in developing some of your talents, you may well have achieved as much or more than he. You are equal to other men. You need only to work as hard to achieve as much as others.

4. *Complexes due to physical defects or handicaps:* Sometimes men are faced with physical defects such as a large nose, large ears, small build, or they are not particularly handsome, at least in their own estimation. They may have more serious handicaps such as a missing limb, loss of hearing, or may be blind or crippled. It is very difficult, sometimes, for such a man to feel equal to men who have no such disadvantages. They are inclined to feel that if they were whole and handsome, they would then cease to feel inferior and could accomplish anything.

Once again I must stress that it is not what a man has or what he appears to be that really counts. It is what he is. A man who is completely whole may be a superior man if he has lived a worthy life, but again he may be a lesser man. The man in the wheelchair may be valiant, masculine, worthy, and in every way a real man. Each must be measured by what he really is, rather than what he appears to be.

One time I met a man on an airplane who was in a wheelchair. He had lost both arms and legs in an industrial accident. After living a vigorous outdoor life, one can imagine the trial he had in learning to use mechanical limbs. But he had learned to do this to a fair extent and had the courage to travel alone. He said he visited friends periodically and had no one to accompany him, so he went alone. Besides this, he had a schedule for several months each year when he would visit hospitals and train other amputees to use an artificial arm or leg. He was in worse shape than any he trained, but yet he had the confidence to cheer them up and help them fight their feelings of inadequacy.

Another great man was Glen Cunningham, who, as a young boy, was so severely burned that he was told he would never walk again. Yet he overcame this handicap and became a champion runner. This tremendous will to amount to something has caused others to use their handicaps as a stepping stone to greatness. Jimmy Durante found that he would never be cast in the leading romantic role because of his large nose. So he exploited this disadvantage, exaggerated it, and made a fortune. He turned a lemon into lemonade.

In summary, we can say that each man must be judged according to what he really is, and not according to what he has. A man who strives to do his duty, to develop his character and be a worthy man has no reason to feel inferior to anyone. His confidence will grow because of his day-by-day efforts to live a good life.

If, however, a man is lazy and indolent, if he is a slothful person who never turns over his hand to do his duty, fails to reach upwards to a better life, then he has every reason to feel inferior to other men. His only hope lies in building a better life and doing things which will justify a feeling of confidence.

DO THINGS TO BUILD CONFIDENCE

Confidence is built upon the qualities which join to make a worthy life. If a man is faithful to duty and earnestly strives to be a better person, to reach higher objectives, confidence will follow. If, in contrast, he is lazy and irresponsible and is content to be an inferior person, he should not be surprised to lack confidence. He cannot expect to gain confidence if he does nothing on which that confidence can be built. The following are measures that a man can take to buld confidence:

1. *Discover your own unique gifts, talents, or abilities:* Confidence will grow if a man will discover his greater abilities and concentrate on making a success of them. Many men have

hidden talents that are never fully realized. In the quiet mind of the average man may lie some hidden ability, some insight or even genius that would be a notable contribution to the world. He may have a faint reflection of these gifts at times, but usually disregards them. To discover these talents and make use of them becomes his sacred responsibility. If God has placed them within man, He also expects them to be used for good. By developing such talents, a man makes the world a more beautiful or pleasant place and advances mankind and himself as well in the feeling of self-esteem he receives.

2. *Increase your knowledge and improve your skills:* If you will learn to do things *well,* if you will improve your skills so that you reach a greater quality in your work, you will have ability upon which to base a greater confidence. A man who produces mediocre or inferior work cannot expect to have confidence in his work.

3. *Build success patterns:* Strive to build success patterns in your work. If you meet with success in the beginning of a project, it will build confidence which will encourage another success. It is like a spiral upward. If, for example, a salesman aims for success on his first try, it will give him greater confidence for the next. If this meets with success, he will have further confidence. He builds a success pattern that encourages both success and confidence. But if, on the other hand, he were to say, "I have plenty of time, I don't care if I lose this first sale," he is apt to fail. His failure undermines his confidence and encourages other failures. The trend is downward rather than up.

Apply this principle to other activities, such as sports or public speaking. If a man is called upon to give a talk, he should prepare to make a success on his first try. This in turn builds confidence which leads to future success, and so the trend is upward. The same can be said of an actor. He should prepare with all diligence for his beginning performances, for they are often the key to success. It is here that confidence is built for future performances.

This same plan should be followed in setting goals. Determine to leave no stone unturned to reach objectives. As you reach one objective, you will have confidence to reach another and another. If a young man will determine in the beginning of his life to reach the worthy goals he sets if at all possible, it will develop a success pattern that will aid him throughout his entire life. If he does not, if he is content to give up one project after another, he will soon

come to think of himself as incapable of reaching goals and will
not have the confidence he needs for success.

4. *Become a good conversationalist:* Usually we are inclined
to think that to be a good conversationalist we must have a great
background of unusual experience, be an authority in some field
or another, be colorful in the use of language, or have an
acquaintance with many special subjects. This is not so. It is not
difficult to be a good conversationalist. One need only have a
superficial knowledge on a few subjects and speak the language
reasonably well to converse with anyone. Here are a few
guidelines which will help increase your ability:

a) *Read widely:* Know something of the main issues of the
   day. To help with this, read the daily newspaper, especially
   the main news items and the editorial page. Take a weekly
   news magazine. Read the Scriptures fifteen minutes a day
   and read superficially on other subjects as you have the
   time to.

b) *Remember human interest stories:* Develop a repertoire of
   experiences or human interest stories. This would include
   incidents you have read about, heard, or observed about
   people—something unusual, inspiring, or otherwise impressive that has happened to them. Also include humorous
   incidents, since people like to be amused.

c) *Be interested in people:* When you are conversing with
   someone, be interested in *him,* in his life, his problems, his
   family, his goals, plans, and interests. Ask about these
   things and show a sincere interest as he talks. If he is
   enthusiastic, be so with him. If he is discouraged, show
   forth sympathy and understanding. Try to build up his self-
   esteem. If he is excelling in some great accomplishment or
   reaching great success, show appreciation for his success.
   It is seldom that men will be enthusiastic about another
   man's success, but it is such conversations as these that
   make warm friendships and leave both parties renewed. It
   is one of the most interesting and rewarding topics for
   conversation.

d) *Avoid the following:* Avoid focusing the conversation on
   yourself too much. Although it is proper to tell interesting
   experiences about yourself, restrain from centering the
   conversation on yourself unless the other party shows an
   absorbing interest. Also avoid bragging, complaining,

gossip, any attempt to demean anyone else, coarseness, loud talking, vulgarity, profanity, or anything which would be offensive to the sensibilities.

e) *Having a positive attitude:* Present a pleasant, positive, optimistic, and enthusiastic attitude about life.

5. *Build character:* And last, if we are to build confidence, we must build *character.* This may be a new thought to you, but it is one of the keys to building an all-encompassing confidence. A man may have confidence in a specific ability or talent, without this quality of character, but he will not have confidence in his total worth as an individual unless he has strong moral character. This is the kind of confidence which can be compared to steel.

In attaining character which leads to confidence, a man will need to acquire the traits described in Chapter IX, but especially the virtue of moral purity. This includes not only purity of actions, but purity of thought. God has said, "Let virtue garnish thy thoughts unceasingly and then shall thy confidence wax strong in the presence of God."

To retain moral purity of thought, it is important to "avoid the very appearance of evil." This would include any type of pornography—trash literature, obscene movies or stage performances, or evil environments where obscene incidents may occur. It may take a great amount of insight to understand in just which way the contamination of the mind would affect one's feeling of confidence, but such is the case.

XII
HEALTH

Let us turn again to the man of steel and velvet. We have learned that his steel side indicates strength, a strength which is derived principally from the firmness of his masculinity and the strength of his character. Completing the picture of his steel side is a strong physical body, one which comes from good health.

What is genuine good health? It is not, as some may think, merely freedom from illness. The man with the strength of steel is in vigorous health. He has a strong body of remarkable endurance and well developed muscles which are beautifully coordinated. There is life to his step and vitality in his manner. The vigor of his healthy body has in a miraculous way encouraged a vitality of spirit which increases his total liveliness. He has, in addition, clear eyes, sound teeth, and a good coloring to his skin. We cannot help being reminded in seeing this wonderful specimen of manhood that "God made man in His own image," and that man is, as Shakespeare declared, "in appearance like a god."

In contrast, consider the man who is not healthy. He is not ill, as illness is generally defined; he keeps up the pace of life, but he is not really healthy. He may have stooped shoulders, a sunken chest, weak muscles, sallow skin, and bags under his eyes. If he is overweight, his waistline is probably larger than his chest. He does not have vigor of spirit and manner for his degenerate body lacks this vitality. He is not in any way "in appearance like a god."

Our modern life has sadly contributed to this degenerate condition. A man's work is apt to be confining, requiring a bare minimum of muscular endeavor. After work he goes from crowded offices into a heated or air-cooled automobile which carries him to a comfortable residence. If he engages in strenuous physical activity at all, it is only occasionally. In past times this situation was not nearly so acute. Life in the country demanded physical activity, and even in the cities men were forced out of doors at least part of the time, walking, riding horses or carriages.

Our food supply is less than ideal. In plentiful America we have depleted crops, grocery stores filled with artificial and processed foods, and an abundance of "junk" foods. Advertisements on every turn incite us to fill our bodies with alcohol and tobacco. The world we live in invites death, not life.

We can, however, take heart in the fact that good health is not out of reach for most of us, even in our advancing years. I have met numbers of men who enjoy good health into their eighties and nineties. But these are men who practice good health habits. Anyone can do the same who will put forth equal effort. The following are the basic principles to follow in attaining good health:

NUTRITION

Foods to eat: Wholesome foods fall into five categories:
    Fresh fruit
    Fresh vegetables
    Nuts
    Whole grains
    Meats (to be used sparingly)

Here are some important guidelines to follow to achieve a balance in nutrition: Eat at least one yellow vegetable and one green leafy vegetable daily. Include some fresh and ripe fruit. Eat a third or more of your food raw (unless stomach trouble prevents this). Whole grains should be used rather than those which are refined such as white flour and white rice. Wheat was given to man as the staff of life and should be eaten daily.

Eat very little meat, if any, and avoid the fat of animals, including those found in milk and other dairy products. Note: Recent studies have aroused questions as to whether meat is a healthful food at all. If it is used, it should be sparingly and the fat completely removed.

A guide to proper eating is to use fruits and vegetables as nearly as possible in the state God prepared them—apples, peaches, bananas, etc., as they come from the tree instead of in some rich dessert. Some fresh foods are available all year. Each season produces fruits, nuts, or berries and some fresh vegetables. Eat the foods which are in season at the time. Grains remain fresh all year, so should be eaten at all times, as do beans and other dried foods.

The taste of food is not a safe guide to nutritive value. Bad foods often taste very good. The taste of good food, however, can be cultivated so one will come to prefer the taste of wholesome foods.

I have heard some people argue that nutrition is not essential to health. To deny its importance is to reveal ignorance. For years it has been known that the growth, health, and quality of animals is directly affected by the way they are fed. The rancher cannot feed his animals inferior foods, or neglect and ignore proper nutrition without immediate harm. He has learned without doubt that he has only to apply the rules of nutrition to his stock to insure good results. Can a human being be less affected by his intake of food?

Foods to avoid: Our food supply has been contaminated by preservatives, refining, and processing which is harmful. Question all food which comes "packaged." Read labels to see if they contain harmful preservatives. Prepared meats, such as wieners, bologna, and sausages usually contain several preservatives and are also about one-third fat. Avoid foods which are refined, such as white flour, white rice, white sugar, macaroni products, etc. Valuable food elements have been removed. Even when they are enriched after milling, they are inferior to the whole grains that God prepared for us. Avoid processed foods such as mixes, chips, and crackers. The rule is, eat foods as much as possible in the natural state.

Avoid overeating. In the world's highly developed countries there are more people dying from over-eating than under-eating. Eating limited amounts of food is conducive to good health. It is better to arise from the table not quite satisfied than to eat until all desire for food is gone. In an ideal situation it is probably better to eat two meals per day, rather than three. Simple meals are better than the feasts. Time of eating is also important. It is wise not to eat late at night. Some serious students of the subject advise that one should not eat after 4:00 p.m. Certainly anything eaten later in the day should be light and easily digestible. Being overweight is a serious problem for many, for excess weight tears down the body and brings on ill health and shortens life. The extra burden imposed on the heart and other vital organs is too severe to go unheeded.

EXERCISE

There are many exercises which promote good health. These include walking, swimming, bicycling, weight-lifting, jogging, and athletic games such as basketball, handball and tennis. However, if you would like to achieve the maximum in abundant health, also include a complete program of exercise which will bring into play all of the muscles of the body.

For a guide to such a complete program, I recommend that you obtain a good exercise book of instructions from a bookstore. One is called "21-Day Shape-Up Program," by Miss Craig, and another is "Royal Canadian Air Force Exercise Book." There are others. After establishing a daily exercise program, supplement this with some vigorous outdoor activity such as jogging or swimming. The important thing is to engage in something which will cause deep breathing and bring you into the sunshine.

SLEEP

You will probably find that if you exercise regularly and vigorously, you will need less sleep than otherwise. But do get sufficient sleep to feel rested. For best sleep it is wise to retire early and arise early. It has been said that an hour's sleep before midnight is worth two after midnight.

If you have difficulty sleeping, try the relaxing method. First, think calm thoughts. Think of clear water, forests, birds, or a placid lake. Then begin with the top of your head and tell yourself to relax the skull, the eyes, the brows, the mouth, etc. If you think relaxing thoughts, your body will relax. Then do the same to your neck and shoulders, loosening up every muscle and joint so that they are limp and placid. Follow this same method with your chest. When you get to the abdomen tell yourself that your body is very heavy, very relaxed. Do the same with the legs and feet. When you reach the feet, think of your entire body as relaxed and heavy, sinking into the mattress. After this if you have not dropped off to sleep, begin the process again. Do it a third time if necessary. It's not likely you could remain awake longer than this.

FRESH AIR

Fresh air, which until modern times was taken for granted, is now more difficult to come by. It is hoped that the awareness of this important need will be sufficiently felt by everyone to correct the abuses of air pollution and that everyone will contribute his share on an individual basis to keeping the air fresh.

Proper air supply includes both oxygen and moisture. Oxygen is obtained by circulation of enclosed air with that outside to obtain a fresh supply. Outdoor exercise is also important, for it causes deep breathing. The lungs contain thousands of little alveoli which need ventilation. Shallow breathing fails to bring the fresh air into these little alveoli which may remain closed and stagnant. The lungs resemble a balloon and should be inflated to full capacity to expel the impurities which accumulate and rejuvenate them with the purifying action of oxygen.

The lack of moisture in the air caused by inadequate furnaces results in much illness, including colds, sore throats, coughs, and even inflamed lungs. For solutions, install a moisturizer in your furnace or use a room vaporizer while the furnace is running. If necessary, hang wet bath towels in rooms you occupy or boil water. Ideally the furnace should be turned off at night and the windows opened for ventilation.

WATER

All plant and animal life require sunshine, air, and water. Our bodies are made up predominantly of water, being more than two-thirds by weight. As water is required in bodily function, it must be used over and over. Essential to health, then, is a fresh water supply daily. Three quarts is recommended, which is probably much more than the average person drinks.

MENTAL HEALTH

As with the other topics of health, we can only deal superficially with mental health in this writing. Most important is to stress the effect of mental health upon the body. If the mind is at peace, the body is affected in a positive way to induce good health. If the mind is filled with turmoil, unhappiness or unrest, the body is adversely affected and may succumb to illness or death.

The source of mental health lies in attaining good character. We are promised in the Scriptures, "The fruit of the Spirit is love, joy, peace, longsuffering, gentleness, goodness, faith, meekness, temperance." (Gal. 5:22) Anyone who has these virtues does not have mental difficulties.

Dr. J. A. Hadfield, one of England's foremost psychiatrists, has said, "I am convinced that the Christian religion is one of the most potent influences for producing that harmony, peace of mind, and confidence of soul needed to bring health to a large proportion of nervous patients."

The fruits of a deficient character are negative traits such as worry, anxiety, hatred, envy, anger, greed, fear, etc. These traits induce mental turmoil. I would like to especially point out the harmful effects of anger and hatred as they cause mental disability to destroy the body.

The damaging effects of anger were dramatically brought to me by an experience of a man of my acquaintance who owned a dairy. He was by nature short-tempered and impatient, but was otherwise an honorable man. One morning he arrived at his plant to find that someone had failed to assemble some of the bottling equipment properly, and the morning milk deliveries were being delayed by two hours. He became so furious that he felt quite ill and had to return home. On the way he suffered a heart attack in his car which was fatal.

Another example concerns a man who was swindled out of $17,000. His wife related that he was so overcome with anger that he would awaken at night and pace the floor. He also died of a heart attack.

We must all recognize that we are human beings and as such are subject to anger. But this type of deep resentful anger is a weakness of character which is destructive to both body and spirit and must be overcome if we are to maintain peace of mind and health. We must develop strong character, learn the principles of forgiveness, patience, and humility, and overcome an over-materialistic nature by developing a sound sense of values. In this way we will control, if not eliminate, the tendency to anger.

In summary we can say that good character leads to mental health. This in turn induces good physical health which is the physical health that provides the strength of steel found in the ideal man.

That good character can bring forth physical strength may be difficult for some to believe. But, as in many eternal things, it is difficult to prove except by experience of your own. If any man will employ the principles of good health and develop a fine character, he will be able to see for himself what hidden strength it brings to his physical body. He will be able to say as Lancelot did in the *Legend of King Arthur*, "My strength comes from my purity."

WORK

There is something in one's physical make-up which demands that he be employed in useful work if he is to have continued good health. Perhaps this is the reason God cursed the ground for man's sake and commanded him to earn his bread by the sweat of his face. Sustained work, accompanied by a willing attitude, bring forth natural functions which rejuvenate the body. Many people who are in good health into old age attribute their condition to a life of steady work. I read an account of a ninety-year-old cowboy who was still riding the range. My next door neighbor who was ninety-five was still climbing trees, and I heard of a man of 113 years who was still gardening crops on a tractor. Work is a blessing, not a curse.

The benefit of work is not in physical exercise alone. If this were true, those who work at desks would receive little benefit. The greatest effects of work, especially demanding work, is the feeling of usefulness which it brings to the individual, and this, in turn, results in a healthy mental attitude about life.

Retirement from physical work is often a grave mistake. Some men look forward for many years to the time that they will retire and live a life of ease. But when the time comes, they find that the loss of physical activity and the realization that they are no longer needed in the world's important work has robbed them of a feeling of usefulness, and they degenerate physically. It would be wiser for one to cut down his work, if this is possible, than to completely retire from it.

WORK, MY BLESSING NOT MY DOOM

Let me but do my work from day to day
In field or forest, at the desk or loom,
In roaring market place, or tranquil room.

Let me but find in my heart to say,
When vagrant wishes beckon me astray,
"This is my work, my blessing, not my doom.
Of all who live, I am the one by whom
This work can best be done in the right way."

Then shall I find it not too great or small,
To suit my spirit, and to prove my powers,
Then shall I cheerfully greet the laboring hours,
And eventide, to play and love and rest,
Because I know, for me, my work is best.

RELAXATION

The body needs relaxation of three types: 1) Relaxation while working; 2) relaxation through rest; and 3) relaxation by engaging in activities which are a diversion from work.

You may have wondered why some men can work for long hours and never seem to tire, while others weary at almost the beginning of a job. This may be due to the person's ability to relax while working. The muscles work with greater efficiency when relaxed than when tense, and thus have greater endurance. The pianist learns to relax while playing and is able to practice or perform for long hours without tiring. The public speaker learns that if he keeps his voice muscles relaxed, he can speak for many hours without tiring, but when tense, he may tire in thirty minutes. The laborer also can work with less tiring if he is relaxed.

Relaxing at work is accomplished largely by mental attitude. For example, when working at a difficult task, think of the word "relax." Let your mind tell your muscles what to do. You will immediately find that you have mind control over your muscles and that they will obey the command of the mind. When you tell your muscles to "relax," there will be an immediate reaction felt.

Relaxing in activities is difficult for some. They may find that they become so wound up in a game, have such fervor to win or excel, that they become tense. I am not suggesting a lack of enthusiasm or drive in such activities, but rather to enter them with a spirit of relaxation and enjoyment, eliminating a spirit which is overly competitive. Even the champion will verify that to be relaxed is the key to his doing his best.

In summary, we have reviewed briefly eight basic rules for good health. Although the knowledge can serve as a guide, only in application will the benefits be seen. Self-discipline is required to adopt new health habits when one is used to doing things a different way. This is not easy, but the benefits are tremendous.

As a suggestion, if you have been eating deficient foods, encourage your wife to begin your new program by removing all unhealthful foods from your shelves. Then in the future be determined to purchase *only those foods which are nutritious*. As she plans each day's meals, she will have to use more imagination than formerly to create tasty meals, but the results will be better nutrition. By following this rule, she will be forced to prepare wholesome meals.

If you have had little or no exercise, adopt a complete exercise program and practice daily. Doing it only occasionally will not lead you to success. Use self-discipline, and exercise regularly. A good diet and exercise can transform a person's health so that he will feel noticeable effects within two weeks. Six months is required to achieve maximum results. The rewards of good health are difficult to describe to someone who feels run-down. He has probably come to assume that he feels normal and about as he should. But there is a new life blood which comes into the body and a feeling of well-being which makes the effort worth it a thousand times over. It is safe to challenge anyone to a health program for six months with a promise that he will become a devoted believer.

PART II
THE VELVET

We have discussed many of the steel qualities which provide the basis of character and dependability in a man . . . his firmness, sense of duty, dedication to responsibility, reliability in strength to meet the tests and prove strong in the face of adversity. At appropriate times we would see sternness and immovability. Like the great raw buttresses providing inner strength in a building, such are the qualities to sustain a man in his trials and to instill confidence in those who follow his leadership.

But with these qualities alone, a serious lack exists, as with a building having no outside beauty. The velvet qualities we shall study in this section offer the softness, gentleness and tenderness, understanding and refinement of character which a man must have to round himself out as a manly individual.

There may be men who would resist some of these virtues as being unmanly or "sissified." Perhaps standing alone, that might be the case. But as the facing to the building which makes of it a work of art, comfort and beauty, so do these qualities give to a man a refinement that makes him stand forth as a truly polished individual. These qualities of velvet cushion the steel qualities so that they don't stand forth in their sheer raw force to startle or frighten. It gives to the strong hand the gentle touch. To a woman, this is a vital part of a man.

XIII
UNDERSTANDING
WOMEN

In millions of homes every day there are men leaving for work who probably have as their last words, "Who can understand a woman? What makes her act that way?" As Henry Higgins sang in despair in *My Fair Lady,* when he was at a loss to understand Eliza, "Why Can't a Woman Be Like a Man?"

This lack of understanding between the sexes arises from the fact that women are not like men. They do not think as men do. They are different in temperament, characteristics, and needs. They have a different world of responsibility and therefore a different set of problems. And they view problems differently.

And yet women can be understood. To gain such an understanding is to attain a liberal education—one that is essential to the velvet in a man. The following are some of the most basic needs and characteristics to understand if you are to live with a woman in peace and happiness.

The first two needs of women I wish to discuss have to do with love, first *Christian love* and second *romantic love*. It would be easier to explain the emotions of love if the English language had two different words to describe these two kinds of love, for they are not the same emotion. Both, however, are essential to a woman's happiness and feeling of security with her husband. Let us consider these two basic needs in women:

HER NEED FOR CHRISTIAN LOVE

For want of a specific word I will call this kind of love *Christian love*. Christian love can be explained as a concern for the welfare and happiness of another person. To show this kind of love a man must be willing to stand by his wife in all circumstances, to be genuinely concerned about her, both in joy and sorrow. If she is troubled, he shows deepest concern, sympathy and a willingness to help. He never deserts her when she is in real need and he is always a true and loyal friend, not just because she is his wife, but because she is a human being to whom he owes a devotion.

It may seem strange that one must spell out a woman's need for Christian love, for one would assume that if a man loved a woman romantically, he would certainly love her with a basic Christian love as well. But such is not always the case. A man may have tender romantic feelings for a woman but these feelings may be basically selfish. He may love her more for what she does for him than for what he can do for her. He may fail her in times of great need and distress, show lack of concern and sympathy for her feelings and even sometimes desert her in times of trouble.

A man may resent any implication that he lacks basic Christian love for his wife. He may defend himself with the fact that he has always provided for her adequately and done many wonderful things to make her comfortable and happy. He may remember times that he has been self-sacrificing for her sake. But, in spite of many kindnesses through the years, if he does not show his deepest concern for her when she is in distress, he appears to be, in her eyes, "a fair weather friend." A woman *must* have the assurance that her husband will stand by her in *all* circumstances (not just when he feels like it) if she is to feel truly loved.

If a man lacks Christian love for his wife, then his romantic love may strike her as being superficial and insincere. She may even disregard his tenderness because he has wounded her by his neglect in times of distress. Only when Christian love is present can romantic love be of real worth to a woman.

HER NEED FOR ROMANTIC LOVE

Love is to man a thing apart . . .
'tis woman's whole existence.

Lord Byron

The central need that a woman has in her life with her husband is her need for romantic love. This is the center of her happiness.

Romantic love is a tender romantic feeling a man and woman experience for each other. It is, in fact, the all-consuming emotion that brings them to marriage. After marriage, the man needs only a vague assurance that his wife really loves him, whereas, in the woman, this need is intense, and the need continues from day to day for the rest of her life. There are few men who realize this need in women and consequently they neglect her daily need for love and tenderness. The following example is typical of a man's attitude:

The story is told of a man who told his wife on their wedding day, "I want you to know that I love you. If I didn't, I wouldn't have married you. I expect to continue to love you, but don't expect me to say any more about it. Remember, I have already said it." The wife was speechless and, guided by instinct, said, "Oh, I can't remember something like that. I think you will have to remind me again and again." What her husband failed to realize is that as plants need sunshine and water, a woman needs love if she is to flourish as a woman. Deprive her of this and she "wilts on the vine," as in the following example:

A man of my acquaintance who loved his wife dearly suffered the terrible blow of losing her in death. He was left with several small children to manage and in his predicament felt an urgent need to find a second wife. His new bride had never been married before and suddenly found herself with a family and full household to run. She entered marriage hopefully and determined to succeed in her new responsibilities.

Her husband loved her to a degree, but never sufficiently to allow *her* to forget his first wife. He grieved his previous wife's death openly and in the presence of his second wife. His attitude was that his new wife was fortunate to get a ready-made family of adorable children and a husband to provide for her. He felt that he was giving her the essential needs that a woman requires. His appreciation was the type that he would extend to a hired housekeeper.

Denying her the love and tenderness that every woman needs caused a tragedy to happen to this woman. I saw a withering effect take place in her, observed the tender blossom fade on the vine until she was reduced to a common drudge. She lost the vitality she formerly had and became harsh and disagreeable to live with. His lack of love destroyed the finer qualities within her.

Men are not harmed by the lack of love to the same degree as women are. A normal man, if denied love, usually throws himself into his work and finds compensating fulfillment there. Or he may concentrate on achievements outside of his work where he obtains admiration or praise which is his greater need. He manages to survive and make a fairly adequate life for himself. Not so with a woman. If she is denied love, she will suffer as no man could comprehend. Her whole existence shakes at the foundations.

If men realized this human need in woman and the pain experienced when a woman feels unloved, it would be difficult to imagine how a man could be so cruel to another human being as to tell his wife he no longer loves her, or turn to another woman or seek a divorce. It seems that there would be some compassion for her suffering that would prevent this cruelty. He would be driven to plead to God for insight into their situation to sustain him until love could be rekindled.

HOW TO LOVE HER

1. *Cultivate a Feeling of Love:* True romantic love is a spontaneous feeling from deep within. This love is awakened by the woman through the charm of her personality which appeals to a man. As she reveals her femininity, her angelic character and other womanly traits, the man is enchanted, and a feeling of love is awakened in him. Romantic love does not arise out of a feeling of obligation as does Christian love for one's fellow man—a feeling we must extend to all men if we are to be saints of God. True romantic love is inspired by the woman.

With this thought in mind, it might seem on the surface impossible for a man to do anything to awaken his own feeling of love. He would be entirely dependent upon his wife to cultivate this feeling. But the miracle is that there are things he can do. *If a man will apply the teachings of this book—if he will be a man—he can cause a woman to blossom into her full womanhood, to regain lost charms so that he can love her as he once did.* If he will provide for her, protect her and lead her with firmness—if he will treat her like a queen and help her have a feeling of self-worth, if he will treat her with tenderness and all of the velvet qualities—he will awaken her finer qualities so that she will be a better woman. She will be worthy of his love and will inspire it in him. So far as loving is concerned, it is a man that makes a woman what she is by the way he treats her. He can bring out the bloom on her and help her reveal real charm. This is the miracle that cultivates your own feeling of love and tenderness for a woman.

2. *Express Love:* It is not only important that a man feel *love* for his wife, he must *express* it. This love can be expressed in a variety of ways, but since it is to be a daily practice, one can rely upon words and tender affection. A man need not be adept with words as the poets to express the feelings of his heart. A woman is happy to accept the humblest of speech when it is sincerely given. Tenderness seems to be one of the most appreciated expressions of love for a woman. A touch of the hand, a pat on the shoulder or the head, a tender word or term, or any act of affection moves her emotions. She thrives on these small manifestations of love.

3. *Prove Love:* It seems to be deeply embedded in the nature of a woman to count love as sincere only when a man does something to prove it. Perhaps this is why little girls are so attracted to fairy tales in which the hero rescues the princess from a castle wall, or from the clutches of a witch or from a villain who ties her to a railroad track. In each case the hero does something to prove his love. This is illustrated in the story "The Gift of the Magi," by O. Henry:

The story is of two young married people with a deep feeling of love and sacrifice for each other. In near poverty, they had only two possessions of real worth—Della's beautiful long hair and Jim's gold watch that had been his father's and his grandfather's. Della had often looked longingly in a shop window at two tortoise shell combs with jeweled rims—something she knew they could never afford. On Christmas Eve the two young lovers found themselves almost penniless. Eager to prove their love for each other and without knowledge of one another's actions, they made a most noble and willing sacrifice. Della sold her beautiful long hair for $20 to buy a gold chain for Jim's prized watch. Jim sold his gold watch to buy the two beautiful combs for Della's hair. As the author said:

"And here I have lamely related to you the uneventful chronicle of two foolish children in a flat who most unwisely sacrificed for each other the greatest treasures of their house. But in a last word to the wise of these days, let it be said that of all who give gifts, these two were the wisest. Of all who give and receive gifts, such as they are the wisest. Everywhere they are wisest.''

In the mind of a man he no doubt feels that he does prove his love by his hours of toil in providing the living, his devotion and loyalty, his patience with her weaknesses, etc. This, of course, is a very tangible evidence of love and duty, but do not think that this is sufficient in the eyes of a woman. She is inclined to look at these as obligations, just as she has an obligation to serve you meals and keep the house clean. There must be something beyond the call of duty to prove love.

In every case of proving love there is an element of *sacrifice*. There must be some extra effort given, something one goes without, some trouble in attaining the object of proven love. It also requires being *sensitive to her needs*, her desires, deep feelings and even whims.

Without being sensitive to her needs a man may make a noble sacrifice but still fail to prove his love so far as she is concerned because he doesn't sacrifice to provide the exact thing which means so much. For example, had Jim bought a new dress for Della rather than the combs she had been wanting, he would have failed to fully prove his love. Often it is an insignificant item or small favor a woman wants so desperately, but because the man is dense and unaware of these desires, he loses an opportunity to fully demonstrate his love. But, when a man is sensitive to a woman's needs, the effect upon her spirit is profound, as you may now realize. A personal experience illustrates this point well:

We lived in a house with a serving bar between the kitchen and eating area. The eating space was small, and my wife often remarked that it would greatly impove the kitchen if this bar could be removed. I had some doubts about it since it required considerable patch-up of the tile of the cabinet, the floor coverings and the walls. But her desire persisted without much hope. She didn't ask, but I was aware of her wishes.

While she was visiting relatives for a few days, I decided to surprise her by remodeling the kitchen. It was a trying job as most small jobs turn out to be. But when it was finished, it looked great, and I wondered why I hadn't thought of it. I bought a round table and some new chairs and had the job completed when she returned.

I shall never forget her joy in my thoughtfulness. She leaned against the doorway in total silence. Then she began weeping. She has reminded me many times since that this was one of the happiest moments of her life.

Sometimes in desperation a woman will ask a special favor merely as a test of a man's love. She may not feel so much a need for the favor as a need to see tangible evidence of his love. Little children often do this—just a little checking on their part to see if their parents still love them.

There is something in the male psyche which causes him to resist giving his wife something which he thinks she expects. If he also senses that the desire is more to prove love than satisfy a legitimate need, he will probably resent the whole thing and determine to give her nothing. If she hints for a birthday present or to be taken to dinner, he puts the idea out of his mind although he may have previously thought of it. The very thing she wants and needs she is deprived of because in his eyes she made the mistake of asking.

Although it runs counter to the masculine nature to give in to such requests, it is wise for a man to do so and do it in good spirit. There is a biblical scripture which asks of men, "If a son shall ask bread of any of you that is a father, will he give him a stone? Or if he ask a fish, will he give him a serpent?" If a woman needs proof of a man's love, should she be denied this proof? "If she asks for bread, should she be given a stone?"

Proving love when asked is certainly not the most significant way to demonstrate one's real feelings. But temporarily it will fill a need which is very important to a woman. When requests are made, this only indicates to a man that he may have failed to assure her of his love. In the future it is hoped he will seek opportunities to fill this need without being asked.

Romantic love is of great significance. It has always been the theme of impressive music, art, and literature—the very center of the drama of life. To have life center around love is the most sound of reasoning. Is any subject of greater importance to both men and women? Are other efforts a man can render of more worth than love and tenderness in his marriage relationship—the very center of a happy home?

TREAT HER LIKE A QUEEN

Treat a woman like a queen and she will act like one. It is a fundamental fact that if you place a high value upon a person and let him know that you regard him highly, he will tend to grow to be that finer person. Especially is this true with women. If they are held in high esteem, they tend to take on a regal attitude which makes them queenly.

The story of Johnny Lingo bears out this message dramatically. The story concerns a young Polynesian girl who was downgraded by her father to the point that she and everyone else considered her an inferior person. She deteriorated until she no longer combed her hair, and often hid behind the banana trees to hide herself from the mockery of society. So diminished was she in the eyes of everyone that she had no feeling of self-worth.

A young man who lived on another island knew her when she was a little girl. He always remembered her and recognized her true worth. When he grew to manhood, he decided to go back to her island and ask for her hand in marriage. He was evidently aware of her deterioration, but believed in her intrinsic worth and meant to rescue her from her situation.

As was the custom in this society when a man asked for a girl in marriage, he bargained for her with "cows." If a woman was considered ordinary he may have to pay only one cow for her. If she was of great worth and the competition was keen, he may have to pay three or four cows for her. Women took personal pride in how many cows they were bargained for, and there was a special value to them in having their suitors sacrifice for them.

When Johnny came to the home of the girl, he set out to bargain with her father. Her father was prepared to give her away for one cow and feel he had the best of the bargain. But to his astonishment, Johnny offered him eight cows. When asked why he did not bargain for the girl, he said he wanted everyone to know, and especially his wife to know, that she was worth this higher value. As he took her by the hand, a great change came over her—a realization of her worth. Her self-esteem was raised, and she took on the dignity befitting a person worth "eight cows." The girl unfolded like a lily in the spring with the fascinating charm of a real woman. The power a man holds over a woman to either bring out the best in her or to downgrade and demean her is awesome.

Unfortunately, there are men who fall short of making a woman feel queenly. By criticism or slighting remarks they treat women like inferiors. I was surprised to hear a business associate speak of his wife as "the old lady." Men are quick to criticize "women drivers" and yet expect women to drive and run errands for them. Some men make demands on their wives to the point of causing them to feel like slaves. Or they may ignore them or treat them with indifference. Anything which depreciates them in value diminishes their womanliness.

The evil effects of this downgrading of womanhood has more far-reaching and destructive effects than most men realize. Many young women are being lured into the women's liberation movement because they feel men have let them down. Most women would not give the liberationists a second thought if their men honored them in the many ways women expect to be honored. I quote from a pleading letter from a woman:

"Let the men who are contemptuous of the women's liberation activist take a good look at themelves and take a personal inventory of their attitude towards women in general. Perhaps they will develop some insight as to where they have failed as men—failed to appreciate and show appreciation for true womanhood and all that womanhood represents. Perhaps they will come to realize that women are members of the same human race they themselves belong to."

The Russian women are not treated as queens. They are treated as equals with men and required to do the work men do. And now they are crying out for the tenderness and chivalry that men lack. Their hearts ache to be treated with the esteem that women used to be treated with, and they would be better women if they were.

In the film *My Fair Lady,* Eliza complained that Henry Higgins always treated her like a "flower girl." But she said that she would always be a lady to Colonel Pickering because he treated her as a lady, where she could only be a flower girl to Professor Higgins because he always thought of her that way and treated her accordingly. And thus a woman becomes what a man esteems her to be—be she queen or slave.

ALLOW FOR HER MISTAKES

Being human, women sometimes make mistakes. They may be late, or fail to have dinner on time, or the food will not taste just right. Sometimes the house is not well kept, especially if they have little children. They may not handle children wisely or may spend money foolishly. They may make some stupid remarks. The usual tendency is for a man to be harsh and critical at such times of feminine failure. She may have pleased her man in a hundred other ways, but let her make one mistake and he expresses harsh disapproval. A man who expects an angel for a wife, one who does not make any mistakes, has a very unrealistic viewpoint. He fails to realize that women are human and, like themselves, make mistakes.

Allowing for mistakes is greatly appreciated by women. But if a man will go a step further and be forgiving, understanding and sympathetic for her error, and if he will help her overcome the problems caused by her mistakes, he can bring a woman to tears in appreciation. Such a kindly act will probably come as a surprise— it is so foreign to a man's nature—but it will never be forgotten. It is one of those velvet traits in a man that women treasure as a rare jewel. He is set apart from other men who are less understanding and sensitive to the inner needs of a woman. There are two things a man can do to help him learn to allow for human error. They are:

1. *Develop Humility:* A man who has true humility is not quick to criticize the mistakes in his wife. He realizes that he himself is imperfect and subject to error. His mistakes may not be the same ones as he sees in his wife, for where she is weak he may be strong. For example, a man's wife may be habitually late where he is always punctual. If he has true humility, however, he will realize that he does make other mistakes. And his wife is probably strong in areas where he is weak. This attitude of humility makes it easier for him to allow for her mistakes. When she makes mistakes, he is reminded of his own.

2. *Look to Her Better Side:* If a man will look to her better side and concentrate on her virtues, it will be easier to allow for her mistakes. When the spotlight isn't concentrated on the fault, it doesn't seem so important.

When a woman makes continual mistakes which are a burden to others, it becomes her husband's obligation to teach her the need for improvement and, if he is capable, teach her or assist her to secure the instruction which is necessary. For example, if she is a poor housekeeper or a poor cook, let her know how very much it means to you and to the success of your home life for her to learn these feminine skills. She must know that a part of the success in her life is to become adept in these skills, and that a serious responsibility attaches to it. If necessary, help her find instruction in these subjects.

If she is habitually late, help her understand how inconsiderate it is to keep others waiting. She may not understand that such a habit demonstrates a lack of concern for the valuable time and comfort of others. Teach her as you would children if her fault is a childish one. If she spends money foolishly, she can be taught the principles of economy either by yourself or by special instruction. Let her know that it places a burden on you and your responsibilities when she is careless with money.

If this instruction is given with kindness, free of sarcasm or ridicule, and with an assurance that you don't consider yourself as perfect, a woman will usually respond favorably. Otherwise she will resent an unexpected critical remark, especially when she is tired or busy.

In review, we can say that it is never wise to offer critical remarks when a woman makes a mistake. Express sympathy and understanding and be forgiving. Help her to overcome any problems caused by her failure. To fail to do this, to be harshly critical is to compound her problems. She may be suffering already the pains of her mistake, and if you offer criticism where sympathy is needed, you will only increase her suffering. If she continually makes the same mistake, and it has brought burdens to herself and others, teach her the error of her ways, but with patience and kindness.

UNDERSTAND HER RESPONSIBILITIES IN THE HOME

In understanding the woman's role as the wife, mother, and homemaker, there are three important things to understand: 1) Her pressing and demanding responsibility, 2) the tendency for her life to be confining and monotonous, and 3) the importance of her work and her need to feel that it is important.

In viewing the woman's life, we must take into consideration that not all women have the same demands in the home. Some have no children, others have one or two, and others have four, five, six, or more to care for. Some women will have reared their children and may have less pressing responsibility. But all women who are running a household must have some consideration for their duties, and certainly some are very pressed with the responsibility of a young family.

1. *Her Demanding Responsibilities as a Mother and Home-maker:* In her role as a homemaker a woman with a family faces a life of long hours and demanding responsibility. She must prepare meals regularly and for every day of the year. She must continually shop for food, considering costs, nutrition, and pleasing the family appetites. If she is a good cook she may spend hours in the kitchen in a single day, hours which are seldom noticed or appreciated.

She must continually fight dirt and wear and tear in the household. Carpets, floors and furniture become soiled and worn. Clothing must be washed and re-washed. Clothes, shoes and socks wear out and must be replaced by sewing or shopping. If her husband moves her from place to place, she must adjust her household furnishings to the new environment. There is usually painting to do, new curtains to make, and a period of getting settled to make her new place attractive.

Her role as a mother is demanding. Her children are not like little stuffed animals. They are human beings with a need for love and understanding. If her children are small, they need instruction, discipline, attention, and even entertaining. She cares for them when they are sick or injured. She escorts them to music lessons, doctors' appointments and to activities and recreation. Her life is made up of a myriad of tasks, many of them menial. No one of them seems great, but when viewed as a total responsibility, it becomes overwhelming. Her responsibility is different from a man's. Only when her children are sick does she feel urgency. But her demands are continual, often lasting before sunrise and after sunset.

When a young woman marries and has children very soon, she may have a difficult adjustment to this new responsibility. As she faces the burden of family life suddenly thrust upon her, she may lose the bloom of her youth. The light tends to go out of her eyes and the laughter fade as she faces the tremendous burdens of the household. She may have a marvelous attitude—feel life is giving her what she has really always wanted and hoped for and dreamed about, but she may not feel adequately prepared for her new and overwhelming responsibility. There are a number of things a man can do to preserve his wife's bloom both in her young years and throughout her entire life, by understanding her responsibility and seeking to minimize her work.

The first thing he can do is to make certain that he is not the one who is burdening her by expecting too much. Sometimes it is he who makes unnecessary demands upon his wife, requesting special food which takes hours to prepare, demands that his pajamas be ironed, his shirts hand-made, or his shoes polished. If his wife is already burdened, it is thoughtless and unkind for him to add anything to that burden. Often by lessening his own demands, he can ease the load sufficiently to make it quite bearable.

Some men even go so far as to bring home office work for their wives to do, such as typing, bookkeeping, and research work, with no apparent thought as to the burdens she has already. Many sweet wives willingly obey.

Among the first things a man should do is to try to get his wife settled down as early in married life as possible. Sometimes his career will prevent this, but if a man will pursue his career quickly (as when he is still in school) and not waste time on foolishness and aim to get his wife settled down so she can pursue her career of family life, he will minimize her work and problems. Some women want the change and excitement of a move, and some adjust very well. But it is nevertheless difficult for her to function in her role and devote herself to husband and family if she is wandering around on the move.

Next, get her settled in a home of her own. A man would do well to listen to his wife on housing, since it will be the center of her world and responsibility. Consider her feelings, giving them priority over your own. The only thing a man has a right to insist on is that it be within a price he can afford.

Choose a location that is convenient to schools and shopping on a street with a homey atmosphere. Choose a home that is not too large or small for family needs. A man is often inclined to choose a larger home, the utmost of what he can afford. This may be due to his desire for status, or possibly a desire to please his wife. It can turn out to be a disservice to her if management is beyond her capacity. A man should not buy his wife a castle if he does not also supply the servants to keep it up. A woman needs a house she can *manage*. Once you have an adequate house, work to make it convenient for her. Build shelves where needed and good laundry facilities. Buy essential furniture and play equipment for the children. Prepare her for her life ahead.

As the children come and responsibilities increase, help her to minimize her work by getting rid of too many possessions. Often women live in a clutter with too many things around, even too much furniture which becomes a burden. Often it is the man who refuses to part with possessions. Living with a minimum of posessions makes a woman's life simpler and her work easier.

If she is disorganized, a man can often be of real assistance in helping her create a smooth-running system where each one has specific duties. Help her list her responsibilities in priorities and encourage her to concentrate on the important things and let minor details go. Help her see where she is wasting time and energy on nonessentials. Sometimes women try too hard to please on nonessentials and then find it difficult to find time for the more urgent responsibilities. Help her with patience and kindness, assuring her that you are only trying to make her life easier.

One of the greatest responsibilities a woman has day-in, day-out is the meals. If her work is burdening her, the first logical area to cut down is meal preparation. If three meals are too much, have only two. Encourage simple meals which are easy to prepare. Rather than demanding elaborate meals, tell her that you will be satisfied with simple nutritious food. When she voluntarily spends hours in the kitchen preparing food to please you, don't make the mistake of overdoing your appreciation as this will encourage her to spend more time in this pursuit. Instead, explain that although you appreciate her efforts in your behalf, you prefer that she spend her time and energy on preserving her health and beauty.

Certainly not the least thing a man can do to ease the burdens of his wife in her household duties is to pitch in and help her when he is available to do so. There is no way that a man's masculinity is demeaned when he fixes the meals, changes the baby, does the laundry, or cleans the house. Under such circumstances, he is really more of a man when he does.

And last, express understanding for her continual responsibility, and appreciation for her efforts. Somehow, whatever we do, no matter how difficult, seems easier and worth the effort if it is appreciated.

2. *Her Confining Life:* When a woman is tied down with little children, her life can become quite confining and may seem to her like a narrow existence. She may feel a need for a broader view and some diversion from the home scene. The trouble is that when a man comes home, his needs are usually different. If his work has been demanding, he may want to shrink inside his four walls and get away from the world. He does not necessarily want to go anyplace or do anything. This incompatability requires under-

standing of both man and wife. There are several things which a man can do to relieve his wife's feeling of confinement.

First, he can tell her about his life away from home. The broader the picture he can paint, the better. He should be honest and let her know the good and the bad. Some men give a blown-up picture of their life away from home, hoping to win praise and gratitude. Others emphasize the negative view, hoping to find sympathy. An honest picture will help her to see life as it really is and will be more likely to make her content with her own circumstances.

A man should also take his wife out of the confines of her home frequently, especially if she is tied down with dependent children. Even though he doesn't need or desire the diversion himself, concern for her demands that he do it. If circumstances permit, it would be highly desirable for him to let her see distant places, as it will broaden her whole scope of life. I know a man who has a large family, and he has taken his wife all over the world with him, even when they were having children. It has done everything for this woman and made a better mother and wife of her.

If a man is self-employed or circumstances are otherwise favorable, it will also help if he will occasionally take his wife to work with him and let her see him in action. Ask her advice on some of your difficult problems and let her feel a part of your world. Do not think it beneath your dignity to share your world with her. This is customary with men and women who are very close to each other. The counsel a man receives from his wife may well be some of the most valuable he could receive anywhere.

Provide breaks in her routine by entertainment and diversions. Women love going out to dinner, not so much for the meal as for the opportunity to get dressed up and have a break away from the routine of home life. She usually returns refreshed and anxious to assume her duties again.

A woman can also overcome her narrow feeling by giving some type of *benevolent service* away from home. If she can increase the circle of her love and concern for people beyond her own family, she will broaden her perspective. As she becomes aware of the problems of others, her own world expands tremendously and she loses the self-centered feeling she might otherwise have. This requires cooperation on the part of her husband—something he may find hard to give, for she is going to have less time for him and some of the things he has grown to expect. Many men are selfish and feel a woman must spend all her time on him and his household. This attitude is defeating, for although he may demand her time, he will lose the benefits of her broader experience. Benevolence truly enriches a woman's life and makes her a better person.

3. *Her Need to Feel Her Work Is Important:* I read of a doctor's wife who developed a feeling that her work in the home was meager and insignificant when compared to that of her husband who was saving human life. But her husband took time almost daily to assure her that her work was as important as his. She was *shaping* human life, which is as important as saving it. She was a builder of society. Her work in the home was appreciated as one of the most essential contributions for the good of humanity that could be given.

Because men have failed to make women feel important and have even tended to depreciate woman's work, women themelves have felt inferior to men, and many of them have rejected their life in the home because of this. They have pushed out into the man's world, seeking careers and hoping to find a greater feeling of importance. Men can decrease this problem by helping women see the importance of their work in the home, a valuable contribution to society equal to the work of men. In the overall, the role of woman in the home is a more vital one than that of the man. Such an appreciation on the part of a man will give a woman an entirely different perspective of her own life and one that will assist her in finding contentment and fulfillment within her feminine role.

RESPECT FOR HUMAN RIGHTS

A woman's most basic rights in marriage are—a voice in matters which concern her, consideration for her feelings and desires, and a certain amount of personal freedom.

We have already learned of the woman's subordinate position—how she has an obligation to yield to her husband's authority, although she must bear the consequences with him. She is also dependent upon him for a living, for things she needs to have, and for places she needs to go and for the freedom to do things she wants to do. He holds power over her. To a certain extent, her human rights are in his hands.

A just leader will grant her these human rights. He will give her a voice in matters which concern her and will carefully consider her viewpoint, feelings and desires and will respect her need for personal freedom when possible. Not all men are so just and in tune with a woman's needs. Let us illustrate:

A man and wife were building a home. The wife wanted a voice in the arrangement of the kitchen, but her husband had different ideas. He took the upper hand and had it designed his way, not giving any consideration to his wife's desires. She said that she often thought as she lived in that house, not of the inconveniences she suffered in the kitchen, but of how her human rights were denied.

In another case the husband was transferred to another city and went before the family to select a home. His wife's only request was that it be on a quiet street and near the schools. But he became "carried away" with his own desires and bought a house which was on a busy street and quite some distance from schools. Such a disrespect for her only two requests was a denial of human rights. .

Contrast this with an experience Phyllis McGinley relates in her book *Sixpence in Her Shoe*. They were remodeling their home, and she selected blue tile for a bathroom shower. When the shower was completed, she was disheartened with the color which looked so much brighter on the walls than what she expected from the tiny sample. She called her husband at work and asked him what to do. This understanding man, knowing a woman's feelings and her predicament, said, "Have them tear it down. It's cheaper than a nervous breakdown."

Such a man as this is a jewel to a woman. He goes beyond the call of duty, but will receive rich dividends in love and appreciation. The interior of a house means a great deal to a woman. It is her world where she functions, the center of her career. To give her feelings consideration in this sphere, her way when possible and to reason with her when not possible, but still respect her right to ask, is to have a deep respect for human needs.

There are other serious mistakes men make in this regard. Some men hover around their wives like shadows, not allowing them the freedom of a world of their own. When a woman's work is done, they require the remainder of her time and attention and deny her the right to do some of the things she may want to do. They expect their wives to be both queens and slaves, centering all their time and attention on them.

Women need time of their own, money of their own, a world of their own in addition to the one they share with their husband. They need to do some of the things they long to do and have some of the things they long to have. They are dependent upon a man for most of these privileges—his justice rules their lives.

A denial of human rights is one of the major causes of the present feminine rebellion, known as Women's Liberation. Had men been more considerate of women in their subordinate and dependent position, had they respected their human rights and needs, women would not consider themselves in an inferior position and would not be striving for what they call equality with men.

The role of the man and the woman is God's plan. Man is the divinely appointed leader of the family, and the woman is his subordinate helpmeet. This plan is the perfect plan whereby a family can function in peace and harmony, but it is all dependent upon the justice of the leader and his respect for human needs and wants. As God is just, so must man be just. As God will give to those who ask and to those who knock, so must a man heed the heartfelt requests of his family members and "turn them not away." I wish to stress once again that it is not necessary to go against one's own convictions in granting family requests. As God sometimes withholds things from us which He feels in His wisdom is not for our benefit, so must a loving father withhold from his wife and children those things he deems unwise. But in his justice and mercy, he considers the feelings of both wife and children and lets them know his concern for their desires.

HER NEED FOR SECURITY

All human beings need security, but a woman's feeling of security is not derived from exactly the same source as a man's. This is important for a man to understand. A woman's security comes principally from three sources: 1) from her husband's strength as the dominant leader of the family; 2) from his adequacy as the provider and money manager; and 3) from his ability to protect her or shelter her. Therefore, anything a man can do to more adequately function in his basic role as the guide, protector and provider for the family will bring his wife the security she needs. Since we have already covered this subject in previous chapters, we need only stress here that it is an essential part of understanding a woman's needs.

It should also be added that security comes from within the woman herself, in her ability to shoulder her own responsibilities and solve her problems within her feminine sphere. But, even if she is competent as a woman, she will feel insecure if she is denied a strong man to lean upon—unless she develops manly traits which relieve her normal need for the security of masculine care.

HER NEED TO EXPRESS RESENTMENTS OR ANYTHING WHICH TROUBLES HER

Often anger, frustrations, hurt feelings and disappointments can well up in a woman's breast in the form of resentments. If these feelings are not expressed, it can cause her to act strange, distant, and sulky. She has likely been trained to be a "nice person" and will resist "flying off the handle" or expressing anger or bitter thoughts which might offend her husband. She may feel no other choice but to suppress these unhappy feelings, but the price both man and wife pay is a break in their relationship.

The usual treatment a man offers is to leave her alone and hope she will get over it. He may ignore her completely, getting interested in other things, or may even leave the house. His actions only compound her problem, for his lack of concern demonstrates, in her eyes, a lack of love. "If he loved me," she may reason, "he would not leave me alone in my suffering." This will deepen a feeling of resentment.

If she is forgiving and feels secure in her husband's love, she may get over her distress alone. But most women feel too shaken by this apparent lack of concern to be truly forgiving. "How can you forgive a man who has a heart of stone?" they may reason. "If he realy loved me and cared about me, he would not turn from me while I am suffering."

There is a great principle of truth in human relations to follow in this regard: Whenever you detect that someone is offended with you, whether you are guilty or not, it is your responsibility to go to that person and try to be reconciled. If you can follow the reasoning of this principle—it is not the offended person's responsibility to take the first step. It would be too difficult and counter to principles of human relationships for the offended one to seek out the guilty party and express disapproval of his actions. With a little thought, it is easy to see that only when the person who has committed the offense, or supposedly committed it, has taken the first step can good relationships be restored.

Following this basic principle, when the woman has been offended by her husband, or even thinks she has, it becomes his responsibility to go to her and become reconciled. He should first tell her that he can detect something is wrong. Then he can invite her to express herself. As she begins talking freely, he can encourage her to continue until she discloses her innermost feelings. If he can see that he is guilty, he should admit it and apologize sincerely. Then he should go a step further and show sympathy for her feelings and the pain she has suffered. If he is not guilty, or feels he is being misjudged, he should not take a defensive attitude, at least not at the present. Only after she has completely expressed herself is he free to justify himself.

Men resist following this procedure for a logical reason. They are inclined to feel that to admit being wrong is demeaning to them in the eyes of their wife. Actually, just the opposite is true. To admit guilt honestly and ask forgiveness is a mark of humility. To show sympathy and concern for another is a sign of good character. Both are velvet traits women appreciate.

If a man is innocent, after his wife has fully expressed herself and the troubled waters are calm, he can point out her errors in a way as nondefensive as possible and clear himself. Even though it is difficult, he will aid the situation if he will forgive her misjudgment and not cause her humiliation because of it.

If a woman is guilty of harsh judgment or a bitter attitude in general, sometime later, when there is no moment of crisis, a man may give her instructions about developing a more tolerant and forgiving attitude. Sometimes a woman has never been taught the true meaning of humility and will listen to a man's instruction if given out of love and concern for her own feelings. By growing as a person, by developing greater love and forgiveness, she will be able to overcome this tendency to harsh judgment and will appreciate his part in this personal achievement.

Sometimes she may have distressing problems on her mind. Whatever the situation, when a woman is troubled, a man can greatly relieve her by telling her he is aware of her distress and invite her to express herself, showing a kindly sympathy for her feelings.

HER NEEDS IN SEX

In sex a woman's most urgent need is to know for sure that her husband's advances are motivated by genuine love and will be expressed with tenderness and consideration. She wants to know that she is not just a female to satisfy a masculine urge. A common fault with many men is that they use sex as a gratification of the flesh—a degeneration to the animal instinct wherein he fills his own needs without regard to the feelings of his wife.

His failure to consider her feelings frequently causes his wife to be unresponsive and cool to his advances. She may *want* to respond, but cannot, for she doesn't feel cherished. This is not a deliberate action or retaliation, but is involuntary because of the delicate tuning of the female nature.

To assist her to respond more positively, a man should do things to awaken her senses. Such things are beautiful and romantic music, art, the beauties of nature, quiet waters, moonlight, and even tasty food. Tender words are indispensable. It is also important to eliminate the things which reduce her sexual response, such as too much outside responsibility, pressure and deadlines, or worry. She needs to be separated from the nagging problems which occupy her mind throughout the day.

I must emphasize that arousing the senses to a demonstration of holy love in sex is not the sensual arousal that many so-called authorities advocate. To them it may be purely an arousal of uncontrolled passion or lust which, although it may increase responsiveness, does so at the expense of one's finer nature. (It is interesting that this negative arousal, as with all sin, does not produce a lasting response that edifies, but must be constantly reinforced by more absurd stimuli until one is finally consumed in complete frustration.) If a woman is still very slow to respond after using the positive methods described above, one can increase her desire through restraint—depriving her for a period of time.

For this to be effective it must *not* be done as a punishment, but should be done while supplying an abundance of tenderness and loving concern and applying the other positive suggestions we have discussed. Her barriers will be broken down as she realizes your feelings are for her as a person and not because she is a woman who can satisfy a physical need.

When the sexual needs of man and wife are encouraged in this wholesome way, they can expect a long life of sexual satisfaction without the "wearing out" or debilitation which often sets in at middle-age. And this satisfaction needs no further outside stimuli, but blossoms from the pure love that only such respect and fidelity can produce.

We come to the end of this very brief study of Understanding Women in which I have explained some of a woman's most basic needs. It has been said that Sigmund Freud, near the end of his lifetime study of human needs, said that he could never discover what women want. I readily admit that we need a great amount of light upon this subject, but from my own limited experience I have found that the following are some of the most important things women want:

SOME THINGS WOMEN WANT:

1. To be loved, cherished.
2. A master to rule over them.
3. A voice in matters which concern them.
4. Sympathy when they suffer.
5. Appreciation.
6. A feeling that their domestic work is *important work*.
7. Personal freedoms: Time to do things. Right to go places.

XIV
GENTLENESS, TENDERNESS AND AFFECTION

Gentleness is a softness of manner and disposition. A man who is gentle is quiet and refined. He is tender and kind with people, mild and smooth in conduct. His temper is not easily provoked. There is an absence of harshness, fierceness or violence. He is not severe or tempestuous.

This gentleness comes to some men seemingly by inheritance. To most, however, it must be developed, as it is generally lacking. Man's firm, rugged masculine nature does not encourage these gentle qualities. His gentleness must be acquired by subduing the masculine nature as one would tame a wild colt. His hot feelings must be schooled, his harsh temperament restrained. He must be trained to mildness in conduct.

Gentleness is to the steel qualities what mercy is to justice. When justice is meted out alone, it is cold, undeviating, and unsympathetic. Although justice is in reality given for the benefit of the individual, without mercy it appears intent on the suffering or even the destruction of the person. As mercy softens justice, gentleness softens the steel in man.

Because gentleness is strong in the feminine nature, many men avoid being gentle, thinking it a mark of femininity and softness.

This may be true if one is lacking in steel. Without a strong masculine nature, gentleness would be offensive in the male. But the careful blending of gentleness with firm masculinity produces a fascinating combination in a man which is attractive and admirable.

Women especially need the combination of gentleness and the firmness of steel. They need the support and strength of steel, but they cannot take it unless administered gently. This man of steel must not be too foreign to their own gentle make-up. Children also require gentleness constantly. A gentle voice, kindly manner and soft expression build good relationships with children.

Gentleness is a God-like quality and was strongly evident in the life of Jesus Christ. He gathered children about Him—they sat on His knee and He took time to converse with them. When the apostles sought to dismiss them as a nuisance, Jesus rebuked them saying, "Suffer the little children to come unto me and forbid them not, for such is the kingdom of heaven." He was gentle with women, and they worshipped at his feet.

He was also gentle with men. When he knew in advance that Peter would deny him and Judas betray him, he did not rise in angry protest. His gentle nature restrained him. When the angry mob gathered to stone the adultress, he did not grab a sword in her defense, but said, "Let him who is without sin cast the first stone." He recommended that we love our enemies, do good to them that hate us, and subdue the hard and fiery nature with gentleness.

With all this gentleness, He was masculine and firm. When confronted by those seeking to entrap or destroy Him, He stood fearless, and His gentle nature was temporarily masked as He demonstrated a strength which struck fear into the hearts of those who heard Him.

King David was an impressive example of strength and gentleness. As a young shepherd boy, he slew both a lion and a bear. With only a sling and a few pebbles from a brook, he killed the feared Goliath. He led armies and governed a kingdom. And yet he had a gentle nature. He loved music and wrote poetry. He spoke of "clean hands and a pure heart, of roses, lambs and green pastures."

Many men lack this gentleness of spirit, much to the pain of their families. I remember in my youth such a man. He wanted his boys to grow up to be men, not "sissies." Even as small children he spoke to them like a drill sergeant giving orders. He always had a sharp word of criticism for them. His wife and children lived in constant fear and seemed relieved if he had occasion to be out of town. When I occasionally visited the family as a little boy, I thought as I walked up the steps, "I hope he isn't home." One day as we were playing, one of his sons thoughtlessly put his finger in his nose. His father slapped him across the face saying, "Don't you know it's crude to do that?" The little boy was almost too astonished to cry. I have thought since if it were not more crude to slap a child in the face than for him to put a finger in the nose.

As I have followed this family I have observed a lack of closeness for one another. The boy still remembers the slap across the face and has confessed to me that he never liked his father. And yet this man provided an excellent living, they lived in the most expensive house in town, his wife was always well dressed, and there was ample of all life's needs. But what reward did he have for all this service to his family if he killed their spirits by his harsh attitude?

The spirit of God cannot dwell in the heart of a man who is harsh. It is a part of the gospel of love to be gentle and kindly. "The fruit of the spirit is love, joy, peace, long-suffering, gentleness, goodness, and faith." (Gal. 5:22) If the gospel of love teaches a gentle nature, we cannot hope to teach it to our children unless we demonstrate it ourselves. They will not likely listen to out instruction if we fail to win their hearts with a gentle disposition. There are steps we can take to subdue the harsh nature and develop gentleness.

1. *Restraint and Self-Control:* Bring the actions and emotions under control. Bridle the tongue as one would bridle a horse and lead it where it should go. School your feelings—restrain and subdue the harsh temperament. In other words, one must train the fiery temperament to become a mild one. There are impressive words to an old church hymn which give such instruction:

> School thy feelings, O my brother;
>   Train thy warm impulsive soul;
> Do not its emotions smother,
>   But let wisdom's voice control.
> School thy feelings, there is power
>   In the cool, collected mind;
> Passion shatters reason's tower,
>   Makes the clearest vision blind,
>
> —Charles W. Penrose

2. *Develop a Gentle Character:* Man's harsh conduct can be brought under control by restraint, but he will never be gentle in nature until there is a change that takes place within his character—until he has a gentle character which automatically prompts him to deal kindly with people. Gentleness comes as we grow spiritually. As we develop love and forgiveness, learn to concentrate on people's virtues rather than their faults, we develop gentleness.

3. *Develop Humility:* The key to humility is in learning to see our own mistakes and weakness. When this occurs we soften our attitude towards the errors of others. For example, we may become irritated if a child breaks a lamp or spills paint on the floor. This can cause a harsh attitude to well up towards the child. But when one considers that he makes mistakes probably far more serious, despite the fact that he is an adult with years of experience, he is humbled and it becomes easier to face the mistakes that others make with a gentle attitude. Our discipline of children will become one of objectiveness and can be administered free of harshness.

TENDERNESS AND AFFECTION

Tenderness is to be softhearted, expressive of the softer feelings of love, kindness and compassion. One who is tender is susceptible to other positive emotions. He is especially sympathetic to pain or suffering. The Good Samaritan displayed tenderness when he treated the wounds of the injured man, lifted him onto a donkey and took him to the inn. So does a father who comforts the pain or disappointment of his little ones, or shows concern for his wife when she is distressed, or assists an injured bird or animal.

Tenderness and affection are awakened when we have feelings of love or a fond or tender attachment for another person. Some acts of tender affection are a squeeze of the hand, a pat on the shoulder or cheek, a soft, gentle expression, and even a tender tone in the voice. The eyes can display great tenderness and are especially impressive if they are those of a strong masculine man. These tender expressions have a penetrating effect upon the emotions of those they are bestowed upon and are worth a thousand words of eloquent language in explaining feelings.

Tenderness and affection, like gentleness, are often termed feminine qualities, and therefore some men hesitate to display them in fear of being considered effeminate. But again I stress that this may be so if a man is lacking in masculinity. It might then be offensive. But when he is strongly masculine and is a man of steel as was Abraham Lincoln who became a hero because of these combined traits—then will a man be considered the more outstanding, the more manly. There is a poem which beautifully describes the need for tenderness:

> 'Tis the human touch in this world that counts,
> The touch of your hand and mine,
> Which means far more to the fainting heart,
> Than shelter and bread and wine;
> For shelter is gone when the night is o'er,
> And bread lasts only a day,
> But the touch of the hand
> And the sound of the voice
> Sing on in the soul alway.
>
> —Spencer M. Tree

People everywhere need tenderness more than they need blankets. And it will bring more warmth and peace than material things will ever do. Especially does a family need to be brought close together by the warmth of tender affection.

XV
ATTENTIVENESS

An attentive person is watchful, observant, and heedful of the comforts and needs of others. He is a sharp contrast to that person who is so concerned with his own feelings and desires that he ignores, neglects or is indifferent towards others, taking them for granted. This is a particularly easy habit for married men to fall into who may come to expect that the legal contract of marriage is sufficient to assure a woman of one's devotion.

It is indispensable for a woman to know that her husband is aware of her as a person. His thoughtful attention to her comfort is a visible demonstration to her of his love. It provides further a unifying bond between them, for as a man shows this thoughtful concern for his wife, she blossoms as a flower in the sun while he feels an expansion of his better self through remembering her. We shall consider some of the ways a man cam be attentive to a woman.

1. *Small acts of chivalry:* An attentive man will open a car door for a woman, help her with her coat, lift in the groceries, etc. If they are attending a picnic and a small breeze blows up, without a word he will take off his coat and place it around her shoulders. He will see that she has the first hotdog, and will check to see that she is comfortable. When they are on a busy street, he offers her his arm or hand. He pulls up her chair at dinner. He is aware of her needs, and his attentions come automatically.

2. *Notice her:* When she enters a room, he is aware of her

presence. He looks at her, comments about her being there and talks to her. She is not like a piece of furniture. She is a woman, and he notices her as one. If she has done something to look especially nice, he offers appreciation. He notices her hair, her dress, her beauty, her figure, or anything that is distinctively feminine. (She wants to be appreciated as a woman, as you want to be appreciated as a man.) Nothing escapes his glance that is worth commenting on. If there is opportunity, he seeks her company and prefers her to other interests.

Noticing a woman helps her to "come alive." She will have a new excitement in getting up in the morning and making herself beautiful, for there is someone who makes it worth it all. She has a new incentive—someone to please, someone to look nice for. She will enjoy making a new dress, shopping, or standing before the mirror wondering how to wear her hair. She is like a little girl who anticipates a birthday party full of surprises—wondering just how he will react.

Such an attentive man knows her best features. She may have a beautiful nose, shapely figure, well-formed neck and shoulders, a special color or glint to the eyes, long, graceful hands, an engaging smile, or beautiful hair. Whatever her best features are, her husband is aware of them and comments about them frequently. If she is not physically beautiful, she may have a charming laugh or cute manners.

3. *Little attentions, indications of thoughtfulness:* He remembers her birthday, anniversary and every other special occasion. Sometimes without special reason he brings her flowers—her favorite kind. Or it may be only a flower he picked in the yard, but it is of special significance because it is spontaneous. She will probably remember it most. He buys her perfume, a nightgown, a scarf, just to let her know he is thinking of her. She may not need these things, but this only convinces her that it is a gift of thoughtfulness and love. Sometimes he writes her love notes, or delivers the message personally. His language may be simple or eloquent, but it indicates *he is thinking of her,* knows she is alive and is important to him.

4. *Remember heartfelt desires:* An attentive man has an educated heart. He is observant, knows his wife's favorite flower, color, and favorite perfume. He knows which styles of clothes she likes, the kind of sweaters and jewelry she prefers. He is aware of her special desires. He remembers the time she looked longingly

in a shop window at a Spanish shawl. She does not have to hint—he knows her desires.

The movie *The Unsinkable Molly Brown* illustrated this point very well. In early marriage Molly had expressed a deep desire for three items: a red silk dress, cups and saucers that match, and a big brass bed. They had little money at the time, but her remarkable husband kept these almost childlike whims in his mind, and later, when they became rich, the first things he bought for her were a red silk dress, cups and saucers that match, and a big brass bed. Molly was overwhelmed. She hadn't imagined that he would remember, especially after such a long time.

Men are often very busy with many things of great importance. Amid pressing concerns of his business, the family budget, or the stock market, it may strike a man as absurd that he should occupy his mind with the whims of a woman. But he should know that because he is so busy, the favor is appreciated even more—busy men who are attentive are so rare. What it does to the woman may be worth far more to him than his profits in the stock market.

Few virtues stir a woman's heart like attentiveness. If men only knew its motivating power, they would not neglect this virtue. It is one of a woman's greatest pleasures and the lack of it her greatest pain. I have often thought of how many marriages could be restored if a man would show his wife proper attention—if he would bring her flowers, tell her she is beautiful, remember her birthday. It would bring out a response in her that would put new vitality into a disintegrating marriage.

Attentiveness is sadly lacking in most men, and especially in American men. When they come home from work, they take their wives for granted. They are part of the scenery, like the furniture, the walls, the draperies. They are background. The man sinks into the sofa and reads the paper or watches T.V. The woman feels no more significant to him than the kitchen sink. If she talks to him, he mutters a few words and continues to read the newspaper or goes to the basement or the garage to work on his hobby. His wife begins to think, "He doesn't even know I am alive." Is it any wonder that women begin to neglect their appearance? A woman simply has to be noticed to have a reason to be attractive to a man.

I have recently read of Russian women and how they long for the return of chivalry. According to authoress Natalya Baranskaya, "A man will rarely open a door for a woman." She pleads for more male attentiveness for the Russian women. The authoress told of the Russian women's reaction to the British-made T.V.

series, "The Forsyte Saga," which they viewed there. The women were impressed mostly by the courtliness and family fidelity of hero Soames Forsyte (forgetting the social point that he was a plundering capitalist). "How sincere he is. His daughter is fortunate. Everything was for her." The Soviet women cannot even dream of chivalry. And the authoress' appeal to Russian men is: "Men, look after the women."

In another interview with a Mrs. Perevoznikova, the lady was asked what women in Russia want. She replied, "They are looking for those material comforts and conveniences that will *liberate them in the home* and add that touch of glamour and color to life that is still so lacking there." And what do they want from their men? Mrs. Perevoznikova became thoughtful. "I would like above all, attentiveness. When a woman does not feel she is liked and respected, she does not even want to comb her hair."

In the movie *My Fair Lady,* Eliza complains of Henry Higgins because she didn't want to be "passed over," or in other words ignored. She could stand to be corrected, remade, revamped, transformed into a different person, but she could not stand to be treated with indifference. And such is the pain in the hearts of thousands of women who are set aside, like the pictures on the wall.

There are some men who are more attentive than others. The Italian men are known to be so, and the women love it. Women who have not seen this masculine attention so lavishly given are especially impressed when they visit Italy. The Associated Press carried a release from Rome under the title "Women Defend Wolves." It seems that Italian officials were going to take action against the sidewalk Romeos when the American Women's Club of Rome resisted the action. They said, in part:

"An American woman is accustomed to walking the street as if invisible. The fact that Italian men aged 17 to 80 will, without exception, turn their heads at her passing, is a thing of wonder and joy. It may take a bit of getting used to, but it is an adjustment women are happy to make. The Italian attitude is the important thing. If you're a woman, you're worthy of admiration. . . . It's so charmingly un-American."

Italian men also use elaborate language. "Never have I seen anyone more beautiful than you," or "You make the whole world like sunshine," they can say with ease, as though they were speaking about the time of day.

Polynesian men are much the same way and have a lavish way of expressing their affection. Perhaps such expressions seem insincere and overstated. I certainly don't recommend insincerity at any time, but there is something about the wholehearted way these men express themselves which could be used as a lesson in point.

WHY FLOWERS?

Many men are at a loss to know why women so appreciate flowers. A short time ago a young man asked me to suggest something he could send his mother for her birthday. "Flowers," I said, "women always love to receive flowers." "But they are so perishable," said the young man. "That is why they are such a meaningful gift," I replied. "If a man is willing to spend his money on them, it's a token of love." He had never thought of it in this way.

I uncovered this mystery about flowers from the Polynesians. While in their islands I watched a lady making leis. She explained that it was often necessary for the women to stay up all night to make the beautiful leis for early morning ships coming to port. "That's a lot of trouble to go to when they only last a day or so," I said. "That's the beauty of it all," she replied. "Because they are so perishable, they convey only the true meaning of love."

This conception of flowers makes them appropriate to show attentiveness—it is a clear demonstration that a man is perceptible to the thoughts of a woman. A gift of great worth is perhaps a greater method of proving real love, since it indicates greater sacrifice. But since these gifts are given only rarely, they are not the type to be used to show attentiveness. Flowers are fragrant, beautiful, inexpensive, and therefore fitting to carry the message, "I am thinking of you."

OTHER GIFTS TO SHOW ATTENTIVENESS

If a man is careful to observe his wife, he will probably have ideas for gifts. He will know her favorite colors, perfume, and those special things she has been wanting. But if he is lost for ideas, he can rely upon the following suggestions:

1. *Seek the Advice of Women Close to Her:* Closest are her mother, sisters, daughters, or close friends. They will likely know her favorite styles, colors, and taste. If not, they have a way of

finding out. Should your wife learn of your special efforts to please her, she will appreciate it all the more.

2. *Rely Upon the Things All Women Love:* Women always love things which are feminine, pretty, soft, scented, silky, and in any way beautiful. Perfume is always appreciated, but unfortunately the best kinds are the most expensive. Don't buy anything second rate. Sweaters, soft scarves, beautiful purses, jewel boxes, mirrors, vases, pearls, and well made jewelry are good standbys.

3. *Things to Avoid:* Avoid things which are overly practical, unless she has expressed a specific desire for them. Avoid things which, although she may *need* them, she may not necessarily *want.* It is relatively easy to observe what someone else *needs,* but remember the key—does she also *want it?* Gifts should not necessarily serve the purpose of filling needs unless they are also desired. One's needs are likely to be filled anyway, but the special attention that stirs a woman is to give her something she wants very much, but would not likely receive as a necessity of living.

SPECIAL PROBLEMS WHICH ARISE IN GIFT-GIVING

Occasionally a gift will be given which does not fit or suit the need as expected. In this case, if a man suggests it be exchanged or returned, he will save his wife the embarrassment of making the suggestion. It is really not appropriate for her to make such a suggestion, although something very near to the gift given might be exactly what she wanted. If in any way you detect that she is not entirely happy with the gift, you can greatly ease the situation by suggesting it be returned. She will appreciate your sensitivity to her feelings.

There are at least two circumstances when gift-giving can be a painful experience. One occurs when she criticizes the gift; the other is when she complains that it is too expensive. In both cases it can be a cutting experience to a man and humiliating for the woman. There is only one satisfactory solution in such a case. The woman, being unaware or insensitive to the value of gift-giving, needs to be taught. If a man will patiently teach her these values, she will be relieved of future mistakes, and the tenseness of the moment will likely be eased as a man takes the opportunity to express himself.

Unfortunately most men do not behave so wisely. Instead they clam up, resolving to "teach her a lesson" by determining never to buy her anything again. This is a sad mistake. A man should not let her ignorance eliminate the pleasure of gift-giving—an act that can bind love closer together. Teaching her will not only keep open the opportunity to give, but it will ease pain on her part, relieve what could be hidden resentments for the man as he expresses himself, and will therefore greatly aid their daily relationships.

I discussed this once with a woman who years before had criticized her husband because he had purchased a lovely leather handbag which she felt was an extravagance. It was not until years later that she understood her mistake and the effect it had upon her husband. Since he alone realized the impact of her mistake, the ill feelings would have been minimized if he had explained the situation to her. This is admittedly difficult, since she is the one in error. But it is the only practical way to resolve the hurt feelings which are produced under such conditions.

SOME PARTICULAR TIMES FOR ATTENTIVENESS

1. *When She Needs Assistance:* In her household duties a woman frequently gets "snowed under" and needs help. At such a time a man demonstrates his awareness of her needs by doing the dishes, changing the baby, fixing the baby's formula, going to the market, or doing whatever is needed. If these things are done, not by routine, but when such special needs are noted, they are acts of genuine attentiveness.

2. *When She Is Not Well:* This is a time when a woman especially needs attention. An attentive man will look after her physical well-being as a mother does her child. He is the first to notice the tired look in her eyes and suggest that she may be working too hard or needs medical attention. His great concern gives his wife a wonderful feeling of security, an assurance that she can rely upon him in times of need.

Often this attentiveness is sadly missing. I have heard women say, "My husband is the last to notice when I am ill." They feel alone in this emergency. Only when they go to bed or see a doctor themselves does such a husband realize that anything is wrong— or at least only then does he *appear* to notice it. This lack of concern for her welfare can cause a woman to feel like a servant and that she really means very little to her husband.

A well-known newspaper columnist received a complaint from a young husband, married four years, who stated that his wife had lost all incentive to fix herself up or to keep up her domestic duties. Before marriage she was immaculate in grooming and energetic and full of life. Now she let herself go and had become a complainer and seemed always to be tired. He mentioned, as if in passing, that they had four children.

For such a man to be so insensitive as to think a woman can manage four children who are so young and keep up the same energy as previously is beyond understanding. It is obvious that such blindness to her needs could only make them more severe and cause her to feel like a common drudge.

There are cases when a husband will become upset when his wife is ill, being silent and distant towards her. He may have become so dependent upon her that he is frustrated to think of life running along without her usual assistance. Such a selfish attitude is wounding to a woman. It gives her the impression that she is only a crutch in his life, that her value is one of a servant. It shows lack of concern, lack of sympathy, self-centeredness, and even lack of love. Love and concern are inseparable to a woman. Such a letdown on a husband's part is to a woman unforgivable.

Again, some men fail to demonstrate concern for fear it will encourage psychological illness. A wife may so enjoy her husband's attention that she may create an imaginary illness to prolong the pleasure. Usually an opposite reaction is more apt to occur. If a woman feels her husband's lack of concern at the first sign of illness, there is a tendency for her, perhaps unconsciously, to encourage the illness for the express purpose of winning his attention, or seeing to what extreme she need go before he is alarmed.

Husband and wife must realize that they are dependent upon one another, "for better or for worse, in sickness and in health." They need each other in times of joy and health, but even more so in times of suffering and trouble. These are times true love is tested. To let another down at such a time is difficult to redeem. It is a source of great emotional pain for the neglected one.

3. *At Childbirth:* A special time when a woman needs a man's attentiveness is when she is expecting a baby. And yet I have observed men who give this dramatic occasion little attention. I remember a man telling me with an attitude of pride that when his wife was ready to deliver their baby, he drove her to the hospital, dropped her off, and came back that evening to see his newborn child. He had thought of asking her to take a taxi, but felt restrained from doing that. Women suffer pain from such

neglect—perhaps pain equal to that of the childbirth. Yet some women will not reveal their sensitive feelings. It is too humiliating. They also have pride and self-respect. If one must ask for such attention, it means nothing. Attentiveness must be given voluntarily and willingly to be of value.

Every consideration should be given to a woman in childbirth. Traditionally, women want the presence of their husband. They want to hold his hand and feel his sustenance and comfort—they want to know that he is there. This used to be customary when women had their children at home. I observe this tradition returning as fathers are being permitted to enter delivery rooms in many hospitals. They are of little assistance to the doctors, are perhaps a hindrance, but are of real value in giving the wife comfort so needed at this critical moment in her life.

Although childbirth is a natural function of the body and seldom does it result in a fatality, yet there is a moment at birth when the woman hovers close to death. Her heart momentarily stops and there is a time of crisis. I think women must sense this possible danger, which is one of the reasons she instinctively feels a need for her husband to be near. It is also a time of intense suffering, and great joy, strong reasons why the husband should be there to share them with his wife.

4. *When She Has Problems:* Sometimes a man thinks he is the only one who has problems and expects his wife to do all the giving. He becomes frustrated if she is troubled or is not her usual cheerful self. He may even become irritated with her or resentful because she has a problem. But this is a particular time when a woman needs attention. She may be suffering emotional pain or turmoil or perhaps a physical pain.

At such times her husband's concern is essential. And yet, men are not so willing to give of themselves in these moments. There is a tendency for them to become so frustrated at the task of trying to comfort their wife, such a lack of knowledge as to how to handle the situation that they may leave the room or escape from the house in despair. I presume such men do not mean harm, but they cannot think of what to say or do. It is regrettable that they fail to realize that desertion at such times greatly intensifies the wife's problems. Her greater need is for her husband's concern. If this is denied, her problems are multiplied.

The solution is very simple. When a man senses his wife is troubled, he will help her immensely if he will say tenderly, *"I can tell that something is wrong. Please tell me what it is. I want to help."* I challenge any man to keep these words in his wallet, to use them when needed and see the miracle that happens. See the barriers come tumbling down. It is important to listen carefully to her problems and offer sympathy and give all the assistance that one can.

But do not take a negative attitude. In other words, do not make her feel ashamed for her suffering. Do not minimize the problem or defend someone who may have caused it. It is *sympathy* and your *concern* she needs. This is the approach that reduces the problem.

WHAT IF SHE DOES NOT DESERVE YOUR ATTENTION?

Sometimes a man feels that his wife does not deserve his attentions. It may appear that a woman is so neglectful in her responsibilities, so unfeminine, and perhaps unappreciative, that she is not deserving of the special considerations. Like with so many things, it is difficult to be a judge. Certainly she is not going to be perfect, and in some areas she may fail miserably. But she does have a better side. It is well to concentrate on this. During a period of a few years, the meals a woman prepares number thousands: she will likely have borne children and done the myriad tasks incident to that, nursing in illness, feeding, washing, and tending. These may be the "first mile" tasks, but they are certainly worthy of appreciation.

There is the possibility that a man may be responsible for his wife's failures, at least to some degree. But even if convinced that she is undeserving, one might remember that "God maketh the rain to fall on the just and the unjust." Should we not then give to the undeserving as well as the deserving?

Often some small act of kindness will so impress a woman that it is the means of causing her to make a new determination to live a better life. If she feels herself that she is not really worthy of the kindness, it will move her even more. The message that it brings of continued concern and thoughtfulness may awaken a new spirit in her.

We are often inclined to punish the undeserving, thinking that it will somehow cause them to overcome their weak tendencies. Positive motivation is far more effective in changing conduct. It is well to also remember that God has said, "Vengeance is mine. I will repay." It is not up to us to mete out punishment by way of being cool and unforgiving.

WHEN SHE APPEARS TO REJECT ATTENTION

Sometimes a woman will strangely reject a man's attentions and even appear to be irritated because of them. He brings her flowers and she accepts them coolly. He brings a gift and she gives thanks stiffly. Obviously something is wrong.

Perhaps a man should check on himself to see if he has offended her in some way. She may be suffering resentments and consider these attentions a cover-up for bad deeds. Offenses will extend from the most trivial to those of great magnitude in which she may have suffered extremely. For a man who has been unfaithful to his wife and presumes that a gift of flowers will compensate for such a great sin has something to learn about repentance.

In any event, if her coolness is the result of an offense by her husband, proper acknowledgement, retribution and forgiveness are first required. Only then will she be in the frame of mind to fully accept a token of warm feelings.

WHEN SHE ASKS FOR ATTENTION

Is a man justified in withholding attentions when a woman asks for them? This is another instance when the nature of man resists that which is expected.

A business associate once confided to me that when he was first married, he and his wife had the habit of walking each evening down to a certain corner where a lady sold carnations. Each evening he bought one for his wife. This went on for quite a long time until it became a tradition. One day he decided not to buy her one. She was terribly disappointed and wondered what was wrong. She asked him to buy her one. This so irritated him that he determined never to buy her flowers again. He said that in the fifteen years that had elapsed since that event, he had never bought her flowers.

I thought, "Oh foolish man. You deny yourself the joy of giving and diminish your wife as a woman." He could have explained to her that it is better not to ask since the flower would only convey meaning if it were his idea. To withhold this evidence of love was to me almost inhuman. I knew this lady and wondered why she was so harsh and impatient. After hearing her husband's story, I wondered if it could have begun with the flower incident.

Actually the solution is quite simple. If a woman makes the mistake of asking, inform her that it detracts from your joy in giving. But do not make the mistake of denying her the very things she needs to keep her spirits alive.

ATTENTIVENESS WITH CHILDREN

We generally think of attentiveness as being given to the wife only. Children also require it. It is important for a father to greet them when he comes home, acknowledge their presence when they enter a room, and give them the courtesy of listening when they speak. They need a pat on the head, a touch of the hand or a squeeze to convey the feeling of concern and warmth. If a father will sit by their bedside and show them special attention, he can draw them to him and make them susceptible to his teachings.

Little children frequently have difficulty in getting their father's attention. He may be reading, watching T.V., or talking to someone. They must compete with these demands if they want attention. It is therefore imperative that the father take the initiative to give them attention without their having to demand it. They, too, must know that they are considered as important people and are not just "fixtures" around the house.

Little girls need special attentiveness. Their father will train them by assisting them with coats, opening the car door for them, seating them at dinner, etc. In this way they are trained to accept such attentions when they become adults. Children are apt to become spoiled if given too many material things which only clutter their lives and lessen their appreciation for material things. But they can receive such attentions as these which add to their security and happiness and are vitally more important than "things."

In review, consider the following means that one can employ as he demonstrates his attentiveness:

HOW TO BE ATTENTIVE

1. *Extend small acts of chivalry:* Open doors, assist her with her coat, give your arm or hand when walking.

2. *Notice her:* Look at her, notice things about her such as her hair, her figure, her clothes, her better features.

3. *Remember little attentions:* Let her know you are thinking of her. Bring her flowers, perfume, remember her birthday, or something she has been wanting. Write her a love note or tell her personally.

4. *Remember her special desires.*

5. *Help in times of emergency.*

6. *Notice when she is not well.*

7. *Offer attentiveness when she bears a child.*

8. *Offer help when she has problems or is suffering.*

It is masculinity to which femininity responds. The masculine art of attentiveness brings a moving response in women. It melts their hearts and makes them womanly. It makes a finer person of her.

The need for this male act of chivalry is deep and almost haunting. Evidence of this is expressed in a song written for a woman to sing:

LITTLE THINGS MEAN A LOT

Blow me a kiss from across the room,
  Say I look nice, when I'm not.
Touch my hair as you pass my chair,
  Little things mean a lot.
Give me your arm as we cross the street,
  Call me at six on the dot.
A line a day when you're far away,
  Little things mean a lot.

You don't have to buy me diamonds and pearls,
  Champagne, sables or such,
I never cared much for diamonds and pearls,
  For honestly, honey, they just cost money.

Give me your hand when I've lost the way,
  Give me your shoulder to cry on.

Whether the day is bright or gray,
Give me your heart to rely on.
Give me the warmth of a secret smile,
    To show me you haven't forgot.
For now and forever, for always and ever.
    Little things mean a lot.

XVI
YOUTHFULNESS

An attractive characteristic of the man of velvet is a spirit of youthfulness. This spirit is exemplified by a zest for living, an inquisitive and inquiring mind, a love for adventure, and a daring to try something new. It is a spirit of optimism with a sense of humor and an ability to see the challenges of life as opportunities to test one's ingenuity.

Youth is a time for dreams, plans, and enthusiasm. When one of my sons was sixteen years old, I took him with me on a business trip to Australia. His youthful eagerness for life was inspiring. He had a map he referred to constantly. His eyes were scanning every landmark he could identify on the map. Flying high over the Pacific he spotted island groups and atolls which he would identify. Even at night he could scarcely sleep because of his curiosity. At every stop he made the most of the opportunity to investigate everything new to him. Our destination was a ranch in the far outback of the Northern Territory. There he found endless interest in the plant life and the animals and insects. He was like a sponge soaking up everything in sight. I contrast this with the bored attitude of some of the passengers on the plane who drew the curtains and read a detective story with no more interest in life than if they were animals grazing in the field.

Unfortunately men are constantly subjected to the idea that age is overtaking them. Throughout our lives we are continually conditioned to age in a negative way by forever being aware that we are so many years old. This information is required on an endless number of forms. We associate ourselves with our contemporaries we have known in school, at work, or in the service. The passing of years goes on relentlessly, and we are reminded of it as we celebrate birthdays, observe the New Year, and see the inevitable changes that take place in ourselves.

It is true that we have all lived so many years, and this is a matter of record and exactness and cannot be altered one whit. We are so many years old and nothing can change that. But it is well to remember also that this age in years isn't necessarily all important. One's physiological age is more important, since it has to do with the aging process. We realize, of course, that the body does not age uniformly. For example, the brain cells are much slower to deteriorate than the muscle structure. One should find his mind expanding beyond the time when he has reached the zenith of his physical capacity.

This physiological aging or deterioration can be slowed down remarkably through diet, exercise, positive thinking, and constructive work. It is not uncommon to see men aged sixty or seventy who are physically younger than men of forty. These older men have a more promising life expectancy and may have as much as twenty-five or thirty or more years of productive life ahead. It is pathetic to see the negative thinking that invades the minds of so many, telling them they are so old they must limit themselves to playing shuffleboard or checkers. Gray hair does not necessarily limit one's activity in any of the important adventures of life. The thought that one is getting old should be discouraged, for it generally brings with it the concept of being weakened, exhausted, worn out, and depleted of vigor. All of these negative ideas militate against one's attitude and performance. And we must remember the truth . . . age is not so much a matter of years as it is a matter of attitude, and there is something we can do about that.

There are a few unique men who retain their spirit of youth into old age. They are eager about life and noticeably unaware of their advancing years. One such man is the famed anthropologist Dr. Leakey. The *National Geographic* magazine carried a feature on this interesting man. He was photographed in Africa on his hands and knees, a shock of white hair hanging down on his forehead, studying specimens he had uncovered in his diggings. One could tell from the intent look on his face that he was enthusiastic about his work and was certainly not aware that he was well advanced in years. I studied the picture carefully. It intrigued me. I felt respect for this man who had such an obvious zest for living. It reminded me of the writing of Thoreau, who said, "I do not want to find when I come to die that I have not lived." Dr. Leakey had not only lived, he was still living!

I also thought, as I continued to look at this picture, of other men I have known in my lifetime who had lost their spirit of youth at an early age. Some became disillusioned and bored. One such man was a famous movie actor who committed suicide, leaving the note, "I am bored with life." Other men complain that life has dealt harshly with them. They withdraw from the battleground of life to nurse their wounds in self-pity.

My father-in-law was an example of a man with the spirit of youth. I am still amazed when I think of this man who at seventy-three, and after he had retired from the active practice of dentistry, began life anew by opening a dental practice in a frontier town in Alaska. This was a small town entirely new to him, but he threw his heart into his work and soon had a successful practice going. While there he also enjoyed hunting and even slept in the rain in a pup tent.

Another man with zest was an architect who designed his finest creation when he was ninety years old . . . a magnificent building which stands like a monument on the top of a hill. During his lunch hour I observed him poring over his plans as though life had just begun. He enjoyed the mental challenge of his work and even worked out difficult mathematical equations daily just for mental exercise.

To one with a youthful disposition, life is good. He can get excited about a new idea or the prospects of seeing a new place, meeting people he hasn't seen before or doing something which has not been done before. To such a man the endless prospects before him in a world so large and varied stagger his mind. He thinks of all the books he would like to read—not books of diversion only, but books that excite the mind because they broaden his comprehension on the many frontiers of new learning as well as the learning of the past. He wants to be familiar with the customs and problems of people who are far removed from him. He would like to understand them and see into their hearts. He is interested in the earth—the infinite variations in typography, climate, landscape, and peoples. It may not be his opportunity to travel widely, but the opportunities of present day education don't make this a necessity. One can saturate his mind from many other sources.

John Goddard, the famous explorer, is a man of daring who has a zest for living. When only fifteen years old, he outlined 127 goals he wished to achieve during his lifetime. Now in his forties, he has reached more than 100 of them and still hopes to reach the remaining. He has sailed the full length of the Congo and Nile Rivers in Africa, and has also explored the Amazon River and climbed Mt. Kilimanjaro and several other peaks.

While visiting with him, I inquired about his plans. He enthusiastically said that the following month he was going to visit the Galapagos Islands and the month after that was going to do further exploring on the Congo River. There was no sign of lessening of enthusiasm for his adventures. In fact, the past seemed to strengthen his spirit of youth.

One who is youthful has a mind *open to new ideas*. A. P. Gianini, founder of the Bank of America, possessed this quality. Although he was an immigrant and had no experience in banking, he had ideas which he felt would be an improvement to the conventional methods in use. Established bankers who sat in their heavy oak-paneled offices behind marble columns, familiar with all the "sound" practices of their profession, ridiculed his ideas. They wondered at the audacity of one who would suppose he could introduce ideas that were at variance with their time-tested methods. Yet this young man entered their sanctuary and succeeded beyond anything they had known. Here is a direct confrontation between a young man with imagination and faith and those who are set in their ways and closed to new ideas.

A special gift of youth is to ignore the limits of time and age. Youths, of course, ignore it because they have so much time ahead, but some men retain this quality in a most remarkable way into old age.

Several years ago I made an exploratory trip to Brazil to search for some business opportunities. Sometime after returning home, I received a call from a man I had never met who sought my services in assisting him in a similar undertaking. I was impressed with the great enthusiasm he had. He had done considerable studying and planning and felt that the potential in some of the large, underdeveloped countries offered excellent "long range" opportunities, as he put it. Later a mutual friend inquired about our conversation. After explaining I had only talked to him by phone, he said, "You should meet him. He is eighty-nine years old." I never would have guessed. He never mentioned his age, and I'm sure his mind felt no barrier because of it. This man was planning for the future as if he were forty years younger, or more.

On another occasion a man age ninety-five called on me to see if he could accompany me to Australia. He was more agile than most men of sixty. As we talked, he became so animated that he was literally sitting on the edge of his seat. Although he had traveled extensively, the idea of going somewhere he had never been intrigued him immensely. To him the world was an interesting and challenging place.

I am always amazed with old people who disregard their age. They seem so youthful. One such man was a neighbor, age eighty-nine. This man was left a widower after sixty-five years of marriage. He lived alone although several of his thirteen children wanted him to live with them. But he liked the independence of living alone. He worked in his garden, pruned his trees, drove a tractor in the fields part time, and even put up his own fruit.

After several years living alone, he considered remarrying. He went to a physician for an examination to see "what his chances were" for an extended life. After the examination the doctor said, "It looks to me like you have another ten years or so"; so he decided to remarry, and took a bride age eighty-three.

Shortly after his marriage, he decided to climb into the upper branches of a fruit tree to prune it. I was working in my yard and heard his wife say, "Joe, you come down out of that tree immediately or I'll call the fire department." I'll never forget his answer. He said, "They'll laugh you to shame if you tell them to come and get a ninety-two-year-old man out of a tree." This man had certainly learned to resist the limitations of time.

I have observed many such men who defy the press of years. One was a production manager on a television program, age eighty. He was so thoroughly wound up in his work and enthusiastic about what he was doing, almost schoolboy fashion, that I could hardly get his attention to ask him a few questions. His youthful attitude of enthusiasm had greatly preserved his physical appearance and manner, and he gave the impression of being a much younger man.

I have, of course, met other men who have lacked this spirit of youth. One was a friend age forty-two. He had a fine medical practice, a wonderful family, and the esteem of the community. One day I asked him how he was getting along. "Terrible," was his reply, "I won't live to see fifty."

Maybe this discouraged friend was just having a bad day, but it is poisonous to the mind and body to allow such horrible thoughts to dominate. More than that, such an attitude is a direct affront to God who has provided us with life and the exciting opportunities it offers.

Sometimes we slow down because we don't feel good. Someone has said that most of the world's work is done by people who don't feel good. This is probably true to a great extent. Muscles may be sore and perhaps there is a headache. For most of these simple maladies the best treatment is an involvement in some challenging work in which one can raise some enthusiasm. One wonders if many of the common complaints are not due to boredom or perhaps a fear of life.

Those who accept the challenge of a difficult situation and look to the opportunities such difficulties provide, stir the admiration and interest of most everyone. A shut-down of a large industry put hundreds of men out of work in a certain community. Some of these men had been working all their adult lives in this one place and knew nothing outside this familiar community. The article describing these conditions referred to the plight of a particular man who had lost his job and who was now at home while his wife brought in the pay check. He was doing the domestic duties and would have the dinner prepared when she returned from work. It was noted that he was suffering certain emotional blows— adjustments to his ego in not being the one to provide the living.

There are numerous cases where perhaps a man would have to adjust to this, at least temporarily. It turned out in this instance, however, that he had been offered a job in another city, but declined it because he hated to move from the town he was familiar with and leave the friends, the only people he had known all his life.

Here is a man lacking courage and daring. He had a job in another city. The only daring required of him was to adapt to a new environment. Making new friends can be a stimulating and gratifying experience. He voluntarily relinquished his position as the provider for his family to stay in the shell he was used to and avoid the mental exertion of the change. Such an attitude does nothing to raise the level of esteem he has for himself, nor does it encourage the esteem of his family for him.

This brings up the matter of risk. A willingness to take risks is a youthful characteristic. In a very real sense the progress of the world is attributable to those with the daring to do that which has not been done before. Certainly there was a time when no one had flown, and to dream of such a thing would bring only ridicule. Every invention, every piece of literature or art requires an investment in time and money and is therefore a risk. Politicians risk their time and resources in seeking office. Launching a new business requires risk. Doing anything which has hope of material gain carries a counterbalance of risk.

A careful line must be drawn between that which has substance to it and is worthy of risk and that which is foolish and over-speculative. Too frequently the hesitancy encountered by the older-thinking person is a lack of courage, an unwillingness to make an extra exertion. Excessive caution is more likely due to fear than prudence. Perhaps it is a realization that past failures have resulted because of a lack of effort or planning and a new venture would require more dedication than one is willing to give. So it is easy to become an armchair philosopher and content oneself with dreaming rather than doing.

Fear of taking action frequently has its roots in the doubt one feels as to the worthiness of his own ideas. Being open to the new ideas of others is important, but being open to flashing thoughts of inspiration which one occasionally receives himself is also important. It is possible that you might get a sudden insight into something which is obscure to everyone else.

People become so accustomed to a stereotyped procedure or pattern of thought that it is never questioned. To change would almost seem a heresy. So it is often difficult to accept a new idea, especially when we recognize that people hate to be different.

When such negative thoughts enter the mind of one who is striving to gain a youthful attitude, he pushes them aside and deliberately replaces them with some logical positive thoughts. He remembers that the wise are not afraid to appear foolish. He remembers that exploring new paths will invigorate the mind and keep him young despite the passing of years.

SENSE OF HUMOR

A man of youthfulness has a lighthearted sense of humor. This removes much of the drabness from his daily work which is bound to become routine and monotonous at times. Being able to see the humor in commonplace situations makes the carrying of one's load so much easier.

It has been observed that a characteristic of healthy and long-lived persons is a sense of humor. It is as though their optimistic attitude were supplying a physical nourishment to their bodies—a sort of vitamin supplement. These people realize that to take themselves too seriously is a deadly mistake. Life is going on anyway, and somehow things always work out regardless of how gloomy the picture looks at some low point.

Humor will often bring the picture into sharper focus. Abraham Lincoln was gifted in this respect, and through this means cut down gigantic problems to a size he could manage. Bitterness and rancor are impossible when one's sense of humor is functioning. It brings a smile to the face, and everyone succumbs to this touch of human warmth.

* * *

These characteristics of youthfulness are not an exhaustive list but will suffice to indicate the nature of the attitude of a youthful person. It is always to be remembered that youthfulness is a state of mind and not a matter of years. When a man has this quality, he adds a breadth to his personality that is a rare distinction. It is an indication of maturity and is in sharp contrast to the childish men who long for "the good old days" and revert back to the pranks of their youth.

Sometimes men are afraid to learn and adopt these qualities of youthfulness for fear of "losing their dignity." It is only the unsure who would harbor such a feeling. Or perhaps one has let life beat him down to the point that the spark is dead. This, of course, is one of the terrible tragedies which we see all too often.

But it is fortunately true that man is not bound down to having to accept things as they are. The human being is far more adaptable than most persons realize. Even long-established patterns are alterable.

XVII
HUMILITY

Humility is a freedom from pride or arrogance. One who is humble may have many virtues and achievements, but he realizes his own weaknesses, mistakes, and limitations. He does not lift himself up in pride over other men, over his wife, nor over his children. Although he will have achieved in some areas of living, he realizes his lack in others. He knows that other people possess qualities he needs and does not have. He also knows that despite his achievements for which he can honestly be proud, he is far from the man he should be—there is still much more to achieve and overcome.

Humility is not, however, a groveling or self-effacing attitude in which one deliberately depreciates himself beyond justification. It is not thinking of ourselves as less than we are, or more than we are, but just as we are. It is a correct estimation of ourselves as God sees us. Humility is not pretended modesty in which we control bragging for the purpose of impressing others. There must be a quality *within* which causes ony to truly *feel* his own limitations and weaknesses.

The Savior set a perfect example of humility. Although He was the chosen Son of God, having no sin, and was able to overcome all things, yet He lived among the common people and dined with sinners. Although His disciples worshiped Him, He did not rise above them in an attitude of superiority. He demonstrated His humility when He bowed before them and washed their feet. By this act He impressed upon them in a dramatic way the requirement that men remain humble. How can anyone elevate himself above others when he remembers this action of the Savior?

Humility is one of the most desirable traits of human personality. No man is truly great without it. It shows a respect for all life and a greatness of spirit. A humble man recognizes himself and others as participants in a divine plan which glorifies the human potential and recognizes that from the most inauspicious beginnings may arise greatness. Humility adds velvet to a man which tempers the hard steel and balances his self-confidence. Without humility, salf-confidence tends towards arrogance.

ARROGANCE OR PRIDE

Humility can best be understood by reviewing its opposite—arrogance or pride. Arrogance is an ungrounded feeling of superiority over others and an inability to see one's own weaknesses or limitations. This fault can be commonly viewed in the following areas of life:

1. *Wordly goods:* The possession of wealth or earthly possessions causes many to be lifted up in pride. Wealth is easily flaunted and is unfortunately considered a yardstick of success by far too many people. For anyone with a tendency to the sin of pride the temptation to use wealth in this way is almost irresistible. Such persons tend to look down on those who have less as inferior to themselves and sometimes deliberately display or describe their possessions to the less fortunate for the purpose of attaining a feeling of self-importance. This pride, which is really an evil, causes men to glory in the corruptible things of the earth.

Wealthy people themselves are not entirely to blame for this unwarranted emphasis given to their possessions. There is great homage given them because of their money. Others scrape and bow to them and induce in them these feelings of superiority. To eliminate this evil from among us, it is essential that we neither elevate ourselves nor anyone else because of worldly goods. Wealth in itself if not an indication of superiority or worthiness.

2. *Knowledge:* For some persons who obtain a higher education there is a tendency to feel superior because of their learning and to demean those with less formal training. Such a person may

find it difficult to accept a new idea from a man with less education than he has. The truly educated man learns to have an open mind, but unfortunately there are some whose education has not extended this far.

The key to retaining humility is a realization that knowledge is not reserved for the highly educated alone. God sometimes puts it into the minds of the most unsophisticated by way of inspiration. There is the further thought that although a man may know a great deal about some subjects, there is an infinitely broader field of learning about which he knows little or nothing.

3. *Skill, ability or talents:* A man who can perform a skill with great ease as a result of natural talent may feel superior to a man who must strive diligently to acquire the same skill. For example, a man attending a trade school or professional college may notice that he stands out as having more native ability than his classmates. There is a temptation under these circumstances to feel superior because of this natural adaptation.

Other men acquire skill and competence not through talent alone, but because of years of experience. Such a man may tend to look upon men new in his field as inferiors. And yet some remarkable men are able to retain their humility along with great experience. They are eager to find ways of improvement, even from younger men, and are anxious to assist others to achieve what they themselves already have. They have no fear that their station will be less if they help someone else achieve the position they now occupy.

I know a medical doctor who achieved special skills and had earned several degrees and citations beyond his M.D. degree. Yet this man displayed unique humility. When a young doctor joined his staff as an associate, he sought out the young doctor's advice, asked him for the "latest knowledge in medical school," and was respectful of the young man's ideas.

4. *Accomplishments, achievements, honors, position and status:* It seems to be human nature for people to stratify themselves into social classes with preferential treatment accorded to some. There are many things which can put a man "at the top" where he is in a position of acclaim. It may be a high degree he has earned, a special merit or award for fame or talents. Since there is an inborn desire for status among men, when it comes, it may "go to his head." All the applause and attention he received from others may cause him to feel that he is a superior person, deserving such acclaim and honor. The limelight dulls his finer

senses, causing him to think he is something special above other people.

When a man has earned his acclaim through effort and dedication, he cannot help feeling a pride and esteem in his accomplishment. This is certainly a justifiable feeling, but it in no way should cause him to feel superior to other men. One only has to look at certain famous musicians and artists of the past to realize that, although they had talent and often great dedication to a goal, they were human and therefore as full of human weaknesses as other men. In almost every case they did not stand out as superior men, only as superior artists. They had every reason, then, to retain a spirit of humility.

But here again, it is often the clamoring crowd that causes the famous to feel superior. They seek their autographs, follow them in the streets, and are awed by every word they utter. If we would all give credit only where due, then these persons of fame and reputation would not have a distorted view of themselves.

5.   *Good works or righteousness:* Being lifted up in pride for what we consider our righteous endeavors was the great weakness of the Pharisees, the Sadducees and the scribes in biblical days. They took great pride in their long fasts, prayers in the streets, observance of the sabbath and the rituals laid down by their forefathers. They made outward demonstations of piety as a means of impressing others. They reserved for themselves special seats in the temple and avoided the contact with the publicans and sinners whom they felt were inferior to themselves. This group of pretended saints received the strongest castigation the Savior uttered. He condemned them, not for their faithfulness, but for their lack of humility.

There is a great tendency in all of us towards self-righteousness, a feeling that we are better than others, that we are more honest, more fair, generous or dependable or in other ways more righteous than someone else. For this reason we criticize, depreciate or even condemn another person. We do not allow for his mistakes. Rather, we tend to judge. This negative attitude has its roots in one's own lack of humility. If we could see ourselves as God sees us, we would realize our own human weakness. This would restrain us from attacking others. You can count on it that whenever you find a faultfinding person, quick to criticize others, you have also found a person lacking humility. He may say he is humble, he may reason that he is, but he is not so. Somewhere inside he has not regarded himself and everyone else in the proper perspective. He has not allowed for mistakes and errors. He has not softened his spirit with humility.

Because our faults are different, it is easy to find room for criticism. One person, for example, may be more generous than another, whereas the other is more punctual. Because of these differences in virtue, there is a tendency to see the failures in one another. Humans have not the ability to judge. God has never listed the virtues in order of importance, nor has he given us the insight to make a fair judgment under all circumstances. We therefore lack the ability to make a valid judgment.

HOW GOD DISLIKES PRIDE

Where pride arises from a feeling of wealth, knowledge, special ability, self-righteousness, or any source whatever, it is a trait which God condemns with strong emotion. We read the Proverbs 6:16-19:

> These six things doth the Lord hate: yea
> seven are an abomination unto him:
>   A proud look, a lying tongue, and hands
> that shed innocent blood,
>   An heart that deviseth wicked imagina-
> tions, feet that be swift in running to mischief,
>   A false witness that speaketh lies, and he
> that soweth discord among brethen.

It is significant that pride is described as an abomination and as one of seven things God hates, being listed in company with lying, wicked imaginations and murder.

THE MARKS OF PRIDE

Pride is demonstrated in a variey of ways. Typical is an air of arrogance. The person of conceit and vanity shuns certain people whom he feels are not his equal and is harsh and critical in his judgment of others. For such a one to teach others is impossible since his attitude will never allow confidence to exist. Who can take instruction from one who is harsh and whose very attitude suggests a superiority over his fellows? The person with little or no humility is not open to new ideas and will shun and resent an opposing viewpoint, for he is unwilling to submit himself to the changes such learning will demand. Suggestions and opinions of others will probably be taken as an offense so that free and easy communication with others is broken. Characteristic of this arrogant type is an unwillingness or inability to allow for the mistakes of others, thus producing an unforgiving attitude.

PROBLEMS WHEN HUMILITY IS LACKING

The greatest problem comes to the person who lacks humility. From him springs the malicious seeds which make a close relationship with others difficult. His personality is dwarfed by his overbearing ego. With such a hindrance or flaw in his make-up, a man is headed for marital problems and family problems—his relationship with his children will be seriously hindered. It is his duty to guide them, instruct them, and represent to them an example of what they should be. We hear a great deal about the generation gap or communication gap, which seems to be the same thing, and one wonders if the seat of the gap is not a lack of humility on the part of the parent or parents. If one is harsh in judgment, slow to listen, and critical in attitude, he has established an environment which makes adequate communication impossible. He has defeated himself in accomplishing the most important thing he has to do in life—training his family. Of course all relationships with others will be similarly affected.

HUMILITY AND A WINNING PERSONALITY

An arrogant person repels others while a truly humble person draws them to him. People will shun anyone who makes them appear deficient or inadequate, as one shuns anything in the physical environment which makes him uncomfortable. There is a softness—a velvet—about the person who is modest, who, in spite of noble accomplishments, talents, or money, puts himself on a plane with everyone else—considers others worth as much as he is and seeks a variety of ideas as supplements to his own. The truly great people throughout history have exemplified this quality and have won people to them.

HOW HUMILITY CAN CURE CRITICISM

A critical attitude is largely the result of a lack of humility. It follows, then, that the development of this attribute will be a deterrent to criticism. As we acknowledge our weaknesses and mistakes, we will find it impossible to criticize others. There seems to be a tendency to enjoy finding faults in others, since it may serve as an ego-builder for the one criticizing. This is particularly true if the fault in question is not one he has himself. If another's faults are not the same as our own, it becomes easier to criticize with less strain to the conscience.

Or if a fault can be seen in someone of importance, there is a temptation to demean that person in an effort to elevate oneself.

One may even feel that his criticism is a justifiable means to establish better habits and patterns in another person. If one's motive is actually to point out a better way, it should be realized that this is the poorest way to approach the problem. Responding to criticism in a positive way is most unusual, since the natural reaction is a withdrawal from such a person. As we come to see a person's total worth—his weaknesses and his strengths—and as we learn to overlook the weaknesses and acknowledge our own, we develop humility. Biblical teachings point out that it is best to remove the beam from one's own eye before attempting to remove the mote from a brother's.

HOW HUMILITY CAN MAKE A BETTER FATHER

As important as anything in the parent-child relationship is a realization on the part of the parent that he is dealing with another individual with as much importance and worth as himself. In theory no one would deny this, but its practice is a far different matter. How many times, for instance, have you seen a child waiting for service in a store while an adult who came in later is served first? Or how many times have you seen the questions of a child ignored as though they had never been asked? Acquiescence to the principle is much easier than its practice.

Because of their youth, children will naturally make mistakes which an adult would not make. The parent probably made the same mistakes in his youth, and more than likely even later on, but now he is harsh and critical to see this mistake made by another, especially his own child. The lessons the parent has learned over the years he expects will also have been learned by his offspring. But more than this, the parent has not overcome all his mistakes even at his more mature age. He is going to feel very foolish, for example, when he gets a ticket for traffic violation when he knows there was no excuse for his getting it since he knew the law and had probably received citations before. In dealing with his child, a father who is humble enough to acknowledge that he has faults himself is in a far better position to teach. The child will recognize errors on the part of his parents and will resent being criticized or punished for his errors when his parents avoid censure by virtue of their being adults.

A parent will not "lose face" by admission of an error to his child and, if necessary, by asking forgiveness of him. Quite to the contrary, the child will feel that he is dealing with someone who is fair, and his esteem for the parent will increase. This comes through even with a very young child who may be unable to analyze the situation in any logical way, but will only be going by his feelings. When it is necessary to administer discipline, if it is given for the benefit of the child without anger or disgust, even though the punishment might be rather severe, the child will submit to it without resentment. A man who possesses humility will not be unfair in his discipline, but will be sympathetic, knowing that all people make errors, and his purpose is to help his child to overcome the pitfalls and errors with which he is confronted.

HUMILITY AND LEADERSHIP

It is quite evident with just a little thought that a leader, of all people, must be a person of humility. When a man realizes that although he has the position of leader, he does not have a claim on all knowledge and ideas—that others may have ideas worth listening to—he becomes a better leader. As he develops humility, he will respond to the suggestions of others by saying, "That sounds like a good idea," or perhaps, "I would like some time to think about it. I appreciate the thought you've given to this." When Andrew Carnegie was asked the secret to his success in business, he responded by saying, "I surround myself with people who know more about business than I do." Certainly he recognized that if his business was going to expand and succeed to the extent he wanted it to, he was going to have to get more ideas and help than he could possibly come up with as a single individual.

Again we go back to the idea of defining humility as the ability to see oneself for what he is—no exaggeration or depreciation of value, but an honest recognition of real value. To admit that someone else may have a better idea is no threat to one's confidence, since he knows that under certain circumstances he will also be the one to see the problem more clearly than anyone else. But every individual has limitations. As Abraham Lincoln once said, "We are all ignorant, only on different subjects."

Good outside ideas will come to a man whose respect for others is such as to establish confidence in them that they are free to express their ideas. We know so well that sometimes we come up with an idea ourselves which, even before the words are out, we realize has a flaw in it. A person with an idea which he felt truly had merit would hesitate to express it if he thought it was likely to be received with a critical attitude. Certainly anyone who is expected to be a follower, whether adult or child, in a home situation or a business situation or whatever situation, would have a similar response. Good leaders are amenable to the suggestions of others—not necessarily to adopt them, but to listen open-mindedly so a reasonable evaluation can be made.

HUMILITY IN MARRIAGE

Some of the rebelliousness of women is traceable to the injustices they have received from men who lack the humility to acknowledge that women are just as important, just as intelligent—maybe more so in many instances—than are the men. Some men tend to be critical of their wives—critical of their housekeeping, their mistakes, burned food, the way they drive a car, shopping errors, or mistakes in the way they handle the children. This criticism may not be confined to her personally, but may be uttered in public to her great humiliation and embarrassment. Or it may be less personal and be just a "dig" at women generally, suggesting that in some way they are less efficient, less alert, or less intelligent.

Men sometimes tend to feel that they are superior to women, that the work they do is vastly more important than the menial tasks in the home which they feel could be done by anyone with a minimum of skill and ability. As the work of the woman is depreciated, so is her value, and she may come to feel herself, as many now do, that the domestic endeavors are not important or challenging enough to warrant her time, for she realizes that she has skill and intelligence to offer the world which is commensurate with that offered by men.

Since they are the leaders, some men will dominate women, ruling with high-handedness. Their arbitrary rulings and demands produce certain injustices which are offensive and may be unbearable. Certainly such behavior makes a marriage relationship difficult since the woman is made to feel subservient and inferior. As a man grows in humility, realizing that his position as leader is only an assignment of responsibility and that it does not vest him with any qualities of superiority, and as he learns to accept the ideas and suggestions given with an unbiased mind, then he builds a better relationship.

Since men are the breadwinners and must receive special education for this responsibility, it is frequently the case that their formal education is superior to that of their wives. But for such men to suppose that their position is superior by virtue of increased education is a fallacy which is easily exploded. While they may have a more specialized training in one direction or even generally, their innate ability is no greater, on the average, than the woman's. She may be deprived from extending herself only by dedication to goals that are even more worthwhile. The knowledge of any person is tremendously small when compared to the vast store of knowledge available. Should it be that the learning of the wife is less than that of her husband, this does not indicate a lack of brains or ability. Does an attorney feel inferior to an architect because he knows little or nothing of this latter profession?

It is not uncommon to find men who, after they have obtained acclaim or worldly success, desert their wives in later life. The wife who has assisted him to achieve an education or sacrificed to help him get ahead in business is sometimes put on the shelf while he goes out to make a life with a younger woman, or a different woman. His ego would be shattered in many cases if he realized that this younger woman has motives of her own.

The "heart" that a woman puts into the home and marriage relationship is certainly of at least as much value as anything supplied by her husband. A man will gain humility as he sees things in the correct perspective, and with this humility he will contribute much more to his marriage.

HUMILITY AND A MAN'S SUCCESS

A lack of humility is a strong deterrent to achieving success, either in one's business life or home life. As noted, this lack indicates a basic character flaw, pointing up a failure to understand and appreciate the contributions of others or their inherent worth. It is a barrier to growth.

On the other hand, one who achieves humility will recognize his own weaknesses and can work to overcome them. His appreciation of others makes working with them easier; he can influence better and the channel for helpful suggestions will be strengthened. The very nature of our existence demands that we get along with our fellows, and our development of this attribute is a big step in the right direction.

In gaining humility it will be necessary to rid oneself of any feeling of self-righteousness or superiority. Not many people would likely feel that they were guilty of such an attitude, but this is exactly the attitude they have in refusing to listen to suggestions or being self-determined in the pursuit of their course. No one is going to suggest that it is profitable to dwell at length upon one's own weaknesses to the point of allowing self-respect to wane, but it is imperative to be aware in a general way of one's limitations so that improvement can be made. Before casting out an idea, be sure it has been properly evaluated. In any event, the expression of appreciation to the source of the idea is important in the cementing of human relationships. We are going to continue to make some mistakes, so we had better be prepared to expect mistakes to be made by our associates.

XVIII
REFINEMENT

Refinement is defined as a state in which the dross, coarse or vulgar elements have been removed and the pure remains. This is an excellent word, being so descriptive and capable of illustration. We think of gold, for example, which usually occurs in nature in combination with impure matter from which it must be separated. To accomplish this, the raw ore is placed in a furnace where it is brought to the melting point and, through the application of fluxes, a separation occurs, leaving the gold free of the contaminants with which it was originally associated. This analogy is appropriate to the refinement which must take place within an individual if he is to become what he is meant to be.

So desirable is this virtue that one would think there would be no opposition to it. Yet there has been an onslaught on refinement in recent years that is shocking. In the name of freedom some people have concluded that they have an inalienable right to say anything they please or to dress and act in any fashion they choose. Because effort is required to overcome the dross, it is thought to be undesirable.

Refined people do not just come that way. The elements of life tend towards vulgarity, and there are unceasing, unrelenting pressures to tarnish or remove the polish which one would like to grace himself with. "Doing what comes naturally" always roughens one up . . . takes off the sheen. Refinement requires a period in the "furnace" where the dross is burned off. That part of the refining process which has to do with outward manners and courtesies may be learned rather easily, but the refinement which comes to one's basic character through a prolonged period of trial and testing so that it is an integral part of his being is not so easy to acquire.

By his nature a man is coarse and rough. He becomes refined as he subdues this tendency and becomes a gentleman. Although this quality is important in all his relationships, it is especially so with women and children. It is a vital part of the velvet which softens the hard steel.

Refinement, or the lack of it, is seen in varying degrees in the men of the world. In some ways men are like animals that are valued for their refinement. In the training of animals, their value is based upon their breeding and training. It is always an inspiring experience to see a horse show or a dog show where the prize specimens are exhibited. We see to what an excellent state many of these animals are brought. The thoroughbreds may be relied upon to behave in a certain way upon order. They have a majestic bearing and confidence which makes them seem almost human. The well-trained quarter horse will be valued at many thousands of dollars, whereas the wild Australian "brumby" may be worth no more than his hide.

The latent ability lies within the unrefined man to be processed as the ore or trained as the horse to command a higher value.

MANNERS

That anyone would have poor manners is most unfortunate since many times the impression given is far more negative than is justified. There seems to be some corollary between good morals and good manners, but apparent good manners are by no means a guarantee of good morals. I say "apparent" since one of genuine refinement would have the good morals. But occasionally we see a man who is of fine character, but who lacks to an astonishing degree ordinary table manners or general manners.

I knew a young man who had cultivated many of the social graces and gave the appearance of excellent refinement. His appearance and dress were very proper and his language cultured. But his table manners were atrocious. For the period he was seated at the table he seemed to be in another world where only his gratification mattered. Not only did he eat fast and noisily, but he lowered his head to the plate for quick and effective consumption of food which he devoured in quantities to the point of embarrassment. These moments at the table seemed so foreign to his nature as to be a "Jekyll and Hyde" syndrome, for selfishness seemed to move into the front to the exclusion of the finer qualities in his character. The poor impression given was probably out of proportion to the seriousness of the offense, but that is the way it is with something that is so obvious.

CRUDE LANGUAGE

Far more offensive than this is the use of crude, vulgar, and profane language. The language one uses gives himself away in the manner of placing a price tag upon him. By listening to someone speak, particularly upon an issue where strong feeling exists, it is possible to make a rather accurate estimate of his character. You will know in advance what his feelings are on many other issues. For example, one cannot profane the name of God and yet be a reverent person. The two are completely incompatible. Lack of reverence is a most serious character deficiency indicating not only a disrespect for God, but also for all His creation.

Crude language is not only an evidence of a deficiency in the language, loudly demonstrating a lack of competence in expression, but it indicates a selfish disregard for the sensitiveness of others. For anyone who reverences the name of Diety, profane language cuts in like a knife.

While sitting at a noon luncheon with a men's service club, one of the men profaned during the conversation. Noticing a minister at the table, he apologized to him. Why didn't he apologize to the rest of us? Deity is certainly reverenced by people other than clergymen. Had women been there he would have apologized to them also, I presume, but for some reason he failed to realize that profane language is offensive to anyone who loves God and is trying to shake off the tarnishing effects of the crude environment. Sitting in the presence of such an unrefined person is uncomfortable and embarrassing, for at any moment one is subjected to having to correct him on his speech, which will prove embarrassing to both parties. Very likely he is speaking out of habit with no realization of the offense he is creating. Such a person will be shunned by anyone whose sensibilities are offended by such usage.

Such a man places limitations upon his own acceptability—giving himself a handicap, as it were. Getting along in life in all the relationships we find ourselves in is difficult enough at best without handicapping ourselves.

One finds among the advocates of "free speech" an invariable pattern of crudeness and irreverence. While it would be difficult to prove, one may presume that such advocates also lack the basic moral values of sexual purity as commanded by God. Here is a case where their language gives them away. Lacking all restraint themselves, they wish to have their vileness made acceptable to all.

The use of the language falls into all degrees of acceptability. The morbid utterances of the blatantly uncultured represent the more extreme cases, but there are many more thoughtless and unrefined terms used by a greater number of people which brand them immediately. The fineness of one's clothing is no gauge to go by nor is the position held. The need for an improvement in speaking cuts across all levels and strata in the society. It is more unfortunate that the battle to clean up the language is made the more difficult by the letdown in journalistic standards which permit many of our leading publications to express themselves in the "language of the street." It is hoped that one day soon this trend will be reversed, for it seems inconceivable that our human dignity will allow us to accept as a standard the everyday usage we are confronted with.

CRUDE BEHAVIOR

Closely allied with crude expressions is crude behavior. The thought and expression precedes the act, so it is difficult to have the one without the other. Occasionally we see a man whom we describe as "fresh," i.e., he is overly friendly or overbearing. He may touch or pinch the girls and women, or in a variety of ways impose himself upon them. Very few people appreciate such intimacy, and most people highly resent it. In this instance, again, we see a man placing himself under an unnecessary handicap. His type of humor or friendliness is an offense to most everyone, and he is immediately marked as one to avoid.

THE "DIRTY JOKE"

The "dirty joke" is out of place in every circumstance. There is no conceivable place where it is appropriate, for it is always destructive to the finer things in the human being. It is an area where offensive men have belittled femininity and depreciated the sacred function of sex. Suggestive and improper conversation, particularly to women and children, is unthinkable. If done to another man, he can presumably take steps to silence the offender, but it is most difficult and embarrassing for women and children. As we speak of the dignity invested in man as the guide, protector and provider for his family, it is evident that this great calling demands a man of stature, maturity, and grace.

Women are told to reverence their husbands. With such an admonition as this to abide by, it becomes evident at once that many innocent women are up against an almost impossible task. They want to be led, they want an example, and unless contaminated by some unwholesome experience in their earlier life, they want to reverence their husband. But how are they going to do it if he is "dirty minded"? The word reverence is a strong one, and one I would dare not use had it not come from the holy scriptures. But it is here that the commandment originates, so no apology is needed. One can see, however, that when a man is the measure of the "Ideal Man," as we describe him, he would be worthy of reverence, so the term is not inappropriate.

DIPLOMACY AND TACT

This is an art which the refined man will cultivate, for it is like frosting on the cake. It has its roots in a sympathetic understanding for others, a consideration for feelings, and a desire to make life as easy as possible. It is delicate in its nature and very much the velvet we are striving to cultivate. Occasionally we see an individual who prides himself on his bluntness. He is likely to come forth with a comment completely raw and unprepared for serving. He is like a cook, who, rather than place a salad neatly ordered and arranged on a side dish, would toss you a handful of greens with a gob of dressing on it, expect you to catch it and place it on your plate yourself. In each case the same ingredients may be served, but the manner of service is as far apart as the poles.

A salad nicely arranged shows a respect for the one who eats it, whereas throwing it at him may be supplying a need, but shows gross disrespect for the individual. The tactless person is a crude person with demonstrated selfishness, which seems to be the common thread running through all the traits which are unrefined.

Lack of tact may be traceable to a desire to injure another, or a desire to see an unusual reaction under a strained circumstance. Illustrative of this is the anxious person who cannot wait to spread sad or bad news—the death of an old friend, for example.

Tact demands a consideration of the time and place where correction or bad news is given. Correction is bad news to many people, i.e., they may not be very anxious to receive it, although they may need it desperately. The only excuse for instructing people or disclosing some bit of information is to assist them in some way. Doing it in such a manner as to indicate your concern for their feelings is most important.

One of the responsibilities of a leader is to instruct, and a man will find himself in this position frequently. He may be instructing his wife and children almost daily. They expect this instruction, but it must be served with love and consideration for tender feelings. Perhaps some men learn to receive blunt instruction, but the feelings of women and children are more sensitive. They are not the privates being given orders by the sergeant. The ego of a small child can be as great as that of an adult.

REFINED APPEARANCE

Refinement is rooted in self-respect. The story is told of a British diplomat who was assigned as a provincial governor to a small island in the West Indies many years ago. Very few people resided on the island, and his contact with the refinements he knew in Europe was almost nonexistent. In spite of this, and although he ate his dinner alone, he always dressed properly and had a formal table setting. This he did out of respect for himself and the culture he knew. One is not well-mannered, refined and polished because other people will be impressed so much as he is because he believes in such a way of life for the inherent value in it.

One's appearance may be thought to consist of two parts—himself as a person, and the clothing and accessories he uses in dress. Beginning with himself, the refined person is going to see that cleanliness is an inseparable part of himself, that his hair, teeth, nails, complexion, and posture are the best possible. From this point he then dresses himself appropriately. Refined appearance certainly has nothing to do with the amount of money spent, since it is possible to spend considerable and still come out looking ridiculous and offensive.

> What a piece of work is man! How noble in reason! How infinite in faculty! in form and moving how express and admirable; in action, how like an angel! In apprehension how like a god! The beauty of the world! the paragon of animals.
>
> —Shakespeare

For a man to see himself as Shakespeare sees him is to place a value of far greater significance than is ordinarily recognized. A beautiful diamond or ruby is not displayed in a showcase with nails, but is placed in a setting with a velvet background, ruffled border, controlled lighting, and uncluttered so its beauty can be appreciated without distraction. Could we say that a man is less valuable than a precious stone? Why, then, would he slouch around or present himself as though he had no self-respect for the being he is?

Refinement in dress suggests that the appearance be modest and restrained. For a man his dress should be masculine and reasonably conservative. The line between masculine and feminine is being so closely drawn that one wonders which is which.

A Hollywood men's shop featured a fashion show where a young man modeled a full-length coat trimmed in fur. Beneath it he was wearing a femininely tailored suit of light pink. On stage he pointed one foot and raised his chin slightly in turning around for full exposure of the clothing. His manner was so feminine as to be revolting. The fashions of the world are not conducive to the masculine appearance in many instances. Some will argue the point strongly, but for a man it seems evident that a refined appearance is a masculine one.

CONSIDERATION FOR OTHERS

In countless ways one has the opportunity to show his concern and respect for other people. Again, it is the overcoming of selfishness which is the key. In conversation, for example, the ideal man will extend to others the courtesies he would expect for himself. It is commonplace for some fathers to fail to show a child the courtesy of looking up from the paper when a question is being asked. The child may be asking for advice or seeking a favor. In his subordinate position he can hardly demand attention and remain the disciplined youngster you have hopefully taught him to be.

The "cold water" treatment is always deflating and hard to take. Enthusiasm is becoming more rare all the time, and to kill it out when it appears is akin to setting a fire in our diminishing forests. Enthusiasm adds the zest and excitement to life, and when one is burning with it, a refined man will respect it. This is not suggesting that all enthusiasm is justified or that encouragement should be given to something which you cannot support. But out of consideration for another, redirect the enthusiasm if you cannot support the idea. Do it in a way that is positive. It's a little like waking someone from a sound sleep if you must. Rather than shout in a loud voice, jerk off the covers, and physically pull him out of bed, it would be much more appreciated to gently and pleasantly awaken him with music or by opening the shades and allowing the gentle sunlight fo fall on his face. This may not always be practical, but it is illustrative of the idea.

The spectrum of good manners and breeding is so broad as to be a study in itself, and our references to it is only in a superficial way. But it is important to realize that the development of the velvet side of one's nature requires some study in the social graces as well as the more mundane matters of earning a living.

Some childish habits persist into adulthood and become serious blocks in later life. Such include nerve or cheekiness wherein one asks for or expects special consideration and will do so at the expense or inconvenience of others. Such cases go to such extremes as to be almost humorous. There is the case of some friends traveling from another city who, when they found the family not at home they intended to visit (they had not called in advance), found their way into the house and settled themselves for the night—this after they had invaded the refrigerator.

In the close relationship of the home, the privacy of individuals must be respected to insure an atmosphere of love and confidence. Not only does this embrace the obvious restraint to knock before opening, but precludes asking inappropriate or nervy questions. "How much money do you make?" or "How much did you pay for this?" are embarrassing questions to some people and are really not the business of anyone else. The morbid curiosity is a childish trait and will be a bothersome handicap unless brought under control.

MATERIAL-MINDEDNESS—PHYSICAL EXCESS

While great emphasis must be placed upon man's duty to provide for his family, and while it is admitted that he doesn't measure up as a man if he deliberately fails in this responsibility, yet an excessive concern for worldly goods, dependence upon them, or over-evaluation of them shows a coarseness in character. It is like the food we eat which we must have to survive, but which one eats in a proper way rather than to lie on his belly at a trough.

Or for that matter, he wouldn't have to eat with poor manners. The gourmet-type individual who is so concerned over the appeasement of an appetite as to be constantly seeking new and exotic ways of satisfying it is not too much above the level of a glutton.

Material-mindedness leads to ostentatiousness since the material-minded person not only finds satisfaction in his self-indulgence, but loves to parade it before others. Such preoccupation with worldly things is a distortion of values leading into many other problems.

It is a most interesting study to consider the very close tie between the things material and spiritual. They are not unrelated and cannot be actually separated, as a matter of fact, yet gross distortion results when the proper balance is not maintained. In frustration some ascetics have chosen to renounce materialism entirely and have withdrawn into themselves for a life of meditation. They renounce materialism, yet they are an inevitable part of it in ways they probably won't admit. Some extremists will not kill a fly or pluck a plant which would destroy life, yet they find themselves under the necessity of eating. Somehow they rationalize that they are absolved of guilt if someone else does the deed.

The material things of this earth were placed here by God for the use and benefit of man—for him to get his hands into, exploit in the proper sense, enjoy and increase and in every way benefit from their use. But such wealth is not to become an end in itself, but was designed to act as an aid to spirituality—to free men, to elevate them, to expand their horizons and refine their natures.

One sees that refinement, as viewed in this discussion, is far broader than a set of manners that may be learned from a book of etiquette. While etiquette is a fundamental part of it—a vital and important part—it is conceivable that an acceptable amount of the social graces may be applied as a veneer to cover a basically unrefined and calloused character. It is doubtful that the facade would escape detection over a prolonged period, but it might prove deceiving in the short range. Like a steel beam which must be tempered to withstand the stresses placed upon it, so must the character of the man be tempered with refinement which is an actual part of him, functioning whether he be by himself or in affluent and distinguished company.

CONCLUSION

To achieve the steel and velvet is no simple task. Its accomplishment promises rewards thought by many to be completely unattainable. Whereas the cynic has come to doubt that life holds any more than fleeting glimpses of genuine happiness and fulfillment, he who achieves a reasonable measure of steel and velvet knows that the rewards promised are as genuine as any can be.

We learn once again that life exacts a toll for rewards. There is no shortcut to success or happiness. The violation of eternal principles invariably brings frustration and disappointment. But we learn that when we determine to comply with eternal truth, fulfillment is the predictable result.

A false philosophy is teaching us that happiness comes through pursuing the "easy life." Work has been demeaned, and people have been urged to avoid its demands. Doing the easy thing is taught as the desirable way.

As it turns out, everyone has problems and life is never easy. It was not designed by our Creator that it should be. But the source of our problems is worthy of some consideration, as they tend to fall into one of these categories:

1. Problems that arise because of one's own weakness, foolishness or slothfulness. These problems result in unnecessary

hardship as they are the natural consequence of our deliberate actions. Such tend to beat us down and place upon our backs burdens and handicaps which discourage us and deprive us of our greater potential.

2. Problems that arise during the course of living from "acts of God" or the trials which naturally befall man in being in a world that is designed as a testing ground. These trials provide opportunity to gain increased strength by meeting them courageously. These come as a result of the principle that men gain strength as they overcome obstacles. Deity has made our environment one where there is opposition.

3. Problems that arise by setting high goals: A man can provide his own opposition, his own testing ground, by setting worthy and difficult goals for himself. As he engages in a worthy cause and assumes responsibilities which are great, he finds opposition, problems, tests and trials sufficient to prove his worth and refine his character. And the most important point is this: The problems will be of such a nature as to result in greater happiness rather than in sorrow and defeat.

Determining to be a man of steel and velvet is such a worthy goal. While there will be times of disappointment, pain and weariness in achieving this noble objective, all this promises the reward of a full and satisfying life. We determine our own reward as suggested in the following lines:

MY WAGES

I bargained with Life for a penny
    And Life would pay no more,
However I begged at evening
    When I counted my scanty store;

For Life is a just employer,
    He gives you what you ask,
But once you have set the wages,
    Why, you must bear the task.

I worked for a menial's hire,
    Only to learn, dismayed,

That any wage I had asked of Life,
   Life would have paid.

                    —Jessie B. Rittenhouse

From *The Door of Dreams*
Houghton Mifflin Co.

ABOUT THE AUTHOR

AUBREY P. ANDELIN received his D.D.S. degree from the University of Southern California and has practiced dentistry in California and Idaho. His business activities include commercial and agricultural developments in the United States, Australia, Japan and Brazil. He is the founder of a successful publishing business. Dr. Andelin is cofounder of FAMILY LIVING INTERNATIONAL where he has had broad experience in the field of human relations. He and his wife, Helen, are the parents of eight children, and they have thirty-eight grandchildren. Mrs. Andelin is the author of FASCINATING WOMANHOOD, THE FASCINATING GIRL, and ALL ABOUT RAISING CHILDREN.

Heartwarming Books
of
Faith and Inspiration

☐	22886	**JONI** w/ Joe Musser	$2.95
☐	24007	**JUST LIKE ICE CREAM** Lissa Halls Johnson	$2.50
☐	22877	**THE HIGH COST OF GROWING** Joyce Landorf	$2.50
☐	23928	**THE SECRET KINGDOM** Pat Robertson, w/ Bob Slosser	$3.50
☐	23363	**MAN OF STEEL AND VELVET** Dr. Aubrey Andelin	$3.50
☐	22706	**FASCINATING WOMANHOOD** Dr. Aubrey Andelin	$3.95
☐	22739	**CONFESSIONS OF A HAPPY CHRISTIAN** Zig Ziglar	$2.75
☐	23748	**THE SCREWTAPE LETTERS** C. S. Lewis	$2.25
☐	23069	**A SEVERE MERCY** Sheldon Vanauken	$3.50
☐	20831	**THE GUIDEPOSTS TREASURY OF LOVE**	$2.95
☐	20168	**THREE STEPS FORWARD TWO STEPS BACK** Charles S. Swindoll	$2.95
☐	23977	**MEETING GOD AT EVERY TURN** Catherine Marshall	$3.50
☐	22623	**TWO FROM GALILEE** Marjorie Holmes	$2.95
☐	23614	**THE GREATEST SECRET IN THE WORLD** Og Mandino	$2.95
☐	23479	**THE GREATEST MIRACLE IN THE WORLD** Og Mandino	$2.95
☐	24139	**CHRIST COMMISSION** Og Mandino	$3.50
☐	20102	**THE 1980'S COUNTDOWN TO ARMAGEDDON** Hal Lindsey	$2.95
☐	23268	**I'VE GOT TO TALK TO SOMEBODY, GOD** Marjorie Holmes	$2.95
☐	23539	**A GRIEF OBSERVED** C. S. Lewis	$2.95
☐	23166	**WITH GOD ALL THINGS ARE POSSIBLE—** Life Fellowship Study	$3.50

Prices and availability subject to change without notice.

Buy them at your local bookstore or use this handy coupon for ordering:

Bantam Books, Inc., Dept. HF, 414 East Golf Road, Des Plaines, Ill. 60016

Please send me the books I have checked above. I am enclosing $_____ (please add $1.25 to cover postage and handling). Send check or money order —no cash or C.O.D.'s please.

Mr/Mrs/Miss _____

Address_____

City_____ State/Zip _____

HF—4/84

Please allow four to six weeks for delivery. This offer expires 10/84.

The Most Important Voices of Our Age

WINDSTONE BOOKS

This new line of books from Bantam brings you the most important voices and established writers of our age. Windstone. The name evokes the strong, enduring qualities of the air and the earth. The imprint represents the same qualities in literature—boldness of vision and enduring power, importance and originality of concept and statement. Windstone brings you contemporary masterpieces at affordable prices.

☐	22921	THE HILL OF EVIL COUNSEL Amos Oz	$2.95
☐	22741	A WOMAN OF THE FUTURE David Ireland	$3.95
☐	22603	THE REALMS OF GOLD Margaret Drabble	$3.95
☐	13476	WRINKLES Charles Simmons	$2.95
☐	20576	ALICE JAMES J. Strouse	$4.95
☐	23468	MIDDLE GROUND Margaret Drabble	$3.95
☐	20817	THE NEEDLE'S EYE Margaret Drabble	$3.95
☐	20575	HOUSEKEEPING Marilynne Robinson	$2.95
☐	14668	CONFESSIONS OF NAT TURNER William Styron	$3.95
☐	14705	GILES GOAT BOY John Barth	$4.95
☐	14704	DARKNESS VISIBLE William Golding	$3.95
☐	24195	THE LONG MARCH William Styron	$2.95
☐	14666	SET THIS HOUSE ON FIRE William Styron	$3.95
☐	20055	THE STONE ANGEL Margaret Laurence	$2.95

Prices and availability subject to change without notice.

Buy them at your local bookstore or use this handy coupon for ordering:

Bantam Books, Inc., Dept. WD, 414 East Golf Road, Des Plaines, Ill. 60016

Please send me the books I have checked above. I am enclosing $_____ (please add $1.25 to cover postage and handling). Send check or money order no cash or C.O.D.'s please.

Mr/Mrs/Miss_____

Address_____

City_____ State/Zip_____

WD—1/84

Please allow four to six weeks for delivery. This offer expires 7/84.

BANTAM NEW AGE BOOKS

Bantam New Age Books are for all those interested in reflecting on life today and life as it may be in the future. This important new imprint features stimulating works in fields from biology and psychology to philosophy and the new physics.

☐	23564	THE PICKPOCKET AND THE SAINT	$4.50
		Sheldon B. Kopp	
☐	14146	SUPERMIND: THE ULTIMATE ENERGY	$3.95
		Barbara B. Brown	
☐	24147	CREATIVE VISUALIZATION Shatki Gawain	$3.95
☐	22511	NEW RULES: SEARCHING FOR SELF-FULFILLMENT	$3.95
		IN A WORLD TURNED UPSIDE DOWN	
		Daniel Yankelovich	
☐	22510	ZEN IN THE MARTIAL ARTS J. Hyams	$2.95
☐	23550	STRESS AND THE ART OF BIOFEEDBACK	$4.50
		Barbara Brown	
☐	23463	THE FIRST THREE MINUTES Steven Weinberg	$3.50
☐	20059	MAGICAL CHILD Joseph Chilton Pearce	$3.95
☐	24283	MIND AND NATURE: A Necessary Unity	$4.95
		Gregory Bateson	
☐	20708	ZEN/MOTORCYCLE MAINTENANCE	$3.95
		Robert Pirsig	
☐	20693	THE WAY OF THE SHAMAN Michael Hamer	$3.95
☐	23100	TO HAVE OR TO BE Fromm	$3.50
☐	23125	FOCUSING Eugene Gendlin	$3.95
☐	23734	LIVES OF A CELL Lewis Thomas	$3.50
☐	14912	KISS SLEEPING BEAUTY GOODBYE	$3.95
		M. Kolbenschlag	

Prices and availability subject to change without notice.

Buy them at your local bookstore or use this handy coupon:

Bantam Books, Inc., Dept. NA, 414 East Golf Road, Des Plaines, Ill. 60016

Please send me the books I have checked above. I am enclosing $_____
(please add $1.25 to cover postage and handling). Send check or money order
—no cash or C.O.D.'s please.

Mr/Mrs/Miss_____

Address_____

City_____ State/Zip_____

NA—3/84

Please allow four to six weeks for delivery. This offer expires 9/84.

SPECIAL
MONEY SAVING
OFFER

Now you can have an up-to-date listing of Bantam's hundreds of titles plus take advantage of our unique and exciting bonus book offer. A special offer which gives you the opportunity to purchase a Bantam book for only 50¢. Here's how!

By ordering any five books at the regular price per order, you can also choose any other single book listed (up to a $4.95 value) for just 50¢. Some restrictions do apply, but for further details why not send for Bantam's listing of titles today!

Just send us your name and address plus 50¢ to defray the postage and handling costs.

BANTAM BOOKS, INC.
Dept. FC, 414 East Golf Road, Des Plaines, Ill 60016

Mr./Mrs./Miss/Ms. _____
(please print)

Address _____

City_____ State_____ Zip_____

FC—3/84